"Button, Button"

"Button, Button"

(Who's Got the Button?)

Gail Soberg - Sorenson

To order additional copies of this book, contact:
Xlibris Corporation
1-888-795-4274
www.Xlibris.com
Orders@Xlibris.com
53833

In Memory of
Grandma, Dad, Cheryl and Heidi

Dedicated to My Mother and Husband

"May you climb till your dreams come true"

Special acknowledgements:

My children, all six of them, my grandkids, all fourteen of them, siblings and Special friends who have done their level best to keep all thoughts of tediousness out of my life

Special thanks go to

Chief of Police, Bud Nelson (retired)

Other recognition belongs to

Mrs. Margaret Wall
and
Mr. Ed Mako

Part I

"The wind was a torrent of darkness upon the gusty trees,
The moon was a ghostly galleon tossed upon cloudy seas,
The road was a ribbon of moonlight looping the purple moor,
And the highway man came riding—
Riding—riding—
The highwayman came riding, up to the old inn door.

He'd a French cocked hat on his forehead, and a bunch of lace at his chin;
He'd a coat of the claret velvet, and breeches of fine doe-skin.
They fitted with never a wrinkle; his boots were up to his thigh!
And he rode with a jeweled twinkle—
His rapier hilt a-twinkle—
His pistol butts a-twinkle, under the jeweled sky.

Over the cobbles he clattered and clashed in the dark, inn-Yrd,
He tapped with his whip on the shutters, but all was locked and barred,
He whistled a tune to the window, and who should be waiting there
But the landlord's black-eyed daughter—
Bess, the landlord's daughter—
Plaiting a dark red love-knot into her long black hair."

Chapter One

The early morning sun was shining brightly through the bathroom window as Kirsti stepped back from the mirror to study herself. She was dressed and ready to go but needed one last look to see if she was satisfied with her appearance. Her medium brown hair was cropped short, requiring only a blow-dryer to give it some fluff. She wore very little makeup—a bit of eye shadow, liner, and mascara—on her naturally long straight lashes, and that was it. She had cream-colored skin and freckles generously sprinkled over her small nose and cheeks, giving her childlike look that she had barely learned to tolerate; she longed for a more sophisticated beauty. For clothing, she had decided, after spending an hour or two of deliberation the night before—a daily ritual—for a very simple white long-sleeved, button-down blouse, jeans, and a lightly weighted denim jacket with white stitching around the pockets, cuffs, and buttons. She liked the effect of the jacket with the blouse, but she wondered if the jeans weren't just a bit too snug. Was she getting fat? She was a fanatic about her weight, and she hated having to be. She was always on a diet and exercised every night, without fail, another daily ritual. The color coordination between the jeans and the jacket was exact, this was good, but she wasn't really sure she was happy with the fit of the jeans; she was running out of time, she had to get moving. She was a girl on a tight schedule.

She skipped down the stairs in a rapid momentum, her hand breezed over the railing with complacent familiarity. She spun herself around the corner at the bottom of the steps, stopped short in her tracks, and gasped; her heart took a gigantic leap from genuine fright. She let out a slight shriek and made ready to bolt for the front door. There was a man sitting in her kitchen. It took her a couple of seconds to register that the person sitting at her table, in her kitchen, was her dad. After she caught her breath, she was furious. Every person in Kirsti's family knew that she startled easily, too easily actually. Every person in the family also knew that nothing short of a cannon-sized warning could prevent her from jumping out of her skin, and then she would jump anyway.

Her bright blue eyes were blazing as she reflexively shouted out at the one man that meant more to her than anyone else in her overly protected existence, "How in the world did you get in here? Don't you believe in knocking? How about calling first? Don't you ever consider any of these options before you just walk into a place uninvited? You just scared the living daylights out of me!"

Her father laughed; they had had this conversation before. He was notorious for just dropping in unannounced.

"I brought my own coffee," he said as he lifted his cup to her. "Your door was unlocked."

No one in the Poval family ever locked their doors. He had the newspaper spread all over the place; he glanced at the commotion he had made on her table, knowing that this wouldn't meet her approval either. She viewed the mess, predictably frowned at him, and was silent. Kirsti loved her father, but he also annoyed her. He was worse, she thought, than her damned alarm clock on the provocation level. Life would be so much better if there was no need for an alarm clock, but she felt she would never—if ever in her lifetime—reach that goal, that very special day when she could dictate to time rather than time dictating to her. The same went for her father, more or less.

Kirsti sat down across the table from her dad. She didn't have time for this, but she sat down anyway. Somehow, she knew she had to do this. His steel blue eyes grew dark under his thick black brows; she didn't like the look that he was giving her. She didn't have to say anything because he spoke first.

"Your grandmother is in the hospital in Farmington. She had a stroke late last night, and before you ask me a hundred questions, I am going to tell you that she is in a coma but stable and this is all I can tell you right now, so don't ask me any more questions about her condition."

She did have a hundred questions that she wanted to ask, but the expression on her father's face staved all of them. His darkly tanned face was placid and impenetrable. Kirsti could tell by reading his eyes that things were far more serious than he wanted her to know. Kirsti had spent all of her life studying her father. His eyes always spoke things that didn't always meet what he was saying.

Kirsti grabbed the edge of the table with both hands, trying to gather her senses and her equilibrium. She felt like her mind was swimming in tar. This was unfathomable, couldn't be possible. She had just talked to her grandma the night before, and Grandma sounded fine. She spoke to her grandmother every day, again another of her daily rituals. Her father never moved from his chair. He sat there and stared at his daughter with eyes that had turned to a hard-steel gray. Eugene Poval was not a tender man; quite the contrary, he didn't own a pair of kid gloves and never would. He didn't believe in them.

"I can't believe this, not Grandma. I am going to the hospital right now. I have to see her." Kirsti stood up to leave.

"Oh no, you don't, and you won't. You are not going to do that," Eugene said sharply.

"You are going to go to school and finish your exams. You have less than a week of college left, and if she comes out of this coma and finds out that you haven't completed your exams because of her, you will throw her into a whole new series of heart attacks. You know how important your education is to your grandmother. You can do nothing better for her than to finish this up. Go take your tests and call me when you get back home."

Eugene leaned back in his chair and placed his hands behind his head. His eyes softened a bit; they became reflective and almost warm.

"Your grandmother is a tough nut to crack. She has beaten many a wolf off of her front steps single—handedly, and this is only one more. You know that, and I know that, so let's be optimistic. I doubt one simple little thing as a stroke is going to stop her from attending your graduation. And besides, she can't have any visitors, no one, not me, not your mom, not her daughters, not anyone."

He smiled as he rose from his chair; his eyes were no longer a steel gray but a soft deep blue. He took one of her hands and pulled her up on her feet, hugged her briefly, and said, "You are tough, you can handle this. Now I have to go home. It's been a long night."

It wasn't until this moment that Kirsti noticed how tired and drawn her father looked. He left as quietly as he had come.

Kirsti stood there for a few minutes to gather her wits. Her dad was right. There was nothing more important that she could do for her grandmother on this worrisome day but go to college and take her exams. Kirsti knew that this was exactly what her grandmother would be telling her to do if she could bring her out of that blasted coma long enough to ask her.

Grandma had been her reason for going to college in the first place. She had insisted that Kirsti go to college and had helped pave the way. Grandma had let her live in this two-story duplex rent-free for as long as it took for her to get her degree. Grandma had "high hopes" for her oldest grandchild.

"You are going to amount to something, and college is the only way to get this done," she had said to Kirsti over and over again. Grandma had given her money when there wasn't quite enough to cover the expenses. This was their secret. Kirsti had worked part-time as a waitress to make money for tuition and was attending the university because it was the most affordable. And speaking of the university, she had to get moving if she was going to make her first class on time.

Kirsti freshened up her make up and lit out the front door, "Ah, damn it, Grandma, why now, why ever? You cannot make my most frightful nightmare a reality. I cannot imagine life without you. Please, Grandma, I will go to school, you get better. You have to."

As Kirsti made her way to her car, she breathed in the fresh spring air. She had worked so hard to get to where she was today; nothing should stop her now. Come on, Grandma, this is all about you and me! Hang in there. Please, God, be with me today.

Chapter Two

Jack Ireland went into law enforcement right out of high school when all you needed was a high school diploma, an attitude, and a lot of determination. He was so dedicated to his job that he had worked his way through the ranks rapidly and was now chief criminal investigator for Dakota County. His specialty was murder investigations. He had an eye for detail and a sense of reading a crime scene that was nothing short of astonishing.

He had dark wavy hair, rugged features, dark brown expressive eyes, and a body that any linebacker would envy. He was large boned, large muscled and stood six foot one in stocking feet. He was inordinately handsome in the most masculine way possible, and women found his looks and his charming demeanor completely irresistible. What made him even more attractive was that he wasn't aware of how handsome he really was. Jack's mind was on crime, not women. Any type of relationship with women was the last thing on his list of priorities. If he had a flaw, and all people do, his flaw was that he had tunnel vision. This did well for him in his job because his focus was exact, but in other aspects of his life this trait had a negative effect and most especially in his relationships with women. Jack was thirty-eight years old and had never been married, nor was he really interested in getting married.

Like his father before him, Jack was born in New Prague, Minnesota. Both of his parents were of German/Irish extraction. His great-great-grandparents had immigrated to the United States in the late 1800s and settled in the New Market area because of its rich and fertile soil, ideal for farming. Both his mother and father came from large families. His father, John Ireland, had two brothers and four sisters; and his mother had six sisters and one brother. Jack's father was the youngest of the bunch and therefore, chose a vocation other than farming. He became a well-known and well-liked auctioneer. He had loved to listen to Leroy Van Dyke and said, after listening to him, he was going to become an auctioneer. The other reason might have been because he had traveled to many auctions with his own father, all was a part of the farming business; however, Jack Sr. always credited his success to Leroy Van Dyke and his song, "The Auctioneer." Jack Sr. married his high school sweetheart, settled down in New Prague, and had three children.

John Ireland Jr. was the oldest and only son. His dad nicknamed him Jack to save confusion later on. Jack had two younger sisters that spoiled him rotten. They adored him. They looked up to him, waited on him hand and foot, and did everything he demanded of them. John Ireland Sr. didn't take the same notion with Jack as his sisters did in the spoiling department. He was a tough parent and held Jack to a firm line. John Jr. was a spitting image of his father. His mannerisms were identical to his father's: he walked like him, he talked like him, and he thought like him. By the age of six, he could sing out the auctioneer's song as perfectly as his father. John Sr. would place Jack on the edge of the podium, hand Jack the microphone, and let Jack take over for the pure pleasure of it.

Jack did what all kids of his era did. He went to school, graduated, and had intentions of going into the air force. Weeks after he graduated from high school, both of his parents were killed in a car accident. They were coming home from a night of celebration, a wedding. Nobody blamed anyone. His parents' untimely death was written off as a very unfortunate tragedy.

The truth of the matter was that some kids had decided to play the game Pull Tire. This particular game if one wants to call it a game rather than a prank, involved wrapping up an old tire with blue cellophane to make the tire look like a brand-new one that had just dropped off a truck. A long rope would be attached to the tire. With one end of the rope attached to the tire and the other end in the hands of the prankster or pranksters crouching in the ditch, the waiting begins. Someone will come along soon and see the brand new tire just lying there on the road. They will stop, get out of their vehicle, and think they are going to get a brand-new tire out of the deal, free for nothing. The person goes to grab the tire, then the prankster or prankster in the ditch give a hard yank on their end of the rope; the tire goes flying, and the unsuspecting victim is scared right out of their ever loving underwear. This is when the mirth on the part of the prankster is supposed to inaugurate. This particular activity was considered by the area residents to be as harmless and traditional as the other often-used prank, the one of piling hay bales at the bottom of a steep hill for some unsuspecting soul to ram headlong into. There were lots of back roads and just as many steep hills. People in the area were used to these things. No one ever got hurt, just a bit shaken up, which was the whole idea.

Never in the history of the game had anyone ever gotten hurt, let alone killed. Not until this Saturday night and it was Jack's parents who were the ones to pay the ultimate price. The tire was larger than it should have been, and the ditch too deep. Jack's parents came over the hill, and Jack's dad had no time to react. The right front wheel of the car hit the tire lying in the road, at sixty-five miles per hour. Jack Sr. was driving faster than the speed limit, but it was late at night; the roads in this area had no traffic issues, and he was very familiar with these avenues. The force of the right front tire hitting the cellophane-wrapped tire at that speed threw his car into fits; and he wound up rolling down into the ditch, end over end; rear end over front end, and side over side. Both of Jack's parents were thrown through the windshield by the centrifugal force of the tumbling and died from the impact of body hitting hard unforgiving ground. It was rumored that both of Jack's parents had been crushed as the car rolled over them. The person or persons who did this ran off into the field, and their identity still remains unknown. The game of "pull tire" was taken to a far more serious level and considered grounds for arrest and highly discouraged as a means of Saturday night entertainment.

Jack took this all in stride, or so it seemed. He blamed no one because he knew that blame wasn't going to help. His father had told him many times that blame was always a useless way to think nor would blame help Jack raise his sisters who were still in high school. Losing his parents in this manner did, however, help him resolve the question of what next? Jack put his parent's house and 640 acres up for sale and moved to Burnsville. He applied for a job with the

Burnsville police department and got it. His younger sisters graduated from high school under his firm hand; both graduated from college and then got married. One moved to Denver and the other to Fargo. They worked and he worked. Jack put the money he got from the house and property into solid investments. He had an uncle who helped him with this. He only spent enough of the money to get him by with rent and expenses for the first three months; after that, he took it on his own.

Uncle Merle gave him good advice. He told his nephew that he should live as though he had never received the money; and with this piece of advice ringing in his ears, Jack went about his life, struggled to get by, and did as his uncle suggested.

His uncle Merle took care of the money; Jack trusted him, and it paid off. The investments his uncle made paid off royally in the long run. There was a time or two when Jack and his two sisters got into a financial bind, and his uncle would hand him money out of his own pocket and advised Jack to be more prudent. Jack did not know his financial worth until his uncle Merle passed away. His uncle had never married and had no heirs. He was a very unattractive man with the personality of piece of granite, but he knew how to manage money. Jack was in his will to inherit everything from his estate, which was worth more than Jack could spend in a lifetime plus what had been invested from his own inheritance. Uncle Merle had made Jack Ireland a very rich man.

If Jack had a propensity to worry about money, those days were over. John Erin Ireland, Jr. didn't have this propensity. He didn't care about money; he cared about crime. There was nothing noble about any of this in his mind or the mind of anyone who knew him because Jack was not noble, nor did he pretend to be. He simply had no interest in anything that was financial. He just wanted to do his job.

Jack wasn't thinking about any of this as he, Vic and Hank strolled into the Orchard Lake Country Club. He and his two best buddies had decided to take up golfing. None of them knew diddly squat about the sport, yet they had unanimously decided they needed to be golfers. Jack, Vic, and Hank were inseparable in what little time they had to spend together. This was the first day in a long time that the three of them had a day off, all at the same time; and they jointly decided that golfing, next to fishing, was going to be their next challenge. None of them knew a nine iron from a driver, they owned no clubs, and they certainly didn't have the proper shoes. But that didn't matter to these three; they were on their way to a new adventure. They had no idea that they would be stopped at the pass by a simple thing, such as setting up a tee time.

It was Thursday, and it was a very wonderful, warm, pleasant day in spring; and the course was booked for the day. The guys held no membership to the club, which was a requirement to use the golf course; and shortly after a slight bit of wasted argument, the threesome were verbally tossed out on their "proverbial" keisters by one very dour-faced girl one-third their size. Her sense of humor was somewhere below ground level. All three decided she wasn't very good at handling stress. She had no stress before they entered the picture, one might need to add.

While they were deliberating what to do next, Hank's cell phone rang. He flipped it open, placed it next to his ear, and then shut it again. He never said a word until he got off the phone, and then he said rather blithely, "I have a choice to make guys. I can either stand around here wondering what to do next or go have some fun with Erika. She wants me badly, you know how that is. She says she is in need of my muscles. I love the sound of it, don't you?"

Hank looked at Jack and then at Vic, flipped his hat over his eyes, and said, "How silly of me, you two don't have a clue. There isn't a woman in existence that would want either of you. You are both way to fat and way to short."

Jack and Vic gave him a stare as he sauntered off to his car.

"What can I say?" said Jack, with a shrug of his shoulders.

Vic shrugged too. "That boy needs help. Big time. Way to fat and way to short; indeed! How dare he?"

"Yep," they both said in unison. "He needs help."

"Got any idea how were going to get home since we all came with Hank?"

"No idea," said Jack "We'll think of something."

Jack looked at Vic with eyebrows arched mischievously and said, "I wonder if you have to be a member to go in and have a drink in the clubhouse?"

Vic frowned, glanced at his watch, and said, "It is past noon, well past noon, and as I see it, nothing ventured, nothing gained. We have naught to do but try."

"How poetic you are, Victor, please lend me your arm."

Vic looked at Jack clandestinely, stepped back a pace, and then forward again, lifted his arm, crooked it, and said, "Ma damn arm?"

Jack slipped his arm into the crook of Vic's, and up to the clubhouse they ambled, heads thrown back to a break-necked degree, eyes skyward. Halfway there, Jack looked at Vic and said, "Somehow or another, I think we should be stepping into a dance. I have this twiddle de dee and twiddle de dum running through my head. What do you think?"

Vic stopped short, disengaged his arm, glanced at his friend, gave him a huge shove, laughed, and said, "I think you are losing it, my boy."

He was right, Jack was working his best to defy gravity and not fall down from the well-placed and unexpected shove Vic had just bestowed upon him. He did regain his equilibrium after some fancy footwork, and the two of them idled their way into the country club's bar and restaurant.

Chapter Three

The University of Minnesota is located on the banks of the Mississippi River that divides Minneapolis from St. Paul. The full extent of Minnesota University grounds defies this division and sprawls itself across the river on both sides with a west side campus and an east side campus. To say that the University of Minnesota is huge is an understatement, at least by Minnesota standards. Kirsti's father told her if she wanted to be a very small fish in a very large pond, the university was the place to go. He wanted her to attend Augsburg College, his father's alma mater. Kirsti's grandmother sided with her father in the big-fish, small-fish thing, but her grandmother's choice of college was St. Olaf located in Northfield, Minnesota, grandma's alma mater. Kirsti, for expense reasons, chose neither. She didn't feel she could afford a private college. She didn't want to be over her head in debt after she graduated.

Traffic was light as Kirsti made her way to the University of Minnesota this early spring morning in May. She concentrated on her exams as she drove to keep her mind off of her grandmother's situation. She took the same route she always took, freeway all the way. Her father had tried to coax her to take different routes, shorter routes, but Kirsti was a person who liked familiarity; and once set on a path, she rarely veered off it very unlike her father who wouldn't take the same path twice if he didn't have to.

As Kirsti approached the university, she began to worry about parking. She was running late, and she knew the cost of this, parking was always an issue for any off-campus student attending the university. She needn't have worried. She pulled into the student parking area and found a spot almost immediately. The good Lord was working with her, she sent him up a quick thank you. She parked, removed her keys from the ignition, grabbed her purse, changed her mind, threw her purse back into the car, locked the car doors, and made a fast beeline to her classroom located in the building about two blocks from the parking spot. She entered the room just as her professor was taking his seat.

Kirsti's first final exam of the day was all about criminal investigation procedure. She was getting her degree in paralegal. This was an advanced course in criminology. The test would be multiple "guess." Kirsti knew this because all of Professor Grant's tests were multiple choices. She disliked multiple-choice tests because usually, the teacher was then an extremely detailed individual, a stickler for detail to the finest point, and the choices so close in likeness that one had to ponder the justification. The difference could be just a matter of "phraseology," but according to Professor Grant, in the legal system, attention to detail was everything.

Kirsti did, however, have to be fair about Professor Grant because he graded his tests on a curve. If too many didn't make it to a C, then he would review the material again, have the students correct their tests, and hand them back in again. It wouldn't change the grades any, but the review was helpful. He was sincere in wanting his students to have a strong grasp of the material. His tests generally required the full fifty minutes of class time to complete even for the brightest students, and because he knew his tests were hard, he always allowed the slower to take their time and stay beyond if they needed to.

When Kirsti had signed up for the class, she was told by her counselor to give herself an hour break between this one and her next one if possible. She completed the test in forty-five minutes, handed it in, and left the classroom. Professor Grant nodded at her as she set the blue book down on his desk, reached out his hand, took hers, and wished her good luck. He knew she was graduating, and that they would probably never see each other again.

Her next class was at eleven o'clock and in the same building. She had a little bit better than an hour to kill. The next class was a non-elective class. She had taken it to fill in her credits to graduate. Political science was her second interest to law, and surprisingly, they ran a very close second to each other in college requirements. This particular political science class was all about the assassination of President John F. Kennedy. The course had required a lot of reading and research, and the test would be essay. This was Kirsti's favorite class, and she had done well so far, A+ all the way. She also liked the professor. His lectures were fascinating. He had a very wry sense of humor that he wasn't shy about using, and he made his tests easy because he would tell his students exactly what they needed to study to get a good grade. All of his tests were essay, and the more detail provided, the higher the grade. Any student could ace his classes if they loved to write and made their essays interesting to read and did this within the structure of the questions he presented to them before the test. Kirsti used the outlining method she had learned in high school to study for his classes. She hadn't carried anything with her but her black pen, a number 2 pencil, some change, and her nail file; now she wished she had brought some of her notes along.

With an hour to kill, Kirsti decided to head over to Commons located across the street to get a cup of coffee, and on the way, she ran into a classmate of hers from her third class of the day (economics, a requisite), who was concerned about the finals. They walked together into the Commons building, discussing the "all over the map" teaching method this professor used and concluded that it wasn't going to be an easy test. None of his tests were easy. Kirsti had always lucked out and received good grades from him anyway, *luck* being the operative word. This professor also graded on a curve and what that curve would be was about as easy to figure out as the professor himself who wore splashy, obnoxious button-down shirts, baggy pants, and dirty tennis shoes without socks. He was famous for giving pop quizzes, containing only one multiple-choice question; and the guess was? One never knew. Never did any one of his questions relate to his lectures or anything within the required reading assignments. There was a method to his madness, however, but only after the day was done and some reflection was used would the answer come to the fore, or so she was told by some of his previous students. Kirsti was not quite there yet, though she had seen some fleeting glimpses, like whispers in the wind, granting her endless hope that this course had not been taken in vain.

The assassinations test went as expected. Professor Griffin wrote the test question on the blackboard and handed out the blue books. The question was Did Lee Harvey Oswald act alone in the assassination of J. F. Kennedy? This had been the question from day one. The students had been given two other tests concerning this exact question. The first paper was to be a comprehensive argument that he had acted alone, the second was to be a comprehensive argument that he hadn't acted alone, and the final test was to be a comprehensive argument with the student debating the argument, one way or the other. Kirsti had decided that she was going to make her final paper something other than what the professor was requesting and challenge the question. She would be arguing that the question itself was presumptuous and assumed Lee Harvey Oswald's guilt, defying the basic rule that one is presumed innocent until proven guilty beyond a reasonable doubt. She knew it was risky, but she had to do it anyway. Once she put her pen to paper, the arguments came rapidly, and she wrote furiously to keep up with her own thoughts, thoughts that she had spent hours organizing and committing to memory. Was she right? She wasn't sure; was she persuasive? She thought so. She was done within a half an hour. She got up, walked to the front of the classroom, and placed her blue book on Professor Griffin's desk. She was the first one done. He smiled at her, said, "Good luck," and picked up her blue book as she walked out of the room.

Kirsti arrived at her third and final class for the day a bit early. The door was open, so she went in and sat down. She selected her usual seat, front row, right next to the door. Her grandmother had told her before she started college to always sit in the front row, and thus she had always made it a point to do so, if she could. Grandma was a schoolteacher; students sitting in the front row rarely fell asleep in her class while those in the back rows often dozed off. Sitting in the front row eliminated distractions. Kirsti liked sitting as close to the door as possible because she tended to be always in a hurry. To gain this choice of setting, she learned it was always better to be early. She looked at the clock on the wall, and it said twelve fifty, she had about ten minutes to kill with nothing to do but stare at the walls. She reached in her pocket and pulled out her nail file. When all else fails, file your nails—this was a great time passer. She had hardly put the file to her nail when other students started straggling in. She knew none of them but by face. This was one of the disadvantages of commuting. Soon the classroom was filled, and last but not least in came the professor, looking like he had just crawled out of an empty cement mixer.

Professor Miles didn't just walk into the room, he came in hurriedly. He glanced around the room with a puzzled expression on his face, as though he had forgotten something important. He stopped abruptly before he reached his desk. His befuddled eyes looked around the room, not at anyone or anything in particular. When he had everyone in the room wondering if he had finally gone over the edge, he asked if anyone had the latest copy of Time magazine. He said he had left his at home, and he wanted to read this while the test was being taken. His wrinkled wild red shirt with yellow swirls was making Kirsti irritable. He had selected a pair of olive drab green shorts to wear with that ugly, garish shirt, and they were even more wrinkled than his shirt was. She had to wonder if he did this on purpose or was he really that distracted. And to add to the eye irritation even further, he had on his dirty tennis shoes with no socks. His long skinny, knobby knee'd legs were winter white above his bony ankles. Kirsti looked him over from head to toe and then back up again only to realize that his blondish hair matched his outfit perfectly. Had he even run a comb or brush through it? If he had, one would never be able to tell by looking at him. Professor Miles had always reminded Kirsti of the professor in the movies starring Michael J. Fox, Back to the Future.

No one raised their hand, so he went directly to his desk, grabbed the blue books, and absently handed the stack to Kirsti to pass on. He then rushed back behind his desk and stood facing the back of the room and looking at no one in particular, or speaking to anyone exactly, said, "You would all be advised to learn to read and learn to read Time magazine, especially. There is a lot of great stuff in that magazine and even a few things that relate to economics." Miles then turned away from the students, picked up a tiny piece of chalk, and began to scrawl in printed letters on the chalk board. His sketching resembled his hair style and his dress to a wobbly perfection.

Final Test:

Write out a brief summary of any article you have read from the Wall Street Journal this quarter.

Kirsti was flabbergasted. Miles had said on the first day of class that a requirement for the students was to subscribe to the *Wall Street Journal* and had handed out a subscription form to be filled out and mailed in. She had done this, but never had he since mentioned the journal. She had received them daily, and they were piled up in a corner of her living room; some glanced at, others ignored. She had spent hours going over the scattered notes she had taken in his lectures and gone from front to back, reviewing the book required. But because he hadn't mentioned the *Wall Street Journal*, she had given the journal no real attention aside from yesterday. She started to panic.

What had she read in the journal yesterday? What was it? She shut her eyes and tried to focus. Gradually, the article appeared in vague imagery. It had to do with interest rates on the rise, creating an uncertainty in the housing market and concern about pending inflation. As she concentrated, the article she had read came closer into view. She could see the headline now; she wrote that down and then concentrated on what she had gathered from the article in general. She wrote what she thought was an adequate summary of what she could remember, but was not deeply satisfied with the results, exactly; but it was the best she could do on such short notice. Had she only known, and she should have known with a teacher like Miles. She was not the first one to hand in her blue book, not this time. In fact, she was one of four left at the end of the class period. Miles was leaning back in his chair with his feet on his desk reading *Newsweek* when she dropped her blue book on his desk; he paid her no mind but remained steadfast in his reading.

Kirsti walked back to her car with thoughts of how failing two finals could affect her GPA and graduating with honors. She looked at her watch. It was two thirty in the afternoon. She was scheduled to work from five o'clock to close at the Orchard Lake Country Club. What she wanted to do was go to the hospital to see her grandmother. She pulled her cell phone out of her purse and dialed her parents' phone number. She wanted to talk to her mom. She wanted to go see her grandma. She should have felt elated at being done, at long last, with college. She was done with her finals, no more tests. What she felt was something akin to sorrow gripping her, a feeling of anxiety. She wished that she hadn't scheduled herself to work. She wished that she had called Hilde and asked her to go out with her to celebrate. She wished her grandmother wasn't sick and possibly dying. She damned well wished that she had read the *Wall Street Journals*. She was really wishing she could blame everything on her wild-haired, garishly dressed economics professor. Right now, life was making about as much sense to her as he was, none.

Chapter Four

The Orchard Lake Country Club wasn't always a country club. Indeed it wasn't. There was a time when this building was one of the finest ballrooms south of the Twin Cities. People came from miles around to listen to big band music and dance on Saturday nights. The original owner gave the ballroom the name Sea Side Inn. He placed the large building right on the banks of Orchard Lake, which could hardly be called a sea; but there was water, and Orchard Lake is a very attractive lake, and who really cared anyway? The people that came could walk out on the veranda and look over the lake, and if the moon was out, they could get the feeling of being on the shore of any sea in any land and in any country. If the moon wasn't shining, the owner was smart enough to turn on the floodlights, offering a similar effect. This man had vision, or was he a romantic? No one ever knew because he wasn't a local guy, and no one, including the manager, ever saw him. If the manager ever saw him or spoke to him, he never mentioned this to anyone. When he was asked, he would simply change the subject.

When the tastes of the music changed, during the late fifties and early sixties to rock and roll, he offered this to people as well. However, the Twin Cities were growing and crowding this exclusive source for entertainment. Other places opened up to offer a different variety of amusement; people were going elsewhere, forcing the original owner to finally give up the fight and close the place for lack of business. The building remained vacant and gathered a lot of dust and mold for several years until some bright person from Chicago moved into the Twin Cities to expand his father's business, corrugated boxes. He was a young man who loved to golf; he had his mind made up to own his own golf course. He heard about this vacant building from a business source in Savage and decided to take a look. He loved the location and decided he was going to bring the place back to life. This was the spot for his golf course. His friends called him crazy because at the time, there was little interest in golf in the state of Minnesota, especially in Orchard Lake. He knew better. He told his friends that the reason for this was because it was considered a rich man's sport, and the lack of participation was due to affordability rather than interest.

On a whim and a dare and with a lot of money behind him (he was not a person who came from humble beginnings, (plus he had rich friends, very rich friends), he bought the Sea Side Inn along with the sixty acres that adjoined the property, created a public golf course with reasonable prices—no membership required. He had the old building torn down and replaced by one that resembled a country club with all the trappings. He designed the golf course himself with a little help from the professionals. He golfed the course a few times, just to gratify his own curiosity, and then went back to Chicago to take over the entirety of his father's business, a large conglomeration of many facets, because his father had decided to retire. He never did come back to the Twin Cities again. He hired a manager, and then he was gone. He paid his manager well, and within ten years, the manager was able to buy the Orchard Lake Country Club and golf-course, lock, stock, and barrel. He turned it into a membership-only club. Joe only made this a membership club because now, membership clubs were vogue and garnered him more customers. His fees were reasonable but adequate enough to help him maintain the golf course. He was happy, and so were his members. Joe made his rates reasonable.

Kirsti had gone to work for the country club when she was still in high school, bussing tables. Her father had landed her the job. She was fifteen years old. Kirsti liked her boss and his wife, Joe and Hanna. Joe was a navy man. He had quit school to join the navy, at the age of sixteen. He lied about his age, no one questioned him. He had black hair, dark brown eyes, naturally tanned complexion, and an unremitting childish grin. He kept his strong bodied navy physique by notion rather than concentrated effort. He was good looking in an odd sort of way.

His wife was exactly like him in hair color, eye color, and ceaseless smile; but she was fair skinned. She wore her black hair long; she had a very slim waist, oversized hips, and broad lip and smile that revealed sizeable teeth. She was also attractive in an odd sort of way. They seemed to Kirsti to be a natural pair. They even had similar dispositions, but one had to know them a while to recognize this likeness. In fact, they were so much alike they could have easily been mistaken for brother and sister rather than a husband and wife. They ran the country club as a well-harnessed team.

The two of them, in equal measure, took Kirsti under their wing and made it their business to teach her everything they knew about the business. She was promoted to waitress, by the time she was sixteen; and by the time she was seventeen, they had her cooking, working as a waitress and playing hostess or simply standing behind the check register. Kirsti grew up with the Orchard Lake Country Club, and as it grew so did she. She was invited to their home anytime and taken out on excursions as often as her busy schedule allowed. When Kirsti graduated from high school and was on her way to college she got a raise in pay and the schedule was worked to fit her college classes and study time. She loved Joe and Hanna almost as much as she loved her own parents. Perhaps she did love them as much, only in a different way and for different reasons.

Kirsti had phoned her mother on her way home from the university; her Mom had told her that there was no point in going to the hospital to see her grandmother yet. Kirsti had argued, but her mother was adamant and even a little short with Kirsti's insistence. Kirsti and her mother rarely, if ever, got into differences; but this time, there was a tug of uncompromising on her mom's part that made Kirsti edgy. She parked her car next to the employee entrance door; both Joe and Hanna's cars were there. This was a good thing because she knew that she could depend on them to give her a bit of psychological support to face the night ahead. She was scheduled to waitress.

The back entrance door brought her directly into the kitchen where Charlie was busy creating concoctions that only he understood. He was a chef, a certified and double-certified, serious-minded chef. No one could possibly describe his personality because he was completely lacking in one. Kirsti did not dislike him because there was nothing about him to dislike, nor was there anything about him to like either. He spoke in one-word sentences, if he spoke at all, and then only in a very flat tone if you could even get that out of him; generally, he simply nodded. Kirsti had been the only one to get him to speak, and when he did, the whole staff went into a state of temporary shock.

She had been called in to waitress a special party that was going on for a bunch of men from a company that is, in this telling, completely irrelevant. Kirsti's job was to serve drinks and then take their individual orders for food. After many rounds of drinks, these men decided it was time to eat; they all ordered steaks. Kirsti took their order for food then brought them another round of drinks per their specification. She then brought out the food. Each steak was marked accordingly with a little tab marked rare, medium rare, medium, or well done. This saves the waitress from having to guess which meal belongs to whom, right along with trying to figure out which one belongs to whom.

There were twelve happy men that got their food and their drinks as ordered. Kirsti had done her job; her shift was over. She was ready to leave when one of the customers called her back to the table. He wanted his steak cooked a little more because it was a bit too raw for his personal tastes. He was congenial. Kirsti brought the steak back to Charlie and told him to give this one a few more minutes; the customer wanted the steak a bit less red.

Charlie grabbed the plate, looked at the tab, and said to Kirsti, "He asked for medium rare, this steak is medium rare." He shoved the plate back to Kirsti.

She in turn, pushed the plate back and said, "Cook it some more, Charlie."

He gave her a solid, determined glare, pushed the plate back, and said, "No."

Kirsti blew up, pushed the plate back toward Charlie again, and said loudly, "You will put that steak back on the grill. I will not have a customer pay for anything they are not satisfied with. Cook it some more, damn it, Charlie, get real!"

Charlie lost his cool for the first time in his employment with Joe and Hanna. He shouted back, "I will not make that steak medium rare by cooking it more, the customer wanted medium rare, and that is what I gave him!"

Kirsti could not accept as truth the words she was hearing from Charlie. She stomped out of the kitchen and grabbed Joe as he was heading toward the kitchen to find out what all the commotion was about. Hanna was right on his heels. After Kirsti explained the situation, Joe went back into the kitchen to see if he could get Charlie off his high horse. There were a lot of words flung around; words like quitting or getting fired and all such things. But in the end, Charlie did wind up making another steak for the poor customer that had been patiently waiting, and had by now lost his appetite and had long since departed.

Kirsti felt sorry for the customer who could hear all the shouting. Heck, everyone in the place had their eyes and ears turned toward the kitchen. Kirsti had sheepishly apologized to the customer. He was hungry but still, the most congenial one of the group. The rest were not so nice. Joe offered them a free meal and one free drink on their next visit. Two perfectly good steaks were thrown into the trash can that evening, with twelve free steak dinners and one free drink to be collected later, this was an expensive argument for Joe and Hanna. Kirsti didn't get a tip off the table; and Charlie remained, as always, totally unaware that he was at fault for anything concerning the incident. There was a lesson learned by the staff, in all of this business, for future use: make sure to tell the customer that medium rare is a lot rarer than medium rare.

Charlie didn't raise his head from his work as Kirsti came through the back door, and it wasn't because he didn't hear her or see her out of his peripheral vision. He did. He could see and hear just fine. He also didn't raise his head to her as she moved around in front of him, past the grills, and through the swinging doors into the dining area. The swinging metal doors made a very notable flapping noise as she passed through them. She was a bit irritable to begin with, and Charlie made her feel even more irritable; and because of this, she hit the doors just a little harder than usual, just for her own satisfaction. They usually went *flap, flap, flap*; this time they went *flap, flap, flap, flap,* and another little flap as they joined together.

There, she thought to herself. *Take that Charlie!*

"Kirsti is here," Joe said laughingly to Hanna.

Hanna set her placid brown eyes on Kirsti and replied, "She sure is, and she doesn't look very happy." Hanna's large-toothed smile turned almost instantly into a serious frown.

They were sitting at "their table" located right next to the kitchen and right next to one of many large windows facing the lake. This table had the capacity to seat four people and was the only one in the dining area without a tablecloth. The only items on the table were a couple of ashtrays and a couple of cups of coffee. Both Joe and Hanna were heavy smokers and coffee drinkers; the ashtrays were full of cigarette butts. Kirsti looked at the ashtrays, picked them up, dumped them, brought them back to the table, and sat down next to Hanna. She rested her head on Hannah's shoulder, looked at Joe, and said, "Grandma had a stroke last night, and it doesn't look good for Grandma."

Hanna threw a quick knowing glance at Joe and then placed her arm around Kirsti. They sat silently for quite some time before Hanna asked Kirsti if she was all right. The real answer to the question would have been no, but Kirsti said yes. Both Joe and Hanna knew better. They knew how closely intertwined Kirsti was to her grandmother.

"Where is she?" Hanna asked.

"Sanford Hospital, in Farmington, they are keeping her heavily sedated for now," Kirsti said this with a deep sigh. Her eyes filled with tears as she spoke.

Joe got up from his chair, walked around the table, grabbed Kirsti's hand forcing her to her feet.

"I think you ought to go home, you look miserable. You will not be good for business, considering the mood you're in. Besides, you should be out celebrating your last day of college. We shouldn't have scheduled you to work tonight anyway. Hanna will cover for you, won't you, Hanna?" He gave Kirsti a listless smile loaded with empathy.

"No!" said Kirsti fervently, "I would rather you let me stay. It is exactly what I need to keep my mind off Grandma. I need to be busy. If I go home, I will brood. I will probably go to the hospital and then be met at the door by my father who will promptly tell me to go back home. Grandma can't have visitors yet."

Joe looked at Hanna, who was unconsciously nodding her head up and down.

"All right" Hanna said passively, "Go change into your uniform."

Joe laughed affably and patted Kirsti's rear end as she turned and walked toward the backroom to change. Ordinarily, she would have slapped his hand, this time she didn't. After she left, Hanna and Joe looked at each other very seriously.

"This could get tough for her," Hanna said.

Joe nodded and sat back down. He looked at Hanna and said, "This week, when this week is over, things could get tough for us as well. She will be graduating and moving on to another life."

Hanna lit up a fresh cigarette, blew smoke into the air, took a deep breath, looked at Joe, and said, "I don't even want to think about it."

Chapter Five

Kirsti entered the backroom, turned around, closed the door, and made sure that it was locked. She didn't want to take a chance on anyone entering while she was changing into her uniform. She was modest to the extreme. Her unusual degree of modesty was a symptom of her self-consciousness that was cultivated early in her life by circumstances surrounding her and people that she rubbed shoulders with day in and day out and reinforced daily from the age of five when she started first grade until she graduated twelve years later.

Kirsti's great grandparents were one of the first early settlers in Lakeville, Minnesota. The town was less than a quarter of a century old when the Povals immigrated to the United States from Norway. Her grandfather had attended and graduated from Lakeville High School. Her father had graduated from Lakeville High School. Her mother had graduated from Lakeville High School. Her grandfather and grandmother had taught at Lakeville High School. Her aunt had been a secretary for the superintendent for years and, because they were who they were and had done what they had done and knew whom they knew, Kirsti's course was set for her long before she ever started school. There would be expectations that she would have to live up to, and one of these expectations was her choice of friends. She would never really have a choice at all. Her grandmother would subtly handpick her friends for her.

The top echelon of the first-grade class immediately embraced Kirsti. One of these friends was the daughter of the local banker, another was the daughter of the principal, and then there was the daughter of the local jeweler, and so on. These kids accepted Kirsti because their parents accepted Kirsti's family as a whole entity and vice versa. These parents knew who she was and where she came from. Kirsti was invited to all the birthday parties of the children of the movers and shakers in Lakeville, Minnesota.

There were others who Kirsti could have nothing to do with; even speaking to them was seriously frowned upon. The pecking order was established, and Kirsti had nothing to say about it, and she was far too young to even give any of this a thought.

The creation of her self-consciousness was her early awareness of how her prearranged friends would stand around and criticize others that they considered beneath them. Kirsti had been well coached, and she didn't question her right to belong with the best of the best; however, she had not been well coached in how to handle the exact lines of demarcation, making her different from the rest, and the nastiness she heard and inwardly questioned. She learned early in life that if she didn't keep up with her carefully selected peers, she might fall prey to the same treatment that was doled out to others who didn't make the grade for no other reason than because they didn't carry the right name or have the right occupation or those who weren't considered particularly bright. She became a fanatic about her weight, her mode of dress, her grades, and outward appearance.

The manifestation of her self-consciousness was a continual and gradual process, gathering its full grip when she hit junior high where physical education was a required course. The locker room became the source for her not-so-well-intended friends to take stock of everyone less endowed or even more endowed than them, physically, mentally, and every other way under the sun. Kirsti would cringe every time she had to take her clothes off and share the showers with every other female in her class. She knew what was said in the huddles and at the water fountain about everyone who didn't measure up. She knew these good friends of hers could be talking about her behind her back, and she would never know.

All through junior high she had phys ed every day, and showers were a requirement. Her phys ed teacher was a redheaded—obviously dyed—hard-nosed individual who had no idea what the word mercy meant let alone compassion and understanding. If anyone was a female candidate for a marine instructor, Mrs. Larkin was. She was tough, crusty, and she had her favorites. Kirsti was not one of her favorites.

Larkin favored the cheerleaders because she chose them, and though most of Kirsti's friends were cheerleaders, Kirsti wasn't. She wasn't because she really didn't want to be, and secondly, had she wanted to be, she didn't have the physical adroitness required. When Kirsti expressed her frustrations about Mrs. Larkin to her grandmother, she had said with conviction, "She doesn't like the Povals, for some reason or another. She treated your aunts the same way. Don't be discouraged by her. Physical education is not a means to the end where you are heading. Just do your best."

Rumor had it that Larkin had been married at one time. Her students found this hard to believe because they couldn't fathom anyone wanting her in a romantic way. This rumor also claimed that Mrs. Larkin and her husband were in a horrible automobile accident; Mrs. Larkin had been driving, recklessly. The result of this horrible accident had killed Mr. Larkin and put Mrs. Larkin in a deep coma for quite some time. The shock of losing her husband, they said, had caused her to lose all of her thick orange/red hair. When her hair finally did grow back, the color was pure white. This rumor turned to a legend which then became fact. Long after Kirsti had graduated from high school, she learned that Mrs. Larkin had been killed in a motorcycle accident and on a motorcycle; she was driving at the age of sixty-five. Kirsti's only reply was, "Well, that figures." Kirsti never took the time to find out if this was true or not because she didn't care. She didn't care because she had never liked Mrs. Larkin. Kirsti had a thing about favoritism, especially if she wasn't included.

By the time Kirsti graduated from high school, she was fully indoctrinated. She was a high-flying, first-class someone. She had grades to prove this and a way of thinking to match. She had no doubt in her mind that she was the best of the best, came from the best of the best, and belonged to the best of the best. Kirsti knew this because all of her friends came from the best of the best. She judged everyone by first impression based exclusively on what she thought was proper attire, looks, and background. She made it a deliberate point to distance herself from anyone she considered beneath her, which was the majority of the population. She had developed into a persona, with a lot of help from her friends and family that was enormously self-centered, egotistical, and arrogant.

However, if one could get a chance to take a closer look, they would find a girl who was far too self-conscious for her own good and uncertain about most everything in life, including her own attributes. If anyone had stopped her for just one moment and told her that she was a person without her own mind, she would have been shocked, appalled, and then angry—defensively angry. They would be right, but no one ever could, and no one ever did dare to mention this to her. On the other side, she was as charming as the day was long. She vibrated with life; she was nothing short of enticing. She was bright, energetic, and pretty; and even though she thought she wasn't a people pleaser, she was. Oh yes, indeed she was. It would have shocked her to know that many considered her a snob. It would have shocked her even more to learn that this was exactly what she was. She would have probably rebutted with the defensive phrase, "I am not a snob! I am particular." This in translation meant the same thing.

Kirsti had always done the right thing; she never considered doing otherwise. She ran with the right people. She dated boys that came from "respectable" families. She studied hard and kept her grades to no less than a B average. She played in the band and sang in the choir. She joined all the right clubs. Her teachers loved her and so did her family. She always appeared to know exactly what she wanted, and what she wanted, she usually got. She generally got what she was entitled to because she had earned it. How much of this was Kirsti and how much of this was forced upon her could be debated, but she was what she was; a girl with many insecurities aptly disguised by a radiant, self-confident exterior. Kirsti saw herself as others did, self-confident, smart, feisty, and well worth knowing.

Chapter Six

The "backroom" Kirsti entered to change clothes had once been an 18' x 20' storage room, lined with shelves from front to back and down the middle. Hanna decided the room would be a great place for her staff to use as a dressing room and the reasons behind this were plentiful. Hanna was a neat freak. From the inception of the opening of their club, she had insisted the staff wear uniforms. Over the years, the style of the uniforms had changed, but not the quality of care and attention on behalf of the staff. Left to themselves, they would come in wearing the uniform, but she could never predict they would come in wearing a uniform that was clean and pressed. Most of her employees listened to her and did what she commanded, but there were always a few who would come in looking like they had slept in the uniform or hadn't a bit of knowledge of how to clean them. She decided to do something about this problem.

Hanna's mother-in-law was a remarkable seamstress; she was also a retired restaurant owner, and she was bored. Hanna asked her if she would design and sew uniforms for her staff. Hanna's idea was for each waitress to have their uniform specifically designed to fit their shapes and their size. The storage room would be renovated into a dressing room where the staff could house their uniforms and their personal belongs. Hanna and Joe would provide dry cleaning services for their employees. This meant they had to have no less than three available at all times. Hanna's mother-in-law was enthusiastic. The uniform for the busboys and cleanup crew was no problem, standard white oxford shirt, black tie, and black dress slacks.

After a few head banging sessions—well, more than a few—a decision was made concerning the style of the uniforms for the waitresses and hostess. Hanna thought a one-piece uniform that was easy to slip in and out of was what she wanted, her mother-in-law had other ideas; Hanna eventually capitulated. The expense of this grand idea was enormous, and rounding up everyone to get measured was equally as difficult. Joe was in complete disagreement with the whole entire idea of custom-made uniforms, laundry service, and renovation; Hanna won this argument by going ahead and doing what she intended to do. Joe knew she would because he had been with her a long, long time. He loved her, and she hadn't failed him yet. He only protested because he knew she expected him too.

While Mrs. Ramonti was busy measuring, cutting, and sewing, Hanna brought in workers to renovate the storage room. The storage room was located next to the far end of the kitchen and thus didn't inconvenience the rest of their business, aside from the most curious regulars who tended to wonder in and hold up the workers by engaging them in conversation. Hanna would let this go on for a while and then mosey in and shag her customers back to their tables, allowing the workers to get back to their responsibility. The reconstruction took better than six months to complete, and Joe cried about every single bill coming in that had anything to do with this project. He would say with mock exasperation, "I will never get my yacht, not ever."

Hanna would look at him over her reading glasses and quip, "You don't need a yacht. You have me. And besides, in case you can't remember, let me remind you, you hate water. I am the one who wants a yacht, and lest you forget, you took your leave from the US Navy only because you hated spending all of your time around water. You loved the girls and the travel but not the water. Have you no recall at all?" Joe was usually on his way to another place long before she finished her all-too-familiar rendition.

"Where did I find this man?" she would muse with affection.

Hanna was waiting for Kirsti when she came out of the dressing room and was again, as always, amazed at how perfectly the uniform fit Kirsti as though the uniform had been designed specifically for her; and perhaps, unconsciously, it had been. The uniform consisted of three pieces, blouse, vest, and for the bottom half, there were three selections the girls could choose from: skirt, slacks or capris.

The blouses that Mrs. Ramonti selected for the uniform were of soft light-weighted, sheer white cotton material, short sleeved for summer, long sleeved for winter. The long sleeved shirts required cuff links. Hanna selected the cuff links and provided them.

The skirt was very simple, A-lined, the length cut to the middle of the knee. The pants were polyester/cotton blend, pleated in the front, and hemmed to the middle of the heel. The capris were also simple in design with stovepipe legs that came to the middle of the calf. The skirt, pants, and capris were black with loops on the waistband; a belt was required, black with a silver buckle. The vest was black silk in the back with adjustable ties; the front of the vest was burgundy and dark green paisley with a dash of white mixed in. The vest could be worn open or closed. The vest was V-ed above the hip on each side and was waist length. Mrs. Ramonti made one-half-inch black ties for the blouse that crossed at the throat over the top button of the shirt held together by a snap. The cuff links were silver to match the belt buckle and very simple in design, oval and brushed silver plated. Black nylons and shoes were required; the girls provided these for themselves; whatever was comfortable and black was fine with Hanna. She did insist the shoes were clean and polished. Kirsti had chosen to wear the capris this evening with the vest open, exposing the silver buckle of her belt surrounding her slender waist. She wore black, soft-leathered, two-inch-heeled black boots that came to the top of her calves, blending the effect from the waist on down to the toe.

Kirsti met Hanna at one of the waitress stations in the main dining room. Hanna handed Kirsti her tray and bank, twenty-five dollars in mixed bills, which Kirsti folded in half and wrapped around her middle finger, long ends up and outward.

"I hope you are up to this Kirsti, Joe has overbooked us."

"So what's new? Joe always overbooks us" Kirsti replied with a smirk. "Thanks for letting me work. I really do need the distraction."

"True, but tonight, he has really outdone himself. I'm putting you in the lounge. You will be working alone for a while, but Lori will be in shortly."

Lori could always be depended on to come in and help out on very short notice. She needed the money, and she loved her job. Kirsti enjoyed working with Lori; she was young, carefree, and full of the dickens. Lori was in the nursing program and another struggling student attending the University of Minnesota. When times got tough on the floor, which was often because of Joe's propensity for overbooking, one of the girls would quip to the other, "I know somehow or another our trials and tribulations here and now are going to help us in our careers!" And then in unison, they would say, "Not!"

Kirsti was glad she would be working the lounge. She had always preferred to serve drinks rather than food. The tips were ample enough, and there was less physical and mental strain involved. Those large round trays of food could get heavy, and then there were always those customers who refused to be satisfied no matter how exceptional the service or the food. Kirsti had it figured that this was their way of cheating the waitress out of her tip. This was never an issue on a bar tab. There were some customers or "guests," as Joe liked to call them, who would eat in the lounge but not many, generally only those who hadn't made reservations. The waitresses referred to them as drop-ins. The bar had a special menu consisting of a variety of cold sandwiches served in a basket with chips and a dill pickle.

The lounge had been added on to the original building about ten years ago and was supplemented because Joe couldn't stop himself from saying yes to every customer who called and wanted in. The lounge was situated at the right of the entrance, across from the coatroom, and totally separated from the main dining area. The lounge had roughly twenty tables and its own bar. There was a piano and very small dance floor in the back corner of the room. If people had no reservations, they were sent to the lounge. If people were early for their reservations, they were sent to the lounge; if the dining room was full and people were on time for their reservations, they were sent to the lounge to wait for their table, and then there were those who came to the lounge for no other reason than to listen to Cathy play the piano and sing. Cathy was there Tuesday through Saturday, 6:00 pm to closing. She had a beautiful voice, played the piano like a pro, and kept restless, hungry people entertained and happy. The lounge was always packed; oftentimes, it was elbow-room only. This was going to be one of those nights.

Hanna took Kirsti by the arm, pulling her closer, and said with a toothy grin, "It's a good thing you came out of the backroom when you did because I think Tracy was about ready to lock you in."

"Why would she want to lock me in the backroom?" Kirsti asked, genuinely puzzled.

Hanna nodded toward the entrance of the lounge. Tracy, who was playing hostess, was leading two very handsome men to their table; they would be Kirsti's first customers.

"So? Tracy is hostess tonight, so what?" Kirsti shrugged, not fully understanding the implication, tucked her tray on her hip and headed toward the lounge. Hanna shook her head and sighed. That girl is just too naive for her own good. Hanna had been keeping a close eye on Tracy since the first day she came to work at the Orchard Lake Country Club. There was something about Tracy that needed watching. Hanna didn't trust Tracy as far as she could throw her.

Chapter Seven

When Jack and Vic finally made their grand entrance into the restaurant, bar, and lounge of the Orchard Lake Country Club, they were greeted by a pretty, well-shaped, very blond young girl. She was smiling, revealing perfect white teeth, and asking them if they had reservations to which Vic replied with a hesitant and questioning, "No?"

Jack was standing in the background twiddling his thumbs and looking the place over.

The girl—and oh what a gorgeous girl she was—kept the bright smile on her face as she answered Vic with a "no problem" sort of response. She was answering Vic, but her full attention was directed toward Jack.

"I will have to put you in the lounge, if that is all right with you? We are booked up solid." She smiled again and gave them a helpless, very put on childlike shrug. She was trying unsuccessfully to play a little girl flirtation with Jack, but he wasn't buying it.

Jack was a cop; he was taking notice; besides, young girls were not his thing. He spotted this girl to be nothing but trouble.

The girl needs acting lessons, he thought to himself. Underneath that playful smile and childlike behavior was a little girl who was used to getting what she wanted. There is something about the smell of spoiled that stands out. It has a distinct and recognizable odor and is most generally considered rather unpleasant by most everyone who comes close to it. Jack could smell it on himself every now and then. He didn't like the odor on himself or anyone else, for that matter. Tracy, as the saying goes, was spoiled rotten.

Jack was right. Tracy was an only child. She had a very wealthy father, a State Supreme Court justice who indulged her every whim and a mother who ignored her childhood requirements, such as love and affection, and only paid attention to her proper social requirements. Her father brought a lot of business to the Orchard Lake Country Club and had been the one to insist that Hanna hire Tracy as a hostess. Hanna had been very reluctant, but Joe kept pushing her to "give the girl a chance."

Tracy had an undeniable natural beauty about her. She had long lush blond hair. Lengthy dark lashes surrounded her startling deep green eyes; a petite nose and full mouth all encased in a perfectly shaped oval face. Her creamy complexion was as smooth as silk. She was tall and slender and had unusual grace for a girl her age. She was richly groomed from head to foot. She displayed her pampered lifestyle with every move she made. Jack disliked her instantly.

Tracy ignored Vic, pouring all of her attention on Jack as she led the two men to their table in the lounge. After she had them seated, she looked directly at Jack and said, "If there is anything I can do for you, please let me know" Her soft voice purring suggestively.

Jack knew exactly what she meant. He had dabbled with her type before and found them to be nothing less than perilous. He chose to disregard Tracy completely, looked at Vic, and said, "Nice place."

Jack had been down this road many times. Vic, no slouch himself in the business of being a cop, was appraising the situation. He decided to help his friend out a bit.

"I suppose it's OK. Who knows, I haven't been here long enough to judge the place, Jack, give me a little time, huh? What you see ain't always what you get."

Vic gave Tracy a slow once-over from top to bottom. His eyes were evocative and deliberately imposing. Vic wasn't used to making bad impressions, and because of this, his act of lascivious fell flat on its face. Tracy wasn't biting, not in the least and rightfully; however, Jack was getting a big bang out of it.

"Are you going to be our waitress?"

Vic, so busy trying to do his part hadn't seen Jack run his hand across his throat, giving him the cut signal.

"Your waitress will be here in a moment." Tracy was having fun now.

Tracy had caught on immediately and spoke deliberately to Jack, not Vic.

"Why don't I get your first round for you? I don't see your waitress right now."

Before Vic could say another word, Jack interceded, "We'll wait. Why don't you find her and send her over, the sooner the better?"

Jack's eyes were on Vic when he spoke. Vic lifted an eyebrow to his friend and shut his mouth.

Tracy turned and walked away. She wasn't done yet, not by a long shot. She wasn't about to let this opportunity pass her by. The man of her dreams had just walked through the door. This guy was supremely handsome, and she wanted him. She noticed Kirsti heading toward their table.

"Damn it, of all nights to have Kirsti in the lounge, why tonight?"

Kirsti was a problem to Tracy. She held an undiluted hatred for Kirsti because Kirsti was everything she wasn't, and she knew it. Kirsti was well liked by everyone. Tracy threw this thought to the side, for the moment, because there was a line of people waiting for her when she went back to her hostess station. She would think about this later; right now, she had to think about her job. Hanna was watching her; Tracy didn't like Hanna either. Tracy was also fully aware that the feelings were mutual. She moved rapidly back to her station, feeling Hanna's dark eyes watching her every move.

Jack and Vic had hardly gotten settled after their go-around with Tracy when their waitress appeared. She looked at each one of them, Vic first and then Jack. Her pleasant expression insinuated that she had known them for years and was elated to see them. Her smile was so warm and welcoming that both Jack and Vic lost track of themselves for a moment; Jack and Vic were thinking the same thing: cute face, cute body, cute everything.

"I don't think I have seen either of you in here before? Is this your first visit?" Kirsti asked, her clear blue eyes studying both of them closely. She, of course, knew she had never seen either of them before. The question was purely an opener for conversation.

"Can I get you something from the bar, or would you like to go straight to the menu?"

Vic was the first to speak. For some reason, or another he wanted to leap in before Jack got the chance. All at once, and without any good reason, he felt like he was competing with Jack, and for no good reason that he could understand at this particular moment, he wanted to be alone at the table and have this one all to himself. It was foolish and soon he mentally up righted himself and brought himself back to where he belonged, but not without a twist.

"My friend over there, his name is Jack, would like a Windsor Water in a tall glass, I will take the same."

Vic looked at her nametag and added, "Hi, Kirsti, my name is Vic. The ugly guy over there is Jack. You have to forgive him; he hasn't learned to speak yet. He looks smart enough but he is very, very slow. Jack, are you awake? This girl wants to know if you want something to drink. Windsor Water, right? He fancies Windsor Water."

Vic realized, after he said this, that he was being offensive to his best friend. He felt a twinge of regret, only a slight tiny little twinge. In fact, he felt like he had to continue, for some reason, or another and again for no particular reason that he could understand at this particular moment.

Jack gazed intrinsically at his friend and smirked benignly as he said, "I would like a Windsor water in a tall glass, easy on the ice. My redundant buddy over there wants the same. On the other hand, maybe he wants to get to know you better but is to shy to say so. He seems to be acting a bit out of character."

Kirsti laughed and said, "I will be right back with your drinks."

Jack noticed that her laugh was wholesome and larger than her size; it came quickly and instantaneously. She left as rapidly as she had come.

Jack gave his chum a teasing look and said, "I think I am in love."

Vic winced and said, "You are always in love. You are in love with more girls than you know how to handle, and you have more girls in love with you than you know how to deal with. Tell me something new, and besides, it isn't your turn, it's my turn."

"Your turn? Since when did we take turns?" Jack asked with mocked incredulity.

"I think I have just been struck by a moment of temporary insanity."

Vic started laughing from the bowels on up and then so did Jack.

Jack's best friend had spoken the truth. Jack was always involved with no less than three women at any one time. Women loved Jack, and he loved them. Vic, on the other hand, had been dating the same girl for five years. Vic and his girlfriend, Tory, had watched Jack waltz his way through many, many relationships; and for certain this one was way too young for either of them. Vic was loyal to Tory and wanted to remain loyal to her. He was a one-woman man.

By the time Kirsti returned with their drinks, both Vic and Jack had regained their composure. Kirsti set two paper napkins containing the Country Club logo down first and then the drinks. Jack was fascinated with that dimple and those freckles sprinkled across her small nose and cheeks.

"Will there be anything else?" She was applying standard waitress jargon.

Jack lifted his drink, moved his napkin a bit, set his drink back down and said, "One more thing, do you have a last name, Kirsti?" He used a solid Irish dialect.

Vic shifted his long lean body in his chair to an almost sprawling position. This was going to be good. Jack was in action. The movement from the tall blond man brought Kirsti's attention back to Vic. She was a bit taken aback at how long his body was. She liked his face, his neatly cut, straight blond hair. He had an amused look on his face that made Kirsti apprehensive. Two guys out together, in a bar, probably hustling and now making her their sport for the evening. She had seen this before, many times. She looked quickly at their hands for wedding rings and didn't see any. The way that the blond guy was looking at the dark-haired guy, she was almost certain she was right. She could play this game. This was as much a part of a waitress's job as serving food, drinks, and collecting tips.

Kirsti shifted her tray over to the other hip, looked at Jack and said, "I don't think you know me well enough to ask that question. In fact," she said with dead seriousness, "I am sure you don't know me well enough to ask me any questions." She gave him a flash of her dimple, turned, and walked away.

Jack took a sip of his drink and glanced up at Vic and said, "Brace yourself, I think we are going to be here all night."

Vic responded with an overt sigh as if to say, "So? What else is new?"

Chapter Eight

Kirsti walked back to the bar to order another round of drinks; the place was filling up fast. Bud Haveland was tending bar in the lounge this evening, alone or at least, for the time being, another bartender was due to come in and assist him at the same time as Lori was arriving to assist Kirsti. Bud had been with Joe and Hanna from the start and was a deliberate and highly honed bartender. He had stick-straight black hair that he wore in the now-back-in-fashion military cut, tight to the sides and short on top. He had sagging colorless gray eyes and a gnarled, deeply lined face. He was of medium height, long backed, and short in the legs. He was strongly muscled through the shoulders and arms. He did have a slight paunch around the middle, but other than that, he was in great shape for a man his age. The bartender's uniforms consisted of a white short-sleeved shirt, black tie, and black pants. Bud was the only one who would not use Hanna's services; he cleaned and pressed his own. "Too much starch" was his complaint. He had long arms and large hands that were covered with thick black hair. He stooped slightly through the shoulders. The characteristics that made Budrick special to everyone who knew him even remotely was his significant ear-to-ear, effervescent, grin; his equally sarcastic, clever, ever-present sense of humor; and his phenomenal memory.

Kirsti called in the two drinks to Bud and waited as he mixed them.

"Whew," he said, brushing his brow with his large hand, "That was a tough one."

Kirsti looked at Bun and then at the tray, he had placed the drinks on.

"Which one is the Windsor water?" she inquired playfully.

Bud studied the two drinks, shrugged and, with equal seriousness, said, "Why, the one with the single straw in it is the Windsor Water."

Bud used various methods to distinguish one drink from another. A scotch and water and whiskey water look the same in a glass and especially a frosted glass, thus the scotch gets one straw, the whiskey two. He taught Kirsti to listen to the sound of the drink while stirring. A scotch and water and a scotch and soda can look the same but will sound differently. There were many little tricks to the trade that Budrick taught Kirsti to make her job easier. He taught Kirsti to go from right to left around the table and call them to him in the order, she had taken them. He would then mix the drinks and place them on the tray exactly as she had called them in, eliminating all confusion about which drink belonged to whom when she delivered them. Bud never needed anything written down, it didn't matter if it was a table of one or a table of twenty-one, Bud would remember every drink belonging to every person at every table he had mixed drinks for. All Kirsti would have to do is shout, "Another round for table two!" and Bud would have it right every time, ready and waiting for her when she arrived at the waitress station to collect her order. He was amazing, and Kirsti loved him dearly.

Bud let out a laugh, his face lit up with glee, and then he let out a roaring laugh, his face splitting into that wonderful ear-to-ear grin. Kirsti broke into knee-buckling laughter. Bud picked up a shorty beer from behind the bar and took a deep swig. He looked at Kirsti, held it up to her, and said as though he had been caught with his hand in the cookie jar, "Just checking, I wouldn't want to sell bad beer!" Drinking on the job was permitted if it didn't interfere with business, and it never did. Customers were always buying the waitresses and bartender's drinks. The bartender kept a separate tab, and the money the customer paid toward the drinks was given back to the waitresses and themselves in tips.

Kirsti gave him another chuckle. As she reached to take the tray containing the two Windsor waters, Bud grabbed her left hand and squeezed it tightly.

"Be careful, I think Tracy has her sights set on the guy at table number one, the dark-haired guy. She has daggers in her eyes, and they're aimed right at you, Kirsti, so be careful. I think the little bitch has it in for you."

Nothing slipped by Budrick. Kirsti glanced at table number one and then at Tracy, who was standing at the same table, flirting with the guy named Jack. She shrugged and said, "So? Lori is here. She gets them now. I have eleven through twenty to worry about. Budrick, you have got to watch your language! This is a public place. What if someone hears you talk about her that way! Name calling only displays ignorance. Her name is Tracy."

"She doesn't seem to be making much of an impression." Bud was ignoring Kirsti's chastening remark because he had heard it many times before.

Kirsti took another look, Bud was right. The dark-haired guy looked uncomfortable, almost irritated. His friend, however, seemed to be enjoying himself.

"Bud, you are such a gossipmonger. You should be ashamed of yourself! Besides, was I to have my choice of the two? Hmmmm, I like the blond guy. Tracy can have the dark-haired one all to herself as far as I am concerned."

The two men were now on their third drink when Kirsti strolled by their table, filling in for Lori as she made a trip to the ladies' room. On the delivery of the second drink, Jack had tried to extract Kirsti's phone number from Lori but had gotten nowhere.

Jack had seen the young dark-haired freckled-faced girl striding their direction and was ready for her. When she was standing by their table, her tray once again resting on her hip, Jack spoke before she could open up her mouth.

"You seem to have deserted us. I thought you were going to be our waitress for the evening. That girl over there told me so, and I believed her." He pointed at Tracy, who was escorting a group of people into the dining area. "If you won't tell me your last name, and you won't give me your phone number, then maybe you will tell me what nationality you are."

"What's the matter, you don't like Lori?" Kirsti shifted the tray to the left hip and her attention to Vic. "Your friend asks too many questions. Would you like another drink?"

"Jack, be nice. I have to intercede on my friend's behavior, you see, he doesn't accept change easily. Remember, I did mention earlier that he is slow?"

Kirsti was having a hard time maintaining as she played along.

"I am so sorry for your friend, what a good person you are to take him with you. It must be tough to have to travel with a person who is so embarrassingly dull. He seems to have a hard time catching on." Kirsti was trying hard not to show any sense of humor at all.

"All right, that's enough! I can't take anymore of this crap."

Jack tried to laugh, but his gaze toward Vic spoke a different language. Kirsti saw a glimmer of animosity pass through his eyes. Jack was apparently tiring of the game. Kirsti felt no sympathy for him at all; he had started the game, and if he didn't like how it was turning out, tough bounce.

Vic knew he had gone one step too far. He was getting a bit weary of the bantering as well; enough was enough. It was time to change course.

"And yes, both of us would like another drink, but change mine to a Miller Genuine Draft, and what about answering my question. What is your nationality?"

Kirsti was taken back a bit by Jack's change of tone. He was serious. She had been asked endless questions, this was part of the business; but never before had anyone, intentionally flirting with her, asked her this one. She glanced at Vic and could see he wasn't going to be of any help. She glanced again at Jack and carefully considered her answer.

She straightened up and pulled the tray in front of her, holding it with both hands as though to create a barrier, the round, gray tray resting against her midsection. She looked at Jack. Her blue eyes intense, her friendly smile was gone. Jack was beginning to wonder if he had hit a sore spot. He hoped he hadn't.

"Genealogically speaking, my father's ascendants can be considered to be of Norwegian extraction, a hundred percent. My mom's ascendants are of German, English, and Irish, extraction. Her mother comes from German derivative, and her father of the English and Irish, in equal proportions. I will allow you to do the math."

Kirsti then smiled, turned away from the table as though to walk away. She stopped, turned around, and said with a grin, "But my grandparents on both sides were born in the United States, my parents were born in the United States, and I was born in the United States. This makes my nationality American."

Kirsti made her way through the thick crowd of people, toward the bar, leaving Jack to his own thoughts and Vic wondering about his friend. He seemed to be, momentarily, in a world of his own. Vic was beginning to wonder if his friend had lost his marbles; this girl was way too young for him. What was he thinking? Hopefully, this was nothing more than idle flirtation.

When Kirsti brought Jack and Vic their last drinks for the evening, she was rushed about it. She hardly gave either of them notice as she placed the drinks on their table. Jack grabbed her hand and asked, "Would you consider going on a date with me?"

Vic was now really amazed. This was not Jack's usual mode of operation. He could not believe his ears. Jack was not being his normal self. This girl was cute, and she was different than most that either of them had ever had contact with; but really, she wasn't all that special, or was she? If he thought she was, why wouldn't Jack think so too? Jack had beaten him to the punch, once again, as always; now *this* was business as usual. Vic took his mind immediately to Tory to remind himself, once again, that he was not Jack. He didn't think like Jack, and he certainly didn't want to be like Jack even though he cared deeply for him. They were different, and because of this, they were close, not in spite of it.

Kirsti pulled her hand away quickly; her reply was just as quick. "I don't know you well enough to answer that question, and you certainly don't know me well enough to ask me that question, and besides, people don't 'date' anymore. Dating, if you have not noticed, is a thing of the past." Her inflection on the age difference was well noted by both men.

She dropped the ticket on the table, turned, and left Jack and Vic to consider their next move. They were out of her hair now. Kirsti felt a bit off balance. She made a hasty retreat toward the dressing room. Her shift was over; she looked in the mirror, went to the toilet, washed her hands, brushed her teeth, and changed her clothes. When she came back out of the dressing room, Jack and Vic were gone.

Good, she thought. *Good, good, good!*

Hanna was waiting for Kirsti at the bar in the main dining room. Kirsti had changed clothes and was now wearing a navy blue pair of sweat pants, matching sweatshirt, and bright white canvas tennis shoes. There wasn't a mar or a smudge on either shoe. She looked so young, innocent, and vibrant; it was hard for Hannah to imagine she had just graduated from college this very day. She didn't look old enough. Was Hanna serving her drinks for the first time she would have carded her just like everyone else did, much to Kirsti's chagrin.

"I have great news for you, Kirsti. Your mom just called and told me to tell you that your grandmother has regained consciousness and is now in stable condition."

Kirsti gave Hannah a big hug; this was great news.

"Thank you. You have no idea how much I needed to hear this. I will sleep better tonight knowing that grandma is going to be OK. Man that put a scare into me! I can't stand the thought of losing grandma. I just can't stand it! I hope I go before she does."

Hanna hugged her back and said, "I had nothing to do with this piece of good news, and don't talk that way, Kirsti! What a dreadful thought! Here, I have a note for you." She pressed a crumpled up piece of paper into Kirsti's hand.

Kirsti unfolded the note, it read, "Call me if you want to go out on a 'DATE.'" Included was a phone number; the note was signed Jack. She stuffed the crumpled piece of paper in her purse, wishing the note had been from the tall, lanky, blonde guy named Vic. She had liked Vic better than Jack. Perhaps it was because he seemed like the strong, silent type. She preferred the strong, silent types. They always seemed to be more intellectual, more discerning. She had liked his eyes; he had beautiful teeth and a compelling smile. Jack was, well, just too good looking; and men who were too good looking always attracted too much attention. She didn't want a man in her life that every single woman on the face of the earth would be falling all over. She had been aware, all evening long, that there wasn't a woman in the club that could take their eyes off Jack, whatever his last name was. She didn't know, and she didn't care.

Kirsti left the Country Club by the same door she had entered. Charlie was there, his head down. As she was getting in her car to leave, he came out the backdoor and shouted, "Congratulations, Kirsti!"

"Well, Charlie! Thank you!" Maybe Charlie was all right after all.

When Jack and Vic were leaving, they had to clear up their tab with Tracy; as hostess, this was part of her job description. While he was in the business of doing this, Jack asked Tracy if she knew Kirsti's last name. His motive for asking, he explained, was to see that she was the one who got the tip. Tracy was preoccupied with entering the information into the computer and answered without second thought.

"Sure," Tracy said compliantly, "Her last name is Poval."

Jack pressed on, "You wouldn't have her address would you?"

Tracy lifted her head from the task at hand; her mind was now completely in center with what was happening. She said to Jack, and far too obviously, "I can't give you that information. However, I will be glad to give you my name, address, and phone number."

With a perfectly manicured hand, she wrote on a small piece of paper her full name, address, and phone number and handed it to Jack. He took the piece of paper, folded it without looking at it, and shoved it into his pants pocket.

"If I leave a message for Kirsti, will you see that she gets it, along with her tip?" he asked.

She nodded and said, "Sure."

Jack wrote out the note as Tracy ran his credit card through the machine. When Tracy handed Jack his credit card, he handed Tracy a piece of paper folded in half. After Jack had left, Tracy read the note, crumpled it up, and threw it in the wastebasket. Tracy wasn't aware of Hanna, who was standing right behind her, watching the entire interaction. After Jack and Vic were out the door, she moved into stance behind Tracy, picked up the wastebasket, and retrieved the crumpled paper. She read the note and glared at Tracy with repugnance.

Hanna spat out the words she had been longing to say for months.

"Tracy, you're fired, effective this second. Get your belongings and remove yourself by the back door. Leave your uniform here, I will send you your final paycheck."

Hanna turned on her heels and made her way toward the dressing room from which Kirsti was just departing. She would intersect with Kirsti at the bar in the main dining room.

Tracy wasn't the least bit moved or affected by any thoughts of regret; she was way too far into herself to take this but with a grain of salt. She had never needed the job; she only worked because of her father's insistence. She didn't leave directly but went back to the dressing room and changed from uniform into her street clothes, leaving her uniform in a hapless heap in the middle of the floor. Tracy spotted a bottle of bleach sitting on one of the shelves and promptly poured the entire bottle over all of her uniforms, all of them, the one she had been wearing and the ones still hanging in dry-cleaner bags on the rack. She then took her lipstick out of her purse and wrote in large letters, all over the mirror, in large sprawling letters, "Screw you, Hanna!" And as though in afterthought, she wrote in large letters, "And you too, Kirsti! I will see both of you in hell!"

Before she left, she sauntered up to Hanna and said fervidly, "You can keep my paycheck and shove it right up your fat rear end."

Then she made her way, head held high, her thick blond hair swirling behind her, out the back door, giving Charlie the middle finger as she passed, which he never saw because his head was down; he was busy concentrating on one his concoctions. Tracy thought she heard him mutter something under his breath that sounded like "It's about time."

Hanna wasn't the least bit intimidated by Tracy's theatrics, quite the contrary. She gave Joe a toothy smirk and said, "Good riddance to bad rubbish."

Joe grimaced, nodded his head, and thought with quirky emotion, "Where did I ever meet this hardheaded, stubborn, dark-haired, dark-eyed vixen?"

He gave his wife a military salute as he went about his business; it was time to close up shop.

When Joe went out to make sure everyone had left the parking lot after closing, he spotted a crumpled up piece of paper on the sidewalk, just outside the front door. He leaned down and picked it up. The crumpled up piece of paper contained Tracy's address and phone number. He walked back into the restaurant and handed the note to Hanna. She read the note, grinned, crumpled it back up again, put it into the ashtray, lit a match, and set the note on fire.

"What goes around comes around. The chicken always comes home to roost." She murmured to herself.

Out loud she voiced, "I will say it again, good riddance to bad rubbish."

Joe gave her another salute and replied with a certain amount of unusual vigor, "My sentiments exactly."

Chapter Nine

Jack Ireland was yanked out of a hard and sound sleep at five thirty in the morning. His buddy, longtime friend, and partner was standing over him with a pitcher of ice cold water and threatening to dump it all over him if he didn't get his ass out of bed—pronto. Through his sleepy haze, Jack noticed that Vic was dead serious.

Vic placed the pitcher of water on the nightstand and watched as Jack slowly pulled himself out of bed and ambled his way toward the shower. Jack was in no real hurry, but then Jack never hurried much, not for anyone or anything. Jack ignored his friend as he showered and dressed. No words were spoken, not even when Vic handed Jack a cup of steaming hot, very strong coffee, not even a thank you. Vic didn't take this personally.

Vic took the driver's seat while Jack strapped himself into the passenger seat. Jack took a sip of his coffee, opened his window, and dumped it out.

"Whew, that is just about the worst cup of coffee I have ever had in my life. Who taught you how to make coffee anyway?"

Vic ignored his friend, shoved the car into gear, hit the gas pedal hard enough to throw Jack's head back against the cushion.

"Easy boy, what's the rush? You damned near gave me a case of whiplash!"

No response from Vic. They hadn't hit the end of the short driveway before Jack was sound asleep again. Jack had learned to sleep when he could.

As Jack slept, Vic drove with ease and sped to the Credit River area, traveling west on Highway 70, barely stopping at the intersection of Interstate 35. He sped up as he leaned the car into the curves of the road, weaving their way around the numerous lakes to be found along Highway 8. The route to Credit River, west of Interstate 35, was scenic although Vic barely glanced left or right as he took each curve with pronounced emphasis, rarely lifting his right foot from the gas pedal; his left foot never touched the brake until he arrived at the intersection of County Road 8 and what was known as the "red road". The usual forty-five-minute drive took less than twenty minutes.

Jack joined the realms of the living about the time that Vic was parking the car. "Good morning, glad to see you could join me." Vic said wryly.

Jack sat up straight, his eyes instantly alert. He glanced at Vic as he got out of the car, "This had better be good because if it isn't, I am making you a promise. You will never again find an available pitcher in my house, ever. I am going to get rid of every single one I own."

"Single is the right word, you have only one pitcher, and it was dirty. Your blessed Irish mother would have been ashamed of you. I had to wash the thing out before I could put clean water into the darned thing. I thought I might be helping you out. A bath served in bed is usually welcomed by most."

"That's breakfast, you big fat, ignorant piece of owl crap."

"Oh." Vic said with a shrug. "No matter, breakfast, water, what's the difference? Either way you should be grateful that you have such a friend as my humble self to keep you so well attended."

"Humble? What? Did you spend all of last night studying the dictionary? You wouldn't know humble from stumble other than maybe that it rhymes."

"OK then," said Vic, "Rhyme rhymes with crime, and that is why I have brought you to this place so early in the morning."

Dawn was creeping up on the horizon when Jack and Vic arrived at the crime scene. The air had an icy feel to it. There were black and whites all over the place. Jack and Vic pulled their badges out of their pockets and presented them to the first officer they met. The cop who greeted them was an older man, about retirement age. He had a deeply lined likable face. He introduced himself as Deputy Bob Reichter from the Scott County Sheriff's Department. He held a large flashlight in his right hand; he shifted the flashlight to his left hand before he shook Jack and Vic's hand. He then led them to the edge of the road and pointed his flashlight into a very deep, very dark ditch. Jack guessed the depth to be ten to twelve feet if not more.

"I have been around a long time, but I have never seen anything like this. There she is."

Bob pointed his flashlight downward into the ditch. The darkness and the tall grass made everything obscure and hard to see; the flashlight wasn't much help. If there was a body down there, Jack couldn't make it out.

"You've been awake longer than me Vic, what do you see down there?"

"Not a thing. Not in this light. We're going to have to go down."

Bob chuckled. a little, "Sorry, I should have mentioned it. I was just pointing towards the general direction. I have read about these things, but I have never, in my entire twenty-eight-year career, come across anything like this, however, I live in a small town. The paramedics and coroner are here and waiting for some lighting so they can move in. Those people over there are trying to set up lights, but there seems to be some technical difficulty going on. Either that or they have decided to wait until sun up. CID is on their way. I was told you were en route, and I should wait for you before I do anything else, so here I am, now what?"

"Who found the body?" Jack asked as he took the flashlight from Bob and pointed it down into the area that Bob had pointed out to him. Jack could not make out anything resembling a body yet without better lighting. This could wait for now.

"You are not going to like the answer to that question. It was the bar manager's dog."

Bob nodded toward the tavern standing silently on top of a slight incline, about a half a block away. Bob looked at Jack and Vic and coughed out a laugh at the look of alarm on their faces.

"I didn't think you would like it. The dog did a real number on the crime scene, tore it up good, and by the way, the manager tumbled his way down there too."

"Well, isn't this bullshit just the best way to start the day?" Jack was getting aggravated. "Who owns the crime scene?"

Bob took the long tubular flashlight from Jack and stuck it back into his waist belt. He pointed to a young rookie cop, standing in a crowd of black jackets. He gave a whistle, which drew everyone's attention, held up his hand, and hollered, "Jack, get over here."

Vic looked at Jack, chortled, and said, "Well now, ain't this a coincidence."

"Jack, meet Jack." Bob was also appreciating the irony.

Jack spent about fifteen minutes interviewing the young cop, getting as much detail from him as he could. The young cop was obviously shaken. This was his first major crime scene. After he had gotten as much as he thought he could out of the kid, he handed him back to Bob.

Daylight had fully presented itself when the Dakota County CSI unit presented itself and cordoned off the area with bright yellow tape. A special enforcement unit was brought in to direct traffic away from the crime scene and to guard the perimeter from the curious, the press, and anyone else whose presence the investigators deemed unnecessary.

Jack looked to the southwest, the sky was clear. This was a good thing. Rain is a miserable interference with the collection of evidence. After some discussion with his CSI team, it was decided that Jack would go down after the tech team had finished with their procedures. They would take pictures, do scrapings, check the body for anything and everything that might give them information about the victim and about the crime that had been committed, and most importantly, hopefully something about the killer. They would study every inch of the surrounding area. They would be thorough.

Everyone else who didn't belong there was asked to leave. The younger Jack, eager to get home to his wife and new baby, was not going home for many hours yet. He would have to stick around until everyone left, and then he would have to go back to headquarters and fill out a report, and if, and only if, there was no one who wanted to talk to him could he go home. Jack felt sorry for Jack. It isn't any fun to be called to a crime scene of this magnitude at the end of your shift. But then, he is, after all, a cop; this is all part of the job. *So much for feeling sorry for him.* The wife and new baby would have to wait; such was life as a cop.

Jack, Vic, and Bob Reichter entered the tavern via the front door. The manager was sitting at the bar, drinking a cocktail made of vodka and tomato juice. Judging by the empty glasses sitting in front of him, he was on his third drink. The three men who entered pulled out their badges and introduced themselves. The manager lifted his glass to each of them; he looked weary. His eyes were glazed, either from shock or from alcohol, more than likely from both. This sort of thing didn't happen in Credit River. Many people would be glassy eyed before the day was done.

The manager of the Credit River Tavern introduced himself as Harley Blackwell; Charles William Blackwell was his real name. Charles had inherited his nickname Harley because he loved to ride motorcycles and his preference was Harley Davidson. He had saved all of his earnings from birth and, at the age of sixteen, bought his first bike, a Harley Davidson super sport. It was a used bike and in need of a lot of attention, but he had fixed it up himself and eventually traded it in for another newer model that he rode back and forth to work every day, rain or shine, snow, and even over a sleet-covered highway. He was more comfortable on a Harley then he was walking. He was of average height and average weight; there was nothing really remarkable about him aside from his thick growth of hair that virtually covered what might have been a very nice-looking face. He had long brown hair that hung to the middle of his back, neatly brushed, styled, and clean to the point of glistening. His deeply furrowed black/brown eyes looked at the investigators with a sadness that cut right through their durable exterior.

"Why don't you just start from the beginning and tell us how you came about finding the body, and if we have questions, we'll ask them later."

Jack was the first to converse; he spoke softly and reassuringly.

"Fred, my dog,"—Harley nodded toward a German shepherd, lying on the floor by his feet, looking as sad as his owner—"started whining and barking about three this morning. I have a cot in the backroom that I use if I have to run back-to-back shifts. I worked late last night and am scheduled to open up today. I don't suppose that will be happening, huh?"

"No. Most likely not" Jack replied without hesitation.

"I prefer to stay here rather than drive back and forth. I rent an apartment in New Prague, which isn't that far, but we generally don't close until after one in the morning, and by the time I get through cleaning up, it is two o'clock. The boss expects me to have the bar open by 10:00 AM. I am single, live alone, and it really doesn't matter to me or my boss if I stay here or go home after my shift is over. Fred is my watchdog and my only companion. I like it that way. He minds what I say and does what I tell him to do without dispute."

Harley turned around in his stool, snapped his fingers, and Fred came to full attention. Harley snapped his fingers again. Fred jumped on command and placed his front paws on Harley's knees and stayed there until Harley snapped his fingers again. Fred went into an attentive sitting position, waiting for his master to give him the next command.

"Show your teeth and give me a growl."

Fred moved into a lunging position, his eyes moving back and forth surreptitiously; he then began to growl a deep, dark, threatening growl. Harley raised his arm and said, "Attack."

The dog lunged at his master, grabbed him by the arm with a full set of sharp glistening teeth and without effort, dragged him to the floor. Harley yelled out, "Stop."

Fred immediately let go of Harley's arm and began licking him on the face.

"That's enough now. Lay down." Harley's voice was soft and demurring.

The dog moved away from his master, panting in obvious satisfaction. Harley picked himself up off the floor, dusted himself off, and sat down again. The cuff of Harley's shirtsleeve had been ripped up by the dog, but nothing else was the least bit affected. Harley gave the men a shy grin, revealing straight pearly white teeth, "I go through a lot of shirts."

Jack, Vic, and Bob had jumped back about ten feet with their hands on their pistols; they were convinced. Everyone was of the same mind frame; this dog would tear out their throats at the command of his master or would die trying.

"Fred came into the back room and nudged me, trying to wake me up at about three thirty this morning. I know this because I looked at the clock. I thought he might have had to go outside to do his thing. He ordinarily never bothers me in the middle of the night. I tried to ignore him, but he was being very persistent. He was grabbing at the bedding and pulling at me, barking and snarling. I knew that something was going on besides wanting to be let outside to use his bathroom privileges. He was acting frantic. I knew he wanted out because when I got up, he raced to the door and stood there with his body in full attack position, and he was growling. When I opened up the door, he went straight for the ditch, and then I lost sight of him, but I could hear him barking.

"When I didn't follow him, Fred came running back to the tavern, barking all the way. It was dark, man, really dark, and I didn't want to follow him. Shit, I didn't know what was down there, and I wasn't so sure I wanted to know, but Fred was insistent. I knew the only way to get him to shut up was to follow him.

"I went behind the bar and grabbed a flashlight and followed him. Fred made the trip down into the ravine without a problem. I followed him but lost my footing and fell halfway down. It was slippery from the moisture and long grass. I slid on my backside and then tumbled into this body lying there. I think she broke my fall, but I can't be sure, everything became a blur after that." Harley gave a deep shudder. Jack noticed goose bumps rising on Harley's arms.

"How did you know it was a she?" asked Jack, his tone patient and kind.

"I didn't know to start with. I only felt this person or what seemed like a person lying there. I pulled myself up to my feet and then had to find my flashlight. I had lost it in the fall. I groped around for a while until I found it, and then I found her. The girl was just lying there. She looked dead to me. With the dog barking and a body just lying there, I was scared out of my ever-loving mind. I didn't check to see if she was dead, I should have, but I didn't. I think I came out of the ditch faster than I went down. Like I said, things were getting sort of frantic by then, and my recollection is blurry. I remember I yelled at Fred to shut up, and then I ran back to the tavern and called 911." His darkly tanned face went into a deeper frown and his now-black eyes more morose.

"Fred would like to know what is going on, and so would I."

The ditch encasing the body was steep, about a ten-foot drop and almost straight down. The ground surrounding the crime scene was wet with heavy morning dew. Jack had to sidestep all the way down the incline, inch by inch. There was a moment or two when Vic laughed as he saw Jacks arm's waving in the air, trying to regain his balance.

"Hang on, Jack, you can make it!" he yelled laughingly, momentarily uplifting the mood for everyone around him. Everyone was holding their breath as they watched Jack make his way precariously to the bottom of the deep and steep ditch.

When Jack finally reached the bottom of the ditch, he found a young girl with long, blond hair wrapped gracefully around her face. Her beautiful blue eyes were open and staring vacantly to the west. She wasn't any older than twenty-five. She wore no clothing. Her long, lean body was lying on its left side, her right leg resting very casually over the left. Her left hand was clenched tightly. When Jack opened the hand, he found a large purple button. He removed the button and studied it for a moment. There were no strings attached, none, it was stripped clean. He placed the button back into her hand and tightened up the fist again. CSI would remove the button after he left. The bruises on her neck told Jack that she had been strangled, more than likely manually. The rest would be up to the coroner to evaluate.

"Take her," Jack said to the coroner as he grimly made his way back out of the ditch. Harley, his face ashen, denied knowing the girl. Jack believed him.

Before Jack and Vic left the crime scene, he grabbed a hold of the CSI team manager and said, "I want you to keep a very close eye on that purple button that she is holding in her left hand. If that gets lost in the process, I will have your hide."

Jack turned to Harley and said grimly, "I want a list of everyone who has ever entered this bar, and I want a very specific list of anyone who was here last night. Can you do that for me?"

"I will do my very best, sir. How much time do I have?"

"Consider that I needed this information as of yesterday."

Dignity, there should be a sense of dignity to death; this young girl had been deprived of any sort of dignity to her death. She had been stripped of her clothing and her life and left to lie out in the open, in the harsh elements for anyone and everyone to see. More importantly, she died alone and unnaturally. Terror was her last vision of life. Jack carried the insult of this with him as he and Vic left the scene.

With his jaw clenched tight, he looked at Vic and said, "Whoever did this has to pay, Vic. You and are going to get him, and we are going to make him pay, big time."

Vic was once again negotiating the curves on County Road 8. His eyes never left the road ahead of him as he said, "My thoughts exactly, partner."

Chapter Ten

Glenda was sitting at the kitchen table, drinking a cup of coffee, when her sister Kirsti came downstairs. The time was 8:00 AM. Kirsti was dressed and ready for the day. Glenda had heard her get up; she had been up since six o'clock; had showered and dressed quietly so as not to disturb Kirsti. Kirsti wasn't surprised to see her sister when she came down the stairs and into the kitchen because there had been a message on her answering machine when she got home from work, telling her that Glenda would be arriving sometime after midnight, leave the door open, and don't wait up. Kirsti didn't wait up but went immediately to bed. She left the front door unlocked and a note for her sister to make herself comfortable; the guest room was ready for her.

Glenda rose from her chair as her sister entered the room, moved toward her, and gave her a big hug.

"How was your flight, any problems getting wheels?"

"The flight was uneventful, which is always a good thing, and no, I didn't have any problems getting wheels. I have a splashy red Mustang. I called ahead."

The two sisters looked each other over from head to toe and hugged each other again. They hadn't seen each other for six long months. Kirsti was dressed in a pair of tan capris, dark brown tank top, gold jewelry, a jacket that matched the capris, and brown leather shoes—conservative but smart. Glenda was dressed in a Levi shirt, long sleeved, with the cuffs rolled up. The shirt had white buttons, white stitching, and she wore it untucked. She had on jeans that matched the shirt—somewhat—white tennis shoes, and red socks. Glenda didn't wear jewelry or at least no other jewelry than a watch and her wedding ring. Her thick shoulder-length dark blond hair was pulled back into a ponytail with a few stray ends falling around her long oval face.

"You do look wonderful," Glenda said to Kirsti.

"And you are a sight for sore eyes yourself," said Kirsti.

Kirsti poured herself a cup of coffee and sat down at the table, Glenda joined her.

"You've lost more weight, you're getting too thin." Glenda said to Kirsti with a slight hint of disapproval.

"There is no such thing as being too rich or too thin." Kirsti replied. She laughed, looked at her sister, and said, "And you're perfect, I suppose? I see you haven't changed your dress code. What's with the red socks? You've gotten thinner too, but then, you've always been thinner when you've been in love. Nick must be holding your attention."

The last remark was intended to be a barb; Glenda had never held a relationship for very long until she met Nick. Having no desire to get into a sparring match with her sister, Glenda let the remark pass without comment. The girls finished their coffee, maintaining an ongoing bantering type of conversation, neither quite ready to get down to the serious stuff. They chatted about Kirsti's finals, her upcoming graduation, and things in general.

Visiting hours didn't start at Sanford Memorial Hospital until nine o'clock. By the time the girls left the apartment, it was nine forty-five. The drive from Lakeville to Farmington would take roughly fifteen minutes. Glenda drove. She always drove when she and Kirsti went anywhere together. Kirsti was a tail-gaiter; and to make matters worse, she had difficulty keeping her eye on the road, which was a very unhealthy combination. Her driving made Glenda incredibly nervous. Both girls smoked, and the rule was that the one riding lit the cigarettes. They smoked the same brand of cigarettes and always shared out of each other's supply. Halfway to Farmington, Glenda told her sister to light her up a cigarette. Kirsti took a couple of cigarettes out of Glenda's pack and lit them.

"We should really quit this bad habit of ours," Kristi said as she blew smoke into the air.

Glenda took a drag from her cigarette and blew the smoke straight into the air, took a deep breath, kicked the car into fourth gear, and allowed herself the privilege of a moments worth of silence before she made her next remark.

"Sure, everything with you is 'we' on the bad side and 'yours' on the good side. If you want to quit smoking, please do. That will save me plenty. This sharing gets expensive after a while, and besides, we need to talk about Grandma, and while I am having this conversation with you, I intend to enjoy my cigarette."

"What's your problem with Grandma anyway? What do you want to talk about that has you so disrupted and grouchy?"

Kristi rolled down her window and thrust her cigarette butt out the window. "Grandma just had a stroke, she will recover. I know she will. She has the capability. This is only a minor setback for her. Dad said so himself."

"Well, if you consider a stroke a minor setback, you are really in la-la land. For your FYI, I think something brought this stroke on other than old age. She has been very distraught lately. I have been talking to her weekly, and Grandma is convinced that Yvonne is plotting to put her in a nursing home, and this was before she had the stroke, Kirsti."

"This will never happen as long as Dad is alive. Yvonne will never get any such notions past either Dad or Lynn, not ever." Kirsti sounded confident.

"Well," said Glenda, "I hope you are right for Grandma's sake, but I have to say that I have been talking to Grandma, a lot, and she isn't anywhere near as confident about this as you are. You have to also bear in mind that Lynn can be of no help to Dad. She can't stay away from her drinking long enough to stay sober for half a minute. She is probably in worse shape than Grandma is. Lynn's condition has brought a lot of stress into Grandma's life. Perhaps Yvonne is right. A nursing home might at least give Grandma a break from Lynn and certainly it will give Yvonne a well deserved break."

Kristi looked at her sister, her blue eyes were blazing with anger, "Grandma is not going into a nursing home, and I don't want to talk about this any more! What makes you think you know anything anyway! Besides, I talk to Grandma every day of the week, and she hasn't said anything to me about this, not one thing, and she would. I know she would. I think you are overreacting."

"What do you mean overreacting? To what am I overreacting?" Glenda threw back.

"Grandma isn't going to say anything to you because she wouldn't want you to worry. She wants your mind on college. Can you at least try for one minuscule second to think outside what you want and attempt to take a look at what is really going on? This is no time for rose-tinted glasses, Kirsti. Honestly, Kirsti, you cannot ever see things from any other way than the way you want to see things, good, bad, or indifferent. Didn't they teach you anything in college?"

By this time, Glenda had pulled into the parking lot of the hospital and had parked the Mustang in the closest available spot to the front entrance door. The glass double doors were but a few yards in front of her. "Ah," she said more to herself than anyone else. "It pays to call ahead."

Kirsti jumped out of the car the second it stopped. She deliberately slammed the car door shut.

"OK, you don't want to hear it," said Glenda to no one other than herself.

Kirsti was literally stomping her way toward the hospital entrance door. Glenda was familiar with these sorts of tantrums from her sister; they hadn't been sisters this many years for nothing. Glenda took a few long strides and caught up with Kirsti just before she reached the door. Kirsti flung the hospital door open with a force strong enough to cause it to spring back with equal measure, paying no heed to her sister who was by now on her heels. Glenda had to double step to avoid the door closing on her as she entered, but she wasn't quit quick enough. The door hit Glenda in the back of her foot causing her to let out a yelp, something that sounded like "Ouch, gosh, darned it, Kirsti!"

"It serves you right!" Kirsti snarled, not bothering to look back.

"Welcome home and back to the real world," Glenda voiced quietly but not so quietly that Kirsti missed the remark.

Kirsti twisted around and glared at her, her eye's burning with anger, "Just shut up! Just shut up! You are getting on my nerves, big time."

"My, my, my, aren't we being temperamental these days." Glenda was getting a little bit irritated herself.

When the girls came in through the front door of the hospital, they entered the main reception area. The reception desk was off to the right. Ahead of them were padded chairs and a long couch of an indescribable greenish color; to the left was the gift shop. Glenda turned toward the reception desk to inquire into the whereabouts of her grandmother. She was standing at the desk, front and center, when she heard a familiar voice behind her.

"Girls, what in the world is going on? You have got to pipe down! You are going to wake up the whole hospital with your bickering."

Glenda turned around and almost bumped into Kirsti, who was standing right behind her. The person telling them to pipe down was their mother. Glenda swept her sister aside with her forearm, went to her mother, and gave her a big hug; she then stepped out of the way, allowing Kirsti to give her mother a hug. Glenda was taller than her mother by about four inches. Kirsti and her mother were exactly the same shape and size. They could easily share each other's clothing. Their height was 5' 1", and both refused to wear anything larger than a 6. Their size was the only thing that these two shared in common. There was no mistaking Glenda and Mary for mother and daughter; their facial features were identical. Mary's appearance was so youthful that she was often identified as Glenda's sister.

Standing behind Mary was Yvonne. She appeared equally glad to see her nieces. Her smile was welcoming as she embraced them. Yvonne led the group back to the coffee shop. After they had themselves seated at one of four tables and a cup of coffee in front of them, Yvonne volunteered information without anyone asking "the" question.

"Your grandmother is doing really well, better than anticipated. The doctor is in her room right now, and should be finished in a few minutes then you can go in and see her. She is weak, so don't linger too long. We are allowed ten-minute visits every hour."

They then went on to talk about Glenda's trip home from Oklahoma and Kirsti's upcoming graduation. Yvonne steered the conversation. A few minutes later, the doctor strolled into the coffee shop to update Yvonne. The girls took their leave as the doctor, Yvonne, and their mother left the coffee shop for a consultation.

Kirsti entered Grandma's hospital room first with Glenda close behind. Grandma was sitting up in bed. She looked better than either of them had expected. Her coloring was good. She was a short little lady. All stretched out, she might reach 4' 11" and was almost as round as she was tall. Kirsti and Glenda were a year apart and had lived with their grandmother, along with their parents until Kirsti was fourteen years old and Glenda thirteen. Grandma had played as much a part in their daily upbringing as either of their parents had, if not more.

Grandma's eyes lit up as her girls entered the room. "My girls, my girls, how glad I am to see you!" she said, sounding like she had a mouthful of cotton. The girls separated, each to one side of her bed. They hugged her and kissed her and marveled at how well she looked.

"Glenda, you came all the way from Oklahoma, how thoughtful you are. You have always been so thoughtful." Kirsti gave Glenda a glare that spoke volumes.

Grandma turned her sights to Kirsti. "And you are graduating in a few days, I am so very proud of you. Sit down and tell me all about your finals and tell me you will stay with me a long time. Glenda, you have to tell me how your business is going. I have missed you so much. I wish you didn't live so far away. I wish you would call me more often." Grandma couldn't help herself; she was a chronic complainer. This was how she displayed her affections.

The girls sat down and did their best to fill their grandmother in on everything that was going on with them. Glenda had brought her grandmother several magazines, the latest of the latest in fashion and home interior decorating, Grandma's favorite topics. She was a woman of many interests and talents but fashion was her first passion, playing second fiddle only to music. Grandma had paid her way through St. Olaf College by sewing, painting, and taking in laundry. She considered herself the classic example of how a person can get things done when they make up their minds to do so. She was part of the depression generation, making her a hoarder. She never threw anything away. Her house was packed from front to back, upstairs and downstairs with books and magazines that she had accumulated over the years. She referred to them as her friends. To Kirsti and Glenda, their grandmother was an endless storehouse of knowledge and wisdom. They loved her intensely and depended on her. She was their compass.

When their ten minutes were up, almost to the second, Yvonne came through the door.

"It is time for you to leave now; Grandma has to have her rest."

Grandma looked at her daughter with pure belligerence and said, "I will decide when my granddaughters should leave, you go away."

Kirsti looked at her grandmother with shock, surprised by her vicious tone; Glenda was not surprised at all.

Yvonne's eyes turned hard as she said, "Hospital policy, Mother, they have to leave now."

Yvonne left the room to allow Kirsti and Glenda to say their good-byes.

Kirsti and Glenda got up from their chairs at the same time. When they leaned over to give Grandma a kiss good-by, she grabbed their hands and pleaded, "They want to put me in a nursing home, and you have to help me, promise me you will help me."

"We will, Grandma. We will always help you, promise." Kirsti meant it but Glenda knew this was a promise she might not be able to keep.

Yvonne was waiting for them when they entered the reception area. When she told them to sit down, they did. They asked where their mother had gone, Yvonne told them she had to leave, and they were to call her at home when they got back to Kirsti's. She would meet them there later.

Yvonne looked angry because she was angry. She told the girls that Grandma was going to have to go into a nursing home, and if they had any thoughts to the contrary, they might as well keep them to themselves. Grandma was incapable of taking care of herself, and the nursing home was the only alternative plan. She went on to say that she was having enough problems with her sister and brother; she wasn't going to tolerate any from them. Did she make herself clear? Both of the girls were stunned into silence. They had never heard such a threatening tone come from their aunt's mouth. Neither girl had any desire to argue with their aunt. They knew better. Yvonne had always been a strong force in the family; she was highly regarded and deeply respected by everyone who knew her, including every member of the family. The girls were not about to give her any lip regardless of how they felt about her decisions.

As Kirsti and Glenda walked out of the hospital, having been dismissed by their aunt very abruptly and unceremoniously, Kirsti looked at Glenda and said, "I think I am going to be sick."

Glenda looked at her older sister and remarked in return, "Why not?"

They settled into the rent-a-car mustang, Glenda turned on the ignition and said, "Light me up a cigarette. I think I need a drink."

Kirsti lit two cigarettes, one for herself and one for her sister, "Where to now, James? I think I need to be lead astray."

Glenda poured the metal to the floor and spun out of the parking lot, the back tires squealed in protest, the rear end fishtailing.

Kirsti let out a gasp and shouted, "I love it when you do that!"

They looked at each other and laughed until they were crying.

Kirsti slumped back in her seat, looked at her sister who was concentrating on driving, glad that she had her sister with her. They fought over almost everything, but Glenda seemed to know how to handle things; and right now, Kristi needed her sister to handle things. On the way home, they stopped and purchased a bit of beer and a bit of wine. When they arrived at Kirsti's apartment, Mary was waiting for them.

Chapter Eleven

The favorite place in the Poval household had always been the kitchen. This was the place for congregation, conversation, and sharing. The girls and their mom sat down at the table in Kirsti's kitchen. Hilde arrived within minutes. Kirsti got up and poured each of them a glass of wine and put the bottle in the middle of the table. Hilde went into the living room and put a stack of records on the stereo. They would be listening to Jim Reeves, Lynn Anderson, Marty Robbins, Roy Orbison, and Slim Whitman. Hilde always selected the music they would be listening to at their gatherings; this saved at least one argument.

Kirsti introduced the first controversial issue, and the subject was Grandma being put into a nursing home. Both Glenda and Kirsti, interrupting each other, spilled out their anger about this outrage. Their anger picked up steam as they spoke.

Mary tried to calm them down by telling them that Grandma's visit to the nursing home was just a temporary measure until she could manage on her own.

Kirsti was livid. "Grandma will never accept going to a nursing home. I'll stay with her and take care of her. I love Yvonne with all my heart, but I can't go along with her even thinking of putting Grandma in such a dreadful place."

"Yvonne isn't thinking this, it is the doctor, who will not release her, unless she can take care of herself." said Mary.

"What does that mean?" asked Hilde. "What do they mean, exactly, by take care of herself?"

"She has to be able to eat without help. She can't do that right now. She has to be able to get up and walk and at least go to the bathroom by herself. She can't do that right now. When she can feed herself and get up and walk without help, they will let her go home." Mary was trying to infiltrate some optimism.

"When she can accomplish this, we will bring her home. She will require a nurse to come in and check on her daily and have someone provide her with meals and help with some cleaning. Yvonne is working on setting something up for her. Yvonne is concerned about the cost factor. This sort of care can get very expensive.

"Grandma has the farm. Why not liquidate some of the land she owns? This would take care of her for the rest of her lifetime easily." Glenda was looking at her two sisters as she spoke.

"That would be the last thing that your father would ever allow. He will never sell the farm under duress, not ever, and there is another thing that goes along with this that even I don't like. Yvonne is forced to have someone to come into Grandma's house and clean it all up and paint it from top to bottom. She is having this done while Grandma is in the hospital."

"She is going to do this without Grandma knowing?" Glenda was asking; she was astounded. This was a big romper room "no-no". Everyone in the family knew you didn't mess with Grandma's place or Grandma's stuff, not ever. There would never be a forgivable reason to take over Grandma's house without her consent. All three girls looked at their mother like she was growing six heads.

"Grandma is not to know," Mary answered quietly. "That is what Yvonne and I were discussing when you and Kirsti came to the hospital. Yvonne says that to get financial assistance from the state, the place has to be cleaned up, or they will come in and do it for her. Or worse yet, take over the whole affair and then Grandma could very well wind up in a nursing home, permanently."

Kirsti and Hilde stood up at the same time, almost upending their chairs in the process, "Grandma on state assistance? The thought of this is totally audacious. Where is Dad in all of this, I cannot believe this is happening." Kirsti was angry beyond a controllable margin, "Grandma will never stand for this, not ever!"

"The very idea that someone is even considering this might cause her to have another stroke," Hilde murmured, shaking her head back and forth. "This cannot be happening. How exactly is Dad dealing with all that is going on with Grandma? He can't be in favor of this."

"Yeh, just what does Dad think about all of this?" Kirsti asked, repeating the question. "What did Yvonne mean when she said that she was having enough with her brother? That was cryptic. They have always been close."

"He wants to take her home as soon as possible, but I don't think this is going to be the case Kirsti. We have to be realistic, and when it comes to your grandmother, your father isn't always able to be realistic sometimes he has to allow Yvonne to take control of his Mother, she isn't easy to manage and especially now."

Having said this, Mary put her glass of wine up to her lips, took a sip, and said, "Speaking of your dad, I have to talk to you about something concerning him as well."

Mary looked at her three girls; they were waiting for her to speak. She could tell they were far from finished with the first conversation, perhaps it would be better to wait for a better time, but this might be the only time she would be able to get them all together before Glenda had to head back home again and then there was Kirsti's graduation reception coming up. No time like the present? Perhaps it would be better to wait, she vacillated back and forth, her mind in a stir.

Hilde went into the living room and flipped the records over, came back in, and poured all of them another glass of wine. Her two sisters watched her as she did this, waiting for her to sit back down and make some sort of wisecrack that would set them into a fit of hysterical laughter, but nothing came forth. Hilde was by far and away the most cynical of the three daughters; her humor was profound, even bordering on twisted, and always effective. In the worst-case scenario, she could be depended on to offer something that was going to make a difference in the conversation. Not tonight.

After she filled their wine glasses, she looked at her mom and said, "I have heard enough bad news for one day. I am going over to the liquor store and have myself a real drink." She poured her glass of wine into the sink, gathered her purse, her jacket, and walked out the door.

Kirsti and Glenda rose from their chairs as if to stop her, but Mary put her hand out to them and said, "Let her go."

Glenda went into the living room and changed the records, she was tired of country; she wanted something else. She put on Andy

Williams, Neil Diamond, Harry Chapin, and Elton John, in that order. When she came back into the kitchen, Andy Williams was crooning out "I Think I love you."

"So what about Dad?" Kirsti would have to be the first to ask; she had the curiosity of a dozen cats.

"Well," Mary said. Glenda's ears went into full alert; she knew what her mother's *well*s meant. The sound of this *well* was going to lead to something she was not going to want to hear. "Your father went in for tests on the shoulder that has been bothering him for months now."

Glenda knew what her mom was talking about. She had spoken to her dad not more than a week ago about his aching shoulder. He had mentioned his doctor wanted him to come in for tests.

"And there is no easy way for me to tell you this." Mary looked at her two precious daughters and said, "The tests revealed he has lung cancer."

Mary paused and waited for her girls to react. They didn't. They just sat in their chairs and stared at her, as though she was speaking to them in a foreign language.

Mary continued. "The cancer has attached itself to a scar in his lung that he developed as a child when he had scarlet fever. The biopsy they took came back positive. He will begin radiation next week. Fortunately, they caught the cancer early. The prognosis seems good."

Both Kirsti and Glenda sat there silently for a few moments. "Where is Dad now?" Kirsti asked, "When did he find out?

"He was told about the cancer this morning. He is probably over at the liquor store, hobnobbing with his friends. I told him that I would talk to you."

Both of the girls looked at each other and thought about Hilde. She doesn't know. The girls got up from their chairs at the same time, grabbed their purses, jackets, and made for the door. Their mom kept even pace. As they crossed the street, Glenda spotted Lynn's car, sitting in the parking lot. She stopped her mother and asked, "Does Lynn know about Dad?"

"Yes, I think she does, Yvonne knows, and I am sure she probably told Lynn."

"Oh, Lord, have mercy!" shouted Glenda as she ran across the street. "We have to get to Hilde before Lynn does!"

When they entered the Muni, Hilde was sitting at the bar with three tough-biker-type men standing around her. Hilde liked tough guys now and then. She was sipping a Black Russian. The two sisters knew what this meant, and it was not good. She became nasty when she had one too many of those drinks. This whole damned day was going from bad to worse. She knew without being told that Hilde knew about Dad.

Glenda walked up to her younger sister. Trying to be casual, she placed her hand on Hilde's arm and said, "Hey, why don't we go sit in a booth?"

Hilde yanked her arm away and laughed caustically. "Go take a look and see what our dearest auntie is up to. That ought to keep you busy enough and out of my hair for a while."

Hilde was not going to be sitting in any booth with anyone. Glenda backed off a bit. "Have you seen Dad?" Glenda asked as agreeably as she could.

"Sure," replied Hilde acidly, "He left a few minutes ago. I think the sight of his little sister made him sick. If I were you, I'd get in touch with Yvonne. She seems to think she knows how to handle everything. Do you think you could get Yvonne in here to save her? I doubt it. If Dad couldn't handle it, I am sure Yvonne will not even try. She wouldn't be caught dead in this place. Maybe someone ought to call Grandma. She wouldn't be caught dead in this place either."

Hilde turned around and away from Glenda and went back to conversing with her three male friends, newly found friends no doubt. They looked scruffy, but Hilde liked scruffy now and then. Glenda shook her head, joined her mother and Kirsti, who were standing about three feet behind her. They had heard every word.

Sure enough, as Glenda, Kirsti, and their mother turned the corner into the bar area, there was Lynn, having a high old time. She was dancing to the music being played on the jukebox, some old Willie Nelson song. Her greasy blond hair was combed straight back and covered by her infamous multicolored scarf folded into a triangle and tied at the nape of the neck. She had a sneer on her face the size of Texas.

Lynn was dancing and prancing all by herself. Her outdated polyester suit hung on her in floppy folds, its color a gaudy pink. The pants were bell-bottomed with an elastic waistband that she kept pulling on as she danced to keep them from falling around her knees. All three women knew she probably wasn't holding the pants up out of modesty, but to ensure that she could keep dancing without hindrance. A group of men sitting at a table in the corner were clapping and egging her on. The spectacle sickened Mary and her two daughters who had known her forever. They were trying, without success, to comprehend what their eyes were witnessing: the degradation of it all.

Lynn hadn't always been the boozehound she was now; no, indeed not. There was a time, not so very long ago, where she was considered one of Lakeville's most attractive people. She was graceful, beautiful in her own way, and meticulous about everything she did. She could play the piano with the best of them. Against the wishes of her mother and Eugene, she had married young, right out of high school. She married a handsome man who was ten years her senior. She set out to be the perfect wife and homemaker and was more than just a little successful. Her home was a masterpiece of interior design and comfort. She seemed happy and content with her life. She had taken Kirsti and Glenda under her wing, from birth, becoming more the elder sister than aunt to them. Lynn was only six years older than Glenda. When Glenda was going through the tough teen years, Lynn became her mentor and closest confidant.

Then one day she fell in love with someone other than her husband. She not only fell in love but also became obsessive about her lover. She divorced her husband; her lover divorced his wife. Fortunately for the family, Lynn didn't stand out much in the arena of local gossip because everyone seemed to be involved in flagrant affairs at the time. After about a year of fooling around with Lynn, her lover dropped her flat and started a string of relationships with other women. From that point on, it was downhill for Lynn, and a very steep hill it was. She hounded all the bars from one side of Dakota County to the other, searching for her lost lover and, in the process, became a hopeless drunk. The jerk responsible for splitting Lynn's heart in half went on his way without looking back. Lynn's heart never mended. She became mean, vicious, self-centered, and totally irresponsible.

Her mother found solace in denial and became her enabler. She gave her money and offered her sanctuary and a place to rest until the following morning when her day would start over again with the booze and the chasing and the searching for something she would never find ever again. The tragedy of this was apparent to anyone who had once known her as she was before; hopeless love struck her down. She came from a great place and had fallen while others coming from lower positions were rising. The irony of this was lost on everyone but her family.

Glenda was the first to approach Lynn; she unwillingly volunteered for the task because she had always been close to Lynn. Kirsti and Mary stepped back a bit to allow Glenda the opportunity to try to salvage something out of a horrible situation.

"Lynn, let's take a walk outside."

Lynn looked at her niece without recognition. Her eyes were glazed from the effects of the alcohol. She mumbled a few things that Glenda couldn't make out, and then she looked deep into the bottom of her half-filled glass. Her grayish skin color and dissipated eyes were frightening to behold.

"I will dance with you if you buy me a drink," she slurred as she tossed the rest of her drink down in one gulp.

Glenda turned and walked away from Lynn, who was now staring into the bottom of her empty glass. Glenda looked at her mother and said, "I thought she was in treatment?"

"She was in treatment, but there are no locks on the doors. She simply walked out, again." Mary studied her sister-in-law without compassion. "She doesn't want help. She loves this life. She has always been overindulged by her family, my husband included. His answer to this is let her live her life. There might be some sense to this because her sister, her one and only sister, hasn't had any success in trying to control her and get her the help she needs. After nine tries at different treatment centers, one might have to think that maybe there isn't any help for her." Mary sounded a little bitter.

"So then, what do you think we should do, just give up?" asked Glenda, "That's an exasperating thought."

"I don't know about you," said Kirsti, "but I have been down this road before. I'm going home. I am not going to do battle with Hilde tonight, nor am I going to battle with Lynn. Glenda, you can come home with me if you want, stay here and try to manage this fruitless operation, or go with Mom. I really don't care. I'm tired, and

I need to think. Mom needs to go home and be with Dad. She looks worn-out and stressed."

Mary did look totally drained.

They all decided to leave, including Hilde. Glenda drove her mother home. They had a chance to discuss things along the way. Glenda was glad to have her mom to herself for a few moments. The house was dark when they arrived. Mary got out of the car and told Glenda to go back to Kirsti's; it was time for everyone to get some sleep.

On the drive back to Lakeville, Glenda thought about all that was happening. It seemed like a bad dream. She wanted to go home; she wanted to go home very badly. Lakeville wasn't home anymore. This place had become something different. There was nothing left of what was. Things had changed. Life had changed. Glenda was feeling very lonely and displaced when she got back to Grandma's duplex.

Hilde was still up when Glenda entered Kirsti's apartment. She was dressed for bed and sitting on the floor, nursing a glass of wine and listening to music. She looked up at Glenda when she came in and said, "I am sorry, Glenda. I didn't mean to be so rough on you. I didn't mean to be so harsh about Yvonne either. She has more on her plate than she deserves. I don't know how she manages to hold up under all this pressure. I guess I am angry, very angry. The Povals have always been so strong, so tightly knit and directed. We always knew who we were and what was expected of us. We had pride in being who we were. Now it seems our whole way of life, as we once knew it, is exploding into thin air, and it scares me. It is as though Lynn's downward out-of-control spiral is dragging the whole family down with her, especially ours."

Glenda sat down on the floor across from her sister. They shared wine, sang along with the music, and hugged each other for a long time. Then both went to bed, Hilde in the guest room and Glenda on the couch. This had not been a good day for the Poval sisters. Their mother had always told them when they were troubled late in the day, "Now then, go to sleep, things will look much better tomorrow." Mom hadn't said it this evening.

Kirsti, Glenda, and Hilde stared at the ceiling for hours until finally they slipped into a fitful state of sleep. They could perceive that life was taking a turn on them that they were not prepared for. What they didn't want to think about was exactly what they were thinking about and couldn't brush away even in slumber. Their wonderful perfect family, the world as they knew it, was falling apart at the seams. Who was it that said, "Time and tide waits for no man?"

Glenda set her mind to a proverb that came out of a book her younger brother had sent to her recently, "Out of everything good comes something bad, and out of everything bad comes something good." She decided she needed to say a prayer and ask God for help. Sometime during her message to God, she fell asleep.

Chapter Twelve

Hastings, Minnesota, is the county seat for Dakota County. Hastings is located at the convergence of the Mississippi and St. Croix rivers and is the site of the second oldest surviving county courthouse in the state of Minnesota, Stillwater being first and dates back to 1871. The new facility was built in 1974 and was located at the northwestern side of Hastings on Highway 55. The law enforcement building is located on the northeast side and adjoins the Judicial Center.

The 1970s were a time when everything new was in and anything old was out, and this included people with old-fashioned ideas. The powers that were couldn't get rid of the old fast enough. The 50s generation wanted changes, and they were in charge. Along with the dismantling of generations of old brick buildings replaced with strip malls with identical facings came the dismantling of home and family. The shift in the moral fiber of America had worked its way from the extreme right to the extreme left. Housing developments cropped up everywhere. The Vietnam War was over and done with. America had been defeated. The knee-jerk reaction was something akin to mass hysteria where no one seemed able to get a grip or gather control. Life was now a free-for-all. The old-timers shuddered, the middle aged had a lot of fun, and the youth went along for the ride.

"The Times They Are—Changin'" was ripping through the country, and the youth of America were having their way with a boldness that had never been witnessed before, not by anyone who was old enough to make sense out of this, if indeed anyone was. The new became mixed in with the old in such a fashion that even the most lethargic of minds felt the clumsiness of it all. Everything seemed a bit out of order from top to bottom.

It would take until 1989 for everyone to finally settle into the new facility of the Dakota County Government building. The reason being because this brand new facility was not going to be just a courthouse doing judicial business, it was going to be a government building doing all sorts of government business. Everything under one roof had become the mode of the day. Individuality was disappearing into no man's land, and the folk singers that had cried out their protestations in the 70s were now a dying breed.

It was well past noon when Jack and Vic pulled into the staff parking lot of the Dakota County Government building, in fact, it was well past three in the afternoon. The CSI had finished up with their task of collecting evidence in and around the body, knowing much of what they might have found had probably been contaminated, unwittingly, by Fred and Harley. Hundreds of pictures were taken, covering every inch of the crime scene for later and closer scrutiny.

Jack and Vic and a couple dozen other people had walked a half-a-mile perimeter, inch by inch, looking for tracks or traces that could lead them to anything that might shed light on the death of this young girl. They had found nothing. While Jack orchestrated the crime scene, with only a few begrudging glances from the local police, Vic traveled the roads in and out to see if there was a remote chance of finding a clue as to where the killer might have come from, which direction; but he found nothing to speak of. The murderer could have come in from any direction. Once all the preliminaries had been done, the body of the young blond girl was transported by the county coroner to the Scott County morgue for autopsy. Jack knew these people well, and if there was something to find, they would find it; and because crime wasn't a rampant thing in Scott County, he might not have to wait long for the results. This was the only plus so far.

Jack and Vic spoke very little on their way back to the courthouse; each of them was deep in thought. Jack's mind was on the purple button, and as they entered the courthouse from the west side of the building, he said to himself, softly but out loud, "Button, button, who's got the button?"

Along with all the changes coming from the '70s was office structure. Prior to the 70s, the all-important people commonly known as bosses had an office that they could call home. These offices had doors on them that were rarely, if ever closed. To close these doors was considered a symbol of distance not inductive to group thinking, shutting out communication from the rest of the team players. The rest of the personnel were jammed together in one great big room with desks scattered everywhere in some helter-skelter not totally random fashion, and people could communicate with each other without having to get up from their desks.

Somewhere along the line, someone with a thing about sharing space with anyone else decided to change this and create cubicles. These cubicles were good for one thing only, and the word that came to Jack's mind was *isolation*. "Thou shall not see thy neighbor or talk to thy neighbor." A new generational wave of thought had come into vogue, "personal space." "I need my own space." The decided acceptable range was a perimeter of at least three feet.

"Sure puts the kibosh on carpooling, don't it?" Jack had said to Vic when he first got word of it. "Guess you can't ride with me today, I need my space, man."

Jack hated the cubicles. He was glad that he was out in the field and didn't have to sit in one of those isolated places eight hours of each and every one of his working days until quitting or retiring came up for grabs. There were other overrated and highly unnecessary "thou shalt nots" that made him cringe for mankind in general; but these other things would have to wait, probably forever, because Jack was a now person and right now, he had his mind on murder.

Both Jack and Vic did have their own cubicle assigned to them, and were it not for a cleaning crew that came in every day, one would have to ponder the amount of dust that can accumulate in a week's time let alone week after week. Their particular places were clean, organized, and well attended; and neither of these two men had a thing to do with it. They had the best of computers that money could buy at the taxpayer's expense. When Jack and Vic visited their sites, their computers were up and running, waiting for them, offering a soft enticing hum. The background picture on the desktop was of the old courthouse beautifully presented in glory form.

"Times they are a-changing" ran through Jack's mind when he would see the picture on the screen. *Ah, where are the 'Womenfolk' these days? I need to find a copy of their record.*

Brice Buchanan was waiting for the duo when they arrived. He was one of those bosses who kept his door wide open, unless he wanted a closed discussion, and this always meant someone was getting a dressing down. Brice was a tall man; he stood a bit over six feet, three inches tall in his stocking feet, and was slender for his height. His dark brown hair, wavy hair, was gray around the temples, giving him a look of distinction that he well deserved. He was not a man of apathy; this characteristic is what took him to the top of the list of persons to contend with in the Criminal Justice Department of Dakota County. There was nothing casual about the man. His mode of dress was precise, and his demeanor concise.

Brice was thorough, and he tolerated nothing less from those who worked under him. He was the "chief, the commander of the ship." Not a person who worked under him dared call him by his first name, aside from possibly Jack. Vic invariably referred to him as the Chief.

This commander was a man who despised stupidity, ignorance, and slackers of any sort; and to hear him talk, "without stupidity, ignorance, and slackers, there would be no criminals, and thus I could have become a carpenter"—to which he would add—"a very worthwhile occupation and something I wanted to do before I decided to become a police officer."

Anyone who has ever had the raw audacity to ask him why he wasn't a carpenter was in for trouble. The person who dared asked this question would have about three or four minutes to try and explain why they had decided to become a cop and not a carpenter. His men respected him.

Brice Buchanan was born in Minneapolis and came from a family that made their money in the medical field. The family home was located on Lake Minnetonka, a huge sprawling home with a pool and tennis court. His father's specialty was internal medicine. Brice was an only child; his father wanted him to attend medical school and was willing to pay the tab for the best that money could buy, but to his deep disappointment, his son refused the offer.

Brice joined the marines at the time when the battles were most murky in Vietnam. America was losing. The average time of rotation was one year, but Brice stayed in Vietnam for the duration of the war. He hung out in the Marine Corps for another four years and then came back to Minneapolis. His mother was very ill, and his father not faring too well in coping with the suffering his wife was going through. His mother died of cancer a year after Brice came home; his father, a year later. Brice buried both of his parents with profound sadness, and then not knowing what to do with himself, he decided to go to college. His choice of college was the University of Minnesota. After a year of taking required courses, he decided to major in criminology. Eight years later, he had his PhD; his specialty was law of evidence and criminal behavior. He was a very wealthy young man, good looking, well liked; but he was also totally undecided about his lot in life. He, to this point, was what could be considered a professional student.

Then one night, he came home from one of his various social bouts, and he found that his home had been broken into. The window in the back of the house had been tapped, not smashed, the latch unlocked, and one of his most prized possessions was stolen. The frame enclosing the picture of his group of soldiers who served under him in Vietnam had been stolen. The frame had been designed and made for him by one of the soldiers in the picture. The picture taken by the same friend was ripped up and cast aside. The frame might have looked expensive, but it wasn't worth $10 on the open market. The thieves had wandered through the house and toppled everything worth toppling and stolen those things that could be carried out easily. They had stolen jewelry precious to Brice, jewelry that had belonged to his mother. There was lots of jewelry; his mother had loved jewelry, and his father had always bought her the best.

Brice called the police, of course, who came and investigated. They told Brice to make a list of missing items, and perhaps when the "stuff" was pawned, they might catch the thief, but they had their doubts. The jewelry was in a safe, leading the investigators to believe that this was a professional job. Brice went to bed, feeling violated. He wasn't as concerned about what had been stolen as that it had been stolen.

Some people are never allowed revelations about where their life is heading or even a hint of where they should be, but Brice took this as a revelation anyway. He woke up in the morning, pasted the picture back together and yelled, "Stupid, dumb, ignorant bastards!" The torn up, discarded picture was the pivotal point in his life.

Brice then applied for a job and was hired by the Dakota County Police Department. He was hired two days after his first interview. The rest is all history. In less than two decades, he had made his way to the top of the ladder because he simply hated people who commit crimes, and he made it his purpose in life to put them behind bars. He didn't ask for top of the ladder, he liked chasing down criminals; he would have done this without pay. He got hoisted to the top because he didn't seek it. There was nothing political about Brice, but then again, Brice was a man out for justice, not personal acclaim and lord, he certainly didn't need the money. On the wall behind his desk is the picture of his troop that he had pasted together again, many years ago, reminding him every day of every week why he had become a cop.

Brice watched Jack and Vic enter the main area outside his office. They never came in easy. One only had to sit at their desk, shut their eyes, and hear the waves of comments to know that they had arrived. He waited as they worked the room, greeting individuals as they passed with different comments to each one, accordingly. They were full of the devil today. There were none who worked for the Dakota County Investigative department who didn't know these two guys, appreciate them, or want them hanging around. They took the mediocrity out of life. Brice was appreciative and allowed the boys to make their usual rounds.

About the time the two had very likely reached their workstations, Brice gave Contessa a nod. She had been sitting there, waiting; and when he nodded, she pulled her fully formed, actually very rotund body up from behind her desk. Brice grinned as she waddled her way down the isle to hail the boys. How this girl ever got the name Contessa was anyone's guess; she was no more Latino than he was.

Contessa had flaming red, naturally curly hair that was long and pulled into a tangled mess in the back of her head held by one of those claspy gizmos. Her pale white skin had freckles on top of freckles. Every part of her body that was showing, which wasn't much, was heavily freckled. She wore rings on every fat finger she possessed, including the thumbs. Her flare for dress would stun a sloth into rapid motion. She always wore brightly colored skirts, ankle length that rolled and weaved with her very plump body; flat shoes with no heel and normally in a color that defied the skirt in total concept or sense, never black, never brown. The blouse would be of some off color that blended with none of the other colors, and ordinarily were long sleeved, cuffed at the wrist, and always tucked in tightly at the waist—which did nothing to flatter her abundant figure. She was a bangle-and-multiple-necklace person and, of course, none of this jewelry that she wore boldly ever had anything to do with the other part of her gregarious garb. What terrified everyone around her was that her selection in outfitting herself was intentional. Those that knew her better than Brice commented that she took hours putting her wardrobe together.

Brice had inherited Contessa and held on to her because this woman was astute, well-organized, and very matter-of-fact. Maybe one could suppose, given a bit of gracious thought, her wardrobe might be a huge part of her own defined matter-of-fact way of thinking. On the other hand, this might be a stretch. No one in Brice's office had yet to gather a final thought about Contessa. She had worked for him for ten years and still, people wondered, more idly now than before, what she was actually made of aside from a brilliant mass of contradictions. She kept her private life to herself. She was so private about her personal life that no one even knew if she was married or not, aside from Brice, and he only knew because he had looked at her application. It read single. And he wasn't sure about that either because she could have lied on the application. Not to mention that she had been working for the police department for twenty plus years; lots of things can change in twenty years, but in her case, nothing seemed to have. Besides if she wasn't going to spit it out, he wasn't going to ask. Buchanan held high regard for a person's right to privacy.

Contessa scurried down the pathway between the cubicles, chasing after Jack and Vic, yelling without trying to yell, "Hey you guys, hey, hey, Jack, you have to go see the Chief. Hey, are you two fella's listening?"

Jack went around the block, ducking down so Contessa couldn't see him while Vic stopped and waited for Contessa to get closer.

"Vic, where is Jack? The Chief wants you in his office right now."

Vic stepped toward her from the front; Jack crept in from behind. When they were in line, Jack closed in, grabbed Contessa underneath the armpits, and hiked her up as Vic grabbed her underneath the knees and picked her up off the floor. Contessa let out a delicious squeal.

"Whoa there, fellas, you had better put me down right now. I'm getting airsick!"

Contessa was now lofted into the air and being carried back to her desk by her two most favorite people. She didn't fight them for fear of them dropping her. When the boys had her deposited in her chair, they turned around and gave a bow to the audience and then to Contessa. Everyone in the room was standing. When Contessa was finally plopped safely into her chair, the clapping began and continued until both men took another bow, each grabbed one of Contessa's hands, and kissed it gallantly. They made one last bow before they entered their boss's office, leaving Contessa busy trying to tuck her blouse back into her skirt.

"Where's my shoe, I lost my shoe!"

"Was that spectacle necessary? These aren't the good old days, boys. There is public outcry against such antics as this. The last thing we need right now is to be dragged through civil court. If Gloria what's-her-name caught wind of this, why, she would have us all tarred, feathered, and then strung up by our, you know what. Clean our clocks and then drag us through every legal lawsuit she could come up with, including sexual harassment."

"Aw, shucks boss, we were just having a little fun" said Jack as he glanced at Contessa, who was, by now, sitting at her desk, fiddling around with some papers; she had a slight flush on her freckled covered cheeks. "This is undaunted love, Chief, not idle flirtation. Vic and I are going to marry her. Gloria who? I don't know any Gloria. Do you know any Gloria, Mr. Victor L. Melton?"

Jack smiled and blew Contessa a kiss, which she promptly picked from the air and placed smack-dab on her lush, orange-colored lips.

"I want you to knock off those childish antics, and I mean it. We have enough to think about with the Credit River situation, so let's get down to the things we need to be doing rather than all this other attention-grabbing nonsense."

Jack became instantly serious, "Sure, Chief, sorry. I guess we got a bit carried away. You're right, but as far as the death of the girl in Credit River is concerned, there really isn't a lot I can tell you.

"We," Jack pointed to himself and his partner, "covered the grounds carefully and saw nothing that could lead us to the perpetrator. The CSI spent a lot of time nosing around and gathering what they could to try and find something, but I don't think they had any more success than we did. Hopefully, the medical examiner will have better luck."

"Just what makes you think CSI didn't find anything?" Brice was being calculatingly abrasive and a tad condescending.

Ireland understood his meaning. Brice expected more.

"The girl was young, between the age of eighteen and twenty-five would be my guess. She was deposited, not just dropped or tossed into the ditch. The way she was positioned has significance. I think she was strangled. There were dark bruises around her neck. She was probably attacked from behind. Where she was found was not where she was killed, I am almost positive of that."

Jack took a deep breath before he continued, "I didn't see anything underneath the fingernails to suggest a struggle, nor were their scratch marks anywhere or any obvious bruises. She was stark naked, not a stitch of clothing on her. We found no clothing in the area. We didn't find a purse to give us help in identifying her. There were no tire tracks that were recent, nor could we find any footprints. The ditch that she was placed in was deep, leading me to think that the person tossed her down first and then positioned her body in the manner in which we found it. The ditch is thick with tall weeds. Had it not been for the dog, we might not have found her this quickly. I doubt she had been dead for more than three to four hours before she was discovered. She was left or dumped would be a better way to put it, in no man's land."

"Why do you suppose she was dumped in that particular deep ditch rather than some other deep ditch in some other remote place?" Brice was thinking out loud.

"Good question, Chief. Jack and I have been wondering the same thing." Vic had taken over automatically. This was how well this duo related with one another.

"Then we have Fred and Harley, who did a lot of moving around on the scene before we were notified. God only knows how much help this was to the killer. I think that the person who did this has experience and knows how to clean up after himself. There isn't much Jack and I can do now but wait for the coroners' report, which I am sure will only substantiate what we are telling you and not much more."

"Who are Fred and Harley? If I might be so bold as to ask, you assume I know them."

Vic answered this question. He knew his boss wasn't going to like what he was about to hear. Jack remained silent, deep in thought.

"Fred is the dog, a German shepherd. Harley is the manager of the bar. Fred was first on the scene."

"A dog was first on the scene?" Brice was frowning now and shaking his head back and forth as though he were having difficulty processing what he had just been told.

Jack focused his eyes on his boss. Vic had visibly lowered himself into his chair. He knew what was coming next. Brice had moved from his chair and was standing over the top of Vic, staring down at him, as though he were the one responsible for some gargantuan transgression.

"I think I need to hear more about Fred and Harley." Brice was seething; his words were choppy and came out through clenched teeth. He was clearly falling prey to the "displacement syndrome."

"Brice, don't shoot the messenger. The German shepherd got to the crime scene first. It's as simple as that. He brought his master down into the ditch. It's unfortunate, but it is what it is. Harley didn't have any idea he was sliding down onto a dead body, for crying out loud, and the dog was only doing what good dogs do. Had it not been for Fred, we might not have found the girl yet for as tall as the weeds were and as deep as that damned ditch was."

"Harley is making a list of all people who came into his bar last night. He'll be giving the list to the Scott County Sheriff's office sometime today, but no later than tomorrow. This one is different Chief. I think we may have a serial. There was a purple button in the victim's left hand. I believe this is going to be his calling card, this is just the beginning, and we had better be ready and brace ourselves for the worst-case scenario."

The Chief had moved away from Vic and was looking out the huge window that covered the north side of his office; his back was toward Jack and Vic. He stood there silently for a long time. Brice had a habit of staring out the window when he was deep in thought. After a few moments of reflective quiet, Brice turned away from the window, walked past the two detectives, and closed his door. He made his way back to his desk and picked up a paperweight given to him by his ex-wife. The paperweight was crystal with a white rock enclosed; engraved on the rock was one word, Believe. He sat down on the edge of his desk and began rotating the paperweight around in his hands. Both Jack and Vic sat silently, examining Brice's every move.

"We have to be careful, Jack. We can't say serial until we know for sure that we have a serial. The press is going to be all over this one." Brice spoke softly and cautiously as he continued.

"You also know, the minute the press gets on to this, we could have panic all over Dakota County and the surrounding area. Let's not allow ourselves to be the ones to start a wild fire. This is technically a Scott County problem for now. We are only assisting them, but I am going to call Vince Grossman to be sure that we are on the same page. I would be willing to bet that he is as nervous as a cat on a hot griddle. We need to play this very, very cautiously, and no one is to know about the button. You guys might as well go home and get a good night's sleep. Tomorrow, I want you to pound pavement and beat down doors. You will be interviewing the list that we get from Harley, and if he doesn't send the list, you will be wringing his neck to get it out of him."

Jack and Vic nodded in agreement. As they were walking out of the room, they heard Brice say, "Brothers and sisters, have I none, but this man's father is my father's son."

Both Jack and Vic turned around at the same time and asked in unison, "What did you say?"

"Nothing of importance, it's just a riddle that was presented to me by my uncle when I was a child. The riddle keeps popping up and especially at times like these. The riddle helps me focus. Riddles always have answers and right now we are working on a riddle."

Chapter Thirteen

Jack dropped Vic off at his home in Hastings. He had suggested they stop at the Beer Stand for a quick one, but Vic was tired and wanted no part of a longer day. He said he needed time to think. Vic was that way. As he unlocked the door to his three-bedroom rambler, he was thinking *Brothers and sisters have I none, but this man's father is my father's son.*

As Jack ventured his way toward his home on the outskirts of Farmington, he was thinking, *button, button, who has the button?* He already knew the answer to the other riddle.

The sun was setting on the western horizon in resplendent colors of red, orange, and pink. It was going to be another beautiful day tomorrow, "red sunset at night, sailors delight."

Jack started singing "I love Minnesota in the springtime, I love Minnesota in the fall, I love Minnesota in the summer, but winter is the best time of it all."

Jack was singing his own made-up version very loudly as he entered his house. He slammed his door with an extra hard, defiant thrust. He was singing because he was angry and "singing always made his spirits rise." He stole that thought from the musical, *Camelot*. He picked up the phone and dialed a familiar number.

"I am on my way over. I'll be there in about half an hour."

He took his time showering and changed into a soft fleece pullover of a creamy white material; he then slipped on a pair of jeans, white crew socks, and tennis shoes. Doreen loved him in jeans, but then Doreen loved him period and had loved him for over a decade. He then placed a quick call to Vic and told him he was going to Doreen's for the night, and if he wanted to find him in the morning, that was where he would be.

Vic laughed. "You have the car, my friend."

"You have another car, my friend. You can pick me up at Doreen's at about eight o'clock. I'll keep the company car; it beats your broken-down bucket of bolts. See yah on the morrow." Jack hung up before Vic could give him any flack.

Doreen was sitting on the back porch, studying the resplendent sunset when he arrived. She didn't get up to greet Jack, rather he leaned down and gave her a kiss on the mouth. He pulled up a chair and sat down beside her.

"Would you like a beer?"

"No," Jack replied. "Not yet."

"Long day?"

"Very."

"I heard about the Credit River killing. They mentioned your name as lead investigator."

"Yep, we can count on the press to be right on top of everything, can't we? They, as usual, didn't get it right. I am not going to be lead investigator, I will be assisting the Scott County lead investigator." Jack placed heavy emphasis on the word assisting.

"Well, Jack, even you have to admit that it isn't every day that bodies are found, lying around in ditches in Credit River. The press was bound to find this story attractive."

"That's for sure, and ain't that a good thing, huh?"

"What, the press or the lack of dead bodies lying around? Let's go inside. I think you need something to eat. I'm getting cold."

Jack stood up first and pulled Doreen to her feet. He wrapped his arms around her, held her tightly and said, "Ah yes, and what a sweet morsel you are my dear. Let's forget about the press and concentrate on live bodies."

She yelped and tried to pull away from him as he bit down not so very gently on her neck.

Doreen was an import from Wisconsin. She had graduated from Eau Claire High School with visions of becoming a lab technician. She applied for entrance into the University of Minnesota and was accepted. Her father couldn't afford to pay for her education, so she applied for a student loan and got it. The first year, Doreen traveled back and forth with other students and worked as a waitress at one of the many diners in her hometown. During summer break between her first and second year, her aunt's husband passed away. They had no children, and her aunt invited her to come and stay with her while she attended college. Doreen jumped at the chance to be closer to the University and live with one of her favorite aunts. She could have her own room and not worry about a lot of family noise while she tried to study. The situation was ideal.

Her aunt had a small business of her own in downtown Farmington, a sandwich shop and a catering service. Doreen would help her out on the weekends and also during the week if she could. Her Aunt Mattie was insistent that work should never interfere with her education. She allowed Doreen to drive her car back and forth to the university as she was within walking distance of her shop and rarely drove anywhere. Mattie assisted Doreen in every way possible, and Doreen did her best to reciprocate.

A month before Doreen was to start her senior year at the University of Minnesota her Aunt Mattie had a fatal stroke. With no other family to think about, Mattie had willed her house, all of her belongings, and her shop to Doreen.

Feeling the weight of the obligations she had been granted, Doreen quit college and bore down on making Mattie's business a thriving enterprise. Through the progression of doing this, she discovered that she and Mattie were a lot alike. She loved having her own business; she loved the town, the people; and soon she was in enormous demand. She discovered she loved to bake. By the time Farmington got their strip mall, she was ready to expand. She kept her sandwich shop downtown and rented a space in the mall for her bakery, flower shop, and catering service.

On one particular fall day, she will always remember it was in the fall and the date was September 5; it was a Saturday. She was busy cleaning out the ovens and overseeing her workers as they prepared for the day. She had a wedding that afternoon. The young couple had planned an outdoor wedding and reception at their parents' home located three miles east of Farmington. She had taken no time in the morning to shower or apply makeup. She was covered from waist up with flour from baking sweets, pies, and buns for the wedding. She had already delivered the cake.

While she was putting some freshly baked buns in plastic bags, the bell above the door tinkled, alerting her that a customer had just entered. She glanced up from her work, and there he stood, the most incredibly gorgeous man she had ever seen in her entire life, and there she stood with her face powdered with flour. Her first reaction was to run for the back exit, but she couldn't; there was no one else available to help him. This was the moment she fell head over heels in love. She remembered his first words to her, "Hi, my name is Jack. I am new in town, and I heard that you make the best caramel rolls in all the Midwest, and do you know that you have flour all over your beautiful face?"

Jack held all the cards. She couldn't say that he hadn't been decent with her over the past decade because he had. He introduced her to everyone he knew. He wined her, and he dined her. He was as attentive to her as any man could be; the only thing lacking in their relationship was commitment. He would come and stay with her sometimes for days at a time, and then he would be gone, and she wouldn't see him for a month. She always waited for him. She had no interest in any other man. She knew he was seeing other women, but she had no hold on him, none. He had even told her that he loved her like he could love no other woman, but this didn't change things. Doreen never pressured him; she was afraid of losing him forever if she did. Jack could and would not ever be corralled. She had come to realize after many hours of contemplation that this was what she loved about him the most. If it was meant to be than she would have him, if it wasn't than she had him while she had him. Her father had told her never to try and cross a bridge before she got to it. He was a practical man, and she believed him.

Doreen hadn't seen Jack for almost a year, and now here he was on her back porch, biting the heck out of her neck.

"Stop it! Jack, that hurts!" She tried to pull away from him, but his strong arms held her tightly. He seemed irritated when he finally let go of her.

Doreen opened up the back door and entered the kitchen, leaving Jack standing on the back porch alone. She was feeling uncomfortable; Jack was coming on way too strong for her liking. This was a side to Jack, she had never seen before. She went to the refrigerator and removed two beers, one for her and one for Jack. She had two frosted mugs chilling in the freezer. Jack liked his beer served in a frosted mug.

As Doreen was pouring Jack's beer into the mug, she felt her body being lifted from behind. Jack was picking her up and carrying her before she knew what was happening. She was taken so by surprise that she didn't know what to do or what to say, so she didn't do anything but let him carry her to the bedroom. Oddly enough, she wasn't frightened. She was more perplexed by his behavior than frightened. He had never done anything like this before. He appeared heated, agitated.

She didn't fight him when he ripped off her clothing and tossed her unto the bed. His love-making was unusually rough, almost cruel; she didn't want to protest this either. She only felt unrelenting love for Jack, and when he was done and had fallen asleep, she took him in her arms and held him. When she woke up, Jack was gone. For the first time in her long relationship with Jack, she felt ashamed. She felt used and physically and mentally abused. Doreen wept until she ran out of tears.

Chapter Fourteen

Several months later

Spring had turned to summer and summer into fall. Kirsti had graduated from college with honors. She aced all of her final exams, including economics. She sang and danced on this score of unexpected results. Hanna and Joe had thrown her a celebration party at the club. The party was meant to be twofold, a farewell party and a graduation party. Hanna and Joe shed tears as they said good-bye to Kirsti, but wished her well. They vowed they would see a lot of each other, but all of them knew this was not likely to happen. There were over two hundred people invited to the party. The guest list was made up of family, friends, and customers; most of them attended. Hanna and Joe had specified no gifts, at the request of the honored guest, but no one paid any attention to this part of the invitation. Everyone brought a card with money enclosed. Kirsti received enough for a down payment on a new car. She retired her 1972 Maverick, now rusted out with age and countless trips over salt-covered roads. The Maverick had served her well but was long past the age of retirement.

The threat of a nursing home had pushed Grandma into a hard-lined determination to recover as quickly as was humanly possible; she was home after two weeks spent in the aftercare unit of the hospital. Her doctor was impressed, and he didn't impress easily. Yvonne had gathered a crew of ten people, all family; she wasn't going to be the only family member whose head was going to roll—to go into Grandma's house to clean and paint. The task took the full two weeks; every nook and cranny of her house was packed with stuff that Grandma had accumulated over time, including plastic containers from McDonald's. The Great Depression had affected most people of Grandma's generation in this way.

Yvonne did a noteworthy job of restoring her mother's house back to some sense of order, but she would never get a thank-you from her mother because she had breached an unwritten rule. The entire crew, with the exception of Yvonne, did his or her level best to deny any involvement. Eugene refused to participate, and Lynn couldn't because she had been thrown back into treatment again after her escapade at the Muni. Lynn had been arrested by the police and charged with driving while intoxicated, thrown into detox, and then hauled off to a treatment center in St. Paul. It was Yvonne, who had called the police and sent them to the Muni to wait for her sister to stumble out, get into her car, and drive. She didn't make it two blocks. The girls learned later that Eugene had played his part as well. "Masterful" they said to each other.

Yvonne and the crew had to content themselves with a job well done and pray that Grandma would eventually forgive them. Grandma did forgive, but she never said she did. She would lament for the rest of her life about how horrible life is when your very own people come in and invade you and your things without permission. The family knew they had done the wrong thing to Grandma for all the right reasons. If Yvonne hadn't cleaned the place up, the social service structure would have considered her home life threatening and rendered Grandma to a nursing home. Grandma needed a nurse to come in, and because the nurse was going to be provided by social services, Yvonne was caught smack-dab between a rock and a very hard place. The girls recanted their objections when they came to understand that Yvonne did what she had to do because she simply had no other choice.

Eugene Poval had gone through his radiation treatments with some success, but no one was considering that he was out of the woods by any means, including himself. When he started the treatments, he weighed over two hundred pounds, a bit more than he should have been carrying by about fifty pounds. He was now a trim hundred and forty-five pounds and the right weight for his five feet, eight-inch frame. He enjoyed being thinner, though he wasn't crazy about the means taken to lose the weight. He was back to work again and glad to be. He worked for the Dakota County Assessors office as an appraiser.

He had worked for the Dakota County appraiser's office for eighteen years and had never taken a day off, not for illness or for vacation; and the time allowed for this was accumulative, which was a good thing because while he was taking radiation, he couldn't work. After he was done with the radiation, they hit him with chemotherapy that really knocked the slats out from under him. He had by now recovered and was feeling, to quote him, "better than ever."

Yvonne, being overwhelmed by her mother's illness and her brother's bout with cancer, took a different approach to her sister Lynn's drinking problem. Yvonne, with the help of doctors and councilors, had her committed to a place where she couldn't just leave on her own say-so. She would be in the hospital for at least 120 days. Those in the treatment industry had determined that Lynn was more than likely incurable, but they did have one more thing to try—St. Mary's, the toughest of the tough, the best of the best in treating those with any sort of chemical dependency. Lynn had been in and out of every treatment center in the Minneapolis/St. Paul area; she had been admitted eight times in half that many years. Alcoholism was and still is one of the least understood illnesses in existence and especially by the nonprofessional. The family, Lynn's family, was running out of answers. They had no knowledge or comprehension regarding the complexities of alcoholism. To the family, Lynn was deliberately throwing her life away. Like many, they considered her behavior a conscious attempt to draw attention and engulf herself in self-pity.

The fact of the matter was that this family was walking through the shock waves of life, as most do, with one foot in denial and the other, in reality with the lines of demarcation, right from wrong, becoming more obscure with each passing day; but they didn't know this, and they wouldn't for a long, long time.

The evening of Kirsti's graduation celebration, she had been going through her purse to find her lipstick and came across the note that was given to her by Hanna. The note had a name and a number. When she got home, she pulled the note back out of her purse and called Jack. Jack, being used to answering the phone in the middle of the night, wasn't surprised that his phone was ringing; but he was surprised to hear Kirsti's voice on the other end. She had had just enough to drink to give her the courage but not quite enough to make her unaware of what she was doing.

She didn't introduce herself but stated the obvious; it was 1:30 in the morning. "Did I wake you up?" She really didn't know how else to start the conversation.

"Is this who I think it is?" said a sleepy voice on the other end.

"Yes, this is Kirsti. I think there was a night when I heard you mention something about a date. Are you still interested in trying to revive a very old-fashioned idea?"

"Sure," said Jack casually. "I think old fashioned is a good thing and needs to be treated with a lot of respect. How about breakfast, meet me at Perkins, seven thirty sharp."

"Not so fast, buster, I am not going to get out of bed in the morning. I am going to sleep until noon if it kills me, and besides, breakfast doesn't qualify as a date. I want a date. I want dinner with dancing, and you're going to pick up the tab, the old-fashioned way."

"All right, you got me. Where and when?"

"Friday night. I want you to take me to 'Mulberry's on the Lake You can make the reservations. Pick me up at seven thirty in the evening. I am sure you already know where I live, and if you don't, well then, you aren't much of a cop."

"Ouch! You have got to be kidding me! Mulberry's? You are kidding, you have to be, on our first date? That's the most expensive place in the state of Minnesota. I don't do tuxedos.

"You don't need a tux. I'll see you Friday. By the way, white roses are my favorite flower, and I like the smell of your aftershave."

"You can smell my aftershave over the phone? I am going to have to cut back on the amount I use."

Kirsti laughed and hung up.

As ordered, Jack picked Kirsti up at precisely seven-thirty, and he did take her to her selected place, the most expensive restaurant in the entire state of Minnesota. From then on, Jack and Kirsti spent every allowable hour of every day with each other. Jack proposed to Kirsti on September 1 and said she had one month to plan her wedding. She pleaded with Jack to allow her six weeks to get it organized; he conceded.

Almost from Jack's first date with Kirsti, he had been telling everyone he knew that he was getting married. He was finally, and at long, last in love. No one, of course, believed him. He took Kirsti to every function he was invited to so that everyone he knew could meet her. It was no surprise that everyone was surprised when he announced his engagement. He had been making such a big deal of it for so long his buddies had become immune to his proclamations. Besides, they hadn't known each other long enough.

Jack's friends, except for possibly Vic (he thought she was too young for Jack), liked Kirsti and thought she gave Jack something he had never had in his life, something to be happy about. She was young and lively with a personality that made each person feel like they were unique and special. She enjoyed Jack's associates, especially Vic. The men appreciated Kirsti because she was so darned sociable; the women because they knew, with all of her warmth, easiness and flirtations, she only had eyes for Jack and also because she had proven herself to be a loyal female ally.

There was to be a Fourth of July gathering at Vic's place. Vic was the only cop in Dakota County, who had a pool in his backyard. He was having a cookout, and all the regulars would be there, the regulars being the whole police department or anyone who thought to show up; bring your own food and beverage was the only requirement. There was rarely the same crowd twice in a row for these monthly gatherings because everyone worked different shifts on a rotation basis.

This particular day, one of the police department's less-liked individual came and showed up with a date. That he showed up was a curious thing because one and all knew that he knew he was disliked, and to think that he could actually get a date was downright incredible. The girl he brought as his guest was frumpy, dull and unfamiliar. Her long brown waist-length hair was straggly; she wore no make-up; her brown dress was baggy, wrinkled and added to her dreariness; she was overweight and seemed to have a less-than-responsive approach to people and life. This was the group's first assessment.

There is, in every gathering, a certain faction of people who are not kind to those who are less endowed than themselves. Kirsti had seen plenty of this in her lifetime and because of this, she was the first to greet Maggie with open arms and make her feel at ease.

Irv, Maggie's date for the evening, didn't require any sort of special treatment. He was one of those who pushed his way in hard; he was demonstrative and smug. This is exactly what made him disliked by the officers and their other parts. He was one of those types of individuals who claimed to have done everything, seen everything, and not timid about saying so. He was what everybody yesterday, today, and tomorrow would call a fabricator or in more crude language, a bull-shitter. Even Kirsti, who tried her best to give everyone a fair shot, found no reason to like him.

Irv was not a cop. He was a computer man with a degree in computer technology, or so he claimed. He had never worked one day out in the field, nor would he ever spend a day out in the field. He was a source for amusement, and that was the only reason he was allowed to join the festivities this afternoon. Besides it would be considered very impolite to cast him out without a good reason.

After the group had eaten and cleaned up the dinner mess, it was pool time. The girls were getting into the pool, as Maggie stripped down to her bathing suit, Irv stood up and snarled, "You fat pig, leave your dress on. I'll not have you embarrassing me in front of my friends. You stay out of the pool and mind your place girl. If you take those clothes off and get in the pool I will personally come in and drown you myself. Who do you think you are anyway, Marilyn Monroe?"

This was not the first time he had lashed out at Maggie with a derogatory comment; in fact, he had been downright rude to her all day long. Maggie quickly pulled her dress back up; her round face had turned bright crimson from humiliation. Everyone wanted to give Irv a resounding kick but only one person acted.

Kirsti was sick and tired of Irv and his big mouth and decided to do something about it. In her opinion, Irv was an obnoxious jerk. He had no business treating Maggie the way he was treating her, and if everyone else at the party was just going to sit around and do nothing, this didn't mean she had to.

"Come on over here, I want to have a word with you," Kirsti said cheerily, crooking her forefinger at Irv.

She took him by the hand and led him toward the edge of the pool out of hearing range. Irv went willingly; Kirsti fascinated him. When she took his hand in hers, he felt his skin tingle from head to toe. He prayed he wasn't sweating. His pulse had quickened at her touch; he felt hot and flushed and a little bit flustered. His face was beet red.

"Now, Irv," she said very quietly. "Maggie is going to go swimming with us. I want her to go swimming with us and so do the rest of the girls want her to go swimming. She can't do that in her dress, now can she?"

Kirsti maneuvered him into a position where his back was to the pool. He followed her lead, mesmerized by her blue eyes and soft, sweet voice. He moved cooperatively where she led him, a bit too eagerly. The crowd was attentive, especially Jack. What was his little girl up to?

"I like your outfit, Irv. Is this a new outfit you're wearing? Your shirt is the exact color of your eyes."

"Yes" he choked through a dry throat "I bought it yesterday for the party."

"What about the shorts and sandals, are they new too?" Kirsti's eyes were radiantly blue, illuminated by the soft lights surrounding the pool

"Yes."

Kirsti placed her hands on his shoulders and began stroking him gently, her eyes glued to his.

"The sandals were really expensive, but I got them on sale at—"

He had no time to finish his sentence. Kirsti had moved her hands to his chest. She gave him a hefty chuck. Irv fell over backward into the water, landing with a mighty splash. When he surfaced, he heard hands clapping and loud cheers coming from the party now gathered around the edge of the pool

Irv heard somebody say, "Let's go swimming, Maggie. That piece of garbage will be cleaned out of the water very soon." The voice was Kirsti's.

Three strong men abruptly hoisted him out of the pool; two of them held his arms while the third grabbed him by the seat of the pants. His feet didn't touch the ground as they carried him to the parking lot where they unceremoniously dropped him like a sack of rotten potatoes.

One of the men said, "If I was about your shape and about your size, I wouldn't come back in." The voice belonged to Jack

Ireland. Irv hated Jack Ireland. He had, since the first day he met him, detested that man; and now he had someone else to hate, Kirsti Poval, whom he held completely responsible for his present demise. He was embarrassed beyond words, beyond expression and beyond endurance.

From this day forward, Maggie and Kirsti would become very good friends. Everyone at the party took a different view of both Kirsti and Maggie. Kirsti was a lot tougher than she appeared to be, and Maggie, well, she was all right too. Maggie was no longer cheerless but animated, lively, and fun. Maggie appreciated the positive attention she received for the duration of the evening and went home feeling quite different about herself, thanks to Kirsti. Irv went home that night, feeling dejected and filled with overwhelming animosity.

Irv was planning his revenge as he drove home that evening. There wasn't a single person at the Dakota County Courthouse, who knew that Irv wasn't really Irv at all. His name was Willy. Willy Howard was his given name, no middle name. His father had named him Willie because the thought of having a kid gave him the willies. Willie had a younger brother named Morty, also named by his father because the thought of another child brought the thought of mortician into his mind. His father later nicknamed him Shorty because he had a very short male part. Neither of these boys ever really knew their father, and this was probably a good thing because he wasn't worth knowing. He was a mean, vicious person, a hard-bitten and intentionally abusive person. He wandered in and out of their lives infrequently, but when he did, life was not pleasurable. Their mother called him Uncle Fred. The boys called him Uncle Dread. His mother and his father, as far as he knew, had never married. His father always referred to them as his charming little bastards.

He would amble in now and then to get a meal, beat up their mother, and leave again. One time he strolled in with his usual hostility and held each of the boys up against the wall, put a knife to their throat, and said their life was going to be short-lived because he was going to kill them and their mother. He had cackled mirthfully as he ambled back out the door. His son's didn't doubt him. Their mother drank from morning until night; the booze provided to her by her sons, stolen in the dark of night, their father never touched a drop, to their knowledge. He didn't need booze to be vicious, he would proclaim with a spine-chilling intonation of complacency.

Then, came the day, a day of grave magnitude. It happened when Willy was seventeen years old and his brother was fourteen. They had been out scrounging for food in all the best garbage cans they could find. This was customary. They had become thieves, good thieves, and highly creative dumpster divers. They rummaged by day and thieved by night. Neither of them had ever attended one day of school in their lives, no one missed them nor gave this a thought. They became particularly apt at making themselves invisible. Their catch for this day was steak dinner. It was Christmas Eve. They were anxious to get home and show their mother what they had stolen the night before and what their morning hunt had produced. They had gathered a lot of jewelry that they could pawn and one incredibly expensive computer wrapped in the unopened box, it had been originally packaged in for delivery. Rich people. Willy loved rich people. The California mountainsides and valleys were amply populated with rich folk ripe for the "*pickin' and pluckin'*."

Willy's fascination with everything electronic was boundless, especially computers. The run-down, dilapidated double garage next to the run-down dilapidated house was lined from floor to ceiling with electronic gadgets, computers, and computer components. He was becoming a self-taught expert. He had even found his way to the Internet without much trouble at all. Willy was bad, but he was also smart. Shorty wasn't quite as bad, nor was he near as smart. In the few sober moments she had, their mother taught the boys to read. This was the only contribution she had within her to offer them. She told them that they had to read. She had no energy left to send them to school, let alone keep them there so she taught them herself. No matter how drunk she was, her sons had their reading and writing lessons.

The twosome came into the house, hooting and hollering, their arms loaded with ill-begotten booty. They had had an enormously profitable night and morning. They would eat steak for Christmas Eve dinner and give their mom an expensive necklace and perfume as a Christmas present.

When their mother didn't respond to their beckoning calls, the boys decided to see if she was passed out in her bed—this was more likely than unlikely. Willy entered the bedroom first; the light was already on. Their mother was on the bed and as dead as anyone could be. She had been stabbed multiple times; there was blood everywhere. Her face was nothing but raw flesh, barely recognizable. She had been brutally beaten then stabbed and left to die alone. She was stripped down to nothing; she was lying on her side, her right arm placed over her face and her right leg resting gently over her left leg. Were it not for all the blood, the boys might have thought that their mother was sleeping. Her long blond hair, spread all over the pillow, was streaked with blood—red blood; her blood.

Covering the bottom half of her body was a purple coat, her favorite coat, her only coat. The boys took off that day and never returned. Fresh in their minds was their father's last words to them. Their mother's body was found a month later by a hunter, who was curious enough to check out the decaying buildings. Beside the run-down shack of a house was what little remained of what had been a garage. It had been burned to the ground. The identity of her killer was never discovered because no one really cared, nor did anyone notice that her two sons were missing. Not a single person gave them a thought. They never hit anyone's radar of even having ever existed, so desolate was their life and so remotely they had managed to keep themselves from the mainstream of society.

Willie and Shorty made a swift departure from California that Christmas Eve day, never to return again. They did not look back. They traveled around the country doing what they did best; robbing and stealing from anyone and everyone who had in their possession those things they wanted and/or needed. So finely tuned was their ability to remain obscure that no one noticed them or paid them any mind. They moved about as though someone or something was chasing them, and it wasn't the law they were worried about; nope, it wasn't the law. It was the face of his father that Willie saw in his rearview mirror. It was the recollection of an ice-cold blade pressed against his throat that he couldn't escape; a harsh, bitter recollection, causing many sleepless, anxious nights.

Chapter Fifteen

"If you don't stop your wiggling around, I am going to stick you with one of these pins."

Grandma was sitting in a chair and tugging at Kirsti's waist, trying to place pins in the wedding dress for the final adjustment. The dress needed to be tucked by at least a half an inch on both sides. Grandma always allowed an inch in the waist for expansion, but Kirsti hadn't expanded.

"I don't know why we always have to do this at the very last minute! You don't have to tuck it. The dress is just fine as it is; besides this is way too much work for you. Can't we just leave it as it is, Grandma, please?" Kirsti was pulling herself away from her grandmother as she spoke, wishing for a reprieve.

Grandma gave Kristi a slight prick with the pin.

"Ouch, that hurt," yelped Kirsti.

"Well then, stand still. There, that should do the trick."

Grandma lifted the dress from the bottom as Kristi bent from the waist, allowing her grandmother to pull the dress over her head. "I will do the finishing touches and bring your dress to the church with me."

"Thanks, Grandma. I will see you at three. You will be coming with Mom and Dad?" She loved her Grandma immeasurably. Kirsti noticed how bent over she had become. Her long beautiful fingers worked the material with the touch of a master; her thinning gray hair in perfect place. Her pure blue eyes were keen and sharp. Her stout body was the only imperfection this woman owned. As Kirsti watched her grandma, a chill passed over her. It was at this moment that Kirsti realized she could never survive losing her grandma, not ever.

"No," said Grandma. "I'll be coming with Yvonne. You know your dad is always late, and I want to be there early to help you get dressed. I don't want to have to depend on your father to get me there. In fact, your mom is riding with Lynn for the same reason."

Kirsti grabbed her grandmother and hugged her hard.

"I love you, Grandma. I love you more than you will ever know. I cannot imagine life without you."

Grandma turned away and got back to the wedding dress, she didn't respond. Grandma wasn't happy about this wedding; it was too soon. Ah, but kids don't listen. Grandma sat down at her sewing machine and sighed. Kirsti was going to do this whether Grandma liked it or not. Kirsti had always been headstrong.

Kirsti gave her grandmother a kiss on the cheek and dashed away, the front door slamming behind her.

"Be sure and pull the door shut behind you. It doesn't close on its own," Grandma yelled a bit too late, Kirsti was by now out of hearing range.

This was Kirsti and Jack Ireland's wedding day. It was October 10 and a gorgeous fall day in the state of Minnesota. The trees were in full, radiant color; fall colors of red, orange, green, and brown. The sun was shining brightly, the temperatures mild for this time of year.

Glenda was driving, once again. It was one in the afternoon. The girls had just enough time to pick up the flowers in Farmington and get to the church to change into their wedding attire. The ceremony was going to take place at Highview Christiania Lutheran Church, the church where Kirsti was baptized and confirmed. The pastor performing the ceremony was Kirsti and Glenda's first cousin, Greg, Yvonne's son. He had told Glenda that he simply couldn't compete with Robert Wagner as the world's most notable playboy, so he had decided to become a pastor instead. He had this tongue in cheek sense of humor that always kept his cousins on their toes and shaking their heads affectionately. He was part of the pack and Kirsti was thrilled that he could perform the wedding ceremony for her and Jack. The cousins had spent the first part of their lives romping through the fields of the farm together and all holidays. Nothing could be more perfect than him officiating.

Kirsti wanted a small wedding party. Glenda was to be her maid of honor, and Vic was selected by Jack to be his groomsman. Her father was going to give her away. Hilde was her personal attendant. Where was Hilde anyway?

Her father was going to give her away if he showed up. Eugene had hit the roof when he found out his daughter was getting married and had fought Kirsti every step of the way. He was so distressed by his daughter marrying Jack that he threatened not to appear at the wedding at all. No daughter of his was going to marry a cop and certainly no daughter of his was going to marry Jack Ireland.

It wasn't as though he didn't like Jack; Jack was all right on a man-to-man basis, but he had three strikes against him. First of all, he was a cop and being married to a cop was not a good thing for any woman and especially the type of cop that Jack was. He was a man who took risks. Secondly, he wanted his daughter married to someone who could give her some status in life, someone with an interest in the finer things of life, someone more cultural. Jack had enough money, this was clear, but he had little interest in anything aesthetic. Jack was a John Wayne man; his choice of music was Johnny Cash. Of even more serious concern to Eugene Poval was that Jack was a notorious womanizer. Eugene was old enough and wise enough to know that this could and would probably be the biggest of Kirsti's problems with Jack. Eugene worked at the Dakota County Courthouse and was privy to all the gossip. He had heard a lot about Jack over the years, most of it favorable, but there was the other side of Jack that caused Eugene to be bothered.

Nope, his oldest daughter, Kirsti, was no match for Jack Ireland. He would have worried less was his second daughter marrying Jack; Glenda was naturally streetwise and a lot tougher than her sister. Eugene was struggling with his decision. He knew he would cave in to Kirsti, he always had. He had always been a lot harder on Glenda.

Glenda pulled her rent-a-car into the parking lot in front of the church. As she did, she thought about her father and his misgivings about the wedding and had to wonder if he would make good on his threat. Kirsti was positive that he would be there, but Glenda wasn't so sure. Her dad had pulled her aside and had a long conversation with her and Mary about his misgivings. Glenda had no doubt in her mind that if there was a way to stop it, he would. Glenda had never seen her father so adamant about anything. He pounded on the table; he had ranted against participating in a ceremony that he was so dead set against. Neither Glenda nor Mary could calm Eugene down let alone say anything to assuage him; they could only let him blow off steam until he finally exhausted himself. When he was finished ranting and raving, he cried. Glenda had never seen him cry, never; his tears shocked her. He didn't believe in tears, he considered them a sign of weakness; yet there he was, crying like a small child, head in his hands, tears streaming down his face. Glenda and Mary had been rendered speechless. But then Kirsti had always had this effect on their father; she was his firstborn child; his expectations for her and of her had always been a bit too high.

Kirsti was bubbling and babbling as they walked into the church. She was unaware of anything other than her wedding; she was concentrating on only one thing, getting married and getting married to Jack Ireland of all people. Who would have ever thought this a year ago?

Yes, Glenda thought to herself, *who would have thought.*

Kirsti was standing next to a window, looking down toward the parking lot. She was ready now. She was fully dressed and looking as beautiful as any bride could ever hope to look. Her wedding gown fit her perfectly, a simple formfitting, sleeveless white satin gown that went to the floor with a long flowing jacket of the same length made of lace, falling elegantly from the shoulders. Most importantly, to Kirsti, the gown had been designed and stitched by her grandmother. One of her greatest childhood dreams was reaching fulfillment. This would be a perfect day.

The laced jacket was long sleeved and V-ed over the hands, with a high mandarin collar. There would be no veil, just a simple band of white flowers around her head. The flowers were attached to a clear plastic band nestled in her short brown hair. Her grandmother had chosen a three-inch thinly strapped sandal that couldn't be found in the Twin Cities but had to be especially ordered from a source in New York. Her bouquet contained six red roses, surrounded by pure white, lily of the valley. Glenda's floor-length gown was made of a dark green velvet material and was also designed and sewn by her grandmother. Glenda would carry a single red rose.

"Glenda, come here a minute."

Kirsti was still standing by the window.

Glenda walked to the window and looked down into the parking lot where Kirsti was centering her attention. Jack was standing with his hands in his pockets, talking to Vic. They were apparently sharing a joke because Jack was laughing, Vic was moving around animating something. They stood out among the visitors in their tuxedo's; one as handsome as the other. Kirsti's brothers were there as well. They would be her ushers. They were also dressed in tuxedos and as Kirsti would say to them later, "I am proud to be your sister."

"Have you ever, in your life," said Kirsti, "seen a bunch of more handsome men than those standing down there in that circle? I think Jack resembles Tyrone Power."

"Ahhhh, Kirsti, you have always had a crush on Tyrone Power, and no, I don't think that Jack looks like Tyrone Power, not in the least. Actually, I think he looks like Guy Williams. I really do hope that you haven't trapped yourself into some sort of fantasy?"

"What makes you say that?" Kristi turned abruptly towards her sister. "What are you saying?"

"Nothing, dear girl, I was only kidding you. Jack is entirely too fine looking, and I am happy for you. I still think, though, that he looks more like Guy Williams than Tyrone Power, all kidding aside. What do you say, Hilde?"

Hilde was busy fussing with the camera. She put the camera up in readiness and said, "Quite frankly, I think he looks like Boris Karloff." Flash!

The church was filled to capacity as Kirsti walked down the isle to be joined in marriage to Jack Ireland. Greg did a number on the bride and groom as he joined them in marriage, lingering on stories about his life with the bride. He even got a laugh out of his uncle Eugene, who had, at the last remaining second, shown up to walk his daughter down the isle with an expression that showed no joy whatsoever but was instead dark and dour. After the couple took their vows, Greg gave John Ireland and Kirsti Poval-Ireland his blessings, pronounced them man and wife, and sent them back down the isle, hand in hand; the crowd burst forth with shouts of cheer as Jack led his new bride out of the church.

The whole cast of people that attended the wedding traveled from Highview Christiania Lutheran Church to the Orchard Lake Country Club for the reception; horns were blasting loudly as they pulled into the parking lot. Hanna and Joe were waiting to greet them. The reception was Hanna and Joe's wedding gift to Kirsti and Jack. They had attended the wedding and were the first to leave to get back to the club to see if everything was in order. There were 250 invited guests. They had doubled their staff to make sure that the accommodations were perfect. Dinner was served at seven thirty; the band began playing at nine o'clock sharp. The band, by request from the bride, was one that played music from the '30s, '40s and '50s. She wanted music at her wedding that would please her parents. All the invited guests ate, drank, and danced to their maximum capability, including Eugene. He danced with his wife, his daughters, and every other pretty girl who would indulge him. Eugene was somewhat of a womanizer himself. He had always enjoyed dancing and wasn't half bad, besides, dancing kept his mind off his negative thoughts about Kirsti and Jack. And though he saw nothing but trouble on the horizon, he was glad he had attended the wedding. He, in actuality, did want to be wrong about this one.

Kirsti threw her bouquet of flowers as she and Jack were leaving the reception. The bouquet landed squarely into the arms of one of her sisters, Hilde. She quickly passed the bouquet off to Maggie, who decided to keep them for posterity. As the limousine disappeared out of sight, Glenda was overcome by a mysterious sense of urgency.

Out in the parking lot, in a dark, remote corner of the parking lot, someone was watching and waiting. He grinned as he saw the bride and groom leave because only he knew that while he was watching, someone else was busy. Jack Ireland wouldn't be smiling for long.

Jack had planned the honeymoon. They were going to stay at the Hyatt-Regency bridal suite after the wedding dance and leave in the morning for Mexico. They were going to a very quiet place on the eastern coast where there was no hustle and no people, a place where he and Kirsti could be all alone. Very few knew about this location. He had found the perfect spot while searching the Web and by using his investigative skills. The plane was due to leave Minneapolis at ten in the morning, arriving at their point of destination at nine in the evening.

By the time they left the reception, Kirsti had ingested way too much champagne. Jack had no one to thank for that but his roguish pals, and the majority of the blame had to fall on Vic, who seemed determined to get his new wife totally blasted. He had been depressingly successful. As the newlywed couple was led to their room by the uniformed bellhop, with Kirsti chatting nonstop about the wedding, Jack began to notice Kirsti's words were becoming slurred, and she was starting to weave a bit. He had to grasp her arm several times to keep her upright. When they did get to the room, she took one look at the bed and crawled in, wedding gown and all; she glanced up at her husband, and said with an inebriated slur, "Good night, darling, sllllllleeeeee yah in the morning."

Jack's bride was sound asleep in a matter of seconds. He tenderly undressed her and cautiously laid her wedding dress over a chair so it wouldn't wrinkle. He studied his brand new wife's lovely body as he covered her up with a blanket.

"Thanks, Vic," he mumbled, as he slid into bed beside her. "Ah well, tomorrow is another day." He was a bit worn-out himself. The thought of sleep and no sex was too comfortable a thought for him. Jack was beginning to wonder about a lot of things. Soft subtle light was leaking through the window blinds creating an interesting pattern of whites, grays and blacks throughout the room. He surveyed the changes of the patterns as they moved about until darkness overcame him.

A cell phone rang at six thirty in the morning. Jack looked at the clock and then at the caller ID, it was Vic. He ignored the phone for the first three tries; but Vic was being persistent. On the fourth call, Jack shouted into the receiver, "Go away!"

He hung up; the phone rang again. He was determined not to answer it. Jack got out of bed, being careful not to wake Kirsti, who was still deep in slumber-land. Jack was by now wide-awake and irritated. He took his time going into the shower; the phone rang again. He ignored it one more time. His cell phone was ringing when he got out of the shower; this time Kirsti picked it up and answered it.

"Sure, here he is," she said, rubbing her eyes while handing the phone to Jack.

"Good morning, dear husband," she said to Jack as she got out of bed and made her way to the bathroom, seemingly unaware of her nakedness. Jack watched her move; he wanted to follow her but was halted by Vic's voice coming from his cell phone.

"Jack, are you there?"

"You son-of-a-bitch, are you deliberately trying to screw up my life? I am about ready to send out the death squad to exterminate you, you sack of shit." Jack was fuming. "Enough is enough."

"Such language, didn't your mother ever tell you to watch your mouth? You can beat me later for all the previous mischief, but I had to call you, I have been commanded to call you. You and I have been beaconed back into the office. There's been another murder. The Chief gave me orders to call you and get you to headquarters as soon as is humanly possible. I'll meet you there. Do the words, 'purple button', mean anything to you?" Vic sounded calm.

"Another?" Jack was stunned.

"Yes. Another."

"Can't someone else take this one? What about Hank? I'm on my honeymoon, for God's sake!"

"Not this time, Jack. The commander wants you and no one else. He knows what you have going on and wouldn't be troubling you if he didn't think it was necessary."

Jack sat down on the bed; his head was starting to pound. How was he ever going to explain this to Kirsti? If he was called in, he had no choice but to go back in, that was his job; his job held priority over everything else, but would Kirsti see it that way? He wasn't happy to have to know the answer to this question this soon in his marriage.

"I'm on my way, Vic."

"I will meet you at headquarters in two hours, sorry, buddy, I really am." Vic hung up.

Kirsti came out of the shower wrapped in a towel. She had applied her makeup, but her hair was still tussled and wet. She walked over to Jack, who was sitting on the bed, looking really unwell.

"What's going on? You look like you just lost your very best friend." She sat on his lap and hugged him.

"Kirsti, we have a problem." He wrapped his arms tightly around her waist. He wanted to kiss her, but he didn't.

"I know. I had too much to drink last night, and I really am sorry. We have a little time before we have to go to the airport maybe I can make up for—"

Jack placed his hand over her mouth to prevent her from saying more. Kirsti's eyes widened, she became startled, "What's going on? Certainly—"

Jack hushed her again, lifted her and moved her off of his lap. He stood up and walked away from her toward the window.

He turned around and faced her, his eyes full of remorse, "I have to go back to headquarters. I can't put it any more bluntly than that, I suppose. I have been called back in to work on an ongoing case. I can't explain the details to you because I can't. I need to get to the office ASAP."

Jack's face was grim, his jaw set firm. "I don't like this any better than you do, Kirsti, I hope you believe me."

Kirsti could do nothing more than stare at Jack, standing there, telling her that the whole idea of a honeymoon was over. She literally could not comprehend what she was hearing. Jack's expression told her he was serious; he wasn't joking as she hoped he was. Kirsti sat down on the bed; she needed a moment to think. *All the plans, everything they were going to do together.* Is this how the honeymoon was going to end? How could this be possible?

Jack moved toward her with his hands outstretched, "Come here, let me hold you for a little bit, and then I need to get moving. I'll call the airlines and cancel our flight while you get dressed."

"No, you go, I'll call Glenda. She'll come and get me." She stood up but didn't approach him. She was struggling to regain her composure. She felt like screaming, she felt like throwing something at him. Then she was struck with the full impact of the situation, she had married a cop. Not just any cop, she had married Jack Ireland.

Jack appeared different to her somehow; he seemed cold and hard—electric. He dressed rapidly. What she didn't realize was that Jack's life was always like this. He was conditioned to life turning on a dime. After he was fully dressed, he gave her a long kiss and said, "Bye, baby. I love you. Things will be just fine, I promise, but who has the button, darling, who has the button? That's what I want to know."

His mind was now away from her. Tears rimmed Kirsti's eyes as she watched him walk out the door.

What button? What was Jack talking about? Kirsti glanced at the clock with blurry eyes; it was 7:00 AM. Glenda wasn't going to be very happy, but what the hell, she wasn't very happy. She and Glenda could be unhappy together. Fine, if this is how it has to be, well then, this is how it has to be. It wasn't until she noticed her wedding dress neatly draped over a chair that she started to cry. She cried while she showered. She cried while she dressed. She cried while she packed, and she didn't quit crying until she heard Glenda's voice on the other end of the line.

Part II

Dark in the dark, old inn-yard a stable-wicket creaked
Where Tim, the ostler listened—his face was white and peaked—
His eyes were hollows of madness, his hair like mouldy hay,
But he loved the landlord's daughter—
The landlord's black-eyed daughter;
Dumb as a dog he listened, and he heard the robber say:

"One kiss, my bonny sweetheart; I'm after a prize tonight,
But I shall be back with the yellow gold before the morning light.
Yet if they press me sharply, and harry me through the day,
Then look for me by moonlight,
Watch for me by moonlight,
I'll come to the by moonlight, though hell shall bar the way."

He stood upright in his stirrups; he scarce could reach her hand,
But she loosened her hair in the casement! His face burned like
    a brand
As the sweet black waves of perfume, came tumbling o'er his breast,
Then he kissed its waves in the moonlight
(O sweet black waves in the moonlight!),
And he tugged at his reins in the moonlight and galloped away to
    the west.

Chapter Sixteen

Willie was standing at the sink, brushing his teeth when his brother finally hauled himself out of bed and made himself at hand. Willie didn't glance at his brother or even acknowledge him until he had all the debris picked from his teeth. He moved his mouth from side to side as he studied his perfect teeth. He had a thing about his teeth. His mother had always told him that a bright smile would get him through everything. He did have a bright smile. He liked his smile. In fact, he loved his smile. Willie stepped back a few paces from the mirror and admired his body. His body was really quite remarkable, or so he thought. He was just the right weight for his height. He stood at 5' 10" inches tall and weighed a muscled 175 lbs. He was strong, and he knew it. He was also very smart; he knew that too. Smarts was what had saved the day for him and his brother through all these years of traveling together.

Willie turned and looked at his brother who was in his usual fog. Shorty had no idea of how to get anything done without Willie, the curse of being an older brother, he supposed.

"How did it go last night? I would have stayed up and waited for you, but you took your sweet time coming home. I decided you had decided to go out and celebrate."

Willie gave himself another look in the mirror and smiled. Ah, that smile, how enticing.

"I had to wait a lot longer than I expected. She didn't come out of the bar until three in the morning. I think she had something going with her boss. I almost didn't get the job done, but then, there she was, walking out all by herself. The boss, who is probably screwing her didn't even bother to think she might need some looking out for but then girls these days are really easy prey. They think they don't need a man for anything, but what they want them for." Shorty snorted with disgust.

"Sounds like you don't have a lot of respect for women, brother of mine."

"Oh, I respect women just fine as long as they remember that they have a place, and that their place hasn't been dug yet." Shorty chortled and snorted again at his own joke.

"Go brush your teeth and get cleaned up. I have a job for you, we might have to be changing our identities quickly, and I want us to be prepared. Right now, I have to get to the office. There is a special meeting going on that I heard about through the grapevine. Little old Lulu likes me, a lot, she called me about an hour ago."

Lulu worked dispatch. She was madly, crazy wild about Willie. Willie couldn't have cared less about Lulu; she was the skinniest thing he had ever seen in his life, but she served his purposes. Lulu didn't have enough sense to come in out of the rain, but she handled dispatch, and dispatch was important to Willie. He had no problem with keeping her happy, for now.

Shorty danced his way to the bathroom, singing phrases from songs in mixed measure and beat. Willie watched his little brother fondly, picked up a spoon off the table, and threw it at him. "Love you, brother. Stay low."

"Love you too, I will and the same goes for you, every day is a new day."

Willie and Shorty hadn't given a second thought to the death of their mother. Somewhere along the line, they figured this was going to happen eventually, but they hadn't thought of what they were going to do when it did happen. They didn't flee the state because they had a compulsion to do so because that wasn't the case; they fled because they figured the more distance they could put between themselves and their father, the better off they would be. They never had a relationship with their drunk of a mother. They disliked her even more than they did their father. Their father was a strong and intimidating person as far as they were concerned, and their mother was nothing but a complete washout, a weakling, and deserved everything she got. She could have stopped everything had she been stronger, but no, she just sat around and got drunk every day; she was nothing better than a waste of time. They knew who killed their mother, and they actually liked him for it, or so this was what they told each other now and then when they talked about it, which was rarely. He was their father, and though he was a mean bastard, he was better than the whimpering son of a mother that they had to be bothered about from sun up till sun down. Her death relieved them of one great big fat burden, "Thanks, Dad."

Willie and Shorty made their way to Fargo, North Dakota, for no particular reason, but because it was a long way from California and a place where they could hide out for a while until Willie collected his thoughts. Willie haunted the campus and found the name of a student that had no real family and no real claim to fame. This student's name was Irv Jason Wells. Willie remained silently in the background, waiting and waiting until the young man graduated from college and had his degree. Willie planned his moves carefully. While he waited, he studied criminology over the Internet under the name of Irv Jason Wells. The Internet was a new thing and the time long before anyone took notice that there might be a glitch in all the freedom of information being sent through space for anyone who wanted it.

One day, Irving Jason Wells met Willie. Willie wined and dined him. What no one knew about Irv was that he was a homosexual. Willie, having been invited to a sleepover with Irv, took advantage of the opportunity. He shot Irv from a close distance, square, though the chest. Irv never knew what hit him. The boys took his body to a site already known to both Willie and Shorty, in a very isolated area in North Dakota. They buried his body six feet deep; to their knowledge, the body hadn't been found yet. The rest was easy. Willie took on Irv's identity. He stole his social security number. He stole his driver's license, had the picture changed to fit his own image, and he was off and running. Shorty was good at counterfeiting and forgery. These boys had special talents that served them well in their desire for survival.

Willie and his brother then took themselves to the Twin Cities where they hung out for a while, doing their usual everyday robbing and stealing from anyone and everyone that they could rob from and steal from and not get caught. Then one day, Willie met Lulu. She was a bar hound with not a whole lot going for her in her personal life. Willie embraced her, and she became his women, according to her. Willie stood silent on the subject. She told Willie that the courthouse was looking for a computer technician. He set up an appointment, was interviewed; he offered an impressive resume and got the job. He did know computers; his resume had checked out. Irv had seen to that. He was in. This was his first real job ever, and he liked it. He delighted in collecting his paycheck at the end of the week like a normal person. Life was rolling along very agreeably, "Thank you very much!"

Now Lulu had heard rumors about Maggie and things were starting to get sticky between them. He didn't bother to tell Lulu about the pool party. A little bit of jealousy never hurt anyone. Being dumped into the pool and thrown out was something he wasn't going to talk about, not even to Shorty; but he would remember this event forever, and he would get even.

Irv walked into the office well ahead of everyone else, including Brice; and there was Lulu, sitting at the dispatch desk, filing her nails like always. He winked at her; she winked back at him. Lulu will have to go eventually, but not just yet. Irv went immediately to his workstation located in the back of the large square room. While he waited, he cranked up his computer. Irv Jason Wells waited for the man to arrive. First came Brice and then next, in came the infamous duo. He was elated to see that Jack was not in high spirits. *We did good Shorty. We did really good!* Jack never noticed him. No one ever paid any attention to Irv unless their computer froze up on them, and they needed him. Irv didn't care; one day the whole state of Minnesota would know who he was.

Brice was standing by the window in his office when Jack and Vic entered his office. He was staring out the window, deep in thought. He looked tired. There was an enormous amount of pressure being placed on him over the unresolved Credit River case. Someone was leaking information to the press, and being the hound dogs they are and the unusualness of the case, the media were having a lot of fun sensationalizing the story and in the process making the whole police department look inept. The fact of the matter was the investigative team had worked countless hours using every resource available to them in their attempt to put the pieces together and had come up with absolutely nothing. They hadn't even been able to identify the victim let alone track down the killer. Now there was another one, another one just like the other one.

Brice turned from the window and sat down in his chair. He put his feet on the desk, opened a drawer, and took out a bottle of what looked to be antacid tablets. He poured four of them on his desk and tossed the empty bottle into the wastebasket.

"I get the first two; you and Vic can fight over the other two."

Vic, who was sitting on the couch across the room from Brice, declined the offer. Jack picked up the remaining two and put them in his jacket pocket.

"I'll save them for later. They might come in handy around lunchtime."

The men were silent for a long time. They just sat there and looked at each other all of them were thinking the same thing, "What next?"

"Sorry we had to pull you away from your honeymoon. How did Kirsti take it?" Brice spoke first, breaking the silence between them. He knew he had to cross that threshold first, and it was going to be a touchy subject.

"You had a very lovely wedding, Jack. I really am sorry I had to take you away from your honeymoon."

"I'm sorry too," Jack said crossly. "And I don't know how Kirsti is taking this because I couldn't stick around long enough to find out. On the other hand I suppose there is no time like the present to give her a true concept of what my job is all about. I left her at the hotel, her sister was going to pick her up, and what she is going to do with the rest of the day is anyone's guess."

Jack looked up at the ceiling and sighed, "None of this is your fault, Brice, so no need to apologize."

He turned to Vic and said, "Thanks a lot, buddy, for you know what not happening! Now if anyone owes me an apology, it is my interfering partner who is sitting there, trying to act so damned innocent while he and I and the whole world know he's as guilty as Charlie "I never did anything" Manson."

Brice and Vic laughed hard but briefly. It was time to move on to the business at hand.

"You said a while back you knew the Credit River killing was more than likely done by a serial killer." Brice was staring directly at Jack as he went on to say, "I hate it when you are right and especially about things like this. A 'serial' puts a chill into the spine of all mankind."

"I wasn't sure, but it had that look about it. I read a lot, you know, and most of what I read is about serial killers." Jack was trying to be light. "We might want to call in an expert on this. Our team doesn't have a lot of experience in the 'serial' killer department."

"Read?" Vic looked at him dubiously. "How can you find time to read anything? All I ever see you do is chase women and drink yourself into a state of oblivion day in and day out." Vic stretched his arms over his head and yawned. "Read, indeed."

"Oh, I get it. You have the women in your life read to you while you drink. I know you can't read past a first-grade level, and your powers of comprehension are zero, and as far as sex goes, I have heard—"

"Well, aren't we being downright complimentary this morning. I have heard a few to many rumors about you to Melton and if I were you, I wouldn't be sitting in that chair casting dispersions. People who live in glasshouses? Ever hear that one? It takes one to know one, etc. and etc."

Jack sat back in his chair and gave Vic a wide, fake smile. He leaned so far back in his chair, he almost dumped himself over backward. He caught himself in the nick of time. It was Vic's turn grin.

"You are so adroit, Jack, you amaze me sometimes, not often, but now and then you are really quick. If you weren't so damned big headed you would have better balance."

"OK, OK, that's enough, save your incessant quibbling for the streets. I don't want to hear it."

Brice got up from his seated position and moved around to the front of his desk and positioned himself, so he was sitting on the edge of his desk about three feet from Jack.

"Close the door. I don't want anyone else overhearing this conversation."

Jack got up closed the door and sat back down again. Brice rarely closed his door. Vic slid his long, slender body deeper into his chair and removed his locked hands from behind his head. Jack sat up in his chair and crossed his legs, placing one hand on his hip and the other on the arm of the chair. He started unconsciously strumming his fingers. Every action has a reaction, Jack was responding to Brice. He was nervous.

"We do have a serial. This one was found on Highway 169, about a mile south of Chaska. She was placed on the edge of the highway, in plain sight. A passing car found her and called it in at about four thirty this morning. Apparently, this person doesn't want to be involved because he kept right on going. He didn't leave a name or number. The Shakopee Police held the scene until the CSI unit arrived. The MO is identical to the Credit River case. The girl was blond, she was strangled and positioned exactly like the other girl, and she had a purple button clutched in her left hand. Whoever did this wanted her found. We can probably locate the guy who called in, but I doubt he will be of any help at all. I want you to find him anyway."

"What we need to do is find a connection between the two girls. There has to be one. I wonder why they are being dumped in that neck of the woods?"

Jack ran his hands through his thick wavy hair.

"I hate to say this, but I don't think we're going to make any headway on this until there is a third, and there will be a third. The purple button is the key, what does that purple button mean? I know that it connects the two murders, but what is the meaning behind the purple button?"

"I think we need to set up a special task force and keep it tight." Brice had his eyes on the closed door. "We have someone out there who is leaking information so pick people that you can trust to keep their mouths shut. We might have to pull manpower from Scott County, so go over there and talk to those folks. They have the database, and they know the territory. I know you don't like Irv, but he is a brilliant computer man. We need to bring him in on this to set up our own database to cross-check information that comes in. I noticed when I came in that he's here, so let's bring him in my office now."

"What's he doing here on a Sunday?" Jack asked quizzically. "He's office personnel, they never work on Sunday."

Brice said slyly, "Lulu is managing dispatch today. Water fountain gossip claims they are an item."

Jack looked at Vic; Vic looked at Jack. They both rolled their eyes and shook their heads. "Lulu has to be desperate, either that, or she needs glasses or both. I didn't think you paid any attention to that water fountain garbage."

"I pay a lot of attention to many things, including water fountain garbage." The Chief didn't seem to be anything other than serious. "I have discovered that we can learn a lot by just listening. You guys should try it some time." Now he had a smile on his face. "So get out there and do some listening and bring me home a killer."

Jack and Vic rose from their chairs as Brice called Irv into his office.

"We will leave him to you," said Jack. "Come on, Vic, let's get out of here. I need something to eat."

As they were walking out of the office Jack said to Vic, "Speaking of eating, how about you, Tory, Kirsti, and I go out for dinner some Saturday night? Kirsti loves the Red Rooster. I have to do something to make this up to her."

"Sure, name the day and the time?" said Vic.

"We'll talk about it. They have a band on Saturday nights, so we can take in a little dancing too." Jack did a quick shuffle.

"You don't know how to dance. I watched you last night, what a klutz. Kirsti made you look good though, so did your Mother-In-Law. She's a real prize and one you certainly don't deserve."

"Who was talking about the pot calling the kettle black less than an hour ago?"

"I don't know. I have lost track. Am I the pot and you the kettle, or are you in the kettle and me in the pot?"

"I don't know either, but you had better not be smoking pot, that's illegal. You could get arrested."

"By whom"

"That would be who."

"Speaking of who, I think we need to find one of them."

"We? Why we, Tonto?"

Out of the building they went, bantering all the way. Brice shook his head, laughed, and said to Irv who was standing along side him, "Come on in, Irv and have a seat."

Irv was expressionless, "Certainly, sir."

Chapter Seventeen

Glenda had taken less than fifteen minutes to change out of her pajamas and into a pair of jeans and sweatshirt, brush her teeth, brush her thick blond hair and pull it back into a ponytail before she was out the door and on her way to the Hyatt-Regency to pick up her sister. Had she seen her brand new brother-in-law standing by the side of the road in need of help; she would have run over him. Glenda didn't like Jack at this moment; her only concern was for her sister. She liked Jack generally because he was very likable and made her sister silly, but there was a limit. She was giving no thought to the possibility that Jack had a very good reason to cancel the honeymoon. In fact, and for fact, she had no idea whatsoever as to why Jack had been called back in; and as far as she knew, neither did Kirsti.

Kirsti was in the lobby, reading the paper, when Glenda arrived. She hugged her sister and thanked her for coming to get her.

"You look like you just got out of bed."

"Duh? you Think?" Glenda was tired and in no mood for insults.

The bellhop was waiting patiently with the luggage by the large glass-paned entrance doors as the girls made ready to depart the hotel. Kirsti gave him a hefty tip, thanked him; and in a very short time, the two sisters were on the freeway heading south to more familiar territory.

"I get nervous driving through the cities; everything has changed so much in the past three years and since I moved to Oklahoma. Everything is much quieter there than here." Glenda gave her sister a quick side glimpse. "Are you OK?"

Yes, I'm OK, a bit disappointed maybe." Kristi turned her head towards her sister and let out a low groan, "OK, I am a whole bunch disappointed, but it isn't as though I wasn't forewarned about the drawbacks of marrying a cop and Jack in particular. This is all part of the package. I just didn't expect to find out so quickly and on such an important day of my life!"

"Do you know why Jack had to leave you in such a huge rush?"

"No," said Kristi. "Only that it has something to do with a case he has been working on. I really don't want to talk about it anymore."

Glenda decided to leave her alone and not press her. Kirsti would talk to her when she was ready, she always did.

"Do you mind if I turn on the radio?"

"No," said Kirsti. "Not as long as you don't play Country/Western. I don't think I could bear hearing a song by Johnny, Willie, or Waylon today." They were Jack's favorites.

Glenda turned the dial to WCCO; what the girls heard made both of them stare wide eyed at each other with complete surprise and then understanding. The radio announcer was talking about a homicide that happened early in the morning, near Chaska. There was some speculation that this murder might be tied to another unsolved case that happened earlier in the year. The Scott County sheriff, Vince Grossman, would be having a press conference later in the day.

"I knew there had to be a good reason for him to leave as he did! Jack said it had something to do with a case he has been working on. I feel a little bit better now," Kirsti said with satisfaction, "How about you, and I spending the day together. Have you got any other plans?"

"I couldn't be more honored, what do you say we gather the girls, go to your old apartment, open up your wedding gifts, break out the champagne and celebrate?"

"I think I'll try and get a hold of Jack and tell him my plans. More champagne? Whew, this might not be a good idea after last night."

"All right wine and beer. We'll leave out the champagne."

Jack answered the phone on the first ring; he and Vic were on their way to Shakopee; he was relieved to hear Kirsti's upbeat voice. When she told him her plans, he said, "Good. I'm glad. I've been feeling rotten all morning about having to leave you like I did. I might not get home at all tonight, so don't wait up. This is going to be a long day for me and the boys. Remember, I love you. I wish I could tell you more, but I can't."

"I know."

Kirsti closed her cell phone quietly, "Everything is OK, and he said he loves me."

Glenda nodded. She knew this, but something was nagging at her. Jack was now involved in some very serious business; homicide business, possibly serial killer business. Glenda had to wonder how this would affect her sister's marriage and her relationship with Jack. Glenda also knew that her sister was inexperienced with such things; she had always drawn herself to people who never got any dirt on themselves, not even dust. Kirsti's life had been protected from the insults of the streets where Jack walked daily. Kirsti knew nothing about the underbelly of life and, because of this, had no idea of how to relate to the complexities of Jack's world. Her entire arena was made up of bright, cheerful, positive things, not the sinister portions of the criminal world. A bad day to Kirsti was stepping on the scale and finding she had put on a half an ounce of weight.

Only Kirsti would consider everything all right while there was a possible "serial killer" on the loose in their own backyard, and this bothered Glenda, immensely.

It was after midnight when Glenda, Mary, and Hilde took Kirsti to her new home. She had never been there without Jack; the place felt lonely. Jack was not home yet and had left no messages on his answering machine. Kirsti was tired; it had been a long day. She wrote Jack a note and went upstairs to their bedroom, changed into warm pajamas, and went to bed. She fell asleep before her head hit the pillow.

When Jack came home, he found his wife in bed, sound asleep. He kissed her on the top of the head and curled up next to her. Before he went to sleep, he wondered what it would be like to make love to his wife. She had been determined to save her first time for their wedding night, but now that was in past tense. Kirsti didn't respond as he placed his strong arms around her, nor did she respond when he gave her a soft kiss on the lips. He smiled, reminiscently when he caught the faint odor of champagne on her breath.

One more day," he thought. "*One more day. Button, button, who's got the button.*

Jack clenched his fist, as though he was clasping the button in his hand, and then he drifted away into a deep sleep; he was mentally and physically exhausted. He had traveled all day and after fifteen hours of searching, questioning, and interviewing, he was no further ahead on the solving the case than he was when he started. He would make love to his wife in the morning, his sweet, young, beautiful, innocent wife. The very last thought in his mind as he floated off to that mysterious place called slumber land was a vision of Glenda. She was moving toward him, her long blond hair flowing back in the wind. Her bright blue eyes were questioning him, she seemed to be suffering and deeply hurt. She was reaching for him, and in her outstretched hand was a purple button then she evaporated and was gone.

The phone was ringing. The phone was always ringing. Jack tried to avoid answering it, but it kept right on jingling in an incessant and single-minded, purposeful manner. When he came to his senses and realized the phone was not going to quit ringing, he dragged himself out of bed and down the stairs, but wasn't quick enough, the answering machine had kicked in. He looked at the clock on the fireplace mantel; it read five-thirty in the morning. He had been asleep for three hours.

From the answering machine came a muffled voice, saying, "*I am your man Jack. Are you getting sluggish, my boy? Can't keep up? I thought you would have picked up right away, what, am I too early for you? Or just to fast. I am the man with the purple buttons, Jackie, and I have several of them. You will not know exactly how many until the day of your death. When I am done with the buttons, then I am coming after you. Have fun trying to find me, Jackie boy. I am your nemesis. Check out the Web site, Jack. I have created a website just for you. Take a note of this, jackireland/visit/murder.com. Have fun.*" Click.

Jack immediately made a backup of the tape. He felt his adrenaline flowing. He quickly changed clothes, grabbed the tape, wrote a note to Kirsti, and was on his way to the office. He called Vic en route and told him to get his rear end to the government building. Things were on the move.

Jack was pumped. He had also called Brice. Vic, Brice, and Jack entered the parking lot at the same time. The three men did not speak until they were settled in Brice's office. Jack closed the door behind them. He didn't want anyone in on this but his boss and his partner.

"I received a call from the killer this morning, and I have it on tape. We need to have it analyzed. He also gave me the name of a Web site he has created." Jack could hardly catch his breath. "This might be the break we have been looking for."

"Let's get Irv in here to pull up the Web site. We might need his expertise." Brice picked up his phone and started to punch in numbers. Jack stopped him before he finished dialing.

"Let's don't and say we did," said Jack. "I don't like him and I don't trust him."

Vic nodded and said, "I agree with Jack. I don't think we should bring him in yet because I don't trust him either. That guy has a serious personality disorder. Let's outsource this. I know a guy, a good friend of mine, who is as good at computers as Irv could ever think to be. He works for Computer Tech as their engineer. He's good, he's independent, and he probably won't charge us a cent. He loves this kind of stuff. He'll climb on board just for grins and giggles."

Brice was studying his investigators closely. "I guess I don't really understand your apprehension where Irv is concerned, but if you think this other fellow should handle it, I'll go along with it for now. However, I am going to state for practicalities' sake that you had better find a way to justify this quickly. Irv has worked hard to set up a database for our department, and I think we ought to be using it. I'm going to need a formal request from you for the files and his resume."

"Irvie was your choice, not ours," said Jack. Vic nodded again. "He gives me the creeps."

"I know you guys don't like Irv. No one likes Irv. Hell, I don't even like Irv but he is part of the system here and I am going to have a hard time explaining why I am not using our own computer expert on a case this sensitive. People are going to ask a lot of questions, and I might find myself short of answers, this would not be good so get me that paper work right away. Contessa will steer you through it."

"No one is going to ask questions if no one knows. Let's see what light Jamie can shed on this before we mention this to anyone, and perhaps, by not bringing the tape into the light of day, we might get the guy riled up enough to talk to Jack again. This guy seems to need attention."

"Learn that from all your reading, did yah?" Jack chided. "All those books about serial killers and all, huh?"

"No, Jack. Remember? That's your gig. How come you are always blaming me for things you do? I don't get it."

Brice grabbed each of them by the arm and steered them toward the door, "Shut up, both of you. This time I really mean *shut up!*"

"Touchy, Brice, you are so darned touchy these days. What is getting on your nerves so badly anyway? One serial killer amongst friends shouldn't cause you to be so sensitive. Vic and I are just trying to get along, and here you are, making us out to be the villains."

"Yah, Chief," Vic chimed in egged on by his partner. "Your girl friend give you the old heave-ho or what? What's happened to your sense of humor?" Everyone knew that Buchanan was not known for his sense of humor.

"Have your fun, boys, have your fun, but while you are engaging yourself in idle humor at my expense, you had better remember one thing, I have a long memory and payback is hell. Now let's get the heck out of here before the press locates us."

At that moment, Jack spotted Lulu at the dispatch station. "Well, hello Lulu, you're looking lovely today. Don't they ever give you a day off?"

She waved at Jack as she spoke into her headphones. "Nine-one-one, where is your location, state your problem please."

To say that Jamie was a big man would be an understatement. He was massive. Jack guessed him to weigh in at about three hundred plus pounds. Jamie had obviously carried this excessive weight around with him for a long time because he was surprisingly agile and quick on his feet. He had a head full of jet-black hair, black eyes, and deeply tanned skin and not because he spent any time in the sun. His eyes spoke for him; his genuine smile said the rest. He had perfectly straight white teeth that he wasn't shy about showing. Jamie had the capacity to see life in an entirely different manner than most people. He saw humor in everything, and though he did have a perpetual uplift around his mouth, his eyes told a different story. They were intense and oftentimes unnerving to the most serious-minded individuals. He held an inner wisdom that was sometimes frightening and yet fascinating. "What you see is what you get" did not apply to Jamie.

As Vic introduced everyone all around, he added, "You caught my friend on a good day, evidently, he is smiling, and he is talking to. He generally does neither. I have known him to come and visit me and never say a word for hours and then just get up and leave. I have always found him to be rather spooky." Jamie never let loose of his grin, nor did he comment on his friend's assessment of him.

"What do you want to do first, the tape or the Web site?" Jamie inquired as he led them to his computer station. The spot where he was situated looked like something out of *Star Trek*, the latest version. Jamie sat down in the center, pointed to several chairs not being used at the time, and suggested they gather around, which they did.

Jamie considered the bedazzled expressions on the investigators' faces and said, without hint of condescension or haughtiness, "Welcome to the computer world. It is intimidating, indeed it is, and it should be considered as such. There is no greater threat to the privacy of all mankind than what you will see here, right now, in front of you. So now that we know that this is a given, let's see if we can make some use of it in a positive way. Where should we start, with the tape or with the Web site?"

"Let's start with the Web site. We already know what's on the tape."

Brice shifted closer to Jamie as he typed in the Web address. Jamie had to click on three different sites to bring forth the contents of the Web site, and what they saw shocked four men who thought themselves beyond being shocked by anything. Whoever had put this together had created a slide show of the two girls coming and going from different places and at different times. He had stalked them. The girls could have been twins; they were so similar in looks. They were both about the same age, in their early twenties. Both had long blond hair, blue eyes, and adorable faces—young faces, innocent faces, friendly faces. Most of the pictures were close-up, but some were full bodied, showing them walking; and then there were the last pictures of them lying on a cold dark floor, dead, their eyes wide open and glazed, their bodies naked and displayed in full front view. Planted on their foreheads was a purple button. At the end of the slide show came a picture of a note written in brilliant red; it said, "These two are on me, the rest are on you, Jackie. Are you having fun yet? I am."

Jamie was studying the background of the pictures as he reviewed them over and then over again until all had become numb to the contents, which was the general idea.

After several dozen reviews and listening to the tape several times, Jamie turned around, looked at Jack directly, and said, "Whoever did this thinks he knows you, Jack, and he also knows his way around a computer. He has done a really good job of erasing all backgrounds from the pictures, so all we see is the person and the body. However, we might want to study the clothing they are wearing. This might shed some light. I saw in one picture of the second girl that she might have been wearing a uniform of some sort. Was she a waitress?"

"Well, let's take a closer look," said Brice, leaning back in his chair, stretching his arms over his head to get the kinks out of his body and his mind, "I have all day."

For as horrible as the pictures were, the men were not disappointed; the killer had given them something to work with. The uniform gave them a starting point. With the overall meticulous cropping, Jack wondered why the killer had put that picture in and questioned this out loud.

Jack looked at Vic, and Vic looked at Jack; they were thinking the same thing. Jack shook his head.

"No, he doesn't want to get caught, he is teasing us, he will be picking up steam now. As I see things, this is just the beginning. What do you say, Vic?"

"You know, Jack, you could make a very lazy man out of me. You keep up the same thinking as I'm thinking. Pretty soon I won't have to think at all. I can leave all the thinking to you. Now ain't that a fanciful thought."

"I think we need to visit a few bars, and while we're at it, I will talk to you about how little thinking you are really capable of. Reasoning isn't really your strong suit, Vic. I might have mentioned this before, but perhaps we need to go over this subject again."

"Yah, which ones, there are only about a gazillion of them in the twin city area, and while you are in the business of telling me how I am not capable, why don't you let me drive because you can't chew gum and drive at the same time."

"How about we start in Shakopee?"

"Say Jack? How about we start in Shakopee?'

Jack and Vic grabbed the pictures Jamie printed up for them, and then they were gone, leaving their boss to find his own way back to Hastings.

Chapter Eighteen

The Crawford and Crawford law office was a family-owned partnership, father and son. Samuel Crawford was the son of Reed Samuel Crawford I. Reed Crawford I practiced law when the legal process wasn't so specialized. The only type of case he refused to handle was any having to do with divorce. Reed I couldn't stomach the nastiness of the divorce process, in general or in its legal particulars. Prior to the present times of "no fault," there had to be grounds for divorce, such as abuse or adultery. What constituted abuse was loosely written and adultery had to be proven. Which generally meant a lot of expense was handed to the client for the use of a private investigator, whose job was to prove beyond a doubt that one or the other was playing around outside the marital arena and custody suits got down right vicious. Many a lawyer got rich handling divorce cases, and the nastier the divorce was the richer the lawyer became.

It took a while, but eventually the judges, from coast to coast, became impatient with all of this nasty business that was wreaking havoc across the land, from one side of the country to the other, and decided to put a stop to it. Perhaps there was a very honorable reason for doing this, one such as preventing the children from being torn between the two parents. On the other hand, maybe there was too much fault being passed around. Then again, perhaps it was a change of social climate. Perhaps it was the hippie movement, all that "free love," perhaps it was the Vietnam War or the assassination of John F. Kennedy; no one really knew for sure, but the court system found itself a bit more favorable toward thinking about a "No Fault" plan, which thrust half the population of the United States into divorce court. Divorce became so rampant that some wise guy generated a bumper sticker boldly and rightfully proclaiming, "A hundred percent of all divorces are caused by marriage." A new-angled sort of havoc commenced, none of which affected Crawford and Crawford because Reed I simply refused to become a participant.

Reed Crawford I was a trial lawyer and gained a respectable reputation handling civil cases. His specialty was personal injury. He fought for the little guy that was injured on the job. He fought large companies with big names and very deep pockets. He fought valiantly for the rights of the individual; he fought tough, and he fought hard and he, with rare exception, won his cases. When he died of a heart attack at the age of sixty-three, his son Samuel took over his already well-reputed and well-established law firm.

Samuel Reed Crawford went to work for his father after he graduated from Harvard. His father taught him all he knew about the business of law, intellectually and judicially. He told him never to take a case, he wasn't passionate about. When Samuel inherited the Crawford Law Business, it was located in Richfield, Minnesota. He, like his father, became a distinguished trial lawyer.

Samuel looked like his father, walked like his father, dressed like his father, and talked like his father. It wasn't exclusively a gene thing. He did his best to emulate his mentor; he did so consciously and perhaps even a bit unconsciously. There was a time when someone told him that he was the "spitting image" of his father. Samuel had looked at this person and said, "Hardly. If you think that, you never really knew my father, and you certainly don't know me." He took the comment as an insult to his father because he had cleared it in his own mind that he could never measure up to his esteemed parent, but he would, for all intents and purposes, die trying.

Samuel married Mary Jo Stratford. He was thirty-one years old and wealthy. Mary Jo was anything but wealthy. She came from a very poor family who had starved themselves to save money, so she could go to college. Her father was a welder. He had his own business and was certainly busy enough, but he had eleven kids and barely made enough money to support them. What didn't help his financial situation any was his propensity to be a nice guy. A lot of the work he did was never paid for because he didn't charge his friends or family, and he had lots of friends and a huge family.

Mary Jo was the only one of his children who had expressed an interest in going to college. She selected St. Olaf College in Northfield,

Minnesota. Her parents could only afford to pay for her first year; she paid for the rest by scholarships and grants. She majored in interior design and minored in music. Mary Jo came from a family of great musical talent. There was not a one in the bunch who couldn't carry a fine tune. They sang with each other and with groups, but only Mary used her voice to get herself a scholarship from St. Olaf College. The rest of the brood was convinced that singing professionally was for someone else; an avocation, not a vocation, and joined the workforce of society and were more than happy to do so. They would become "mainstream" Americans. Mary Jo had no such thoughts about herself.

Sam met Mary Jo at a party. She was a friend of a friend of a friend. Sam noticed her immediately and asked a buddy of his, who said he knew her, to introduce them. He did. They dated for a year and then married. They moved into a modest apartment in Richfield until one day, Mary Jo came home and told her husband that she had found a beautiful, vintage two-story house in Eagan. She was excited. The house required a lot of restoration, but she was up to the task if Sam would only give her the opportunity. He agreed. They purchased the house, and Mary Jo set herself to making it one of the most unique and desirable homes in the metro area.

The couple lived there until their first and only son was born, Reed Samuel Crawford II. She wanted her son to have all the opportunities in life that she never had. She shopped around until she found an elaborate mansion on Lake Minnetonka. Sam liked his home in Eagan and was resistant at first, but he loved his wife above everything else and caved in. Sam decided to have the house in Eagan transformed into his law office. Mary Jo liked the idea and handled the makeover almost single-handedly. Sam had very little say in the process or the cost of the reconstruction. This was her project. She worked shoulder to shoulder with the people she hired. When they shingled, she was up on the roof, pounding nails; when they painted, she painted; she did everything they did. Rumor had it that she did a lot more than pound nails with her crewmen. Sam could manage a courtroom expertly, but he never did quite figure out how to manage his wife.

Mary Jo wanted to have more children, but after several miscarriages, she gave up. She blamed her husband because she had to blame someone. She came from stock that had great reproductive genes, he didn't. She wanted a daughter badly, but this was never to be. She poured all of her attention on her only child. She put him in a private school. She sent him to a military academy out east. Sam fought her hard; he wanted his son to have a life closer to home, with him, but she did it anyway.

After Reed II graduated from the military academy, she sent him to Harvard. She saw her son over the holidays and summer vacation and then rarely because she had acquired a taste for travel. She soon became inaccessible to her husband and then eventually her son. She had come to love the high style of life and the freedom her husband's money could afford her. By the time her son graduated from Harvard, Sam and Mary Jo were married in name only. She had purchased a villa in France.

"This is where the action is," she told her husband.

Sam remained faithful to his wife, but the same couldn't be said about her. Fortunately, the society pages weren't interested in lawyer's wives when there were bigger fish to fry. The Crawfords were wealthy enough, but they certainly had not been embraced by the "blue bloods". This suited Sam just fine, but not Mary Jo. Sam knew what was going on in France, but he loved his wife and would never consider divorce; he made his life go on without her. Mary Jo never mentioned divorce either. This would have created unnecessary complications for Sam and especially Mary Jo, financially speaking.

Reed Samuel Crawford II graduated from Harvard. His grades were adequate, but not exceptional. His strong suit was criminal law. His specialty was defense. Reed Samuel Crawford II was not like his father. He didn't look like his father, he didn't dress like his father, and he didn't think like his father. He was a progeny of his Mother. He cared deeply for his father but considered him a bit too soft. He held his father in respect for his better attributes, but his mother was the one he considered the example of what independence was all about. When Mary Jo died a year after his graduation from a rare untreatable virus, he laughed. He found no reason to mourn her death because she had lived her life to her own satisfaction.

"Rare virus, indeed, I doubt it" was his answer to her death. Samuel Crawford grieved deeply; his friends and associates wondered why, but he knew why. Mary Jo was the essence of what life should be about, freedom of choice and freedom to be herself. His recollections of his wife went deep and private. Reed's reflections on his mother were steeped in bitterness. He thought only of a mother he never had, could never have, would never have; and in truth, he was right. Mary Jo was many things, but she had never been a loving, nurturing mother to her son.

Chapter Nineteen

Kirsti had transported her sister Glenda to the Minneapolis-St. Paul International Airport at eight in the morning. They had left Lakeville early, hoping to avoid the morning rush hour traffic. Traffic had been light on the freeway but not so light at the airport.

"What is this? Is everybody in the state of Minnesota leaving town today? We're going to have to park so far away from the building that we'll have to catch a taxi to bring us to the front door."

"I told you to drop me off, but no, you had to have things your way. Be patient, would you, we have plenty of time."

"Yah, but now we will have to lug your suitcases a half a mile. Ah, here is a spot, it's a good thing I drive a small car. I hate airports."

By the time the girls checked Glenda's baggage and walked down the long, long corridor to the waiting area, it was time to board the plane.

"Gosh, I wish you didn't live so far away, Glenda. I miss you already!" Kirsti said, her eyes filled with tears

"Don't you dare shed a tear, us Povals don't cry. You just concentrate on taking care of that handsome hubby of yours. If you need me, you know where I am. I love you. I'll call you when I get back home." As Glenda boarded the plane, she blew her sister a farewell kiss.

Glenda walked down the narrow isle of the Boeing 747 looking for her seat. She had selected a window seat right behind the right wing of the plane. Nick had told her that this was the safest area on the plane. She pulled a paperback out of her purse, opened her carry-on bag, stuffed her purse inside the carry-on, and shoved both underneath the seat in front of her; both seats next to her remained empty as the plane took its flight into the skies and out of the Minneapolis-St. Paul Airport. She watched as the plane moved upward, leaving the ground at a rapid rate, the evidence of life beneath her getting smaller and smaller as the plane ascended into the air. She then realized how much she missed her life in Oklahoma, her pilot husband, who was always flying off somewhere, and her small antique shop. She was anxious to get home, to settle back into her life. She wondered if her husband would be there to pick her up at the airport when she arrived. He promised he would, but life was always on the go for him.

The flight from Minneapolis to Oklahoma City took three hours; Glenda was glad to see her husband's gorgeously handsome face as she came through the exit door. Jack Ireland had nothing over Nick. While Jack had a dark, brooding, handsomeness, Nick was his polar opposite. His thick blond wavy hair was a sharp contrast to his bronze-colored skin. He had brilliant, sky blue eyes that sparkled with mischievous delight. His naturally muscled body was shorter than Jack's by about three inches. He was not much taller than Glenda. What Glenda loved about Nick was his unwavering let's get it done attitude and his desire to live life to the fullest every minute of the day, every day of the week. He was mature in thought and in action. He was six years older than she was and solid. His eight years in the Air Force had launched his career as a pilot. With Nick came stability, a characteristic that Glenda needed in a relationship. Glenda was impulsive without reservation.

"Where have you been hanging out these last few days? I was beginning to think you were never going to come back to me." Nick grabbed her bag and set it down. He wrapped his arms around Glenda, pulling her close to him. "I sure have missed you."

Glenda pulled his head down towards hers and gave him a long, lingering kiss.

"No one knows where a hobo goes when it snows, and besides, you say that to all your wives."

"Hobo, huh? Well, little miss hobo, let's get out of here before one of my other wives catches me fooling around. I want to take you somewhere and show you something you might not have ever seen before."

"I hope it isn't Mt. Vernon because I am tired of traveling."

"Nope, it ain't Mt. Vernon. Where we're going no one has to worry about hobos, snow, or anything else either. You look tired. Let me be your doctor. I will fix you up just fine."

"I am tired. This was a long, hard week."

"You want to talk about it?" Nick became serious.

"No, not really, I want to think about you, and what we have here if that's OK with you. I am going to let you be my doctor, but if you don't do it right, I am going to go get a second opinion."

"All right, my little hobo. Let's go home. After I am finished with you, I promise, you will not need a second opinion."

The Crawford law firm had hired Kirsti before she graduated from college. She had been interviewed by both Samuel and Reed Crawford and had found both these men ultra collected and somewhat intimidating. They permeated wealth and success. Kirsti knew at the outset that these two men were the driving force behind the company, each in a different way. Samuel was casual in his approach to the interview while Reed was direct and sometimes harsh. Her last interview was with Jerry Lucas, who would be her direct boss. He was "the man" in command of research. He had a staff of four. Kirsti would be the fifth.

Jerry Lucas was thirty years old and not near as sophisticated as the two lawyers that had hired him right out of college. The interview with Jerry was more comfortable for Kirsti because he was as personable as the day was long. Jerry knew how to research law and just about everything else as well. His prime interest in life was research, period. His friends called him "The Genius. They had developed a game called "Let's ask Jerry". If Jerry couldn't give an answer to any category of question off the top of his head, he would research and have the answer in an astoundingly short period of time. No one ever asked Jerry to play Trivia Pursuit. The question for this day was, how old was Elvis Presley when he lost his first tooth?

It was Samuel, who hired Jerry to be his own personal paralegal. What Sam liked about Jerry was his matter-of-fact way of approaching the interview. Jerry had told Sam on their first and only interview that he had researched every law firm in the country and his choice of place to work was at Crawford and Crawford. He didn't sell himself, he went about selling Samuel on what a great law firm he had and how meaningful the cases were to the many clients he had represented and he would be quite satisfied doing his part in making a contribution to tasks that still needed to be finished. Jerry had boned himself up on the pending legal issues that Sam was concentrating on and cited many areas of research that would benefit Sam in winning these cases. Sam was impressed and hired him. He placed Jerry on the same wage as all of his starters and got no disagreement from Jerry. Sam placed Jerry in management over the rest of the paralegals, against Jerry's better judgment, and even though he was the team leader, he didn't think of himself as that. He worked elbow to elbow with his personnel. His style of managing was not to manage.

Jerry had argued feverously to persuade Samuel and Reed to hire Kirsti. They thought she was too young and too inexperienced to handle the job. He disagreed. They wanted somebody with no less than five years of experience. Jerry won by sheer dogged persistence. He had researched Kirsti as thoroughly as he would have researched anything else, and he wanted her on his staff.

Jerry's direct boss was Samuel. Sam had liked Kirsti's straightforward personality; he was also impressed by her resume. And with a bit of pushing and shoving from Jerry and because Sam outranked Reed, Kirsti was hired. She had now been with them for three months and had already established herself to be worth her salt. She was bright, and she was resourceful. Sam noticed that Kirsti took her job seriously. Jerry appreciated her innovative and meticulous approach to whatever assignment she was handed.

Reed, of course, held no such regard for Kirsti. She might have dazzled Jerry, and she might have dazzled his father, but to Reed, she was just another skirt with a lot of stars in her eyes. Sure she was good, but could she take the heat? Reed had a lot of plans for his father's law firm and in his estimation, there were going to be some who would not be on board when he took over; and one would be Kirsti, the other would be Jerry. He was making his moves and with the showdown in the foreseeable future; he needed to make sure that there would be no interference from the paralegal department.

Kirsti parked her car in her usual spot. It was a cloudy, heavily overcast, gloomy day; and the predictions were for more of the same into the following week. The air actually felt icy as though winter was hiding its unpleasant self right around the corner, exhaling its cold breath into the atmosphere, belligerently extending advanced warning of its pending arrival. All the splendid colors of fall seemed to have suddenly disappeared and had turned into a cold, dreary, dullness.

Kirsti hadn't called in ahead of time because she didn't think she needed to. She had put in for two weeks' vacation, and the thought had crossed her mind that her premature return to work might be rejected by Jerry if he were asked, so she didn't ask. She needed to get back to work. She had mentally braced herself for the onslaught of questions that would more than likely come her way; she was supposed to be on her honeymoon, not here, not at Crawford and Crawford, not yet.

Kirsti had not seen her husband, at all, since the Sunday morning after their wedding. He had left cute little notes for her attached to the coffee pot, but she hadn't seen him. They were like two ships passing in the night. The only means she had of knowing he had been home was by the notes he left for her and his dirty laundry. He was living on a few hours of sleep at home, some nights he didn't come home at all. Better than a week had gone by since she'd seen him; she was feeling isolated, alone, and detached from her husband and the life she had anticipated, she would have with him.

There was not a single person at the office that didn't greet her as though this was an average afternoon, including Jerry. The fact of the matter was that Jerry had counseled everyone on staff that morning to be gentle with Kirsti if she came in; he had a feeling that she would. The law firm, by need, kept up with what was going on in all the surrounding twin city area. They were abreast of the news; locally and nationally. They had heard, when Kirsti did, that her husband was the lead investigator on—what the mass media was boldly insinuating to be—serial murders.

Kirsti climbed the stairs, making her way to the law library. She didn't look left, and she didn't look right. She had no desire to witness the stares, questioning glances, or shocked expression on people's faces. People greeted her as they passed, but she had nothing to say. If she acknowledged them, it was only by a glance and a nod. She didn't say a word to anyone. Everyone, of course, expected this. Jerry had done his prep work well; the staff let her have her passage in her own way. There were a few who smirked, but not many. Most were sympathetic, but she didn't want that either.

Jerry observed quietly as Kirsti plopped herself down in her chair at her workstation. Her computer was already up and running, but she did nothing more than stare at it. She looked like she wanted to punch a hole through it.

"Before you do what you are thinking of doing, I would consider the repercussions. You might destroy half of my life's work." Jerry got up from his chair and walked toward her but came to a halt when she put her hand out as though to stop him.

"Jerry, please, I just need to be left alone for a minute, if you don't mind. Being here at this moment is a reminder of where I shouldn't be, and I need to have a second to adjust my thinking. I didn't realize it was going to be this difficult."

As Jerry stepped back to his station, he said, "Tough break, kid, but you are here now, for your own reasons, so what do you say we get to work?"

"So, to get started, why don't we do some research on the life of a cop; dedicated and seasoned cop?" He wasn't kidding. "I think that you had better brace yourself for the long haul on this one because Jack is embroiled in one of the most complex cases ever to hit him and everyone else that he is working with also, for that matter. The pressure on Jack is going to be enormous, if it isn't already."

"Fine, Jerry, thanks a lot for your kind, consoling words. That's just what I needed."

Jerry turned to his computer screen and said, without antipathy, "My job is not to console you, Kirsti. If you need consolation, I'd say, you came back to work too soon. You might as well just pack up and head back home again. This is a law office, not a hospital for the mentally disturbed. I need you to be focused and geared to take on the responsibilities of your job and our clients. If you can't, then be on your way."

Kirsti was not completely shocked by Jerry's harsh words; she knew he was right, and she said so. "Sorry, Jerry, I'm staying."

Samuel had seen Kirsti enter the building and make her way up the stairs. Life was about to get tougher for his new paralegal and for Jerry as well.

Both Jerry and Kirsti stood up as Samuel entered the law library. This was a reflex reaction to his bearing as he entered the room. The expression on his face was grim.

"I need to see both of you in my office immediately."

Samuel turned and strode out of the room as quickly as he had entered, leaving both Jerry and Kirsti staring at each other. They took only a half a moment before following him down the stairs and into his office.

Samuel went immediately to his desk and sat down. Reed was sitting in a soft brown leather chair in the corner of the room. He had a smirk on his face. It was apparent that he and his father were in serious disagreement about something. Jerry touched Kirsti's hand ever so slightly as they entered the room, sensing the strain between father and son; Kirsti unconsciously reached for Jerry's hand but drew it back immediately. The two paralegals took a standing position in front of Samuel's desk until he pointed toward two soft leather chairs identical to the one Reed was sitting in with his legs crossed and a smug look on his face. Samuel told them to take a seat, which they did, without hesitance and gratefully.

Jerry made a deliberate production of getting comfortable. "With all of your wealth, couldn't you afford to buy better chairs for your guests? What's up, boss?" The air in the room was thick to the point of stifling.

Kirsti knew that Jerry was trying his level best to lighten the mood and eliminate the dense atmosphere that was almost smothering them, but his attempt at humor fell flat on its face when Samuel didn't react at all in the way he ordinarily would have. A deep red crept up Jerry's neck and made its way upward to his cheeks and ears, and worse yet, this hot flush of embarrassing color was happening without any comprehensive reason that Jerry could grasp on to at that precise moment. Nothing like this had ever happened to him before, not ever. He had always been careful not to put himself in a position where he might be humiliated.

The look of hostility coming from Sam's eyes made Jerry rise from his chair and move behind it.

"Do you mind if I stand, sir? I seem to have a cramp in my leg." He didn't have a cramp in his leg. He just needed to not sit. He was uncomfortable and when he was uncomfortable he needed to move away from that which was making him uncomfortable.

"I would prefer you sit. I think you're going to be glad to be sitting down by the time this meeting is over with." Sam said sternly.

Jerry sat. He had been hearing rumors he had chosen not to believe. He wasn't prepared for what his inclination suggested he was about to hear. He bore a long hard look at Kirsti, as if to say, "Grab your britches, the devil is about to rise."

Kirsti, innocent Kirsti, never picked up on his silent message. She had no inclinations; she only sensed the pressure in Sam's tastefully decorated office. She turned her attentions towards Jerry and with deed serious concern said, "You're going to have to walk that cramp out of your leg. I don't think you should make him sit down Sam because he needs to move around awhile. I get cramps in my legs all the time, and it's the only thing that works. You probably have low potassium. You should be eating at least one banana a day."

Her request was painfully sincere. In fact, it was so sincere it made Jerry wince.

Samuel ignored Kirsti's plea; his attention was now on Reed, "Do you want to do the honors, or should I?"

There was a strong layer of sarcasm in Samuels' voice; there was also a faint trace of frustration that Kirsti didn't like to hear. She had heard through the gossip mill that Reed was attempting to overpower his father and take over the law firm. These had only been rumors; she hadn't seen any indication of this happening, but then she was the new kid on the block and was still learning office politics. She glanced at Jerry and noticed that he was losing his color. Did he know something that she didn't? What was that pained look on his face all about? Sam should let him stand and walk the cramp out of his leg. Why was he not doing that?

Reed rose from his chair and strolled to the window, observably enjoying the moment. His expensive pin-striped suit was designed to make him look taller than he was. He never did like the solid fact that he stood a mere five feet six inches aboveground level, but one wouldn't guess that by first glance. It was no well-kept secret that Reed wore shoes specially designed to add another inch to his height. His white blond, curly hair was cut to precision, enhancing every single ringlet. His round cherubic face could be deceivingly pleasant, and yet the gray-blue eyes evoked something cold and callous.

As Reed turned and situated himself in front of Kirsti, she felt a chill move up and down her spine. She felt something stir within her, but she didn't know exactly what it was. She somehow knew that there was something in all of this that was meant for her. She wanted nothing more than to get up and walk out of the room, but something froze her and told her to stay. She glanced at Samuel; he was standing now and making his way toward the door. He seemed to be moving in slow motion. He could not stand to look at Jerry or Kirsti on his way out.

"See you later, Dad." Reed seemed very pleased with himself. The words *full of yourself* came to Jerry's paralegal mind.

Reed strolled nonchalantly around the desk and sat down in his father's chair. "Well now, what do you think of this? Me, just little old me sitting in my old man's chair, in my old man's office.; who would have ever thought this day would come?"

The question he was asking, both paralegals knew, was nothing more than pure, unadulterated rhetoric.

"I understand that you are the two best researchers we have on staff, this is exactly why you're sitting in this office right now. I have taken on three new clients this week. These three cases will be your top priority. You will be working with me and for me. I expect to win all three. Got it?" This wasn't a rhetorical question.

Jerry and Kirsti bobbed their heads up and down in keeping with their absolute confusion. They could hear just fine, but what they were hearing was not sinking in.

Reed reached to his left and picked up three files from the top of his father's desk and tossed them antagonistically at Jerry. He smiled, looked directly at Kirsti, and said, "Good luck. Both of you had better keep to the foreground of your mind that I expect to win, no matter what it takes. I don't want any foot dragging or shenanigans. If I see any or hear of any negativism on either of your parts, I will fire you."

Kirsti, I know that you can and will do your job impartially."

Reed stood up from his seated position and escorted them out of the office. He grinned maliciously as he shut the door. He would have his father's business in no time, and then he would have his day with Kirsti. Money and power could buy everything.

Wouldn't it be nice to kill two birds with one stone? Now that would be simply gratifying. Reed was enjoying himself and promptly decided that he needed a bit of reinforcement and sexual gratification.

He reached for the phone and with his left hand forefinger, he pressed a button. Two seconds later there was a rap on the door and in waltzed his secretary. Andrea, his golden haired, blue eyed vixen; she knew a lot more about sex than she did about taking shorthand. When she entered, she said slyly, "And in your father's office no less.

How wicked you are; how scrumptiously void of scruples you are."
She locked the door behind her.

Jerry followed Kirsti back up the stairs to the law library. They
were both feeling a bit off kilter. Jerry opened the files and began
reading them out loud to Kirsti.

Three young girls, sixteen years old, had been brutally raped and
assaulted. Three young men, college freshmen, had been charged.
All three were presently out on bail, pending trial. Included in the
file was a copy of retainers amounting to a million dollars each. The
primary investigator and the arresting officer was Detective John
Ireland. His report was included. There was a final note from Reed.
It read, "Pay attention to the retainers, how much defense can three
million dollars buy?"

"Hang on, Kirsti. This is a real mess, but we'll get something
worked out. Maybe I will have a one on one with Samuel. I have to
believe he isn't backing any part of this. He might listen to me. I'm
shocked, he let it get this far. Something is radically wrong with this
whole scenario, and I intend to get to the bottom of it."

"I wish I could believe that, Jerry, but now I don't think so. Reed
couldn't take on these three cases without Samuel's approval. If you
go to Sam, it is going to be viewed by Reed, as "shenanigans" and
you will get fired."

"Perhaps getting fired would be a good thing."

"Perhaps getting fired wouldn't be a good thing Jerry. This is Jack's
case. He was the arresting officer. I cannot be involved, not if my
marriage means anything to me and it does. Jack has a real issue with
defense attorneys who work the system and put criminals back out in the
streets. He doesn't even want me working as a paralegal for that reason.
He has been on me about changing careers since the day I met him. He
wants me working on the side of the prosecution or get out of the legal
business all together. Can't I use conflict of interest to remove myself?"

Kirsti's mind was in a tail spin; she was starting to ramble a bit.
Her eyes were wide open and startled. Her expression resembled
someone witnessing a train wreck.

"I had to defend my employment here by convincing Jack that
we didn't handle criminal cases, and that this law firm's reputation is
impeccable, and now I get this? Jack is going to flip if he finds I will

be working on these three guys' defense. He might demand that I quit my job, Jerry. What am I going to do?"

"I honestly don't know, Kirsti, how can I advise you on anything? I can't get my mind centered on how Sam let this happen to begin with, let alone what happens next. From what I can see, just from the top of the heap of issues, it looks like you, and I have to make some serious decisions, and I suppose my first question is, 'am I going to work for Reed Crawford'?"

"I think I need to get out of here for awhile Jerry. I can't think in this place. What do you say we just cut out early and go find ourselves a quiet spot where we can talk this over and have a drink?"

"Sounds like a very good idea to me. Where do you want to go?" Jerry was already heading for the door.

"I don't know, where you lead me, I will follow. Just get me out of here!"

Reed was standing by the window and in the process of buttoning his shirt when he spied Samuel's two highly praised paralegals leaving the building. He had succeeded in his goal. He had put his father in an impossible position by accepting the retainers from the families of the three young men. Jerry and Kirsti would either have to quit or work for him; either way, it was a win-win situation. He seriously doubted that Jack Ireland would allow his wife to work for a lawyer, who was defending three guys he had dragged off to jail, and Jerry? He'd quit. There was no way in hell that Jerry would ever spend one second as his paralegal. He was sure of it.

Win, win, win, this has been a great day.

He slapped Andrea on her bare rear end, gave her a tap on the mouth with his forefinger, implying, *keep it zipped,* and strode out of his fathers office leaving the door wide open when he left. Andrea could hear him chuckling as he departed. A second later Sam was standing in the doorway.

Chapter Twenty

(A few weeks later)

The parking lot of the Red Rooster was not nearly adequate enough for the amount of people who flocked there to eat on any given Friday or Saturday night. The place boasted of the finest broasted chicken in the Midwest. Kirsti had suggested this restaurant because she loved broasted chicken. Jack, being an American boy, liked a good steak any time. Judging from the crowded parking lot, the people who owned this establishment were living up to their reputation. Jack was not having any success at finding a place to park and was getting a bit irritated. After he had circled the lot three times, he stopped the car and said, "Any of you three have a second choice? I'm about to get out of the car and dole out a few parking citations."

Jack was trying to hold his composure to a steady level, but not doing very well. This was his wife's night out. He wanted it to be a special evening for her but there are limits. It was raining when they left home. In December, this made for dangerous traveling conditions. The rain could easily turn to ice, followed by snow and then there could be a possibility of all three of these things happening at the same time; windshields crust up with frozen rain and then, hello ditch. Jack was thinking a nice quiet dinner at home would have been nice, but this was Kirsti's first and only choice.

Vic took a pen and note pad out of his pocket, wrote something down, tore the piece of paper off the note pad and handed it to Jack.

"What's this?"

"Why, it's the number for a towing service. Do you want to borrow my cell phone?"

Jack wrinkled up the piece of paper and threw it at Vic. "Very funny."

For lack of any other alternative, Jack wheeled the car under the protective canopy by the front door and stopped.

"Why don't you girls get out here while Vic and I park the car? I guess we're going to have to park down the street a ways. Hopefully, we'll be able to join you before the joint closes."

Vic didn't miss a beat on this one. He looked at Jack and said, "Whoa, there fine fellow and chauffeur, I am going to accompany these two lovely ladies into the restaurant while *you* park the car. These girls can't go into the restaurant without an escort. Why, that would be downright indecent. What would people think?"

Vic opened up his car door, stepped out, and motioned to the women in the backseat to follow suit. He grabbed the umbrella, opened it, assisted the ladies out of the car, tipped his hat to Jack, and waltzed the girls into the restaurant. As Jack looked into his rearview mirror, he saw his best friend kissing his wife on the cheek, on purpose. Vic gave Jack a salute adding insult to injury. *While he was playing the role of valet, Vic seemed to think he was Sir Galahad.* By the time he parked his car three blocks from the restaurant, the rain was falling in a torrential downpour.

The three were amused by Jack's appearance when he finally came rushing into the Red Rooster. His hair was saturated and had started to twist into tight little curls. He shook the water from his head, removed his raincoat, and handed it to the girl at the coat counter, paying little attention if any to her. He had put rubbers over his shoes; this thought came to him as he got out of the car and stepped into a puddle of water. The rubber overshoes were on the floor of the backseat, luckily, so was his raincoat. Not a cop in their right mind went anywhere without raincoat, galoshes, and an umbrella. Jack could barely see beyond the water dripping down his face from his hair and long black lashes. Kirsti tried to help him wipe the water off of his face, but he brushed her helping hands aside.

"Stop fussing over me; I can do it myself."

Kirsti's sweet, poignant laughter only served to irritate him further. "All of this effort had better be worth it." Jack was scowling deeply as he addressed his wife. "How long are we going to have to stand around and wait before we get seated?"

"Not long at all," said a vaguely familiar voice. "I am ready to seat you now, just follow me."

This has to be some sort of hallucination, to much water in the ears or something, Jack thought almost out loud but not quite, he was having difficulty time, trusting his own eyes.

Tracy was looking better than ever, if that was possible. She had a deceptively innocent, angelic look about her that all men found enormously appealing, if not totally irresistible. Since the day that Jack had first met Tracy at the Orchard Lake Country Club, she had not let up in her pursuits of him. While Jack had set his sights on Kirsti, Tracy had her sights set on him. She had located his phone number; how she managed this, she never said. She had found out where he lived; he never could get her to disclose how she managed this either. She called him often; she came to see him often. She would just drop in uninvited. She seemed to know when he would be home and when he wouldn't be. This aspect alone would be unnerving to anyone. She was a relentless temptress; Jack had finally given in to her seductions, and while he was pursuing Kirsti, he was sleeping with Tracy.

Now here she was, her shimmering blond hair flowing sensually around her shoulders and down her back. She tossed her head indicating the direction they would be heading. Tracy had matured into something that was nothing less than stunning to behold. Her dark green emerald eyes were flashing as they looked directly ahead of her. Her make up was applied to accentuate every part of a near-perfect face. Her lithe, slender body was magnificently sculpted from hours in the fitness center and a very expensive trainer. She had a rich bronze tan that came from a very expensive tanning booth. Tracy looked expensive; everything about her, from head to toe, spoke of money, lots of money. However, even without all the pampering and expense, Tracy would have been considered a, '*stop dead in your tracks and take a good look*', beauty.

Tracy's attention went straight to Jack as she seated the two couples. She knew Jack was coming. She had seen his name on the list of reservations. She had requested that she be allowed to not only be his hostess but his waitress. The owner/manager had complied because he and Tracy had an affiliation that went beyond employer-employee relationship and one that his wife would not approve of if she knew, but she didn't know, not yet. His wife took no interest in his business and never had.

"Hi, Jack, it's good to see you again. I've missed you."

She grabbed his left hand with her long fingered, professionally manicured hand, "Oh, I see that you have a wedding band on. You got married, no wonder I haven't heard from you lately." Tracy looked at Kirsti and winked, "Just kidding."

Kirsti was busy explaining to Tory how they knew the waitress and was unaware of the barb. She was absolutely oblivious to the malevolent look in Tracy's eyes as she spoke to Kirsti. Had she been looking at Tracy, she would have not seen it because Kirsti held no animosity towards Tracy and had this misguided notion that if she didn't dislike someone than they had no dislike for her. She had always been relatively unaware of Tracy even when she worked with her. To Kirsti, Tracy was a non-entity. One could easily argue that this would have been all it would take for Tracy to pursue Jack with the dogged and acute intensity that she did, to the point of hiring a private investigator to find out where he lived, his schedule and every other minor and major detail she needed to succeed in her conquest. Victory would not be hers. She was going to marry the detective. This would be her triumph over Kirsti. When she heard that Jack was going to marry her arch-rival, she went into a spiral of anger and deep rage that had not yet met its peak.

Tracy was fluid motion as she handed each of them a menu, and then she disappeared into the subtle light of the restaurant towards the bar. Jack's discerning eyes followed her as she moved away and out of sight. This could get tricky; Kirsti had no idea how involved her husband had been with Tracy, but then, there were a lot of things about Jack that Kirsti didn't know. Things could get sticky real fast.

The food had surpassed their expectations. The foursome spent the remainder of the evening, enjoying the music and the band. They danced and drank the night away. It was Jack's turn to be designated driver; he remained sober. Jack was a bit relieved that Tracy had only served to make him uncomfortable by her presence and no one else. As far as Jack knew, Vic wasn't aware of his past relationship with Tracy. They had never talked about it. This was Jack's private affair. Tracy was the epitome of graciousness, which was more discomforting than had she been the other way. Jack felt like he was waiting for a bomb to go off. He became nervous, edgy and short with Tracy. She would only smile. While Jack was waiting for the bomb to drop, the rest partied on. Tracy would give him a knowing grin now and then and did nothing to assuage his expectations, in fact, quite the opposite. She was sending him all sorts of subtle signals. She knew she had him hanging out to dry, and she was taking satisfaction in every second of it. She had the cool cop sweating, literally.

None of these contrived antics, verbal and non verbal, slipped by Jack's partner. Vic was aware of the devious glances Tracy had cast in Jack's direction. He heard the insinuations and the innuendo's, every one of them and while the girls were in the powder room, he asked Jack, in a casual way, if there was something going on between him and Tracy that he should know about. Jack had replied in an equally casual way, "There is nothing going on between Tracy and me. Why do you ask?"

"I'm a cop. I get paid to notice things that don't quite fit."

"You also have a very vivid imagination. I repeat, there is nothing going on between Tracy and me."

"All right, if you say so, Ireland." Vic didn't sound like he was convinced, but he said nothing more. The subject was closed.

Jack wasn't pleased that he had to lie to his friend, but he didn't want Vic to get the wrong idea either; and besides, he didn't have anything going on with Tracy, it wasn't a total lie. Had he been honest with Vic about his relationship with Tracy, he might have also told him the rest of the story. He might have told him that when he broke it off with Tracy, she had become vicious to the point of violent. She had threatened to get even with him, if it took her the rest of her life. She had stalked him for weeks and made countless threatening phone calls.

Now he was asking himself why he hadn't told Kirsti. There was no very good reason not to with the exception that Kirsti would have insisted he break off the relationship immediately, and she would have been emotionally injured by his lack of faithfulness. He was a man who needed sex in his life all the time and Tracy gave him all the sex he desired. She was as sexual as he was. Kirsti had held him back from all sex until they were married. Her dream in life was to come to her husband as a virgin. He had tried to persuade her to change her mind, but she had denied him saying, "*Love had everything to do with respect and if he respected her he would honor her desire to be clean for him when he married her.* She had gone on to say, "*I am a one man woman and I hope that you will take into your heart what this means. I expect that you will think of us as couple and if there are others you will remove them from your life and make me your one and only. I cannot and will not share you with another".*

Jack had agreed to the first part of, no sex with her, until they were married, but he couldn't bring himself to do the same. He didn't say no but he didn't say yes either. He allowed Kirsti, by no comment, to think he was agreeing. Tracy was still right there. She was far too available; way to willing and much too lushes to let loose of, at least for the time being.

Kirsti interrupted his musings with an impatient, "Jack, what is the matter with you tonight? You are not yourself!! Come on, get with the party please. I need you to come and dance with me. I have requested our song." As she led Jack to the dance floor the band started the intro to *"Can I Have This Dance for the Rest of My Life"* or something like that, made popular by a female singer from Canada. Jack wasn't quite sure about any of the details at this point. He didn't even remember it being their song. His mind was back on his young wife, so young, so innocent and so totally uninformed. He wrapped his arms around her and pulled her close to him. Kirsti rested her face on his shoulder; the top of her head barely reached his chin. She sighed and said, "I love you Jack, why are you so distant from me these days?"

There was someone else at the Red Rooster this same evening. This someone was wandering around the bar and restaurant, back and forth, deliberately making himself indistinct. He had nothing to drink, nor did he have anything to eat. In a smaller crowd, someone might have noticed him; but because this place was packed to the rafters, no one paid him any mind, which was exactly what he wanted. He found a spot where he could keep an eye on Jack and his precious wife, Kirsti. The only fun he had that evening was watching as Jack squirmed under the subtle pressure coming from the long-legged, blond-haired, emerald-eyed beauty that was doing her level best to see that Jack was uncomfortable. She was clever, maybe too clever. Tracy was being paid abundantly, and how irritating it was to learn that she probably would have done this for the pure pleasure of it and maybe even for nothing. If there was such a thing as the devil incarnate, he had found her.

Tracy had her instructions. When he held up his hand with four fingers showing, Tracy went to the bar and ordered a round of drinks for Jack's table.

"We didn't order another round," Jack said as Tracy was setting the drinks on the table. Now he was getting irritated. He wanted to leave. He wanted to get out of this place and away from Tracy. He had done his time and given Kirsti the evening she wanted, now it was time to leave. He was becoming intolerant, exceedingly intolerant. He was becoming impatient with his own impatience and knew it.

"I know you didn't, some guy ordered these for you. I'm just doing what I am told to do."

"Who was *this* guy?"

"I don't know, I didn't ask him his name. Last time I saw him, he was standing over there next to the bar.

Tracy pointed toward the back of the room. Jack turned completely around to get a better look at whom she was pointing at but garnered no satisfaction. There were lots of people standing "over there", but not the man she was looking for.

"He was over there a minute ago, now he's gone."

"Was he alone?" Jack asked with annoyance.

Tracy was now in a differential mode. "How would I know if he was alone or with someone? The guy asked me to deliver a round to your table, he paid me and so, here I am."

"Tell him thanks. Oh, by the way, what did 'he' look like?"

"What's with all the questions, Jack?" Tracy asked with unreserved indifference. "He was standing in the shadows. I didn't get a good look at him and besides, I had no special reason to remember him. He told me to bring a round of drinks to this table. I gave the order to the bartender, the guy gave me cash, told me to keep the change, and I delivered the drinks, this happens all the time.

"Now, if you're finished with the inquisition, I have other customers that need my attention." Tracy turned on her heels and with her beautiful, slender hips sensually swaying back and forth, she moved slowly out of sight. Jack felt a tug in his gut as he watched her disappear into the crowd. He hated himself for still wanting her.

The man was standing about five feet from the table; he heard the conversation in its entirety. He was pleased with Tracy's performance.

He waited for Jack to take a sip of his drink, but Jack didn't, instead he pushed all the drinks towards the center of the table.

"I think I've had enough of this joint. I don't think we need another drink. Let's get out of here."

Jack wasn't asking, he was telling. Vic sensed something very mysterious going on, but it could wait until tomorrow. He agreed with Jack on the shoving the drinks aside.

Never take anything for free, unless you know exactly where it is coming from, 'rules and regulations, class 101'.

At exactly 1:15 AM, the man made a phone call. "I will be home very late tonight. I will be bringing home a package.

I will be waiting. My task for the evening is completed," said the voice on the other end.

"Were there any problems?"

"Not anything that I couldn't handle."

"Good, is the basement ready?"

Yes, the basement is ready, why?

"Never mind why, just get yourself to bed. We'll talk in the morning. Go to bed and get some sleep."

"I want to wait up for you."

"No, no, no, you go to bed, I don't know how late I will be."

"You will wake me in the morning and show me the surprise right away, won't you?"

"Sure, now go to bed. Do what I say."

"All right but I would rather wait up. I'm not very tired. Can't I watch TV for a little while? I might go to sleep easier if you let me do that."

"I think I already answered that question! No. I want you to take your pills and go to bed. I'll be home when I get home, and if you value your life you will not wake me up in the morning and you will not go down the basement without me. Do you understand me?"

"I think so. Well, maybe not."

The voice on the end of the line became menacing, "You will do what I tell you to do. You are well aware of the consequences if you defy me. Now go to bed. I will see you in the morning, and if you are a really good boy, I will let you in on a very nice surprise."

"I like surprises. I will go to bed now. Good-by."

Chapter Twenty-One

Temperatures had dropped radically overnight, turning the rain to ice and then to snow. The state and county road crews were ready and by morning most of the ice had been handled with liquid salt, and the snow on all major highways had been pushed aside.

Minnesota residents pay large tax dollars to see to it that they can come and go unhindered by the challenges of their unique weather conditions be it snow, sleet, or ice in the winter or the violent storms in the summer coupled with oppressive heat and humidity. It is a rare day in the state of Minnesota when its populace will be held up by inclement anything. Minnesota winters are legendary, and yet though rarely mentioned as a factor, their summers can be equally as unpleasant. The pendulum sweeps in equal direction on both sides of the seasonal spectrum in the state of Minnesota.

The determination of the immigrants who came into Minnesota at its earliest inception set the standard of what would be required to become a permanent inhabitant of the state, "Rough and tough and hard to bluff." Can't and impossible are two words that are left out of the Minnesota vocabulary almost entirely except for stating with impatience, "Don't think that way! There is no such thing as can't be done. All things can be done. Whether or not it should be done is the question, not whether it can or cannot be done."

Sunday morning found Hilde and Glenda sitting at the kitchen table in Grandma's duplex. Hilde had taken Grandma up on her offer and moved into the duplex after Kirsti married Jack. Grandma didn't want the place empty, and Hilde was willing to move in under the provision that she would pay her Grandma rent. Hilde didn't want anything even closely related to "conditions" placed upon her. "Besides," she voiced to Glenda, "I don't want to take advantage of Grandma." The insinuation was obvious.

Of the three sisters, Hilde was the most brilliant and the most like her father in disposition. She had graduated from Lakeville High School with honors. She was taking evening classes at the University of Minnesota with intentions of getting a CPA degree. She was blessed with a photographic memory, a quick wit, and was a bona fide skeptic. Her sense of humor was often caustic because of this. She was well liked by everyone who knew her and voted "Most Likely to Succeed" by her classmates.

Hilde was born overweight. She was constantly trying one diet or another to shed the extra thirty pounds she carried from her waist on up to her neck. She secretly envied Kirsti and Glenda, who always managed to maintain their weight without any apparent effort. She longed for the day when she could shop for clothing and be able to pick anything she wanted off the rack, put it on, and look good in it. Little did she know, very few people could actually do this, including her mother, Kirsti, or Glenda. Hilde wore her medium brown hair short, like Kirsti's. They used the same hairstylist. Her complexion was flawless; like Kirsti, she required very little make up, a touch of eye shadow, eyeliner, and mascara, and she was ready to go. Her eye color was also the same as Kirsti's, true blue.

Glenda had flown in from Oklahoma the evening before to spend time with the family prior to the holidays. She was the exclusive owner of an antique shop, which also sold new and used books and offered snacks and coffee for its customers. Glenda had a manager she could depend on when she wasn't there, but she was a hands-on person; and though she would like to be with her family on Christmas Eve and Christmas Day, her business came first and so did her husband. Coming early was better than nothing. Hilde had picked her up from the airport and insisted that she stay with her for the week. Glenda was more than happy to comply.

The sound of the snowplow going through town woke Glenda from a sound sleep; she was the first to get up. While she was making coffee she glanced out the kitchen window at the freshly fallen snow. There were several inches of pure white piled in soft display on everything permanently situated. The sun was shining brightly, creating a crystal-like wonderland. She liked living in Oklahoma, but she missed the change of seasons in Minnesota and her family. She amused herself with the thought that many from Minnesota went south for the winter, and she wanted to come north. Ah well, there is no such thing as a perfect spot. The freshly fallen snow, the ice, the slippery roads reminded her of Christmas past and how the planning of the events surrounding Christmas had always been important to each member of the family. The same traditions repeated year after year after year. The continuity and the predictability of these special moments in life offered a consoling rhythm to the rest of life's unpredictable nature. Since she had moved to Oklahoma, she had felt a subtle shift, a change in the basic core of her existence and the purpose of it. She laughed at herself, and as she poured herself a cup of coffee, she heard her sister come down the stairs. She grabbed another cup and filled it.

The conversations between Hilde and Glenda were as a general rule, always animated and lively. They had developed a deep understanding over the years. No matter what the discussion might be about, inadvertently, one or the other always seemed to take the opposing side. Their debates could get very heated and rarely, if ever, did they come close to an agreement; that wasn't the purpose of the debates. They were engaging each other for every reason other than that. Reasoning was the reason; nothing more or less, was intended to come out of these sparing matches. Hilde who housed a complicated mind loved bouncing things off Glenda, who thrived on simplistic thinking.

Hilde, as always, started the debate. It was an election year. "What do you think about those Republicans trying to take our president to the mat over a few extramarital dalliances? How disgusting and totally hypocritical they are. No one will tell me that the accusers aren't guilty of the same, and if they might not be, so what? The private life of a politician should remain private, don't you agree? Just because he has an affair doesn't mean that he lacks capability to do his job as president."

Taunting words before the first cup of coffee was poured? Glenda studied her sister and let out a long, deliberate and exaggerated groan. She knew that Hilde was toying with her, she wanted to get something started, otherwise, she wouldn't have used the word, they.

"Do we have to start our day with an argument?" Glenda responded. "I'd like to enjoy a cup of coffee before we get into a political debate. Can't I at least get a big hug and a 'Good Morning', or even a 'hello', first? What woke you up on the crabby side of the bed this morning anyway?"

Hilde rubbed her eyes. "Sure I suppose you can have a hug if you think you need one. All of this hugging business is over-rated as far as I'm concerned."

"Man, you really are in a grumpy mood. Maybe I should leave for awhile and come back when you are in a better mood." Glenda was getting snappy.

"I don't want to start an argument," said Hilde. She looked at her sister sharply, "I simply want your point of view."

Glenda scrutinized her younger sister warily "I don't think you want my point of view on this," said Glenda, looking down into her coffee cup and back up to Hilde, "I think you want a debate, and I am only going to give it to you because I doubt you will leave me alone until we have hashed this over. Your question was conclusive in how you think. So what do you want me to say, pray tell?"

"I think all of this mass media hype regarding our president's transgressions is misplaced, misrepresented, and contrived as a means, by the Republicans, to get him out of office." Hilde was not going to be sidestepped. Whether Hilde actually believed what she was saying was another part of the deal. Hilde often times took the exact opposite stance to clarify what she believed to be true. This was her way of untangling things.

Glenda's blue-green eyes settled on her sister, and she chose her words carefully, slowly and very solicitously. She didn't mind debates if they were going to lead somewhere, but she hated arguing for the sake of arguing, something her younger sister thrived on. She had to be careful to avoid becoming entrenched in one of Hilde's mind games. This whole operation could start with a political debate and wind up in an argument over the price of tea in china if she wasn't careful.

"I couldn't agree more with you on the idea that this is a political ploy on the behalf of the Republican Party. The whole concept behind these elections has always been based on partisan differences, and you can bet your boots if the shoe were on the other foot, the Democrats would be having a field day. What did he actually think was going to happen, Hilde? Do you think he publicly denounced his relationship with other women because he was trying to fool his wife? Heck no, he was trying to fool the public and why would that be?"

Hilde got up and poured herself another cup of coffee, "Well, what if society is wrong, and they are placing emphasis on the wrong thing and the anti-adultery conception within our society is completely out of sync with mankind or human nature? What then? There are extramarital activities going on all the time, and there have been since the conception of man. Perhaps having more than one relationship going on at the same time is more human than we like to think."

"Perhaps you are right. Perhaps we are all too hard on each other and expect way too much, but I don't think so." Glenda got up from her chair, moved to the counter, and looked out the kitchen window.

"Hilde, I don't care if the president had twenty affairs in his life. That is his prerogative, what I didn't like was when he was caught with his pants down, so to speak, he pointed his finger at the American public and said, "I didn't have sex with that woman". He was overtly condescending in his tone. Like 'How dare, we question his integrity?' But he did have an affair with that woman, and he had done much more with other women. Does this really matter? I think it does because he holds the highest office in the land. He is our leader and if he can't live a life with some sense of regard to the standards he proclaims are necessary for you and I, well, then, why would I want to go out and vote for him? Let alone campaign for him."

"I was disappointed because I could see that he might have just sold himself short. For sure he sold the American people short and worse yet, he was following in the footsteps of another fallen president, Mr. Richard Nixon. When you are caught red handed with your hand in the cookie jar, what is the point of denial? A good explanation would be better than insulting the intelligence of those people who were there to support you in the first place. People, as a general rule, prefer honesty, even when it isn't necessarily convenient. Truth isn't always easy but it does seem to work out better in the long run. I hold no contempt for him. I only say that he is a politician playing political games, and sometimes I would like to see somebody in office who could thrust himself above all the bull shit."

Hilde thought for a moment. Her brow was planted in a deep furrow, her eyes were glistening, "Really, Glenda, did you expect him to get up on public television and admit to the world that he had had an affair? How silly that thought would be."

"Actually, no I didn't expect him to do that. I expected him to do exactly what he did. He played his cards and then got caught in a bold faced lie on public television with millions of viewers watching him, including all the news pundits. That is what I didn't like. I simply believe that there is a certain part of everyone's private life that should remain just that, but to keep a 'something' private, one has to act more responsibly than he did."

"This country is hell-bent to slaughter the people that they elect, and therefore, one has to be careful about how they manage themselves and especially if they vie for public office, from ground floor up. It isn't that people don't understand how these things can happen, they do and always have, but duplicity has never been treated well in our society. You cannot preach family values and expect people like me to sit around and see the very person doing the preaching get caught with his 'you know what' in the mouth of anyone other than his loving wife and especially in the Oval Office of all places. If it didn't appear so pathetic, it would be downright comical. Not to mention that the last thing this country needs right now is a president who comes off as loose and out of control in his private life as our current president has. Trying to blatantly dupe the American people is not a wise course of action and especially in the long run. He left himself wide open for attack, and that is what makes him unsuitable for another term as president. If he isn't any smarter than that, then I don't want him representing me anywhere at any time, and I don't care how good-looking he is or how charming he is. I need a president I can *trust* to make the crucial decisions that need to be made concerning this country."

Hilde looked at her sister directly and said, "How moral of you. How quickly you climb up on your high horse."

Glenda examined her sister earnestly before she continued, "Don't you dare make this a personal issue, Hilde. If you want to talk about me, let's do it. This conversation has nothing to do with me aside from the fact that you decided to push a political debate in front of me this morning. You wanted my opinion and I have given it to you. Maybe morals don't have any business in politics, but I am hard pressed to believe it."

At that moment, the front door burst open, and Kirsti came through, interrupting their somewhat heated debate; both sisters were surprised to see her. She looked like death warmed over. She had no makeup on; this was unheard of. Kirsti never left the house without being fully made-up. Her eyes looked tired, blood red and swollen from crying. Her short hair, usually in perfect order, was standing up in every direction when she pulled off her hat. Kirsti ripped off her bright orange jacket, wrapped it in a bundle, and threw it angrily across the room. Glenda had to duck to avoid the onslaught of a flying object coming directly her way.

"Whoa, Kirsti, what the heck is going on? Take it easy! What in the world is going on? If you are having a bad morning, join the group."

"Get out of my way Glenda and I mean it!"

Glenda backed off immediately; her sister was in a total state of rage.

Glenda and Hilde stepped aside as their oldest sister stormed into the living room, both of Kirsti's sisters were rendered speechless, as she plopped herself down on the couch. She was sitting Indian style, one leg crossed over the other, seemingly unmindful of her surroundings. Her eyes were glazed and startlingly imperceptive. Glenda and Hilda moved cautiously toward her. Glenda sat down next to Kirsti on one side, Hilde on the other. They sat there for a long time, waiting for Kirsti to speak. Kirsti stared straight ahead, her blue eyes were now calm, thoughtful, and soaked with tears.

Glenda, taking what she thought was her rightful position, spoke first. Her question was easy and direct, "What's wrong, Kirsti?"

Kirsti answered without hesitation. "I have married the wrong man. I never want to see him again in my life. If he calls, tell him that I am unavailable. Oh Glenda, I love him so very much. What have I done, what have I done?"

After this puzzling question, Kirsti had nothing more to say, instead she looked at her sisters with tear-filled eyes and climbed the stairs to find repose in the bed most familiar to her. Glenda and Hilda followed closely behind her. Kirsti seemed unaware of them as she entered the bedroom and closed the door. The sisters knew that Kirsti needed this time to herself. They would just have to wait.

"Seems our sister has a problem of some sort or another" Hilde couldn't help but say something blithe. This was her way. "And might I add, it would seem the biggest part of the problem might involve her husband? I would like to know, who, if anyone, is going to find this surprising?"

Glenda, who was following Hilde down the stairs, tousled her sister's hair lightly as they reached the bottom of the stairwell and said with an offhanded tone of authority, "You'd have to be sound asleep not to see this one coming."

"So than," said Hilde, "where did we leave off in our conversation before we were so rudely interrupted."

Chapter Twenty-Two

Traditions are one of the very few things in life that get passed on down from one generation to the next with few, if any, alterations. There is a reason for this. Traditions are always based on those things worthy of preservation. Traditions nurture the mind and the soul in a world that can be dismal, lonely, and unpredictable. Traditions do to the human spirit what a worn-out, frayed, and tattered wool blanket does for the body on a cold winter's night.

Sunday, in the history of the Poval family, as tradition would have it, was a day of recompense. Sunday was the day for reflection, a day of gratitude, a day of rest, a day for sharing. This was, after all, God's day. More times than not the city relatives, and there were plenty of them, would journey to the Poval farm to spend the afternoon, almost always without prior notification. The city and country cousins would explore the 360-acre farm or, if weather was foul, utilize the outdoor buildings, especially the hay barn. The adults would gather around the kitchen table and discuss what adults thrash out at kitchen tables. The coffee pot boiled all day long. The women would help prepare the evening meal.

When there were no guests to entertain, a very uncommon occurrence, the day was spent quietly. The children were in their rooms, reading books that they brought home from the school library, playing board games, or catching up on homework. The operative word was *quiet*; the children could do whatever they wanted to do so long as there was no noise involved. Kirsti, Glenda, and Hilde shared a large bedroom; and generally they would come home from church, change into casual clothes, and spend the day in their room. They would help each other with their homework. They would read to each other and share information about the books each was reading. They would share their thoughts and their feelings about their friends, their teachers, and about things that they did not do together.

This particular Sunday was going to be anything but quiet or playful. This day was not going to be a day of rest, not for the Poval girls and not for Eugene and Mary.

Kirsti had slept restlessly for about three hours. She glanced at the clock by her bedside; it was almost noon, time to get up and face the day. When Kirsti reached the bottom of the stairs, she faced two sisters who looked like they had been sitting in the same spot for hours, waiting for her to make her descent from above. She knew she was in for a grilling session and wasn't quite sure she was ready.

"What are you two staring at? You look like you are about ready to have me for lunch."

Kirsti gave each of them a "you had better back off older sister look" that both sisters recognized instantaneously. She found her way into the kitchen, poured herself a cup of coffee, and said for sake of distraction and perchance control, "How long has this coffee been sitting here, it smells like dirty feet."

This comment should have brought a response, but when it didn't, Kirsti knew that they were just playing the waiting game, and she might have to squirm a little bit. You simply did not throw a jacket at your sister without a reaction, and you didn't leave them sitting in the lurch. They would have to have their questions answered, and they had had a few hours to think about the ones they were going to ask. She was quite sure that she would not be able to satisfy them with anything other than the bold-faced truth and there was no way she was going to give it to them. She wasn't ready. She didn't think she would ever be ready. In fact, she was quite convinced that there was nothing that was going to drag the truth out of her. She came down the stairs defiant, her sister's first clue.

Glenda came into the kitchen and sat down at the table, one leg under the other. She placed her hands flat on table, directly in front of her.

"Kirsti, do you remember a day not so long ago when you came to my house; hmm, probably about nine in the morning or so, you came through the door in all your put-together self. You didn't say good morning, you didn't even say hi, you didn't say anything like that. Oh no, nothing near that nice. What you said was, 'What is the matter with you? You look like hell." Do you remember that Kirsti?

"So, because I firmly believe, because you have always said so, that there is a time and a place for everything and one good turn is always deserving of another; I have something I would like to ask you. What in the world is the matter with you? You look like hell!"

Glenda's normally blue-green eyes had turned to a brilliant translucent green, the first signal to everyone who knew her personally that Glenda was angry and no longer in a mood for compromise, complacency, or crap. So rarely did this ever happen that when it did, it was shocking to the eye of the beholder. It was an 'unwritten' rule in the family, never to get Glenda inordinately upset. Glenda did not rile easily but when she was riled, her temper could be darned near fatal. Eugene had once declared that out of all of eight kids, his daughter Glenda was the only one he had that housed the natural, unmodified killer instinct and if pushed too far, she could be deadly.

"You are a mess, and I want to know why, and I am not going to wait until the next decade to find out either."

Hilde stepped forward and grabbed Glenda by the arm, pulling her away from the table and backward a few steps, "Calm down, Glenda, don't let your temper get in the way of your better judgment. This isn't helping Kirsti any. Don't you think you should let her have her first cup of coffee before you have at her?"

Glenda took a deep breath, yanking her arm away from Hilde; she said with a barely controlled voice, "You're probably right. I'm going to take a walk. I need some fresh air."

After Glenda left for her stroll out in the cold, winter air, Kirsti said to Hilde with a moan. "Whew, Glenda is really upset, isn't she?"

Before she responded Hilde went to the refrigerator and grabbed herself a beer, "Well, it is noon somewhere."

She cracked open the beer and handed it to Kirsti, walked back, and got herself one.

"Glenda is very upset with you right now. You just decided to take off and leave your husband without any explanation. You waltz in here and decide that we don't have a right to know what is happening with you. Maybe you have situated within your mind that Glenda wasn't in favor of you marrying Jack in the first place, which is true by the way. However, I don't think that her opinion about your marriage to Jack is going to grant you any special favors with her. No one knows you better than she does and that includes me. In fact, she has become rather fond of Jack."

Kirsti glanced up at the clock and laughed, "I don't want to argue with you or with Glenda, but if you think that Glenda knows me, you are wrong. She doesn't know me at all. She sees me the way she wants to see me. She has never understood me, and I think she is jealous of me. I think she resents who I am and what I am and she resents my relationship with Grandma, Yvonne and my father. I think she has always harbored a deep dislike towards me."

None of what Kirsti said shocked Hilde, she had heard this before and to Hilde the implications were comical, so she replied with unusual complacency, "You have to talk to us, Kirsti, you know that. We would like to know what's going on with you. I don't think I have ever seen you this upset before, about anything. Well, let me take that back. You did get this upset one time when I borrowed one of your books and bent the front cover and dog-eared the pages. If you have negative thoughts towards Glenda and have no faith in her motives or her intentions, then I feel sorry for you, not her. You are clearly walking down the wrong path if you think that Glenda bears you any ill will at all. You had better bear in mind that you have no closer ally than Glenda, and from where I have seen things over the years, you are the one who has been the one to shove her aside in her hour of need, not the other way around."

Kirsti was listening but Hilde had to wonder if she was paying attention. She continued with her litany, mindful of this possibility.

"There is no doubt in my mind or anyone else's whose opinion is worthy of consideration that you have always held the position of front and center. The most important members of our family have made you their heir to represent them properly, and you have done well, even if you haven't realized the consequence of all of this to the remainder of us. Glenda has walked in your shadow since the day she was born. I have never heard her speak one negative word about you or her lot in life. She accepted her place in the family unquestioningly, and now at this very point in time, she still maintains her loyalty to you and will defend you to the very end of her days. You have really been unfair to her. You always have been."

Kirsti had been listening carefully to what Hilde was telling her. She didn't like what she was hearing. Hilde was always pushing her into a fight. It had been that way since the day Hilde was born. Glenda would always back away from a down-and-out battle, that was a given, but Hilde wouldn't. On the other hand, the only person who could manage either of them, when they would get into a hostile debate, which would lead to a huge fight and downright nastiness, was Glenda.

Hilde knew she was pushing hard against Kirsti; she could read her as though Kirsti were herself, and in more ways than not, this was true. When Kirsti finally hung her head and said, "You are right, Hilde, you are wiser than you think you are, and thank you for refreshing my mind."

Hilde smelled defeat and was genuinely elated. Not because she had done a good deed, but because she had won the argument. Winning an argument to Hilde meant she was right, and to be right was reassuring. She rarely lost an argument to anyone other than Glenda or her father. However, she was really over-indulging herself to think she had actually won this one because having the last word has nothing to do with much of anything and especially in this case. Kirsti had merely capitulated because she needed time to think. She was playing her younger sister, to get her to back off. She never worried about Hilde, she was, however, very concerned about Glenda. Glenda didn't argue. She might debate but when it came to a fight she could and sometimes would become very slippery. She would very rarely argue unless she knew she was absolutely right and unlike her sisters, she detested game-playing, verbally or otherwise. Hilde had no control over Kirsti but Glenda did. Glenda had left to cool off. On the one hand, this was good; on the other it was bad. This meant that Glenda would not be easily convinced or placated.

Hilde, not ever one to leave a stone unturned, replied with "You say that now, but you won't say that tomorrow when life gets back to normal again. Then I will return to my predestined position of little sister, and you will be back to bossing me around again, scolding me, directing me, and making me want to replace you with a different older sister."

Kirsti didn't laugh as she was supposed to, so she continued and spoke more seriously, "Besides, I think I know what happened. I think that you and Jack had your first big fight. Right now, you are angry and so is he. Come tomorrow, you will both be over it and back into each other's arms, promising each other your undying love, forever and ever, amen."

"What do you know about love and marriage?" Kirsti asked with a revitalized lightness about her. "You don't even have a boyfriend and only because who in their right mind would put up with you?" Kirsti was laughing now. This was indeed a positive sign.

Kirsti's sister shifted in her chair and as though speaking to an audience of a thousand said dramatically, "I should have countless suitors if we are going to use 'right mind' as a criteria and not sex as the main power behind healthy relationships, for whom in this world is ever in their right mind, I should like to know. Don't you think I deserve to be appreciated for my mind and not my body in an everlasting relationship? How many men do you know that go for the mind first? I suspect I shall never marry." This was not a question; it was a statement and part of Hilde's whole view on life. She was being theatrical but she meant every word she had just said.

"Hilde, you say that with such sincere conviction that I am tempted to take you at your word."

"Who's to say I am not serious?"

Kirsti laughed again; with Hilde, one never knew. She, in all likelihood, was serious.

The ice-cold crisp December air had successfully done what Glenda wanted it to do, cool her off. When she came back into the apartment, she heard her sisters laughing and teasing one another. The three girls had snapped themselves into a different frame of mind entirely. They had managed in their own special association with one another to recompose themselves. Glenda apologized to Kirsti for being so ferocious and unsympathetic. She didn't do this because she actually felt apologetic, but because she knew her sister, and to get her to reveal what was happening in her life, she needed to.

After Glenda had taken off her jacket, hat, mittens and boots and had seated herself, once again at the table, Kirsti began to tell her story. Glenda and Hilde sat and listened with cautious ears.

"I am the one to blame for the fight, you know. I have replayed the scene repeatedly in my mind. I started the fight, and I finished it. I don't want you or anyone to think that Jack is the one at fault because he isn't, not really.

As you know, he took me out to dinner to make up for all the time we have lost since the day we were married because of his job. He knew that the weather was going to be bad, he knew this, but he was willing to risk going anyway, for me. We had a wonderful time. He wined me, he dined me. We danced the night away. He made me feel as though I was living in a dream, but this dream was real. There were moments when I felt the need to pinch myself to fully conceptualize what was happening. There were moments when I could feel everyone's eyes on us as he waltzed me around the room, but I suppose all eyes were on him, not me. He was the best-looking man there. He is so damned good looking." Her eyes filled with tears again. She stopped talking for a moment.

Kirsti shifted in her chair as though this might change the rest of the story, or she had to shift to tell the rest of the story. When she had regained her equanimity, she continued. Glenda was hearing every word her sister spoke and watching as Kirsti's eyes grew dim as she mentally traveled to some faraway place.

"I was pretty light-headed by the time we left the Red Rooster, in fact, very light-headed. I had drunk only four glasses of wine, and one would have thought that with all the dancing we did, I would have sobered up. But, in reality, I'm not so sure whether it was the wine that made me light-headed, the romantic evening, or both. Vic and Tory had met us at our house, and after they dropped us off, they left right away because the roads were getting really treacherous.

"At some point," she continued, "between the front door and the stairs to the bedroom, it hit me that I could not let Jack take me to bed without being completely honest with him. I didn't want anything between us. There was something I hadn't told him that he needed to know."

Kirsti shifted in her chair once again. She was starting to look exceedingly pale. She put her head down on the table to rest for a moment. When she lifted her head back up, her eyes were starting to glaze over, "I didn't want to breach client/lawyer privilege you know."

Glenda was the first to see what was coming. She lunged out of her chair and caught her sister as she slumped to the floor. Glenda was a strong person, but the deadweight of her sister caught her off guard; both went down in a heap, Glenda in a sitting position and Kirsti drooping across her lap. She had passed out cold.

Glenda held her tight and yelled at Hilde to call 911, who being equally aware, was already putting in the call. Glenda kicked the chair Kirsti had fallen from back and away from them, enabling her to place Kirsti into a lying position, flat on the floor. Hilde, with phone in hand, ran to the living room; she grabbed a pillow and a heavy blanket. Glenda placed the pillow under Kirsti's head and wrapped the blanket around her sister, tucking her in tight.

Glenda attended to Kirsti until the ambulance arrived five minutes later. Hilde stayed on the phone with dispatch. The paramedics came through the door with a flourish and took control. They were communicating with the hospital as they did what they were trained and instructed to do. Glenda and Hilde got out of the way and let them do their job. They stood by the door as they watched the paramedic's wheel Kirsti to the ambulance and then there was a pause. One of the paramedics turned around and made a track back toward the house, the girls waited for him, watching him as he hurried their direction.

"Which one of you is Glenda?"

"I am." Glenda pointed to herself. Hilde silently pointed to Glenda.

"She wants to talk to you, but make it quick; her blood pressure is dropping fast."

Glenda ran in what seemed like slow motion toward her sister, her heart was racing, her legs seemed weak and unable to carry her. In her mind, the trip from the door to the ambulance, a distance of a few yards, seemed to take forever. She felt as though she was running through tar.

Kirsti's eyes were open when Glenda finally reached her. She held out her hand reaching for her sister. Glenda took Kirsti's hand in hers and let Kirsti pull her down toward her. Kirsti whispered something, but Glenda couldn't hear her; she leaned down farther and put her ear to her sister's lips. Glenda was alarmed to hear her sister say, "He raped me, Glenda. Jack, he did this, but please don't tell anyone, please don't speak of this to anyone, you have to promise. Oh, Glenda, look at all the beautiful flowers!"

Kirsti passed out again; her lovely, freckled face was ghastly white.

Glenda kissed her sister on the cheek and smiled. "I won't tell a soul if you don't want me to."

Behind her back, she had her fingers crossed. "Not yet anyway." She said to herself, "Not yet." Kirsti was gently loaded into the ambulance and, within seconds, was whisked away. On the way back to the house, Glenda glanced at her watch. She was in rapid action, but it seemed to her that she was crawling. It was two fifteen in the afternoon. Her flight out of Minneapolis to carry her back home was scheduled for nine o'clock the following morning. It was two days before Christmas Eve. She knew that she wouldn't make the flight home. She looked to the west, the sky was a deep unwieldy black mixed with gray; dark clouds were swirling toward her. Glenda gave a quick glance to the east; her long blond hair had come loose from its confinement and was fluttering around her face obscuring her vision. The sun was shining radiantly where she was heading. The contrast was strange. Glenda shivered as she ran toward the car where Hilde was waiting.

"Grab my coat and my purse, Hilde; we have to leave, now!"

Hilde was already in the car in her arms were a hat, coat, mittens and purse, Glenda's. Hilde was always thinking ahead.

Chapter Twenty-Three

The sisters followed the ambulance to the emergency center at Sanford Memorial Hospital. The ambulance rolled along at a constant pace, just a bit faster than the sixty-five-mile-per-hour speed limit allowed. There were no flashing lights or sirens. The two girls, as a means of self-appeasement, took this as a positive sign. By the time Glenda and Hilde arrived, Kirsti had already been taken into the emergency area and had disappeared from sight. An elderly nurse, dressed in white from head to foot, led them to the waiting room at the main entrance of the hospital. She didn't bother to introduce herself, and the girls weren't the least bit curious to know her name. If they had been asked a half a minute later what she looked like, they wouldn't have been able to describe her because she wasn't the point of concentration; and humans, by sheer force of survival, cannot concentrate on more than one thing at a time.

"The doctor will be with her shortly. You can wait here if you like; there is a coffee shop over there." The elderly nurse pointed to the gift shop. "The doctor will see you after he has finished his examination." She did an about face and swiftly walked away.

Glenda stepped toward the large window, facing the parking lot. Eugene and Mary had arrived; Hilde had called Mary on their way to the hospital. Mary had called Eugene. They came in separate vehicles. Glenda also spotted another important person making his way across the parking lot. Jack Ireland had arrived on the scene. *This could be awkward*, she thought to herself. Eugene and Mary didn't know anything about Kirsti and Jack's state of affairs. Glenda felt a twinge of anxiety as Mary and Eugene waited for Jack to catch up with them at the front door. As they entered, Glenda overheard Jack explaining to Eugene and Mary that he had heard about Kirsti on his police radio. He looked exhausted and worried. Glenda reasoned, and not easily, that Jack did have a right to be here even though what she really wanted to do was haul off and punch him and then throw him back out into the street.

Glenda and Hilde, having been taught that manners came first, greeted Jack cordially, and then they proceeded to fill the parents and Jack in on what had happened. They left out the part about Jack's fight with Kirsti. Without this piece of the story, the information was sketchy, at best. Eugene's keen instincts told him that the girls were not disclosing everything, but he knew better than to pressure either of them. He had learned from experience that his girls would not tell anything on one another, no matter what the consequences might be. He would have to wait. At that moment, a tall dark-haired young man came toward them from behind the information desk.

"You must be Jack Ireland?"

"Good guess," Jack said with weary smile.

The tall, trim, well-groomed young man reached out his hand to Jack. "Hi, I'm Bill Schraeder. I need you to come to the front desk and fill out some paper work."

Jack shook Bill's hand and followed him to the information desk.

The girls, Mary, and Eugene went into the coffee shop, found a place at one of the three tables. While they removed their coats, a young candy-stripper took their order, "Just coffee, thank you."

When Jack completed filling out the necessary paperwork, he took a seat in the waiting room. Eugene invited him to join them, but he declined. This puzzled Eugene and Mary, but not Kirsti's sisters. The waiting room was quiet, very quiet; the group kept their conversation light.

Dr. Fielding had been with Sanford Memorial Hospital for no less than thirty-five years. He had practiced under Dr. Sanford and had been Mary Poval's doctor for no less than twenty years. He had delivered all but two of her eight children. During this age of family practice, he had treated all of Mary's children for major and minor ailments from their births to the present time. He knew the Poval family almost as well as he knew his own.

Eugene introduced Jack to Dr. Fielding. "Husband huh? I didn't think Kirsti had graduated from high school yet. Time does fly doesn't it? Why it seems like only yesterday that I delivered her." Kirsti was one of the two out of the eight that Fielding hadn't delivered. Mary refrained from correcting him.

The doctor's eyes, behind his thin-rimmed glasses, were sharp, and so was his tone. He turned his full attention to Mary when he spoke.

"We are going to have to keep her for a few days, maybe three, maybe four. I won't release her until I have the test results back."

Dr. Fielding made a concerted effort to lighten up the mood a bit; he let out a chuckle and said, "We gave her a mild sedative before we took the blood tests. It took three nurses and an orderly to hold her down, but once the sedative took hold, we could get the blood drawn without any of us receiving a brutal beating. I have never seen a girl so completely panic-stricken by the thought of a needle, and I have been in this profession for many years."

He turned toward Glenda, "You are easy by comparison."

The Doctor laughed with self-appreciation at his own assessment and at the expression on Glenda's face. He truly liked the Povals for their open way of being. With these people, there was no second-guessing. They let you know exactly how they felt, and what they thought about everything, in spite of their own reluctance to do so. What he liked about them most of all was their lack of need to hide from the truth. Eugene had voiced to him on more than one occasion, "How am I going to know how to deal with anything if I am not afforded the full picture? I can only properly contend with the most miserable aspects of life if I am granted the faith from others that I do indeed have the ability to handle the unvarnished truth. I cannot know in advance how I will handle difficulties, so it is unfair for any other to assume that I can't, I won't, or don't need to."

"What's wrong with her? What caused her to pass out like that?" asked Mary. She stated this so calmly, one would have thought she was discussing the time of day. Dr. Fielding had this effect on her.

The short bald-headed, bespectacled doctor became musingly solemn, "She is resting comfortably. Kirsti wants to talk to you and only you for now, Mary. I will take you to her room. She has asked that she be the one to talk with her family about her health issues.

This will be the first time in my history with your family, I have been sworn to doctor-patient confidentiality, and that comes as quite a surprise to me."

Peering over his glasses, the doctor turned his attention to Kirsti's husband. He stepped back a couple of steps. He budged his narrow-rimmed glasses to the top of his head. He pushed his hands deep into the pockets of his white jacket. His eyes were razor-sharp; he spoke quietly but firmly, "Jack, she told me to tell you that she doesn't want to see you right now. I am sorry to have to relate this to you, but as her doctor, I have to honor her request."

He then turned to the group and said, "As for the rest of you, I want you to keep your visit brief. She needs to rest, and she needs to remain calm."

Mary handed her coat to Glenda and followed the doctor down the hallway. Eugene and Jack stood shoulder to shoulder with identical expressions on their faces, deep frowns furrowed their brows; their eyes had narrowed to an icy hot that declared their displeasure with Kirsti's decision to leave them out, intentionally. Glenda and Hilde moved to the far side of the room hoping to avoid the interrogation they knew was heading their direction. Wild horses might not be able to drag the truth out of them but Dad and Jack working as a team was another matter entirely. They decided to leave the hospital and go have a cigarette. Maybe out of sight out of mind might work, for now.

Kirsti was resting, almost asleep, when Mary quietly entered the room. The sedative was taking a relaxing hold on her. Dr. Fielding didn't come into the room but went on down the hall to check on another patient who was about to have a baby. He was tired, it had been a long day; maybe he could get in a nap before the baby needed to be delivered. He guessed he had about four hours before she would be ready. He had been delivering babies for so long that he could almost predict the minute a new child would enter this very challenging universe. He had not yet lost the feeling of exhilaration he was granted every single time he heard a newborn baby cry out their first protest to a brand-new existence. There was no experience he had ever had that gave him the same euphoric sensation, aside from maybe his Jaguar.

Kirsti heard someone enter the room. She knew without looking it had to be her mother. She also knew beyond any doubt that her father would come in later, deliberately defying her instructions to her doctor. She was most worried about Jack. She did not want to see him, she wasn't ready to see him and she didn't know when she would be.

"Hi, Mom" she said weakly as she lifted her arms to give her mom a hug.

"Do you want to sleep, or would you like to talk?" Mary inquired as she gave her daughter a hug. She was surprised to see that Kirsti was hooked up to an IV machine. She was being given a blood transfusion. What surprised her even more was that Dr. Fielding hadn't warned her of this. An alarm bell went off in the back of Mary's mind.

"I want to talk and then I think I am going to want to sleep." Kirsti was groggy.

Mary pulled a chair up close to the bed and sat down. "OK, let's talk."

Kirsti stared up at the ceiling, she couldn't make herself look at her Mom; she wasn't sure where to start. Mary sensed her difficulty, "Tell me what Dr. Fielding told you and why you're receiving a blood transfusion. Can we start from there?" Mom was not pleased.

"He isn't positive, but he thinks I have fibrous tumors. He took some blood tests and is going to get the results back in a couple of days, and then I will know for sure what's happening with my body, in the meantime, I guess I have to get some rest. I have been having a lot of difficulty with my periods this past year. It comes randomly, and when it comes, I bleed heavily. This time, I lost enough blood to make me pass out. One way or the other, I am going to have to have surgery, but I won't know the details on any of this until Dr. Fielding gets the test results back.

"Mom, I am sorry I haven't told you about this before now. I thought it might just go away. I didn't want to worry you."

Mary sat down on the edge of the bed and held her daughter's hand. She was wondering why her daughter hadn't shared this information with her before now. She was having a difficult time believing it had anything to do with causing worry on her behalf. No, there had to be more to it.

"Dr. Fielding told me that the first surgery will be to remove the tumors, but eventually they come back, and I will probably have to have a partial hysterectomy."

Kirsti let out a sigh. "I am really tired, Mom. I want to go to sleep. Would you tell my sisters that I would like to see them, but not right now, please? I don't want to see anyone else, and I don't want to talk to anyone else either. I'm tired. I want to go to sleep, and please, please make Jack go away. He's out there, isn't he?" Kirsti twisted her head away from her mother and closed her eyes.

Mary tucked the blankets tighter around Kirsti, hugged her, and gave her a kiss on the top of her head. "I will pass this on to your fan club. You go to sleep now. I love you."

As Mary tiptoed toward the door, she heard Kirsti whisper, "Mom, will you stay with me tonight?"

"I planned on it."

Jack was standing by the front door, talking to Eugene, when Mary returned to the reception area; their conversation seemed to be light-hearted. Eugene had come to like Jack, not Jack as a husband for his daughter but Jack as a man. Glenda and Hilde were at the desk chitchatting with Bill. He had been a friend of theirs for years; he was the first to spot Mary. He nodded to the sisters when he saw her. The group instantly gathered around her; their anticipation was palpable.

Jack was studying Kirsti's mother with the trained eye of a cop as he approached her. She looked troubled through the eyes, strained. He sensed that what she was about to tell him, he wasn't going to like, and he was right.

Mary spoke to her husband first.

"Why don't you go see your daughter? She's supposed to be resting, but you can poke your nose in anyway. Don't disturb her if she's sleeping."

Eugene was already on his way.

"She's in room 113."

Now she must deal with her other daughters who she knew would be chomping at the bit to see Kirsti. Contending with them was going to take a bit of firmness. She decided to be blunt.

"Kirsti has been heavily sedated and is sleeping. She told me to tell you that she would see you tomorrow."

Both girls started to protest, but Mary cut them off quickly, "We won't know anything until the test results come back, and there is no sense in speculating. I will only say that she is having female problems. She has lost a lot of blood and is getting a transfusion to replace what she has lost. She'll be in the hospital for a couple of days. The results will be back, hopefully, by the end of the day tomorrow, and then Dr. Fielding will fill us in on the rest of the details. Right now, she needs to rest. Dr. Fielding doesn't want her upset or disturbed in any way."

Glenda felt a bit weak in the knees and sat down on the couch. Hilde stood face-to-face with her Mom. "I won't excite her, and I won't disturb her, Mom. Just let me go down and sit with her awhile."

"Absolutely not, you can, tomorrow. As for right now, I suggest both of you go home and get some rest your-selves. She is in good hands. Do what she wants, that is the best thing you can do for her. This is what your sister asked me to relate to you, and she did say, please."

As Mary was arguing with the girls, she caught sight of Jack out of the corner of her eye; he was rapidly moving down the hallway toward Kirsti's room. She caught up to him about halfway to his point of destination. Mary was a very small woman, but when she grabbed Jack by the arm, the force behind it was that of a person three times her size. She spun him around and hissed, "Oh no, you don't! You and I are going to go back to the waiting area and have a little talk. I saved you intentionally for last."

Jack knew better than to argue with Mary. He instinctively knew he was in no position for a face off with either Mary or Eugene. He followed Mary back to the waiting room. He had no idea what she knew or didn't know; none of the Poval clan had given him any indication, not even a hint of what Kirsti had told them. *Play it cool, Jack, play it cool. You have too much riding on the line. Don't argue and don't resist.*

He was a cop, and cops don't jump to conclusions, Rules and Regulations 101.

Mary steered him toward the large-paned glass doors. Before Jack could say otherwise, she had him out in the parking lot. He had it figured correctly by the time they reached the parking lot that this was going to be a one-sided conversation.

"You have to leave Jack. Kirsti does not want to see you. She made it a point to tell me that she doesn't want to see you. Now I don't know what's going on between the two of you, and for now, I don't want to know. I don't care to know. What I do know is that I want you to leave this hospital and not return until you get a clearance from my daughter."

Jack pulled his body up to his full height, as he did this; he not so gently disengaged himself from Mary's strong hold on his forearm. His brown eyes sparked with anger as he gazed steadily into hers. They held eye contact for a long time. He didn't say anything, nor did she. Then he offered Mary a crooked, shy little grin and said, "OK, whatever you say, Mary, but I think you have got this all wrong."

Jack put on his coat and gloves. Mary went back into the hospital. She was shivering from the cold and from nerves. Mother and two daughters watched as Jack strolled casually toward his car, started the engine, and drove off. As he sped away from the hospital and turned toward the west, Glenda noticed he had his cell phone to his ear.

Mary looked at her daughters and said, "That was too easy."

Glenda and Hilde said nothing.

"I am going to spend the night here at the hospital. I need to be sure that Kirsti rests without interruption."

Glenda and Hilde nodded absently in unison. Mary looked at both of them. *What are these girls up to? What do they know that I don't know? What are they not talking about?*

Kirsti wasn't sleeping, she was thinking. She was lying on her side pretending to be asleep. Her father was sitting next to her bed; she wondered what he would have to say about what she was thinking. She knew that he would tell her to be honest, to tell the truth, to tell Jack the whole truth; but she wasn't going to do that. She knew that she wasn't going to do this because she knew that it would make the difference in whether or not Jack stayed with her.

What she wasn't going to tell anyone was what Dr. Fielding had told her about her tumors. Yes, they could remove the tumors, regardless of how many there were; her doctor thought she had at least three of them. Surgery was no cure because fibrous tumors always grow back and generally very rapidly. Her window of opportunity to get pregnant would be about three to six months. What she had never told anyone in her family, her father and mother in particular, was that she never wanted to have children, not ever. She hated the whole idea of parenthood, childbearing and child rearing. She wanted no part of it, and she never would.

Kirsti didn't want to share Jack's attention with anyone or anything. She wanted her career, and she wanted Jack, in equal measure; kids played no part in her plans, not now not ever. She had made up her mind to this a long time ago.

Jack had not raped her, why had she said that to her sister? They had fought over her job and Reed taking on the rape case. She had known Jack wasn't going to like it one bit that the law firm would be taking on this case, let alone her being the paralegal and working on it herself. She had anticipated that they would fight but not to the extent that they had. They had fought ferociously, and in the end, it was she that had verbally attacked him when he had told her he wanted her to quit her job, the sooner the better and think about having a family. She had told him that she would never quit her job for him or anyone else; she liked her job, and this case was just part of the package, just like his job was part of the package; furthermore, she wasn't going to have any part of getting pregnant and having babies, not for him or anyone else. She told him she hated kids and always had. She would never be a mom, let alone a stay-at-home mom, not now and not ever, not in this lifetime or the next.

Jack had been shocked by her harsh words; he had wanted to leave to catch his breath, and regain his composure, but she wouldn't let him, and that's when things had gotten ugly. She had insisted he make love to her because this was the only way, in her mind, he could prove to her that he loved her unconditionally, and when he couldn't she had demeaned him and physically attacked him. She had pounded on him, beat him, and berated him. When he could take no more of her physical and verbal abuse, he had walked out of the house and left her alone. She had waited up all night for him to return, but he didn't come home. And at last, in the early morning hours, she got into her car and went to her sister's apartment at the duplex. There she found Glenda and Hilde together. She had forgotten that Glenda was coming into town; this shed a different light on things. She could get around Hilde, but she had never been able to get around Glenda. She had to find a way to make Jack the bad guy, and rape was the first thing that came to mind. It was wrong, but not something that couldn't be dealt with later. Right now, she was elated at how things were working out for her.

She knew she was having female problems, but never had she counted on her body being so cooperative toward her long-range goals. Dr. Fielding could never speak of this to anyone because of doctor-patient privacy. And now she would, indeed with the help from her body, never have to worry about having children again. She would stay on the pill until she had to have that last surgery with no one but her, any the wiser. Jack would have to accept this, and her sisters would too. Now she could sleep, and she did. Her mind was made up. God was working with her. She felt no guilt nor did she feel any remorse.

After Kirsti had fallen asleep Eugene left the room: Kirsti hadn't fooled him any. He knew she wasn't sleeping. Kirsti had been playing this trick, since she was a tiny child. So then, what was it that she was so hell-bent not to talk to him about? He would find out eventually. It might not be today, and it might not be tomorrow but eventually the truth would be revealed to him. The truth always came to light; a person only needed to wait and push all the right buttons.

Glenda and Hilde made their way back to Lakeville in uncharacteristic silence. Their mother had told them that there was no need to speculate, but that didn't stop them from thinking about the recent events they had witnessed, concerning their oldest sibling. There were too many questions with too few answers. They, each of them separately, held a piece of the puzzle but were, at this point, unwilling to break confidentiality. Neither would share and thus neither would know the total truth which would have granted them the proper understanding necessary to appease their own minds; but then it could have been that these two girls, from what little they had experienced in life, inadvertently knew that truth does not always offer a safe mental harbor. Glenda did not believe that Jack had raped Kirsti, and yet she did not want to believe that Kirsti would intentionally lie to her.

Upon arriving at the apartment, Hilde went upstairs to change clothes; she said she needed a shower. Glenda pulled out her cell phone and called Nick.

"I guess I won't be home for Christmas, Nick."

"You sound like you could use an early visit from Santa, I can be there by morning, just give me the go-ahead."

"Right now, dearest husband of mine, I don't know what it is that I need, Santa might be a bit too much for me to handle. At this moment, what I want and need is a glass of wine, a long hot shower and some sleep."

"It's that bad, huh?"

"Hmmm, I guess it is that bad."

"Family problems are the only things that put you in this frame of mind. What's going on?"

"Kirsti's in the hospital. It isn't critical, so don't get yourself all charged up. She's going to be OK, or so Mom says. I couldn't go in and see her because Mom said she needed to get lots of rest, doctors orders. No excitement allowed."

"I'm coming up. I'll see you tomorrow morning. Don't worry about picking me up from the airport. You do what you have to do, I'll find you. I don't want you going through this alone, Glenda, and especially over the holidays."

Glenda hung up the phone and looked out the window. The winds were picking up, and the snow was starting to swirl in large swooping circles. She grabbed the remote and turned on the weather channel. The predictions were not encouraging. She called Nick back and told him to hold tight; she didn't need another anxiety in her life right now. There were ten to twelve inches of snow blowing in from the northwest, and she didn't need her husband in the middle of this mess. Nick agreed to stall. He was a pilot after all. He paid keen attention to weather patterns nationwide.

Glenda was glad she had her Christmas shopping finished. She placed a call to her trust-worthy assistant and told her she wouldn't be back until after Christmas. Her assistant said, "We will miss you, but life is going well on this end. Good luck and don't worry, everything is under control."

Ah, if only that were true. Glenda needed some music. She set a record on the turn table, a record from the "by gone" days. Perry Como was soon singing, "Don't Let the Stars Get in Your Eyes"; and as he sang, she walked up the stairs, heading directly for bed. She didn't bother to change into her pajamas; she didn't take a shower. She fell asleep as Rosemary Clooney crooned "Beautiful Brown Eyes." Her last thoughts as she fell asleep were of Scarlett in Gone with the Wind, something about starting all over again tomorrow. Yes, tomorrow is another day.

Hilde had showered, changed her clothes, and went out into the night. She left a note for her sister, "I'll be back sometime tomorrow, went to see a friend."

Chapter Twenty-Four

Willie had gotten up early in the morning, much earlier than usual. He was so excited he had hardly slept all night. The Christmas season was upon them, and he was keyed up. He took his time in the shower, languishing at the delights of the day to come, and what he had been planning. He loved to plan things, he had always loved to plan and then see his plans materialize, one step at a time. He and his brother were going to decorate the Christmas tree. He loved Christmas. Life buzzed loudly around the holidays, and he liked being a part of it all.

He dried himself off with a towel and slipped into his robe. He liked to refer to it as his "round two" robe. As he was thinking about what he was going to wear for the day, he put his face up close to the mirror. He did this automatically and without thought. There were some days when he would think he knew the person gazing back at him, but for the most part, he didn't know this person. He always considered the reflection in the mirror a person estranged from himself. A life form he had never come to know or understand. The image was someone of little interest to himself or anyone else, for that matter. There stood a man who was not very handsome at all, in fact, quite unattractive. He had large bulging, angry eyes; thin, sparse brown hair; and a pocked complexion. The mouth was thin and mean. The teeth in this person's mouth were not straight and well formed but crooked and tinged with a dark gray color and pushed away from the gums in a sort of hideous fashion.

The shape of the face was drawn, narrow, and hollow with a shallow, weak jaw line; the complexion, sallow and pasty. This was not his face, this was the face of his father that he saw, certainly not his own. He would shake his head, mentally will the image to go away and in a flash his other face would come into the foreground. This face was handsome, strikingly handsome. He had thick, dark brown wavy hair. His eyes were clear, bright, kind, and gentle and deep golden brown. His complexion was naturally tanned, his lips full, his teeth a bright white and immaculately straight. This was Willie's image of himself. Could it be possible that he and Jack were twin brothers? How could he look so much like Jack and not be his brother?

Willie exited the bathroom wearing his "round two" robe and slippers; his brother was sitting at the table, slopping down lumpy oatmeal using an oversized spoon. His razor sharp vision honed in on the disorder that Shorty was creating, and it sickened him. The wobbly table was cluttered with leftover residue of milk and sugar that had missed the bowl. The countertop was littered with an assortment of cereal boxes; the stove was covered with the remainder of the oatmeal that hadn't made it into the copper-bottomed kettle, but Shorty was smiling. He was grinning from ear to ear with milk soaked oatmeal dripping down the sides of his mouth and off his chin.

"This is really good stuff, Willie, you want some? I put in some more sugar and cinnamon, and it tastes really good. I wish I had an apple. I love apples in my oatmeal, don't you Willie?"

Willie grabbed a neatly folded washcloth out of the drawer, pouring hot water from the tap onto the washcloth until it was soaking wet and dripping. He held his brother by the back of the head and began roughly wiping his face. His younger brother fought him a bit but not much. "Stop fighting me!" Willie snapped "You're a sloppy mess."

"This is going to be a good day, huh?" Shorty gasped as his brother tugged his head back farther and gave him another swipe with the warm, wet washcloth.

"This will be a better day if you're thinking about cleaning up your mess. You know how I hate this sort of disregard for cleanliness. You are the biggest slob in all of God's creation; you know it and you don't care. You don't even try."

Shorty chuckled and said, "Sometimes you sound just like Ma. She used to say that, didn't she?"

"Your Ma used to say a lot of things; most of what she said wasn't worth listening to." Willie gave him a slap in the back of the head with the washcloth for emphasis. One of the ends came around and flicked him in the eye.

"Ouch, that hurt!!" Shorty started to pout, "This is Christmas time, why are you pick in' on Ma? You know she doesn't like you picking on her. All of your life, you've been blaming Ma for everything, and I don't think that's fair. She was a good ma. She was pretty. I wonder what happened to her. What happened to her, Willie?"

Willie knew better than to get Shorty started on his Ma kick. He distracted his brother by changing the subject; sometimes it worked, sometimes it didn't. Shorty's obsession with his mother disgusted Willie to no end. This was an area where Willie and his brother shared nothing in common.

"You are going to think this day better than you expected, dear brother of mine, but first I want you to get this kitchen cleaned up, chop-chop. When you're done, we're going to set up the tree and decorate it, and then I have a real surprise for you, so let's get with it. Get a move on brother:"

As Shorty was doing his chores in the kitchen, Willie went outside to gather up the Christmas tree that he had brought home the day before. He was proud of himself because he had actually paid for the long-needled Norway pine. This was a first. He had taken one step further and bought Christmas decorations: lights, bulbs, garland and a couple of packages of silver tinsel. The decorations were new in the box. Willie knew that Shorty would be elated, and he was. To Shorty, this would mean that they had reached a new level in life. They could afford to buy something rather than steal. Shorty was a misguided moralist, but Willie loved him anyway.

After they had decorated the tree, the two brothers sat down for a while and marveled out loud at their creation. Now the time had come to get down to the business at hand. Shorty was sitting contentedly in a beanbag chair, appreciating the lights flickering on the tree. They were celebrating with a mixture of eggnog and very expensive brandy, also bought and paid for. "We didn't do a half bad job, did we Willie?"

Willie gazed at his brother fixedly, "Did you get the job done last night?"

"I already told you that I got the job done last night. The lights on the tree are beautiful. They remind me of Ma. She was beautiful.

She shined like those lights, didn't she, Willie? I wish she was here to see this, Willie. She would have loved it, her two boys setting up the tree, decorating it themselves, going out and buying presents and not stealing them. She would have been happy to see this, wouldn't she, Willie?"

Willie didn't need or want Shorty's small mind fixated on Ma.

"I need to know the details, Shorty, come on; talk to me. Give me all the details."

Sometimes, Shorty wasn't good at talking. He was good at doing but not talking, especially when he didn't feel like talking and at this moment. Shorty wasn't much interested in talking about anything other than what he wanted to talk about. Shorty kept his attentions focused on the tree. He wasn't done absorbing the one and only good thing they had ever done in their entire lives.

Willie jumped up from the couch. He grabbed Shorty by the neck, his thumb and forefinger clutched Shorty under the jaw, pressing into his windpipe, making it almost impossible for his brother to breathe.

"I want to know exactly what happened last night, and I need to know now. You are avoiding the subject, and I want to know why."

After Willie had made his point, he released his fingers from around Shorty's neck, shoving him violently back into his beanbag. Shorty winced with pain.

"You hurt me. I hate it when you hurt me. Why are you always trying to hurt me? I have done what you told me to do. The pictures are on the camera. You can see for yourself." Shorty was rubbing his neck as he pointed to a digital camera lying on the kitchen counter.

"I got it done, Willie, the pictures are on the camera. You can look when you want to, but for now let me enjoy the tree."

"Were there any problems?"

"Just one." Shorty tossed this out with unsettling pacification.

Willie whirled around, he was livid. "Just one? What do you mean by just one? I know what I mean when I say just one!"

Shorty sat back deep into his chair, placed his hands behind his head, and stared into the lights, "Yep, just one."

Willie stood up and began to pace, "What would that 'just one' be, Shorty?" Willie landed hard weight on the just one.

Shorty shifted his eyes from the tree to his brother. His expression had turned from complacent, almost innocent, to rigid. "There was a possible witness."

Willie was stunned beyond belief, "What do you mean there was a possible witness? You had better explain this to me in detail, and I mean every stinking, rotten major and minor detail."

Shorty sat back in his chair, rubbed his neck, and purposefully grimaced. He was amassing a lot of enjoyment tormenting his brother. One good turn always deserves another, and payback was hell.

"You need to look at the pictures. There is no witness. There was, but there ain't no more. I took care of everything just fine."

Shorty accusingly, rubbed his sore neck again. "Now if you don't mind, I would like to sit here and enjoy the tree."

Willie thrust his body back into his chair; he was appreciating his brother's method of trying to outwit him and make him suffer. "You're sure you covered everything?"

"If you don't think, so go check it out for yourself."

Shorty was done talking now. The blue in his eyes were reflecting the sparkling colors of the Christmas tree. Willie knew that it would do more damage than good to continue pressuring his brother for more information. Shorty had said as much as he was ever going to say on the issue.

"You actually bought this tree and all the lights and garland. This is going to be a special Christmas, huh, Willie."

"Yah, this is going to be a very special Christmas, Shorty, but we are going to have to be on our toes. I think it's time to create some distractions, and I think I know just how we're going to go about it. Let's go down the basement. I have a surprise for you. Call it an early Christmas present."

"Will it fit under the tree Willie? We need to get some more packages under the tree!"

"I don't think so Shorty, I don't think your early Christmas present is going to fit under the tree."

Chapter Twenty-Five

As Jack spun out of the Sanford Memorial Hospital parking lot, he spied towards the western horizon, thick blue/black bellowing clouds heading his direction. The wind was picking up momentum and starting to blow small flakes of snow in a senseless swirl across the road. His intention was to head home before the predicted storm hit hard and made driving difficult, if not impossible. He was well aware that Minnesota storms could move in quickly and with a nasty vengeance. He was bone tired and anxious to get home and get some badly needed sleep. He was stunned by the news of his wife, and the thought that he had been excluded from her side while she was in the hospital distressed him. He was her husband; he should be the one sleeping in the chair next to her bed. He was confused by the actions of his wife and life in general; he needed time to regroup. He wasn't confused about his love for his wife, but he *was* bewildered about Kirsti. He had no idea what had come over her lately. She certainly wasn't acting like the Kirsti he had fallen in love with.

He picked up the phone, called a florist, and ordered a bouquet of white roses to be sent to his wife's hospital room. This was the best that he could do for now. He made a stop in downtown Farmington to finish up his Christmas shopping. The only family that was in proximity to him for the holidays was the Povals. As if there might have been a question about what the plans were going to be, Kirsti had informed him in a definitive language that they would be spending Christmas Eve and Christmas Day at her parents. In other words, there would be no debate allowed. The subject was closed.

Jack knew his two favorite Poval girls loved jewelry, so he bought a pair of pearl earrings for his mother-in-law, a diamond necklace with matching earrings for his wife, and a watch and cigarette lighter for his father-in-law. He thought about his sisters-in-law but decided that to buy them something might be considered a payoff, or was he being a bit over sensitive? Nothing had been said about a gift exchange, and if there was one, Kirsti had probably already handled it. He hadn't had time to assess the gifts already under their elaborately decorated tree. Kirsti never did anything in half measure. He picked up a few stocking stuffers for his wife; a family tradition, she had warned him about ahead of time. He charmed the clerk into wrapping the gifts for him, and then he was done.

The long, curved driveway leading to the house was beginning to plug up with snow as he turned into it. He was glad he had a four-wheel drive. He kicked the jeep down into low gear just for kicks; the snow was coming down so forcefully he could barely see three feet ahead of his front bumper. The automatic garage door opened at his command; he pulled in, parked his jeep next to the Mercedes and entered the house through the side door.

Kirsti's cat met him at the door, not because she liked him (Abby didn't like anyone (very much), but because she wanted to go outside. She was an indoor/outdoor cat, more outdoor than indoor. He ignored her as he took off his outer clothing. She didn't need to be let out, it was too cold and blustery, but she didn't seem to want to believe it. The cat kept rubbing against his leg while he made himself a cup of hot chocolate; she was determined to pester him until she got her way. Jack finally picked her up, gave her a talking to about how disagreeable it was outside. He let her out anyway. She would come back quickly enough. Jack had come to know the cat well in the last few days. As he opened the storm door, a package fell to the floor with a thud, a five-by-seven manila envelope. There was nothing written on either side of the package. Jack picked it up, placed it on the counter, walked into the living room, and turned on the television. He sat down in his lounge chair and fell asleep instantly.

He woke up to the sound of his cell phone ringing. The clock on the wall indicated he had been sleeping for 10 minutes. He thought about the cat; she was still outside. He raced to the door and let in a very angry, snow-covered tabby cat. He glanced at the caller ID screen on his cell phone; the numbers and dashes on the screen belonged to "The Boss Man". He was calling from his home phone. It had to be important, Jack answered immediately.

"You wouldn't be calling me from home, unless there was some urgent business needing my attention."

"I just got a call from the Dakota County Sheriff's office. Mac Durkin has put in a missing person's report on his daughter Tracy. According to Mac, no one has seen her since late Saturday night. I don't think I have to tell you how important a person Mac is or how powerful he is. We have to pull out all the stops on this one or there is going to be hell to pay. From the top all the way down to the bottom of the totem pole, heads will roll if we don't find her."

Jack reacted as though someone had just clobbered him with a bat. He dropped his cup of hot chocolate, the cup shattered as it landed on the floor, spewing hot brown liquid from one end of the kitchen to the other.

"Shit, shit, shit!" Jack yelled; the cat let out a screech and scampered out of sight while Jack was busy trying to brush the chocolate milk off the front of his pant legs and socks; he ignored the brown fluid seeping all over his kitchen floor. Stepping carefully he made his way into the living room. The Christmas tree was flashing its multicolored lights, which unwittingly seemed to add to his aggravation and confusion. "You've got to be shitting me, Tracy Durkin is missing? Are you sure?"

"Yes, I'm drop-dead sure. If Mac is sure, then I am more than sure. He doesn't know the meaning of the word panic. I have already given the go ahead on an APB, but with this weather, I doubt that anything can happen until this storm passes. All roads have been closed throughout the entire state, no one is going anywhere. The snow plows have been pulled off the roads and won't go back out until the wind dies down. I want you in the office as soon as travel permits. I'm on my way over to Durkin's house now. I've also contacted the FBI. They should be at Mac's; by the time I get there. I don't care if you have to come by horseback. I want you in the office first thing in the morning."

"FBI? Then you think Tracy might have been kidnapped?"

"Yes, I think she might have been kidnapped but bear in mind, the operative word here Ireland, is 'might'. Mac's not taking any chances, nor am I. I want you and Vic in Hastings the second you can get there." Click.

Jack turned his attention to the mess he had left in the kitchen and his saturated shirt and pants. He changed into a pair of jeans and sweatshirt, put on fresh socks, and went into the kitchen to clean up the broken glass and hot chocolate, which was everywhere: all over the floor, splashed on the cabinet doors, and dripping off the counter top. Jack was reminded of the envelope as he wiped off the counter. After he had finished cleaning, he opened up the package. Inside the larger envelope, was a small plastic envelope containing a 1GB memory card most commonly used in digital cameras.

"Now what?" he thought out loud. Abby came out of hiding and meowed as she sauntered casually to her empty food dish. He poured some dry cat food into her dish and gave her fresh water, "There now. That ought to do you for a while. Now go away and leave me alone. I need to think."

The computer was set up in one of the spare bedrooms on the first floor located right off the living room. He had enlarged the doorway to fit oak double doors. His office was his favorite room in the house. On the walls was a collection of original wildlife paintings that he had purchased at auction sales. He had designed and constructed the oak shelves that covered one entire wall from floor to ceiling. Jack liked to read and had saved every book he had read since first grade. His impressive gun collection was encased in a large glass cabinet that he had designed and built in his spare time. Along the same wall was a large safe that contained important papers and family keepsakes, including a full genealogy chart on both sides of his family given to him by his sister. All of his most cherished possessions were housed in this room. The computer sat on a scarred-up old oak desk that he had hauled out of a junk pile. Jack had methodically stripped the desk down to raw wood and refinished it.

He punched the 'on' button on his year-old, already-out-of-date computer. While he waited for the computer to run its start-up procedures, he removed the memory card from the plastic bag it was housed in by dumping it on the desk; he prodded inside the manila envelope with a lead pencil, looking for a note and found none. Using a tweezers and the eraser end of the pencil, Jack pushed the disc into the smart card attached to his computer and let Windows XP do its thing. After the computer downloaded the pictures, a drop-down menu appeared. He clicked slide show and waited patiently while the photo software did what it needed to do.

The house was too quiet; he missed Kirsti. He selected a CD from his collection done by the Bee Gees, popped it into his CD player, and turned his concentration back to the seventeen-inch flat screen, which was now displaying the pictures from the card, one at a time.

The computer had told him there was a total of ninety-eight pictures. Ninety-six of these pictures were of Jack and Tracy doing the things that they did together, each of them was dated. The pictures were astonishing to observe, in more ways than one. Jack sat there with his eyes glued to the monitor; he couldn't accept as true what he was seeing.

Someone had been following them, stalking them. This aspect alone was disconcerting to the detective and downright vexing. That a person could get this close to him without him knowing it gave him chill bumps all over his body. He was trembling as he fixed himself a double scotch, straight up. Jack felt as though he had been stripped of all of his clothing and was standing in town square bare-naked and shamefully exposed.

Whoever had taken these pictures had a gift for photography. The pictures were vivid, some were close-up of them kissing; others were from a distance, showing them dancing provocatively. One whole set was taken of them at the beach, their suntanned bodies entwined in the water or on the beach, playing, kissing, laughing and covering each other with sand.

Jack sat in his chair, completely mesmerized by the bold display in front of him. Each picture was a work of art and beauty. Jack so dark and Tracy so blond, they made a striking contrast to one another. Jack got so caught up in the splendor of Tracy and himself, and what they were together that the second to last picture caused an electrical current of shock to pass through his body, literally making his hair stand on end. The picture was of him and Kirsti. They were looking deeply into each other's eyes. The picture was so close and tight that Jack could see the pore of their skin. It too was dated. The last picture, number ninety-eight, was a note consisting of letters cut from magazines and pasted one letter at a time, in multiple-color. The note read, "*Hi Jackie, I hope you enjoyed the show.*"

Jack carefully removed the disc from the computer before he shut it down; he glanced at the clock, it was 1:00 am, one day before Christmas Eve. He sat back in his chair and stared at the ceiling;

outside, the wind was roaring violently, rattling the windows and siding of his house. He rose from his chair and looked out the window but saw only darkness. Sitting in the office doorway, patiently waiting was Abby. He looked at her, and she looked at him. He walked over to her, leaned down, and scooped her up into his arms.

"I think I am in trouble, Abby." She purred as he scratched the back of her neck. He set the cat down when she started to struggle; he picked up his cell phone, punched in a number, and waited. It was now one fifteen in the morning.

"Hi, Vic, this is Jack. I hate to wake you, buddy, but I think I need you. Get over here as soon as you can."

"I think you might want to take a look outside. There seems to be this thing they call a blizzard going on. Do you think this could wait until the storm blows over?"

The call from Brice earlier and now these pictures had Jack's mind in a tempest that matched in equal ferocity what was going on outside. The Christmas tree lights gave one last flicker and died. Lakeville and Farmington had lost electrical power.

"Yah, Vic, that's what I meant, but get here as quickly as you can. I have something serious going on here. I gotta go, I just lost electrical power."

Jack cut off his conversation with Vic, grabbed his flashlight, went down the basement, and kicked on his battery-operated generator. He would have heat and light, but many wouldn't. There wasn't much left for him to do but grab the cat and go to bed. If he couldn't have Kirsti, at least he could have her cat. He had never liked cats very much thus this ridicules thought amused him. Abby snuggled up next to him and started purring loud enough to wake the dead. He ran his hand over the cat's back, smiled, and said softly, "Now here is an animal that knows something about stalking. Maybe I need to take a few lessons from you, Abby. I do believe the person who has been stalking me might just be the one who has all those purple buttons. Then he thought, *button, button, who's got the button? Those damn purple buttons and just how many of them does the ass-hole have anyway? Where in the Sam-hell is Tracy?*

Abbykitty was now tired of Jack. She let out an angry growl, pulled away from him, and jumped out of bed. She was, after all, a creature of the night.

Chapter Twenty-Six

Shorty had a strong sense that something had changed; something different was going on, something out of the ordinary. He wasn't the brightest brick in the building, even he knew he wasn't as smart as his brother, but he did have a lot of intuitiveness to make up for some of the difference. Willie was acting a bit weird today. He seemed unusually charged up, and Shorty had himself convinced it had something to do with last night and the basement. Willie gave his brother a set of black coveralls and a black stocking hat that covered his head completely and was long enough to tuck into the neck of the coveralls. Willie had also given him two plastic bags to put over his feet and had instructed him to tighten them securely with rubber bands. Then he handed him a new set of thick white plastic gloves and had been quite specific about making sure that everything was tucked in so that no skin showed anywhere.

"Tuck, tuck, tuck, tuck. Tuck rhymes with struck, which rhymes with luck." Shorty loved rhythm and rhyme.

Shorty was singing as he did what his brother instructed him to do. Shorty was always singing. When he was ready Shorty hollered at his brother, "Come on, Willie, what's taking you so long? I'm getting hot. This seems like an awful lot of stuff to wear just to go down the basement. I don't understand why I have to wear all of this stuff."

When Willie came out of his bedroom, he was also covered from head to toe with dark clothing, no skin exposed. The only thing different in the garb was that Willie had a special mask over his face that distorted his voice when he spoke.

"I guess we're ready now, do you have the camera?"

Willie sounded like Darth Vader.

"Now before we go down into the basement, you have to listen to me carefully, Shorty. Are you listening?"

"Yah, I'm listening, but you sound so strange!" Shorty started laughing. He was soon laughing so hard he could barely stand up. "You sound really funny!"

"This isn't funny. I am doing this for a reason. Listen up, you stupid moron. I have had it with you. This is important. Do you want to go downstairs or not?"

"Yah, I want to go downstairs, but you look hilarious, and you sound worse than you look." Shorty broke out into a new fit of uncontrollable mirth.

Willie hit Shorty along side the head a bit harder than he intended to. Shorty let out a belligerent, "Hey!"

"One more time, Shorty, you give me any more trouble, and I'm going to call the whole thing off and deal with this myself. I have had it with you."

Shorty wasn't laughing now. "You don't need to hit me!"

Shorty sat down on the floor, put his head between his knees, and started to rock back and forth.

"OK, Shorty, I am sorry that I smacked you, but please, you have got to pay attention. You're wearing me out before we ever get started. I don't know why you always have to be so damned difficult."

Willie was pacing as he spoke. Shorty didn't like it when Willie paced. His father used to pace when he got mad and beat up on his ma.

"All right, I'm listen'n." Shorty ran a gloved hand under his nose. His tears did not register with Willie. Shorty was sensitive to violence, especially when it was doled out on him. He stood back up again, grabbed his brother, and gave him a hug. "I will be good. I promise. I won't laugh anymore. I promise, but you still look silly."

Willie broke stridently away from his brother. He was starting to feel a murderous hatred toward Shorty. He inhaled a few deep breaths, soon the mood would pass; it always had before. He took another deep breath and let it slowly hiss out through his clinched front teeth. He counted to ten, twice. It was then that Shorty knew that his brother was creeping up to his edge; Willie wasn't nice when he reached the hissing point, and Shorty had the scars to prove it.

"We are going to go downstairs, and when we get down there, I don't want you to say one word, not one. If you say one word, I am going to kill you. Do you understand me?"

Shorty shook his head up and down.

"Say you understand me. Say it so I can hear it."

"I understand you."

"Good, because, I want you to take pictures, lots of pictures. Do you understand that part?"

"Yes sir. Don't talk and take lots of pictures. I understand." Shorty did a zipper motion over his mouth and lifted the camera for his brother to see.

"There, I think you've got it, let's go."

"I still think you look really weird and sound totally weird."

"Shorty, would you just please put a clamp on it?"

Clamp rhymes with stamp. Stamp rhymes with tramp, all women are tramps. Shorty couldn't shut up his mind. *Willie hates tramps. Willie tromps on tramps.*

Tracy had been awake for a couple of hours. She didn't cry out because she couldn't. Her mouth was taped shut. She had no idea where she was because she couldn't see anything; she was blindfolded. She heard sounds from above. The movements sounded like footsteps, she thought she heard muffled voices. Her sense of smell told her that she was in a very old place. She could smell mildew and mold. Her hands and feet were bound tightly, her hands were tied behind her back, and her feet were crossed at the ankles and tied together. She was lying on something soft, probably a mattress; it smelled new. She wasn't cold, nor was she hot. She could hear a furnace running. Tracy was using every ounce of mental stamina; she had to ward off fright.

Breathe through the nose and let it out. Again, breathe through the nose than let it out. Don't think about the mouth, breathe through the nose.

She hung on to the thought of breathing in and out, over and over again, until she was calm and had complete control of her thoughts. She fought the constraints to no avail.

My father is behind this. I know he is. Who else would want to do this to me? Nobody else would want to do this to me, not one freaking soul in the world would do this to me but my father. My darling dad, that's who. My most precious, self-righteous, never wrong daddy is attempting to scare me to make a point. Mom is going to kill you, Dad! You just wait and see. Mom will have your ever-loving hide for this, you can count on it!

Her father had been after her for a long time to straighten up her act; it would be just like him to pull something like this. She had long ago decided never to put anything past her hard-line father.

"It isn't going to work, Dad! It isn't going to work!" Now she was yelling, but no one could hear her. She had tape over her mouth.

Tracy heard a door open from somewhere above her. She lifted her head when she heard a switch being turned on, and from behind her blindfold, she saw something brighten a bit. This was more power of suggestion than a reality. Her blindfold was tight; there was no luminosity coming through, but Tracy saw light nonetheless; her imagination was running in overdrive, or was it?

"Dad, if that is you, then you had better let me loose. Do you hear me?" She was screaming, but no one could understand what she was saying. Her mouth was taped shut.

Out of the dark silence came a voice, a very strange voice, a voice that sounded like Darth Vader. Her mother had made her watch all the stupid *Star Wars* movies. They might have been good had she not been forced to watch them.

"All the kids love Star Wars," she would say. "Let's see why."

She, to her mother's consternation, had never liked what other kids liked. "Why must you always be so contrary?" her mother would bemoan.

"Maybe it's because I am just like you, Mother."

She wasn't being insolent with this retort; she was merely stating the obvious. Lord knows she had heard this said by others often enough. Her father had said this at least a million times in her short lifetime and always when he thought she was out of line. Why was she thinking about this now when she should be thinking about where she was and why she was bound and gagged? *Focus Tracy, focus!*

"Hello Tracy. How nice it is having you as a guest in our little mansion. I hope you don't find our need for you being here too inconvenient."

Tracy detected a hint of sarcasm in the muffled, resonant voice. *Was that the sound of a camera clicking?* She resituated her body into a sitting position and held her breath.

Dad, is that you? Please, don't do this. You're scaring me. You are scaring me really badly now. You don't need to do this. I promise I won't ever give you any more trouble if you just stop this. I promise, I promise. No one heard her plea. Her mouth was still taped shut.

The deep muffled voice spoke again. "I am going to remove the blindfold and the tape from your mouth now. This is going to hurt a bit. When I do, I don't want you to make a sound. I don't want you to speak, if you do, you're dead. Do you understand me?" *Click, click, click,* and more clicks. She nodded twice.

She gasped as the tape was being yanked away from her sensitive skin; she inhaled and held her breath for a few seconds. She tried to focus but saw little. Her vision was completely blurred; all she could see was shadows of two men standing very near her. She heard more clicks. The dark shadows moved towards her. One grabbed her by the right arm, the other by the left. She winced as one of them cut the ties to her hands. Each held one arm as they clasped on a bracelet of some sort. She heard chains rattling, as they did the same to her ankles. Her vision was starting to clear a little but not enough to allow her to make out who the shadows were.

"You're not my father, are you? Did he hire you to do this to me?"

"No, I am not your father" snarled Darth. "Your father can't save you now. Only you can. And, no, he didn't hire me."

Tracy had finally regained full vision. Standing in front of her were two men. Both were covered from head to toe with black clothing, making their identity impossible; one seemed to be of average height, the other a lot shorter. The taller one did all the talking; the short one had a camera in his hand and was taking pictures. They walked around freely as they gave her time to take in her surroundings and her circumstance, the taller of the two leaned against the wall with his arms crossed over his chest, the shorter continued walking around her clicking away with his stupid camera.

She was in a basement, a very small and very old basement. The cement walls and floors looked freshly painted, and as she had thought, underneath her was a brand new mattress, a very expensive one. To the left was a toilet which seemed to be new and in working order. Tracy studied the cuffs around her wrists and ankles. They were metal bands thinly lined with soft suede to prevent irritation. *How thoughtful.* Attached to the steel bands was a strong set of chains that lead to round steel rings that were cemented into the floor. She noticed that the length of chain gave her mobility the width of the room in all directions. It was somewhat of a relief, if indeed there was any relief to be found in this set of circumstances, that she wouldn't have to yell for help every time she needed to go to the bathroom. She would just have to drag a ton of chain along with her.

To the right was a small square table, and on that table sat her rations for the day, a box of dry cereal, milk, a plastic bowl, and spoon. Underneath the table was a case of water in plastic bottles.

Tracy looked at her captors and said, "Do you mind if I walk around a bit? I'm a little stiff." She was stiff and sore and needed to use the toilet, badly.

The man with the Darth Vader voice said, "Go ahead. Knock yourself out."

She did, and as she expected, she could reach everything conveniently and exactly. These men intended to keep her for a while. It was at this point she realized that her father probably wasn't behind this. Something in her mind clicked. She had been kidnapped. A wave of nausea moved over her; she felt weak. She fought off the nausea by taking in deep breaths through her mouth. Next, with full force, came a wave of panic, overwhelming, stomach wrenching panic. She decided she had better sit down. She felt moisture seeping between her legs. She had lost all bladder control. She didn't want to mess the bed so she sat on the floor.

"What do you want? Why are you holding me here? Is it money?" she asked, her voice barely above a whisper.

"No, this isn't about money, darling, this is all about love. You have nothing to fear but fear." Darth was having a lot of fun watching the girl struggle with the actuality of her situation.

The two men walked up the stairs, turned off the light, and shut the door, leaving Tracy in the dark. Just as she was about to let out a blood-curdling scream, the door opened up again, bringing light back down into the basement. The muted man cautioned, "I wouldn't bother to scream, no one will ever hear you from here, screaming only makes me angry, and my anger will only shorten your life." Ultimate darkness surrounded her again.

Tracy groped for the blankets that had been positioned at the foot of her bed. Folded within the blankets was a small flashlight. Now she was scared. She turned on the flashlight, looked around and saw no way out. These two men had done their homework. She yanked at the chains; they mocked her with their rattling. She was stuck, and she knew it. She groped her way to the toilet and threw up. She concentrated on cleaning herself up.

All about love, what did they mean by that? What do they want from me? How long are they going to keep me in this dungeon?

She left the food on the table untouched. She knew she had to think and think hard. She tugged at the chains one more time and turned off the flashlight; she didn't want to wear out the batteries. In the dead, black silence, Tracy heard the wind blowing from somewhere far away and was reminded of her father. He would save her; she just needed to hold on to her composure until he arrived. She would not let these two little men get the best of her, no way.

Tracy stretched out on the bed staring up at a ceiling she couldn't see. She tried to shut off her bad thoughts by filling her head with songs but a definite thought started creeping in, a very important thought wanted to be heard. Time, time wanted to talk. She had never thought much about time. She had no reason to. Now time was making itself her prime focus. How much time did she have? What time is it? What had they done with her watch? She wanted her watch. How could she keep track of time without her diamond studded watch? *Breath in, breath out.*

Chapter Twenty-Seven

Many of the old-timers who had lived in Minnesota their entire lives reflectively stated that this storm reminded them of the winter of 1963 when there had been a record snowfall of seventy-two inches. This was the year when blizzards lasted a full three days. The storms blew in weekly with temperatures dropping down to 21 below zero. Spring's thaw created massive flooding of the Minnesota and Mississippi rivers; traffic between Burnsville and Bloomington came to a halt for days because the bridge was buried underwater so deep that the barges were passing over the bridge rather than under it, or so the old-timers claimed. After the water subsided, debris could be found dangling high in the top branches of the trees that lined the freeway, and those who had no reason to make the journey from the south side of the river to the north side of the river traveled to see the site. People born and raised in the state of Minnesota are accustomed to a wide variety of severe weather conditions and are not easily intimidated; they know what to do when a storm is heading their way: stock up and sit tight. They will not be caught without lots of food, lots of water, lots of fresh batteries, several flashlights, candles, plenty of warm blankets, and a dependable tractor with a front-end loader or better yet a pickup truck with a blade, and if one has neither, maintaining a friendly relationship with a neighbor that does, helps immensely.

Jack was born and raised in Minnesota. He was not a city boy, he was a country boy; he knew what to do. He wasn't at all taken aback by the amount of snow piled up in his driveway the following morning. Jack took this in proper stride. He was set up for snow removal. He used his snow-blower to clear a path from his garage to his outbuilding, which housed his 620-wide front-end John Deere with a front-end loader. He had inherited the tractor from his father. He climbed aboard, gave the key a turn, and without any hesitation, the 620 gave him the trademark putt that John Deere tractors are noted for. The distinctive rhythm of the engine relaxed him. He drove the tractor out of the building and began the process of systematically pushing the snow into banks. He had done this many times before. When he reached the end of his driveway, he noticed that the main road had been cleared to some extent; it was passable.

He parked the tractor back where it belonged, giving the hood a pat and a thank-you before he climbed down. He cranked up the snow-blower again and walked it up the incline to the garage, moving snow along the way, easily and casually. He cleared away the remainder of the snow, in front of his garage, that couldn't be removed with the bucket, and then he was done. He was mobile again, and oh, how important that is to a Minnesota farm boy. According to his watch, he had been pushing snow for two hours.

Jack heard a phone ringing as he entered the house from the garage. It was the home phone beckoning him, not his cell phone; this meant personal, not work related. By the time he could shed his boots the answering machine had kicked in. Jack reached the phone in three long strides and managed to get in a hello before the end of the message. He hoped whoever it was hadn't already hung up, in fact, he was hoping it was Kirsti, but it wasn't.

"Jack? Is that you?"

"Yeah, it's me."

"You sound a little out of breath. I almost hung up. I hate those damned answering machines. Whoever thought this invention is the answer to anything important needs to be strung up by a piano wire."

Jack couldn't help but laugh; he had heard this before, more than once. His father-in-law refused to be dragged into the twentieth century and not because he wasn't capable of learning all there was to learn and effortlessly but because he simply refused to be dragged anywhere for any reason. Eugene was also very tight-fisted with his money and most likely one of the only creatures left on earth that believed money created more problems than it solved. His concept was, to quote, "The more money you have, the more people there will be, trying to snare it away from you. I know lots of people who are totally preoccupied with one thing only and that's hanging onto their money and as far as I'm concerned that is no way to live."

Eugene never bought anything that was brand-new if he could possibly avoid it, and he always could. Mary wasn't so wild about his way of doing things; and if Eugene did buy something new, it would be for her sake, not his because, after all, she did deserve something new now and then if for no other reason than because she was putting up with him.

He was fond of saying, "People are always getting rid of things simply because they are tired of it and want something brand-new. I like these people, and there are lots of them." He loved using the barter system. The less cash he had to carry around or spread around, the happier he was. No one knew what his financial status was, not even his banker. "My finances are nobody's business." Mary didn't even know what their financial situation was. She knew all about her kids but nothing about their finances.

Jack was visualizing Eugene, sitting at his kitchen table, his steel blue-gray eyes under thick heavy black brows, steadily watching him and talking. A cigarette was undoubtedly hanging out of his mouth, a Chesterfield King, just hanging there, waiting to be lit; and in his right hand, between his thumb and forefinger, a lit match was burning down rapidly as he spoke. The listener now not only fascinated with what Eugene was talking about but also the burning match.

Will he get that cigarette lit before he burns his fingers had crossed the minds of every single person who had ever had a conversation with this complicated man.

Jack learned, as did everyone else, over time, Eugene never burned his fingers. The more intense the conversation and the stronger the point Eugene was intent on making, the more matches it took to get the cigarette lit. He would, of course, eventually light the cigarette and always just before the flame reached his finger tips.

"I was out plowing snow; so what's on your mind? Before you say any more, light that cigarette, I can't stand the suspense."

"I didn't realize you were buying my matches these days, Ireland." Eugene replied with a '*whoof*'.

One match down, how many more was this conversation going to require? Thought Jack with a grin.

"Have you ever thought about investing in a lighter?"

"I have a drawer full of them. I don't find them to be as effective."

Jack new exactly what he meant. He heard another match being lit. Match number two.

This was turning into a game that Jack knew he couldn't win, so he decided to change the subject.

"I have to get into the shower and to the courthouse. My boss is waiting for me as we speak."

"I can't get my driveway unplugged because my tractor won't start, and Kirsti needs to be picked up from the hospital sometime today."

"Does she want me to come and get her?" Jack was fishing.

"What does that matter?" Eugene said impatiently. "Today is the day they are releasing her from the hospital, someone has to be there for her. You live a lot closer than I do, and you are her husband. Who would be better than you to get the job done?"

Jack thought he heard the striking of another match, but then perhaps this was merely a figment of his overtaxed mind.

Jack was working on an answer for his father-in-law when his cell phone rang. Jack picked up his cell phone and looked at the caller, it was Brice. He let the cell phone ring out and went back to Eugene.

"I am going to have to be solid on this one, Eugene. Kirsti has made it very clear to me that she doesn't want to talk to me until she is ready. I have given her the time she wanted, and she has made no attempt to get in contact with me. This would be my first reason not do as you ask. My second reason is because I have a meeting with the head honchos concerning the Durkin case as soon as I can get myself shoveled out of here. I am shoveled out, and when you called, I was heading for the shower, but I doubt I have time for that now. My boss just called and is waiting for me to call him back. Eugene, I see it this way, you have your duty to your daughter; I have my duty to my job. On this particular day, I wish you, and I could reverse roles, but I don't see that happening."

Eugene didn't take much time before he answered, "I'll see to Kirsti. Good luck, Jack." Then the line went dead. Jack stared at the receiver for a few seconds, wondering if he had done the right thing. He had never felt this disoriented before. He glanced at his cell phone, grabbed it, found Brice's cell phone number, highlighted it, hit the call button, and waited for him to answer. Brice answered on the first ring.

"I need you here now. What's the hold up?"

"I just got myself shoveled out to the main road. I'm heading for the shower now. It has taken me all morning to clear a path to the main road. We did have a blizzard, you know, and I don't exactly live a block from the courthouse."

"Can you be here within the hour?" This was not a question.

"Is that an order?" Exasperation was edging in on Jack. Abby was rubbing against his leg, she wanted out.

"Your doorbell is ringing; you had better go answer it." Brice hung up. Jack grabbed the cat and threw her into the hall closet, for the time being. He didn't want her running out the door; he'd never get her back in before he had to leave.

It was of no small wonder that Brice had heard the doorbell ringing. When Jack opened the door, he found Vic standing there with his shoulder pressed against the button. This was one of Vic's favorite tricks.

"Get your damned shoulder off of that bell before I break your neck."

Vic stood upright and held out his right hand to Jack.

"Hi, I am your Avon Lady. I think I have a catalog somewhere."

He started digging through the various pockets of his olive green army-issued jacket. When he came up with nothing, he took off his olive green, fur-lined, ear-flapping cap, held it out to Jack, and said, "I am a soldier of ill repute, and am looking for a hand out," The corners of Vic's mouth lifted, "no pun intended sir."

Jack yanked the hat away from Vic and threw it into the house then he grabbed Vic by the front of his jacket and pulled him into the house with such force that Vic stumbled over the threshold and almost fell.

"You are of ill repute. It only surprises me to hear you admit it. Between the blasted storm, the phone, and the damned cat, I'm about to go crazy. So if you wouldn't mind taking some responsibility for once in your Godforsaken life, answer the phone while I take a shower and get the cat out of the closet, but don't let her talk you into letting her go outside, or you will be chasing her while I head for Hastings."

As Jack was climbing the stairs to shower and change, Vic noticed Jack had lost a lot of his normal bounce. Jack always gathered strength and energy from his job. He had always thrived on the challenges of beating up on the bad guys. He was the very best at disassociating himself from everything that surrounded him as he focused on what he needed to do to bring the criminals he met, day in and day out, to justice. Jack was as tough as nails, and he was thorough. Something was not right with Jack; and Vic, who was no slouch himself at being investigative, knew that it wasn't about the Purple Button Case or about anything concerning his job. Nope, something was going on in his life. There was only one person in Jack's life that could have this effect on him, and her name was Kirsti.

Vic charged out of the driveway with his usual spin-of-the-tires velocity. He loved to give it gas as he rounded the driveway onto the main road, stirring up whatever was beneath the tire. He glanced in his rearview mirror with satisfaction; snow was flying every which way and in every direction.

Jack was staring blankly out the passenger window and said "Did anyone ever tell you that you are an overgrown child?"

"Not lately, but lately' is a relative thing. I can't ever recall you telling me this before; however, as we age, memory is a fleeting thing. What's gotten into you anyway?" Vic was aware of his partner's change of mood. He had known Jack for a long time.

"Plenty has gotten into me. I'm being stalked."

Jack took the plastic bag containing the digital memory card out of his jacket pocket. "This memory card contains enough information on it to topple my entire career as an investigator."

Vic did his level best to disguise his alarm, "All right, maybe you should tell me what's on that memory card before we get to Hastings. You don't have much time."

"Then I will make this brief. There are ninety-some pictures of me and Tracy and one of Kirsti and me. Sorry, buddy, I should have told you about Tracy long before now. Whoever took these pictures was damn near standing on top of me, and I never saw him."

"Well, I haven't seen the pictures yet, but I think I have a pretty good idea what they are all about. I have known about your relationship with Tracy almost from the beginning. I didn't need confirmation from you, Jack. Your life is yours. It isn't any of my business unless you want it to be. Shit, Jack, I wouldn't be worth a tinker's damn as a cop if I hadn't seen that one coming. Tracy had her mind made up the first moment that she laid eyes on you that she was going to have you. It was only a matter of time before you would give in to her relentless approach, and why not? You could do a lot worse than the daughter of a State Supreme Court justice.

"Now the girl has come up missing, you get the pictures delivered to you, and I know you have got to be wondering what this is all about. Honestly, Jack, if it were me going through what you're going through, I wouldn't be very clear headed about anything either, but I am not you. I know you well. We have been partners a long time, and the only thing I can see that might be giving you some trouble is how you are going to handle this with Brice, and you have probably decided, already, not to share the pictures with him. Which, by the way, I am going to argue against if you will allow me. You are dealing with something personal. I know it, and you know it. You might as well fess up and give Brice the pictures. You will save yourself a lot of trouble in the long run if you do."

"Vic, listen to me for a second," Jack leaned his head against the window and sighed deeply before he continued. "I have been mulling this over all night long. Can't you see the bags under my eyes?"

Jack turned toward Vic and pulled down on his upper cheeks with his forefingers. "See? I am getting bags from lack of sleep." A wisp of a smile passed over his face and then he grew serious again. "I don't know what I've decided to do yet. I'd like to keep this from Buchanan for a while. I want some time to work on it myself." He chuckled more for his sake than Vic's. "Who was it that said 'Life gets complicated when you get past sixteen.'?"

"I think it was the Statler Brothers." replied Vic in a monotone voice.

"Odd, isn't it, that I should meet them on the same day. Gives me reason to pause and think about fate. But right from the beginning, it was Kirsti that I wanted, not Tracy. I never expected to fall in love with either of them, and I suppose I thought this was just another one of those things for me, but Kirsti really got to me. She was so doggone different than anyone I have ever had a relationship with before. She was so self-assured and completely aboveboard. She was like a breath of fresh air to me. She was clean in a very dirty world. I don't think I want to talk any more. Let's just be quiet for a while. I need to concentrate on this day and what's ahead of me." Jack was staring out the window again.

"That is fine with me, pal, think away." Vic had heard all he needed to hear. He now knew what was causing this despondency in Jack. Something was going on between Jack and Kirsti. This is what had his partner in a stir, not the 'button' case or the 'Durkin' case.

Jack was silent for a long while. He placed his thumb between his brows and pressed hard as though he were trying to work out a cramped muscle. Vic had seen him do this many times. It was an unconscious mannerism Jack used when he was battling stress.

"You know, Vic, I am going to bring this bastard down. I don't care what it takes to get the job done. This guy isn't even close to finished with his killing spree. He has a lot left to do. Mark my words, he is only getting started. The killer thinks he knows me, Vic. He is going to wish that he had never messed with me. One day I will have him in my clutches, and when I do, I will never let him go. His days as a killer will be over. I am going to nail this son of a bitch or die trying."

"That's the spirit." Vic raced into the parking lot of the Dakota County government building. It was Christmas Eve, and though it was Wednesday, the middle of the week, the Dakota County government was operating with a skeleton crew; for all intents and purposes, one could say that the courthouse had shut down for the holidays. Brice was waiting outside by the front door for his detectives when they arrived. He was smoking a cigarette. All thoughts of Christmas, wives and family, were now set aside. These three men had a job to do.

"I thought you quit smoking years ago" Jack quipped.

"I did."

"It's a dirty, filthy habit, and it ain't good for you."

"Has anyone ever told you to mind your own business?"

"Sure, lots of people tell me that."

"Yeah but listening isn't one of Jack's strong suits in case you haven't noticed" Vic said with an undertone of gravity.

Lulu, who had no family nor any ties to Christianity, had volunteered to handle dispatch over the Christmas holiday. She watched as the three men strolled by her, deep in conversation. Each of them nodded to her as they passed. A mannequin could have been sitting there and received the same nod for as absent it was in awareness. Lulu lifted the receiver from her desk phone and punched in several numbers with the pointed end of her nail file.

"Hi, darling, they are here."

Lulu set the receiver back into its cradle, leaned back in her chair, glanced at her nails, blew on them, and turned her attention to the computer screen. She had pulled up a Web site on horoscopes; she clicked again on the one that would open the door to Scorpio. Her boy was a Scorpio. Lulu was a Libra/Scorpio "cusper". She chuckled as she read. *Passionate was right; they had hit the nail squarely on the head.*

Chapter Twenty-Eight

A lot of different people had taken a lot of time and energy, not to mention personal expense, attempting to make a square brown brick building feel festive. There were reminders of Christmas in every hallway and on every desk. Even the windows had colorful reminders of this celebrated time of year. Today, there were no people chattering, the desks were empty, the hallways vacated, and the phones were deafeningly silent. Perhaps this was part of the reason Brice seemed agitated as he led Jack and Vic toward his office. Both men saw the deep furrows around his brow and mouth that rarely, if ever, revealed themselves on his unusually smooth exterior. He seemed to have aged overnight. He had the television on and set to the local news channel. Brice walked behind his desk, picked up his remote, and began changing channels; he did this for Jack and Vic's benefit. The press was in a feeding frenzy over what they, without proof, had already dubbed the kidnapping of Tracy Durkin. Buchanan scanned the cable channels; the top news of the day was the disappearance of Tracy Durkin, daughter of Mac Durkin, Minnesota State Supreme Court justice. Jack and Vic quit watching the television in a matter of moments; they got the picture. They knew what Brice was telling them without telling them.

Brice knew Mac personally. They lived next door to each other and had, for years, shared many a cocktail, for many reasons and sometimes and mostly for no reason. They golfed together and now and then even took a hunting trip together. Mac was not a State Supreme Court justice to Brice. Mac was a very close and dear friend. Mac was smart, cultivated, and a highly-respected individual. He was well known throughout the legal community as a hard-line judge. He believed in punishing criminals, especially repeat offenders, with the full weight of the law. He also believed adamantly in the jury system and was a tough appellate judge because of this. Mac and Brice came from the same legal mind set. Because of the friendship and the familiarity the men shared with one another Brice knew Tracy up close and personal; he had watched her grow up and was cognizant of what she meant to Mac and his wife. She was their only child.

"Mac isn't messing around" Brice said grimly. "He has called in the state criminal investigators and the FBI, and he is dealing with them on a firsthand basis. Mac intends to walk with them every step of the way. This case belongs to Washington County. However, he wants me equally involved, and this means I need the two of you. I know you have enough on your plate with the Purple Button Case, but I have to consider the ramifications of not getting this one resolved quickly. I am pulling you from the Purple Button and moving you onto this one. Of course, you will work quietly and behind the scenes and be careful not to step on any one's toes. You know how sensitive those FBI boys are."

"Mac will not be easy to handle through this ordeal. He's a raging bull. I will handle Mac. I don't want either of you anywhere near him. We have already had one go-around about the press. I wanted him to wait. He went against my advice and decided to involve the media. He feels the more exposure the better because in his mind, he knows this is a kidnapping, and I think he is right, either that or something worse. If Mac is nothing else, he is a realist.

"If this is Washington County and FBI, what do you want Vic and me to do?"

"I want you to investigate this independently and report back to me directly."

"Dust off our old worn-out sleuth shoes, huh? Then I suppose you should begin by bringing us up to snuff on what you know already.

Jack was seated in his usual chair in front of the desk. Brice was standing by the window, staring down into the parking lot. He turned around, walked away from the window, and sat down in his chair. Vic, who had been standing, closed the door to Brice's office, sat down in his usual chair, and took out a pencil and notepad. In his long ongoing partnership with Jack, he had always been the note taker; Jack always asked the questions.

Brice paused for a while before he spoke, giving himself some time to gather his thoughts. He threw his long legs on top of the desk crossing his feet at the ankles, leaned back in his chair and folded his arms across his chest, closed his eyes and started talking.

"Tracy was last seen at the Red Rooster on Saturday night." Because his eyes were shut and so deep in thought he was—and to their relief—Brice didn't catch the astounded looks that were exchanged between Jack and Vic.

"She was supposed to meet her mother yesterday morning to go Christmas shopping, but she never showed up. According to Mac, this was unlike Tracy. Gloria, Tracy's mother, tried many times to reach Tracy at her apartment and on her cell phone but got no answer on either phone. Pressured by his wife, Mac went to Tracy's apartment to see if she was there; she wasn't. He knocked on the door a few times, and when she didn't answer he used his own key to enter the apartment. He went through every room, calling her name, but she wasn't there. Her bed was unmade, but Tracy never bothered to make her bed. There were dirty dishes in the sink, but that didn't mean anything either. Tracy wasn't the sort to keep up with housecleaning tasks. There was little evidence, leading Mac to believe that anything was amiss, with one exception, her car was gone and there were no tracks in the snow to indicate she had been home and left again."

"Maybe she couldn't get home because of the storm and is holed up in some motel someplace or at a friend's house." Jack interjected.

Buchanan continued, paying no heed to Jacks remark.

"He then called the Red Rooster and was told that Tracy's car was still in the parking lot; the doors were unlocked, and the keys in the ignition. Her purse was on the floor on the passenger side."

Hmm, thought Jack, there is the answer to that question, dummy, and as though he were reading Jack's mind, Vic let loose of a sarcastic cough and a chuckle.

"Mac went to the Red Rooster to verify that it was Tracy's car. He didn't tamper with anything but left everything the way it was and called the Washington County Sheriff's office. Dean Thomas, the chief of police for Washington County, sent out a patrolman to secure the scene and called in his forensic people. Because of the storm and the snow piled around the car, there was no way of telling if it had been moved. The car has been towed to the FBI impound in St. Paul to be combed for evidence, there are no results back yet on what they found or didn't find. Thomas told me he is walking it through the system himself and should have the paper work done by sometime this afternoon."

"Mac notified me first. He wanted to give me a heads-up before the press got wind of it. I called you, and Mac called in the FBI. Those boys work twenty-four hours a day. The State Investigative Agency is also involved, Mac says more is better."

Brice snickered ruefully, "He might be right. I only hope, for Mac's sake, that this works better than it has in the past. As they say, 'Too many cooks can spoil the broth'. I guess that's all I have for you now until I get word from Thomas. What I want you boys to do is revisit the scene and go to her apartment and take a look around. I'll get a hold of Thomas and tell him to give you a pass. He's a good guy; I've known him for years. He won't give you any trouble."

"OK boss. Come on Vic, let's get out of here." Jack stood up and waited for Vic to do the same. He didn't, he just sat there staring at Jack. The two men were now in an eye-ball to eye-ball show down. Vic broke eye contact first; he had made his decision.

"Are you going to tell him or am I?"

Jack held his silence but if looks could kill Vic would be dead. Vic pressed on—ward, he knew he had to for his sake and for Jack's. He was not going to allow Jack to destroy his career because he was having a temporary moment of insanity and wasn't thinking clearly because of his own personal involvement. Buchanan would cream both of them for holding something of this magnitude back.

"Before we leave I think Jack has something he needs to share with you Brice." Vic was watching Jack closely as he said this.

Jack reacted violently. His face had turned a deep red from the neck on up.

"Damn you, Vic, just shut the fuck up! We don't know if this has anything to do with Tracy's disappearance. Damn it, Vic!"

Jack's demeanor was threatening; his fists were clenched as he moved toward Vic. Vic was out of his chair in an instant, preparing to physically defend himself from whatever Jack had in mind. He had expected this.

Jack's mind was in a blur as he went after his best friend, but what he walked into instead was Brice, who had moved quickly from behind his desk and positioned himself squarely between Jack and Vic. He gave Jack a hard shove in the chest, almost knocking him over. Jack stumbled backward; the only thing preventing him from falling on his rear end was the corner of Brice's desk. The sharp edge connected squarely with his tailbone with such a force that it caused Jack to yell out in pain and buckle to his knees with a thud.

"Sit down!" Brice wasn't fooling around. "What in the world has gotten into you, Jack? What the hell is going on? Somebody had better start talking fast, or I will have both of you locked up in county until you're old and gray."

Jack grabbed the edge of the desk and very slowly pulled himself back up on his feet again neither Brice nor Vic offered him a helping hand as he tried to pick himself up off the floor.

"Sorry, commander" Jack groaned, "I would like to follow your order, but I think I am unable to right now, can you give me a minute? I don't think I can breathe let alone sit down."

Jack's face was twisted with pain as he limped around the room, rubbing his tailbone as he walked. The amount of sympathy he was getting from the other person's in the room would have fit in a thimble with room to spare.

"Damn it, that hurt!"

He limped around the room, shaking both legs, trying to stave off the numbness that was taking control of his lower extremities. When he thought he could, he sat down in his chair. The anger he felt a few moments ago was now replaced with insolence.

Jack glared at Brice, still rubbing his backside and said with a lot of conviction, "I hope you didn't just crack my tailbone, it sure feels like it."

Jack's face was ashen, and he had broken out into a cold sweat. Vic was wondering if it was from the pain of his currently injured tail bone or from fear of the thought that he was now involuntarily obligated to bring out the truth about him and Tracy which, at this stage of the game, could very well cost him his position as investigator on this particular case and maybe a whole lot more. He had intended to withhold vital information from his commander. This was a number one romper room, no, no and grounds for immediate termination. Jack was in serious trouble, he knew it and he had no one to blame but himself.

"I knew a guy once who had a cracked tailbone, and he was laid up for a long time. Months and months are the thought that enters my mind. He gathered full pay while he was lying around and watching television. He even got full benefits. He had his meals delivered to him every day, three times a day, at the taxpayers' expense. I don't think I can be of much help to you in the pending investigation if I have a cracked tailbone."

Buchanan knew exactly what Jack was doing. He was doing what Jack always did in moments of stress—fudging.

Brice retorted, "Losing you for a few months would be a blessing, but until you have proven yourself qualified for 'workman's comp,' let's cut the bull and get down to work. Let's hear what you have to say about what Vic was talking about before I really haul off and give you a medical reason for time off. I might even enjoy a lawsuit, could be a really nice distraction."

Vic stepped up behind Jack and placed his hand gingerly on his right shoulder.

"Jack, I apologize for stepping out of line on this one, but I do believe you have got to include Brice in on what you know. He needs to know."

"I want you to think before you act Mr. Buchanan" Vic said gazing steadily at his boss. "I am saying here and now, that if Jack gets fired over what you are about to learn, I will be leaving with him."

Jack was still miffed and still in pain. He shrugged Vic's hand off of his shoulder.

"Give him the card Jack." Vic said softly.

"I guess I don't have much choice now, do I? You should have let me decide, Vic. You just took it upon yourself to decide this all on your own. Thanks a heap, buddy; old pal of mine. So, here it is."

Jack reached into his jacket pocket and extracted the package containing the memory card. He tossed it on Brice's desk, got up and limped towards the door.

"Take the damned thing and do with it what you will, the two of you. Vic hasn't seen the contents yet, might give him a thrill. I need a drink, a strong one. Where's the coffee machine?" *As if he doesn't know*, thought Vic.

Brice carefully reached for the large Ziploc bag containing a five-by-seven-inch manila envelope. He reached into his pocket and put on a pair of rubber gloves before he opened up the envelope. He used the tweezers to remove the small plastic bag from its outer envelope. Brice, with surgical precision, slid the disc into his smart card and waited for the computer to download the contents and then pressed slide show when the drop-down menu appeared.

Jack and Vic left the office to get a cup of coffee while Brice studied the pictures being displayed on his computer monitor. Jack and Vic had to walk by Lulu to get to the coffee machine. She was sitting there, grinning like a schoolgirl as they passed. She was unimaginatively filing her nails. Neither of them paid her any mind. Lulu wondered why Jack was limping. He wasn't limping when he had arrived. He wasn't limping as badly on his return trip. The two men were having a hushed conversation; and this time, as they passed by her, they did pay attention to her. Each of them nodded and Jack said "Hi, Lulu, nice nails, Merry Christmas." Lulu blushed.

When Jack and Vic reentered Brice's office, coffee in hand, Brice was sitting back in his chair, arms folded once again across his chest, staring intently at the computer screen. Jack's spontaneous anger at his friend had subsided upon the realization that Vic was right. He was now more concerned with Brice's reaction to the pictures and what they could or could not mean. After the two men were sitting in the same chairs they had left a few moments before, Brice veered his gaze from the screen to Jack.

"So, Jackie boy, it seems we have a situation going on here."

He was angry. Jack had expected this. What he hadn't expected was the horrible look of disappointment set deep in Brice's eyes.

Brice turned the monitor around so Jack could get a good look at what he had been concentrating on. It was the note, the last picture on the disk.

"When did you get this?" Buchanan's voice was constrained and covertly low.

"Last night. It was stuck in my front door. I had to let the cat out, and it fell out of the door. It was after I got home. I didn't look at it until after you called and told me about Tracy. I had no idea what it was all about so really didn't give it much thought until I was cleaning up my kitchen counter and saw it laying there. I opened it up and there was the card. I put it into my computer and saw what you are looking at right now."

"Why didn't you call me back last night and tell me about this Jack?"

Brice hit slide show again. Jack saw his life with Tracy flashing in front of his eyes, one more time, picture after picture, bringing that part of his life into full resplendent color on the screen for him to remember. That someone could get that close to him made him extremely uncomfortable. Brice watched Jack squirm. He watched every facial expression as Jack sat with his eyes fixated on the monitor. The last picture was the one that grabbed Jack the hardest, the one of Kirsti kissing him. Had Brice not been so disturbed by the implications of this, he might have felt sorry for Jack, but he was far too angry to give him any sort of sympathy at all. He hit the 'off' button on his computer; the monitor went black. He stood up and walked to the window and stared unseeing down into the parking lot. Brice was observably working very hard to regain his equanimity. When he finally turned around, his facial color had returned to normal; he was unbearably quiet.

"I think you have a very good idea why I didn't call you." Jack wasn't being defensive, he was being pragmatic and that is exactly how Brice saw it too. Jack had said what needed to be said to get Brice back in his corner.

There would be some who would say that the next phase would be considered an act of leniency on Buchanan's part, but they would be wrong. Buchanan didn't know how to be lenient about anything. He let Jack off the hook because and only because he understood him, and because he would have done the exact same thing as Jack had done, under the circumstances. He also was very aware of the fact that Vic was probably the best partner Jack would ever find in his entire lifetime and vice versa. He had been in the law enforcement for many years, and he had never seen a team, a duo, so suitable to each other than Jack and Vic and he didn't see any benefit to mankind to do other than let them do their job and specifically together.

Brice had to choose his next words carefully. He would let Jack off the hook but that didn't mean the rest of the world would and Jack needed to be aware of this, if he wasn't already. He also couldn't afford to let Jack know that he was off the hook either. He didn't want it to get around that he was soft and more importantly he didn't want Jack to get any foolish ideas.

"I'm going to give you what you want Jack, or at least, for the time being I am. I should fire your ass but right now I can't afford it.

Your best bet is to get this Durkin thing resolved as fast as is humanly possible. I will have to turn this card over to the FBI and then, well then, things could get sticky. The other reason I can't let you out of my sight is that I believe, now, that the Purple Button Killer is directly connected with the Durkin case and you are going to be the conduit the killer is going to use to lead us to him."

Jack and Vic got up from their chairs to leave. The meeting was over. As they were leaving, Lulu walked into the office and handed Brice an eight-by-ten manila envelope.

"This just came in. I went to the bathroom, and it was on my desk when I got back."

Lulu placed the envelope on Brice's desk, turned, and scampered out of the office. She gave Jack and Vic a nod as she left. She seemed distracted. Lulu was never distracted. She reminded Vic of a cartoon character that he was familiar with, but he couldn't recollect which one. He hadn't watched cartoons for years. Then he had to wonder why he was thinking about Lulu at all, what did she have to do with anything?

As Jack and Vic were making their way out the front door of the courthouse a guard stopped them. "Mr. Buchanan is wanting you back up in his office right now."

Brice was sitting at his desk. He silently pointed to an envelope, a picture, and a note that were spread out across his desk. The picture was of two women, apparently very dead. They were side by side; shoulder to shoulder. They were lying on their backs, facing the sky; they were completely naked. One had long blond hair and blue eyes, the other dark short hair and brown eyes. Pressed into the middle of their foreheads was a large purple button.

Jack's eyes focused on the envelope lying on Brice's desk. The only thing written on the envelope in black maker was, "Attn Brice Buchanan; Urgent."

The letter sent along with the pictures was also stenciled not written in freehand. Without a word, Jack picked up the letter. The paper was standard white printer paper. The writing was done in marker and also stenciled, but this time, not in black but in bold red letters.

He mouthed the passage to himself first in a low whisper, and then he melodiously read the words out loud.

Where the pines grow tall and the rivers bend,
Two lovely ladies have met their end.
Jack, be aware of things to come.
It 'will be bad for you and worse for some.
Your troubles will last for many a day,
And soon you will pray, I would just go away.

"Well, take a look at this, Vic, the jackass thinks he's a poet!" Then Jack started to laugh. He laughed until he had tears in his eyes. He was laughing so hard, he had to sit down. His laughter was contagious. Soon Vic was laughing just as hard as Jack was. He too had to sit down.

Brice didn't laugh; in fact, he failed to see the humor entirely.

"Well, sure enough, this guy isn't much of a poet, but he sure knows how to kill women. This makes four. You boys are in for a long day. You can laugh now but I am betting that a minute henceforth you won't be laughing."

The boss man was right. When Jack and Vic left the courthouse it was as though a cloud of doom had just passed over their heads. They were somber and still.

Lulu was sitting at her desk and getting bored when her cell phone rang. She let it ring three times. She waited and then punched in a number, this time with broad end of her nail file.

"Yes, I delivered the envelope, and no, I have no idea what was talked about. Brice shut his door, and I couldn't hear anything. I even stood outside his office but still couldn't hear anything. I think the three of them are about to leave now. No, I don't know where they're going. How would I know that?"

Lulu shifted the cell phone to her bony chest and watched as the three men passed her station. "They're leaving the office now and none of them are looking too good. They seem kinda sad, actually."

It was Christmas Eve, the phones were quiet; there was no one around but the guards who stood a vigilant watch by the entrances. None of them came in to speak to Lulu. They spoke to each other by two-way radio, but they did not speak to her.

"When am I going to see you again?" Lulu asked seductively.

"Soon, my darling, very soon."

Chapter Twenty-Nine

The house was dark and still when Jack came home from a long grueling day of intensive interrogation. Brice had given the memory card containing the pictures of him and Tracy to the FBI agents immediately upon their arrival at state headquarters in St. Paul. The FBI had their way with him first, and then the commander of the State Criminal Investigative Unit had questioned him for another long two hours. Brice had sat in on the interrogations but remained indifferent throughout. Six hours later, both teams decided that Jack probably wasn't involved in the disappearance of Tracy, but the very insinuation that he might be was degrading and an embarrassment for Jack. Vic, because of his close association with Jack, was also subjected to a long and hard question-and-answer session by both parties and finally cleared of any involvement. The entire ordeal had been demoralizing for both of them.

Jack made his way into the living room, poured himself a scotch and water, and sat down in his recliner. He turned on the television just for some noise. The channel was set on Fox News. He liked Fox news, fair and balanced. The disappearance of Tracy Durkin had hit national television and the pundits were having all sorts of fun speculating. They were turning Tracy's life inside out and upside down looking for scandal, and they were finding lots to talk about. There was no mention of him. He turned off the television, leaned back in his chair, and shut his eyes. He fell asleep instantly with his drink in his hand. When he woke up, it was morning, late morning. He must not have moved much during the night because his half-filled glass was still clutched in his hand. The sun was shining brightly through the wide bay windows. The beautifully decorated Christmas tree reminded him that it was Christmas Day, and from there his mind switched in the direction of his wife and the Povals.

The only packages left under the tree were the ones he had put there, all the rest were gone. Kirsti had apparently been home and then left again. Under the tree, there was a white envelope with his name written on it. Kirsti had left him a note. He went into the kitchen, taking the note with him. He needed a cup of coffee. He was almost afraid to read the note for fear of what it would say, but curiosity got the better of him. While he was waiting for the coffee pot to finish brewing, with trembling hands, he opened the envelope, removed the note, and began reading.

> *Hi my darling husband,*
> *3:30 PM: Christmas Eve*
>   *Glenda and Hilde picked me up from the hospital. I stopped at home to pick up the Christmas packages I needed to bring with me to Mom's. I am going to be spending the night at my parents' house. Dad insisted. If you get home early, give me a call. Tomorrow is Christmas Day. The whole family will be at Mom's, so I hope that you will be able to join us, dinner will be at 1:00, but you can come anytime you want. I am sorry I have been so hard on you. I love you with all of my heart. Please don't be too mad at me. I heard about Tracy, and I am guessing that is what you are working on today. I will be waiting to hear from you. I love you! Merry Christmas! Your dearest and most loving wife!*
>   *Oh, by the way, I have Abby. I didn't want to leave her not knowing when you would be back. Thanks for taking care of her.*

Jack sat down on a bar stool. "*Abby, I forgot all about Abby!*" Kirsti would never forgive him if anything ever happened to Abby Kitty while in his keeping. He should have thought about Abby when he didn't see her when he came home. "Boy, Jack, you have got to get a grip, you are really slipping."

The clock on the coffee pot read 8:30 AM. He raced up the stairs, taking two at a time. He was going to see Kirsti today; things were truly looking up. Jack hit the shower first, shedding the clothes he had slept in; he kicked them into a corner and left them there. He took his time in the shower, allowing the hot steamy water to roll over his head, down his back and legs to relax him. When he stepped out of the shower, he grabbed a large, thick towel, dried himself, and then wrapped the towel around his waist to cover himself while he poured warm lather over his face and shaved. He hummed a tune that vaguely resembled "It's Beginning to Look a Lot like Christmas."

Kirsti was an old-fashioned girl. She kept him generously supplied with Old Spice. She never told him he had to use it for her sake; she only implied that it was one of her favorite fragrances on men. He spread it liberally over his face and neck imagining her soft voice whispering in his ear, "umm, you smell so good!"

The bedroom that he and Kirsti shared was done to her tastes. The rough stuff had been removed and replaced with soft lace and delicate, soft pastel colors. Eugene had warned him when he married Kirsti about women's invasive behavior. He had put it this way, "Jack, your home will never be your home again. Once a woman moves in, everything you own will be replaced with something they find more suitable to their tastes. Your home, from here on out, will be referred to as Kirsti and Jack's not Jack and Kirsti's and even more likely, you will be left out entirely, and it will become Kirsti's. You mark my words, Jack. From now on, what's yours is hers, and what's hers is hers. This is a fact of life with the female gender so brace your-self."

How true were his words because the bedroom was where Kirsti started her home improvement project, and she wasn't anywhere near completion. Everything he had owned was now sitting in an outbuilding and everything she wanted was now in the bedroom. He didn't even dare to mention the closet. He had to use every ounce of investigative skills he owned just to find a pair of socks, so busy was his wife in changing and rearranging things. She and her Grandmother were constantly chatting about renovations to his house. The kitchen was next and then the other bedrooms. When she started parking her home interior design magazines in his office, he put his foot down, firmly. She could do whatever she wanted to do with the rest of the house but his office was off limits. He even went so far as to put a "Do not disturb" sign on his door. The whole "Poval" family got a bang out of that one, especially Eugene.

Kirsti had been home. Stacked in the middle of the bed were three ornately and perfectly wrapped Christmas packages. Jack didn't need to guess who they were from, there was a note attached that read, "To Jack, from Santa." The boxes were numbered. He opened the gifts by the numerical system his wife had devised. The first one contained a dark green sweater that had a front view picture of Rudolf embossed on the front and Merry Christmas artistically embroidered across the chest. The nose of Rudolf was red plastic. "Push me," it read. He did. The nose got bright red and started flashing. Cute, he thought. The second box contained a white turtle-necked, long-sleeved pullover, obviously to be worn under the sweater, and a pair of socks that matched the sweater—green with Rudolph printed all over them. The third box contained a pair of black jeans, and underneath the jeans was a red-and-white Santa's hat. Jack dressed himself in the clothing that Kirsti had bought for him, looked in the mirror, and laughed. "OK, if this is what she wants, this is what she gets!"

The large graveled circular yard was packed with cars when Jack arrived. He had a heck of a time finding a place to park. He placed the Santa hat on his head using the rearview mirror to guide him. How does one wear a Santa hat? When he opened his car door to get out, there stood Kirsti. She was dressed in clothing identical to his. He took one look at her and laughed, he grabbed her around the waist, picked her up, swung her around in a circle, set her down, and kissed her long and hard. He looked deep into her soft blue eyes and said, "Merry Christmas, Kirsti, I have missed you. I have missed you very much."

Kirsti pulled away from him, grabbed his hands, and said auspiciously, "I have missed you too. Can we start over?"

"Your dad must have gotten his rickety old tractor started up and running; either that or he has a good relationship with one of his neighbors, which one is it? Knowing your dad, he probably had the boys out here, hand shoveling." He was kidding, of course. Then again, the hand shoveling was not beyond the realm of possibilities. He had heard plenty of stories from Kirsti's brothers to make him believe that Eugene would indeed insist upon this if he could get by with it.

This was not what Kirsti had expected to hear; she frowned as Jack steered her toward the house. Eugene was standing in the doorway as they entered; he greeted Jack with open arms, gave him a hug, and invited him in. Hilde and Glenda also hugged him and wished him a Merry Christmas. Mary was busy in the kitchen, helping Grandma prepare the dinner, and didn't greet him at all. Eugene poked the nose of Rudolf and then let him pass, but not without a remark.

"As long as I live, I will never understand women and the lengths, they will go to embarrass the men in their lives."

Eugene was dressed in a bright red button-down shirt and dark green pants. His tie was black and loaded with little friendly faced Santa's. On the top of his head was a red and white, furry Santa hat. His had a round brass bell hanging from the end of its tail that jangled when he moved. When he caught Jack paying mind to this, he said without reservation, "I am the only one in this family who gets the bell and when I ring it everyone had better be standing to attention." To prove his point he took his hat off and rang his bell. Jack burst into laughter as he glanced around the room. The whole entire clan looked like escapees from the JC Penny Christmas catalog and all were standing at attention waiting for Eugene to say something. There wasn't a single person in the room who wasn't wearing a red and white Santa hat.

"See? This is not the first occasion I have witnessed when it is beneficial to be the oldest surviving male."

"As far as I know," Jack said, his eyes twinkling, "You're not the oldest male in this house. Yvonne's husband is older than you are. How do you explain that?"

"I don't have to. He is an interloper such as your-self. He's only invited to this party because he happens to be married to a Poval. One day he might inherit a hat from his own family, but I know his family and they aren't into this and the truth be known, I'm not crazy about it either but it pleases the women in the family." He pointed directly to his oldest daughter.

Dinner was served first. The menu of Norwegian tradition consisted of peeled, boiled potatoes, cranberries, lefsa (everyone's favorite), lutifisk (no one's favorite), fresh rolls, sweet soup, white sauce and melted butter for the lutifisk, and lots of hot steaming coffee. Before dinner was served, the family sang the Norwegian dinner prayer and "Silent Night."

After everyone had finished eating and the dishes had been cleaned up and put away, Yvonne picked up a school bell and rang it to get the group's attention.

"Would everyone take their seats please? Greg would you escort Grandma to her chair, please?

"Ordinarily we would open gifts now, but the family has a special gift they want to present to you first." Yvonne was speaking to her mother. "We are going to give you your own special church service here at home in honor of your ninetieth Christmas."

Yvonne handed her mother a program that Mary had created and designed for the occasion. "So let's begin."

Greg, Yvonne's pastor son officiated the service by reading scriptures from the bible, explaining the birth of Christ. His wife opened the music program with a solo. Her rich soprano voice did wonderful justice to "It Came Upon a Midnight Clear". The grand children sang "Away in a Manger" and "Jingle Bells." Eugene and Yvonne sang, "What Child Is This." Their soprano and tenor voices were an ideal blend. Next to sing were Kirsti, Glenda, and Hilde. They sang "Living for Jesus," a song they could sing without any practice. Kirsti's brothers sang, "Little Drummer Boy." Yvonne's second son and his wife did a spine tingling rendition of "When a Child Is Born," and last but not least Brandon, Yvonne's youngest son, who was music director at a state university, ended the concert with a mind-shattering, knee-shaking, heart-tugging "Oh Holy Night." When he was finished singing, the entire group got up and sang "How Great Thou Art".

To close the concert Greg went to Lynne who had been playing the piano masterfully throughout the concert. He took her by the hand and bowed to her. The entire family gave them a standing ovation. Then they all turned to Grandma and gave her a standing ovation because they all realized and appreciated that she was the prime force that had made all of this possible. They all knew, as a family, that there was nothing more important to Grandma than her family and nothing gave her more satisfaction than music.

And what was Grandma's reaction? Her exact words were, "All of this, just for me."

She did not clap, nor did she offer any emotional display. She simply sat there with a small, indiscernible smile on her lips. Her eyes were intense and her ears listening to every note with the inquiring instincts of a master. That she had not frowned one single moment throughout the entire performance was the key to assessing her appreciation. There were no frowns, there were no tears, the family had pleased her, and they were elated.

By the time all the gifts had been opened, daylight had passed, and the darkness of night had moved in. The remainder of the evening would be spent visiting and playing board games. Jack was starting to feel a bit restless and in need of some fresh air. As he made his way slowly through the crowd toward the front door, he literally ran into Mary.

After they had both gathered their equilibrium, she said, "I haven't had a chance to properly thank you for the gift you gave me, Jack. It was way too generous."

"You are very welcome, Mary. I need to go outside and get a breath of fresh air. Why don't you join me? I'd like to visit with you awhile, but I can't see this happening in here. You are in demand everywhere."

"Sure, let me get my coat. I could use a breather too."

She wasn't gone long and as they strolled out the front door together she heard someone calling her. She kept right on walking. "If it's important they know where to find me," she said with alacrity.

The contrast between the warmth inside and the extremely cold, crisp air outside made both Jack and Mary gasp.

"Are you sure you're going to be warm enough in that coat Mary? Perhaps I should take you back inside. Damn, it is cold out here!!"

Mary offered an affectionate sort of laugh, an almost condescending type of laugh before she responded with, "Jack, please, I have lived in Minnesota all of my life. I'm tougher than I look."

Jack burst out in merry filled, appreciative heart reeling laughter. He was laughing so hard he almost fell off the steps. Soon Mary was laughing with him. He tried to explain the humor, but every time he tried, he burst into another fit of excessive hilarity. When he finally managed to get himself back into control again, he hugged Mary and said, "Forgive me Mary, it's been a long life. You are precious. Now, let's take that walk we talked about and breathe in this bitterly cold air! I'll let you know when *I* need to go back inside."

"You have quite a family, Mary" Jack said as he assisted her down the steps to the yard, "so much talent in one small group of people. The program they put on was extraordinary. Every one of them could be singing professionally if they set their minds to it. How long have they been working on this?"

"Yvonne decided to do this over Thanksgiving. This bunch has been singing together forever, so it really wasn't much of a stretch for them. They all did their own individual practices when they could and had one final run through yesterday morning. Brandon did a terrific job of keeping this wily family focused. The excellence belongs exclusively to Grandma. She has never been one to settle for second best, and every single person who sang tonight knew that they had better be sharp or don't bother performing for her. Do it right or don't do it at all has been her chant with every single member of her family from the very beginning of their existence."

"Well, it certainly sounded perfect to me and what a dynamic gift for Grandma. I hope someone was taping it for Grandma."

"Yes, it was a grand performance, and it all came from people who have no realization that they are as talented as they are and that even includes Brandon. This was just playtime for them, something to do when they are not doing something else. Yes, Bobby was in charge of the technical operations. She was taping the whole program for posterity."

"You mean Bobby, Kirsti's little sister? She's only thirteen! How can you depend on a girl so young to do a job of this importance?" asked Jack incredulously.

"Honestly Jack, you really do have to start playing closer attention to things. She had her cameras set up and running and didn't you hear the trumpet in the background of "Little Drummer Boy"?"

"Sure I did, but I thought it was a tape."

Mary laughed ingenuously.

"So then, there was Lynn at the piano and Bobby with the trumpet. I noticed that Lynn didn't use sheet music. What about Roberta?"

"Grandma considers sheet music unprofessional. Not one in this whole bunch would ever stoop to using it. It just is not an acceptable thing in the world of performing, and Grandma is right. Grandma has always said, 'You cannot read while you are singing, and you cannot sing while you are reading and do accurate justice to either one.'"

"You like Grandma, don't you."

Mary paused for a moment before she answered, "You know, Jack, I have never given that question a second's worth of thought.

She is one of the most important figures in this whole entire family, including my own. It has never been a matter of liking or disliking her. It has always been about getting along and making things work out. She is who she is, and I am who I am and thus far, it has worked out rather well."

Mary and Jack had walked three wide circles around the yard as they conversed, strolling along at a slow and easy pace. Mary was starting to shiver.

"I'm getting cold, perhaps we should think about going inside."

Jack took off his jacket and wrapped it around Mary's small shoulders, giving her an affectionate hug in the process.

"I really want this to work out between Kirsti and I, but I don't know now if it is possible, Mary. I am caught between really loving her and wanting to protect her. I am now starting to realize that I should have thought this out a lot further than I did before I ever got involved with her. A man in my position should never marry. There is too much risk involved. There are things going on right now that I have no control over, and I strongly feel the things I am facing right now are going to rip Kirsti and I even further apart."

"Do you love her?" Mary asked with a shrug of her shoulders, pulling Jack's jacket around her. Snow was starting to fall in large flakes around them.

Jack didn't answer immediately. Mary looked into his dark eyes; they were burning with intensity. His mouth had tightened into a straight line. Who could not love this handsome man, this strong, masculine, kind and gentle person? As he was about to answer Mary, his cell phone rang. He glanced at the time on his phone; it was 11:25 PM. There was a text message.

Jack grabbed Mary's arm firmly and started walking her double step toward the house. His brusqueness startled his mother-in-law. When he had her planted firmly in front of the door, he removed his jacket from her shoulders.

"Thanks, Mary, for sharing this time with me. Tell Kirsti that I had to leave. Tell her that I got a call, and whatever you do, do not let her leave here tonight. You have got to keep her with you. I can't explain right now, I don't have time. Promise me!"

Mary responded without thinking.

"I promise. Jack, where are you going?"

Jack gave Mary a firm hug and kiss on the cheek before he left a troubled Mary standing on the porch. He took long, rapid strides to his vehicle, got in, started the engine, and was gone, leaving a whirl of snow behind him.

Eugene was standing by the door looking out the window when Mary came back in the house. He had seen Jack leave. Mary was shivering but not from the cold. Eugene took her coat and led her into a separate part of the house where no one could be and would be listening.

Eugene wasn't gentle with Mary, he never had been. He wasn't tender with her because she wasn't the sort of woman who thrived on it and that was why he loved her as he did. He respected her because he didn't have to treat her with kid-gloves. He had once told his mother that he never had to worry about Mary because if anything ever happened to him; she was perfectly capable of taking care of herself and others as well. Mary was a woman who was accomplished at taking things in stride and had the ability to always come out on top, no matter what. This was the highest compliment Eugene would ever give to anyone.

Now here she was, trembling. He had at first thought she was shivering from the cold, but now he knew differently. She was speaking to him, but he was having a hard time concentrating.

"You should have seen his eyes Eugene. Something is going to happen. He took a phone call, and then he was out of here. You saw him leave!! He raced out of here. Something dreadful is about to happen, I know it. I can feel it. Jack is in trouble, deep trouble. I know it Eugene."

He grabbed Mary by the shoulders and shook her, "Stop it Mary. Stop it right now. Start from the beginning, you're not making any sense. I can't help Jack if you don't get a grip on yourself!" Eugene's eyes were disturbingly forceful. He was a man with zero forbearance.

"He said we have to keep Kirsti here at all costs, don't let her leave this house tonight, and then he left."

Mary's husband took one breath and said, "I'll handle this Mary. You calm down and go back to the party. Kirsti can't know that anything is going on. I am going to have a talk with Glenda. She is the only one who will be able to persuade Kirsti to spend the night and keep her mind off of Jack."

"What do I say to Kirsti when she asks about Jack?"

"Tell her he was called back in on the Durkin case and then after that be the Mom you've always been."

Chapter Thirty

As Jack was negotiating the snow-packed driveway out to the main road, he placed a call to Vic on his cell phone.

"You need to meet me at my house as soon as you can possibly get there."

He didn't wait for Vic to respond before he hung up the phone. He didn't slow down at any stop signs along the way. Jack didn't care about stop signs at this moment, and if anyone was in his way, they would have to wait. It was Christmas Day; the roads were vacant of all travelers between the Poval's and his place. Large flakes of snow were falling on his windshield, promising a lot more to come. His wiper blades moved back and forth, in a steady rhythm, helping him to concentrate. By the time he reached the end of his driveway, the snow had lightened up a bit, but his wipers kept right on flapping, back and forth, back and forth, *click, clack, click, clack*. Jack wasn't aware that the snow had turned to smaller flakes. He wasn't thinking about his wiper blades, nor was he thinking about snow.

He brought his jeep to a halt about fifteen yards from the house. Right about the place where the driveway ended and the yard began. The house was completely dark; this was what he expected. He sat in his jeep and waited, the engine running, the headlights on; he shut off the wiper blades, they were starting to annoy him. Vic pulled in and parked his jeep alongside Jack's. Vic was the first to get out of his vehicle; he left it running with the headlights on. The combination of lights illuminated the entire front of Jack's house in an eerie, ghostly fashion. Melton walked around the back end of Ireland's jeep. Jack watched him in his rearview mirror as he passed by the back window and strolled around to his closed door. Jack didn't move as he approached, but kept staring out his front windshield at the building in front of him.

When Vic yanked open the door, Jack said without any emotion, "You must have broken some speed limits to get here this quickly from Hastings. If I were a cop, I'd give you a speeding ticket."

Vic wasn't the least bit amused.

Jack thrust open the door and stepped out, his long legs carried him to the front of his jeep, the headlights casting long shadows as he passed by them. He leaned back against the grill, one foot on the ground and the other one resting on the front bumper. He reached into his jacket pocket and pulled out a pack of cigarettes. With his thumb and forefinger, he extracted a cigarette, placed it in his mouth, and lit it with a lighter he had simultaneously removed from another pocket. He then pointed the pack of cigarettes toward Vic and asked all too offhandedly, "Do you want one?"

Vic viewed his friend with an arched eyebrow. On an average day, he followed Jack's lead without a whole lot of question, but now he was beginning to wonder if this was always the wiser course to take. Jack was not above playing games with him. He and Hank and Jack were always trying to get one up on the other. If this were the case tonight, on Christmas Day, well, Jack would pay—big time.

"I didn't break any speed limits to get here. I was in Farmington when you called. You just broke up a very lovely evening I was having with my favorite girl, this had better be important, and besides, I thought you quit smoking."

"Oh really, which 'favorite girl' would that be?" Jack asked feigning surprise.

"Ah, Jack, jealousy doesn't become you. Are you going to explain why I am standing out here in the cold with you, improperly dressed I might add, and not in the arms of my girlfriend or are you going to keep me guessing until I simply have to throttle you? Damn it, Jack, it's fifteen below zero out here. I don't do well in subzero weather."

Vic was losing his cool. It was damned cold; and worse yet, he had to remain just as calm, cool and collected as Jack appeared to be while he figured out what was actually going on. He had been standing in front of Jack, directly in front of him, as he grilled him. And when he got no response whatsoever, he took the same stance as Jack: his butt against the grill, left foot on the ground, and the other on the bumper.

Jack's demise was relaxed; his full attention was directed toward his house; now and then he would peer at his watch. The lighted green numbers read 11:55 PM.

"I did quit smoking."

Jack blew on the lighted end of the cigarette, causing it to blaze a bright red. He put the cigarette to his mouth and took a deep drag, "Now I only smoke when I'm nervous." Vic watched as Jack reached inside his jacket and unsnapped his gun from its holster.

"Give me a cigarette, Jack."

Jack pulled the package of cigarettes out of his jacket pocket again and handed the pack to Vic. Vic took a cigarette and handed the pack back to Jack. Jack then handed him his lighter. Vic lit the cigarette and handed the lighter back to Jack. It was a consciously intended ceremonious transaction.

"I thought you quit," Jack said with a grin.

"I did."

"Then why are you smoking?"

"I only smoke when I'm nervous."

Vic reached inside his jacket and unsnapped his gun from his holster.

"I think I need to ask you one more time why are we standing out here in the cold, leaning against this pile of junk when we can be in your house having a nice warm cocktail in your living room with the Christmas tree lights flashing brightly and a nice warm fire glowing in the fire place. Why is that? In fact—"

Jack took another look at his watch. It was 11:59 with fifteen seconds to go before midnight.

"I needed you here as a witness was what I was thinking."

After that, everything seemed to happen at once. Jack took another drag from his cigarette, threw it on the ground and gave his partner a gigantic shove. Vic hit the ground as the first explosion resounded. The earth seemed to quake underneath him.

Jack also tried to hit the dirt but didn't quite make it. He got midair before he was thrown hard against his jeep. He was lifted backward over the hood, his head smashed into the windshield. He never heard the second blast because by then, he was unconscious.

As Vic felt himself being thrust to the ground, he had to wonder why Jack had pushed him. He heard the first blast when he landed, he felt the second as the ground shook beneath him; his first thought was, earthquake. He covered his head, waiting for the third; it came instantly after the second. Debris was flying in every direction. When he finally dared to get up and look around, his automatic response was to look towards the direction of the blast, which was toward the house. What little was left of it was in flames. He reached into his pocket, pulled out his cell phone, and dialed 911. His next thought was of Jack.

Vic found Jack sprawled across the hood of his jeep. The windshield was cracked, and Jack was unconscious. When Vic tried to move Jack from where he was, he saw blood trickling down from the back of his head and unto the collar of his shirt. He gently moved Jack to the ground where he could get a better look at him. The fire from the house helped, giving him the light he needed to see how badly his ornery buddy was hurt. Jack had a gash on the back of his head that was bleeding profusely.

Vic remained on the line to 911, giving them the information, they needed to find them. Within minutes, there were red lights flashing everywhere. The place was starting to resemble grand central station at rush hour. First came the cops then came the ambulance then came the fire trucks. All of them had their sirens blasting and red lights flashing, now all that was needed to add to the excitement was a band playing the "Star Spangled Banner."

"Wake up, you son-of-a-bitch, you have a lot of explaining to do, you bastard!" Vic grabbed Jack by the shoulders and shook him hard. "Don't you dare die on me, you insensitive, ill-begotten derelict!"

"Goddamn it, Jack, wake up!"

When Jack finally did open his eyes, he looked at Vic and said weakly, "Hi, Vic, what's up? I think I feel a headache coming on. There seems to be an unusual amount of commotion and racket going on. Is someone having a party that I don't know about? Derelict, indeed, Vic, is that what you think of me? You can always tell who your friends are when the going gets tough. I don't think anyone has ever called me an insensitive, ill-begotten derelict before."

Vic didn't know whether to hug Jack or kick him. He did neither. He sat down next to his buddy and said casually, "You wouldn't have a cigarette handy would you? I seemed to have lost the last one I was smoking when you gave me that rather unpleasant shove, and I can't find it anywhere."

Jack reached painfully into his jacket pocket, pulled out his pack of cigarettes, and handed them to Vic.

"What's the matter, Vic, are you nervous? I think you just told me you never smoke, unless you're nervous about something."

"No, Jack, I am not nervous, what would I have to be nervous about. I just thought I would sit here and have a cigarette while we watch your house burn to the ground. There is nothing more relaxing than a couple of friends, sitting around a bonfire and sharing a smoke. The only thing I can think of that might be missing is an icy-cold beer, but I can live without the beer for now."

Within seconds, the paramedics were attending to Jack. Vic looked at his watch; the time was 12:10. Jack was really dazed and not functioning very well. The paramedics made him lie still while they administered to him. The younger of the two took his vitals, the older of them looked at Jack's eyes and said unemotionally, "I think he has a concussion, we need to get him to the hospital."

Jack fought off the paramedics as he tried to struggle to his feet.

"Vic, pull me up, will yah?" He sounded drunk.

The older of the paramedics shook his head no. Vic grabbed Jack by the shoulders of his scuffed-up leather jacket and yanked him to his feet. Jack's head was pounding hard, and his vision was blurred, but he held himself upright with a little help from his friend.

"Thanks buddy. Man, my legs feel like spaghetti. Who is the officer in charge? I need to talk to the officer in charge. Vic, where is my cell phone? I need my cell phone. Damn, my head hurts!"

One of the paramedics was trying to put a cold compress on the back of Jack's head, not an easy task considering Jack was moving his head around fitfully, trying to dodge the hands of the paramedic.

"You're bleeding, son, we need to put this compress on the wound, so stand still. Vic, can you get him to stand still long enough for us to administer to him, or do we have to knock him out?"

"Go ahead; knock him out if you have to. I don't think he is in any condition to do anything to stop you, and besides, he isn't listening to me, are you, Jack?"

By the time Vic retrieved the cell phone from underneath his jeep, Jack was vomiting. Three strong police officers and two paramedics lifted him and carried him to the ambulance. He didn't fight them this time; he couldn't because he was unconscious again. Vic stood by and watched with concern as the paramedics loaded his partner into the ambulance. When they were on their way down the driveway, sirens blasting away and lights a-flashing, he turned his concentration on Jack's cell phone clinched tightly in his right hand. He snapped it open, hit a few buttons, and a text message appeared on the screen.

The message read,

> Mery xms Jkie
> Fire wks yr hse
> Mdnt
> Enjoy the show!

Interesting, very interesting, thought Vic as he stuck Jack's phone into his jacket pocket. He strolled over to the cops who were waiting for the firemen to finish their job, so they could start theirs. The firemen were busy dousing water on what was left of the house. There was little remaining of what used to be a house and garage; the water was just a precautionary measure. This was going to be another long night. Vic brought out his badge, showed it to one of the policemen, and introduced himself. He handed the officer in charge his card.

"Jack is my partner. If you have any questions, they're going to have to wait because I'm going to the hospital. Any of you have any objections? I didn't think so."

No one moved to stop him. As he got into his jeep to leave, he made a phone call. Eugene answered; the time was 12:27 AM.

Who is doing this to you Jack? Vic paid no heed to speed limits as he raced to Burnsville. He never did catch up to the ambulance which he viewed as a bad sign.

Chapter Thirty-One

The parking lot was empty, allowing Vic to park wherever he chose. He pulled into the slot nearest the front entrance of the hospital. An elderly very white-haired, bespectacled woman was sitting at the reception desk, reading a novel, which she begrudgingly set aside when he entered. When he asked her how to get to the emergency room, she directed him somewhat impatiently to follow the red lines, not the blue or the yellow, but the red. She then stood up and pointed with long gnarled fingers flaying about in the general direction where he should be traveling. Vic looked where she was flaying, spotted the red line, thanked her, and went on his way.

The red line led him down a long dimly lighted hallway. He passed closed doors to the left of him and to the right of him; all were identified with a green-and-white sign above the door, sticking out like street signs. He turned left at the end of the hallway and followed the red line to the end of another hallway. When he reached the end of this hallway, he noticed six chairs lined up against the wall to the right. Straight ahead were double doors. On the doors was painted in large, bold red lettering, "Do Not Enter, Authorized Personnel Only". To the left was a large window-sized opening.

"Ah," he said to the young girl sitting behind a desk. "I'm glad to see a friendly face. The not so friendly woman up front sent me down here."

The girl behind the desk hadn't heard him coming, "Oh my goodness, you startled me! Can I help you? The gal up front? She's not a regular. She was called in as a replacement. She gets hostile when her schedule gets disrupted."

"I see. How about a date Friday night? Better yet, why don't we leave now?"

The dark-haired, dark-eyed girl gave him a mock frown, lifted her left hand, wiggled her ring finger, and said, "Sorry, I am already taken. My husband might not like the idea of me spending time with another man."

"How very unfortunate for me and lucky for him, but it never hurts to try, or so they always say. I am looking for Jack Ireland. He was brought in here a few minutes ago."

The girl picked up the phone, punched in a number, and made some inquiries, while she did that, Vic noticed that her nametag read Vicki Mills. *Sweet.*

"He's in x-ray right now. The nurse I spoke to said it could be a while before the doctor has anything to report. You can sit in one of those lousy chairs and wait, or you can go to the coffee shop and wait. Neither of the options are all that great, but it's the best we have at this hour of day and especially over the holiday." The girl sounded sincerely apologetic.

"I don't suppose you can tell me how he is doing or approximately how long I will have to wait?"

"No, I can't give you any information at all. I can only tell you that Jack is being well taken care of, if that helps."

"Yah, well, I suppose he is, and that it does. I am going to the coffee shop and get me a cup of coffee, and then I'll be back. I suspect his family will be here shortly. If they get here before I return, tell them where I went. Can you do that for me, Vicki?"

Vic was on his way down the hallway before Vicki could reply. Maybe she would, maybe she wouldn't; this wasn't his first trip to a hospital. He wasn't going to count on it. Hospitals, like many things on God's green earth, were and always have been a people idea, a human idea. Humans are far from perfect and thus as unpredictable as Minnesota weather.

Vic was halfway back to the reception area when he saw Kirsti and Mary moving rapidly toward him. The hallway was so dimly lit that Kirsti was almost upon him before she realized who he was. She picked up stride when she saw him, wrapped her arms around his waist, and held on to him for a few seconds before she spoke.

She looked up into his face; she had been crying. Her eyes were red, strained, and moist with tears.

"Is he going to be all right? What happened? Dad didn't tell me anything except that Jack had been hurt and was being brought here by ambulance. I tried to make him tell me, but he wouldn't. He just said I should get going. I would know soon enough. Is it serious?"

Vic wrapped his arms around her and held her tightly, "Yes, Kirsti, he is going to be all right. He's in x-ray right now. It's going to be a while before you will be able to talk to the doctor, so let's go get a cup of coffee. Jack is a tough old farm-boy. You don't have a thing to worry about except how ornery he is going to be when his head quits pounding and realization strikes. Your father didn't tell you anything because he doesn't know anything other than what he told you. I am supposed to call him later and fill him in on the details."

There was no one in the coffee shop, and the only coffee brewing was in one of the several vending machines that lined the wall. Vic bought each of them a cup of coffee. Mary and Kirsti were now sitting at a table for four, waiting for him to return. Neither of them spoke as he set the three cups of coffee down in front of them. Vic was taking the first sip from his cup when he noticed someone walking through the doorway. He really wasn't surprised to see that it was Brice Buchanan, and on his heels was another man that Vic didn't recognize. Vic had worked for Brice Buchanan for a long time, and still he was impressed by how Brice carried himself, his self-confidence, and his unflappable and charismatic demeanor. His unyielding determination was a source of strength to all who worked for him. Vic stood up as his boss entered the room.

Kirsti and Mary remained seated as Vic stood up to receive Brice. Kirsti recognized him right away and greeted him with a childlike awe. Brice shook Vic's hand when he reached the table and smiled warmly at Mary as Vic introduced her.

"Vic, this is the Farmington Chief of Police, Walt Stanhope. He needs to talk to you. How is Jack?" Brice was matter-of-fact but congenial.

Vic shook Walt's hand, "Sure, no time like the present. I'll tell you everything I know, which isn't much. Your timing is perfect. Jack is in x-ray, and I have been told it could be a while before we can speak to Jack's doctor. I know that Kirsti has a lot of questions too, so I might as well get this done all at one time."

Melton sensed that the chief of police wasn't warming up to the idea of a group therapy session, and it didn't take him long to say as much.

"I'd rather visit with you separately, Detective."

The hard edge to Stanhope's voice was apparent to all, including Kirsti, who appeared to be having a difficult time grasping the situation; and why not, this was all news to her.

"This is police business we're talking about and—"

Vic cut him off, "I hate to appear uncooperative, but it is either going to be all of us, or your interview with me is going to have to wait."

Vic wasn't in the mood to be talked down to, not by Stanhope or anyone else, for that matter, and this included Buchanan. His mind frame was slightly off-kilter; Buchanan knew this, so he so let the comment slide like hot grease off a Teflon surface.

"Then I will wait," Walt said shortly. "I think while you people visit, I'll go down to the emergency room and nose around a bit."

Brice interceded, "Walt, hold up. Why don't you sit in on this conversation? I think that Kirsti needs to know what's going on, and while Vic talks to her, you might pick up a few things. I think you can see that she is very distressed and has lots of questions for Vic. It wouldn't hurt now, would it? Perhaps we can all learn something by an open question-and-answer session."

Walt, who was halfway out of his chair, sat back down. Brice had that effect on people. Walt had a daughter about the same age as Kirsti. He was glad she hadn't decided to marry a cop and but by the grace of God, she hadn't. He shuddered at the thought.

Vic opened up the conversation with a question for Walt Stanhope. "Have you been out to the site?"

Vic was looking at his watch. The time was 1:08 AM. A lot had happened in the last hour. To Vic, it felt more like a day had passed.

"Yes, I just came from there. I spoke to the patrolmen and the fire marshal, but they aren't concluding anything yet."

Walt glanced warily at Kirsti, who was having a hard time holding herself together. The attractive more mature woman with her seemed to be very composed considering the circumstances.

"How much is left of the house?" Vic asked. Kirsti glared at him, her sky blue eyes widening with unabashed stupefaction.

Stanhope had followed Vic's gaze toward Kirsti, and by doing so, he became aware of where Vic's question was leading. Vic had wisely placed the monkey on his back. Brice knew this too; he sat back in his chair and gave a silent nod of approval. Let the impartial be the bearer of bad news. Stanhope was a tough cop, but he was also a man with a highly tuned sensitive nature. He was a cop but he was also a family man.

Stanhope directed his next words to Kirsti.

"Kirsti, may I call you Kirsti?"

Kirsti nodded her assent and leaned toward Stanhope as though her life depended on hearing every word he had to say.

"I have known your husband for many years. We have worked together on several occasions. Your husband is probably one of the best police detectives in this state. I have relied on him more than once to help me with some of my most difficult cases. I want you to know that I regard him with deep respect and admiration."

Kirsti nodded, her expression was one of someone in shock; dull and slow. Mary shifted in her chair so that she was facing Stanhope. She moved her hands from her lap placing one on Kirsti's upper thigh and the other on her cup of coffee. She had become guarded, defensive.

While Vic was paying attention to Kirsti, Brice's attention was on Mary. He was drawn to her, as though she held a magnet on him. He had never met her before. He had met Eugene many times over the course of time. They crossed paths often at the Dakota County Courthouse. Eugene was someone everyone had learned to reckon with because he was who he was and absolutely refused to be anything else. He was probably one of the most genial men he had ever met and yet the most controversial. He was also one of the most intelligent men that Buchanan had ever had the pleasure of doing verbal combat with. Now he sat across the table from his wife. She was perfect for Eugene. She was regal without being regal. She was compliant without being compliant. She was perfectly formed without being perfectly formed. She was controversial without anyone ever knowing it. She said all of this without ever speaking one word. Brice was here because Eugene had called him and told him to get his ass down to the hospital and find out what is going on. Eugene wasn't interested in mincing words. The phone call had taken all of about fifteen seconds and Poval did all the talking.

Walt continued, "I was on my way to bed when the call came over the radio that there was a fire at your home, Kirsti. I have lived in Farmington my entire life. I recognized the address immediately. I knew who lived there. When I arrived at the scene the fire department was still working at putting out the fire. In fact, I was pulling into your driveway when the ambulance was pulling out. We almost had a head-on collision as we met at the end of the driveway, scared the living shit out of me!"

Stanhope was doing a masterful job of easing the tension. Buchanan soon realized that Stanhope wasn't speaking to Kirsti; he was speaking to her mother.

"I didn't think we needed another accident, but to avoid one, I almost wound up in that deep ditch at the end of your driveway."

When he chuckled, the group had to at least give him a grin. Mary saw the humor, and laughed without reservation. She was a visual person.

Instantly, Stanhope got serious again, trying to choose his words carefully, he said, "Kirsti, there was nothing the fire department could do to stop the blaze. They did an admirable job of trying to put out the fire, but it was out of control before they ever got there. They could only keep it contained so that none of the other buildings would be affected. The house is gone and so is the garage. I don't know any better way to put it, and I am sorry to have to be the one to give you this bad news."

Kirsti visibly cringed as though she had been struck, she gulped in air, trying to catch her breath and swallow at the same time. She was staring at Stanhope with complete and utter disbelief, "There isn't anything left? Nothing?"

"Well, not everything, exactly. We did find a safe that had dropped into the basement after the floor collapsed. A very large metal safe. This type of safe would have survived a nuclear blast. Other than that, everything is gone. The house is burned to the ground, there is nothing left but ashes, and again, I am so sorry to have to tell you this."

Kirsti was unable to speak. She slumped down in her chair, trying to absorb the impact of what she had just heard. Mary wasn't quit as dazed; she was thinking about Jack's parting words, "Whatever you do, do not let her leave. You have got to keep her with you tonight." She was remembering Jack's cell phone ringing. She was remembering his abrupt departure. Had he known this was what was going to happen?

Mary was the one to ask, "Do you have any idea what caused the fire?"

She was positive she wouldn't get a truthful answer. Somehow she knew that they knew but wouldn't tell her, nor would they tell the full story to Kirsti either. Not yet anyway, she was right; she got what she expected.

Stanhope answered, "No, not yet, we are waiting for the fire department to finish their investigation."

Mary got the answer she had known was coming. They knew, they just weren't saying. She drew Kirsti out of her chair, "Let's go down to the emergency room and check in on Jack. I think these men have a few things to talk over."

Brice got up from his chair at the same time as Mary, "I think I'm going to tag along. Jack ought to be back to his room by now."

Stanhope removed his hat and gloves from the table. "I think I might as well go back home." As he walked out of the coffee shop, he said, "I will be waiting to hear from you, but don't take too long."

Both Melton and Buchanan caught the implication and gave him a salute.

The two men took the lead with Mary and Kirsti following behind. None of them spoke to each other; each person was deeply entrenched in their own thoughts. When they reached the waiting room, Brice went to the window to talk to the receptionist while Mary, Kirsti, and Vic sat down on three of the six red plastic chairs that lined the wall.

Kirsti turned to Vic and said with a sort of quiet resolution, "There isn't anything left of the house, huh?"

"No, there isn't anything left of the house or anything in it, Kirsti."

Kirsti's shock was gradually turning to anger. She turned to Vic and asked with a quiet, controlled voice, "And I suppose, you are not going to tell me what this is all about, and Jack won't either, will he?"

Vic hadn't quite caught on to Kirsti yet and replied, "Kirsti, we cannot tell you what we don't know. We are all shocked by this turn of events. There is no explanation for what has happened, you have to believe that."

Kirsti leaped out of her chair and glared heatedly at Vic, "Oh, you know what this is all about and so does Jack. This didn't just happen. These things don't just happen. Never, in all of my life and the life of my entire family, have these things happened, not ever! Not on purpose or by accident. There is something you are not telling me, and I am not going to wait around here, in this dismal, dark hospital and wait for you and Jack to decide when I should be included. No way. You tell Jack to give me a call when he gets his shit together, until then, he is on his own. I don't want to see him nor do I want to talk to him! I cannot tell you how badly I do not want to talk to Jack right now. I'm out of here!"

Kirsti picked up her coat, her purse, and started running down the hallway; and as though it occurred to her that she might be forgetting something, she stopped, turned around, and said, "Mom are you staying or coming home with me?"

Mary was already trailing behind Kirsti.

"Yes, I think it is time to go home and get some rest, everything will look better tomorrow."

Kirsti stared at her mother like she had lost her mind and retorted, "Yah, right!" As Kirsti stormed down the hallway, Mary turned, shrugged her shoulders, waved, and then followed her daughter down the dimly lit hall.

As the two men were left standing and gawking at the departing women, Brice said humorously "That little gal has some spark to her, doesn't she? And her mom ain't half bad either. This is going to be very interesting. Eugene has his hands full with those two."

"Interesting isn't the word, Commander. You might find all of this a tad bit funny, but I don't think Jack will. Right now, I wish I was sitting in Palm Beach sipping a martini. I think I have had all the 'interesting' I can handle for one lifetime. Can I put in a request for a different partner?"

Brice laughed again and wrapped his arm around Vic shoulders. His golden brown eyes sparkled, his dimples deepened, the wrinkles around his eyes uplifted and all but disappeared as he said complacently, "Now you know I don't like this, and you don't like it either, but what the heck, we can't let Jack Ireland know he's getting the best of us. Why that would be a crying shame!"

Part III

He did not come in the dawning; he did not come at noon.
And out of the tawny sunset, before the rise of the moon,
When the road was a gypsy's ribbon over the purple moor,
The redcoat troops came marching—
Marching—marching—
King George's men came marching, up to the old inn-door.

They said no word to the landlord; they drank his ale instead,
But they gagged his daughter and bound her to the foot of her narrow bed.
Two of them knelt at her casement, with muskets by their side;
There was Death at every window, dark window,
For Bess could see, through her casement, the road that he would ride.

They had bound her up at attention, with many a sniggering jest!
They had tied a rifle beside her, with the barrel beneath her breast!
"Now keep good watch!" and they kissed her, she heard the dead
    man say,
"Look for me by moonlight,
Watch for me by moonlight,
I'll come to thee by moonlight, though Hell should bar the way."

She twisted her hands behind her, but all the knots held good!
She writhed her hands till her fingers, were wet with sweat or blood!
They stretched and strained in the darkness, and the hours crawled
    by like years,
Till, on the stroke of midnight,
Cold on the stroke of midnight,
The tip of one finger touched it! The trigger at least was hers!

The tip of one finger touched it, she strove no more for the rest;
Up, she stood up at attention, with the barrel beneath her breast.
She would not risk their hearing, she would not strive again,
For the road lay bare in the moonlight,
Blank and bare in the moonlight,
And the blood in her veins, in the moonlight, throbbed to her love's
  refrain.

Chapter Thirty-Two

One, two, three, four, one, two, three, four.

Tracy Durkin was counting under her breath as she lifted her legs up and down in a mentally contrived balanced rhythm. She wished she had some music to listen to, anything but this deafening silence. She had no idea how long she had been in this hellhole. She was losing track of the days. There were moments when she thought she was losing her sanity because she had started looking forward to seeing the one and only person she was having contact with; the short guy. She hadn't seen the tall one since the first day of her captivity. The short one brought her one meal every day. The meal he brought her was always in a plastic container and was usually something left over from one of their meals. He would come down later in the day and collect the plastic containers. He would turn the light on in the morning and turn it off again at night. The light hadn't been turned on yet today, so she felt safe in assuming it was probably still night-time. It was impossible to tell. The two undersized windows had been covered with wooden boards, blocking any natural light from seeping in. She had no watch or clock. She moved her lithe body into position for push-ups and started counting again. Exercising was the only thing that was helping her maintain a grip on her situation, but the exchange for this was one repugnant smelling body. She was seriously starting to dislike the smell of herself, and aside from using the water in the toilet to try and freshen up a bit, there wasn't much she could do about it.

A bath and a change of clothing would be nice, but she didn't see that coming without a fight; and even with a fight, she didn't see it happening. The little guy was immune to her. She had thought she could turn him around like she had many men in her life, to her way of thinking, but he rebuffed all of her advances, sexual or otherwise. He never spoke when he came down to give her food; he just did what he needed to do and then left again. Sometimes, he would come down the stairs, sit on the bottom step, and stare at her, covered from head to toe in black. He wouldn't say anything; he would just sit there and stare at her and then go back up the stairs again. The only thing keeping her sane was a rigid exercise program. If she ever survived this ordeal, she knew she would never fight with her father again. She had no idea what they wanted from her or why she was being held captive. She had asked many times, but her question was met with stone cold silence.

The door at the top of the stairway opened up, and brightness came tumbling down. The short one had turned on the lights and followed the tall one down the stairs. The short one was carrying something. The tall one spoke first in his Darth Vader voice, "Hi, Tracy. My, you are looking a little dirty these days. I don't think I like you smelling up my basement. My partner here finds the stench so distasteful, he doesn't want to come down and feed you any more. He says the smell of you gives him a migraine. He insists we need to get you cleaned up a bit."

"That would be nice." Tracy replied a bit too sarcastically.

"I see you haven't lost your attitude yet, but that's fine with me. You will."

Darth nodded to the short one who had a gizmo in his hand that alarmingly resembled a neck collar and a leash most generally used on dogs.

"We're going to take you upstairs and let you have a shower."

The short one moved toward Tracy; the tall one pulled out a gun, pressed it to the side of her head, and said without any feeling at all, "Sit down and be very still."

Tracy did as she was told. A shower was the first pleasant thought she'd had in days; she wasn't about to blow this opportunity by getting mouthy.

Once the collar was fastened tightly around her neck, the short one removed the shackles from her wrist, waist, and ankles then he blindfolded her.

"Hand me the lead. I should make you beg. I should make you bark like a dog, but this is your lucky day. I don't have time to screw around with you."

The short one gave Tracy a mean push from behind, causing her to stumble as she was being yanked up the stairs by the throat.

"Move along, child of mine, move along. You will shower first, and then there is something I want you to see."

As she tried to make her way up the stairs, the short one would poke at her from behind, causing her to stumble. When she fell, the tall one, Darth, would wrench on the leash without mercy, causing her to scramble to catch her breath. They were having a lot of fun at her expense. When she felt her endurance starting to dissipate, she began counting. She was no longer thinking about her father or her mother or God; she was only thinking in numbers and planning her revenge, once she escaped, and she would escape, indeed she would. Her mind was made up. These stupid jerks would slip up and when they did, she'd be gone.

"I am now going to remove the collar and the blindfold."

Tracy's eyes adjusted rapidly. She was standing in a small standard-type bathroom. It contained a toilet, sink, and shower. There was no window in the bathroom. She was somehow hoping there would be; this might have been an avenue of escape, but on the other hand, she thought, I should have known better.

The short guy handed her a towel and a change of clothing, a sweatshirt and a pair of dull-looking sweat pants, gray in color, size small. They would fit. There was no underwear included in the package. There were no socks. When she asked about this, she was told she didn't need them. Tracy immediately decided she didn't want to know why.

"I have no desire to see you naked, so feel free to undress and shower. I am going to be standing right outside this door while you shower so don't get any bright ideas. You have exactly ten minutes from start to finish. I have already wasted one minute of your time."

Tracy, being grateful enough to even be allowed to take a shower, didn't argue but got undressed immediately; she showered, dried, and dressed under the nine-minute time frame. There was a hairbrush sitting on the sink along with a tube of toothpaste and a toothbrush. When she was done, she felt refreshed, renewed. She made no comment to either of the men as they collared her and blindfolded her again. She didn't speak as Darth, pulling her by the neck collar, dragged her back down to the basement again. She didn't speak at all as they put the chains on her wrists, and ankles or when they removed the collar and blindfold. She was still alive, and she was clean. This was a good start to this new day.

Darth commanded her to sit on the bed. After she was seated, he went back upstairs. When he came back down, he had two newspapers in his hands. He tossed them on the mattress and said, "This is your reading material for today."

He laughed insidiously as he went back up the stairs, the short one following close behind.

Tracy sat down on the bed and spread both papers in front of her, side by side. She had no idea how much time they would grant her. One of the two newspapers was the *Star and Tribune*, the other was a special edition of the *Dakota County Press*. Tracy looked at the *Metro Star and Tribune* first. On the front page of this newspaper was a large picture of herself and her father taken at her high school graduation. Boldly written was **"DAUGHTER OF MINNESOTA SUPREME COURT JUSTICE IS MISSING."**

She went on to read that there was a massive search in progress to find the missing girl. The State Investigative Office and the FBI were working in cooperation with each other to find Tracy Lynn Durkin.

Her stomach turned upside down as she turned her attention to the second paper. The headline read **MASSIVE FIRE CONSUMES HOME OF LOCAL RESIDENT.**

The article went on to state that the owner of the home, Jack Ireland, was transported by ambulance to the hospital. The cause of the fire is still unknown, and the whereabouts of the owner has not been revealed.

As Tracy was working her way through the article about Jack, she heard the door open. Darth came halfway down the stairs then stopped.

"Are you enjoying your reading? He asked snidely.

"Perhaps with a bit of help from me, you will figure this out before Jackie does."

Vader turned and climbed back up the stairs, again singing a familiar song to her titled, "I Shot the Sheriff."

"Sweet Dreams, Tracy."

When he reached the top landing, he switched off the light, leaving Tracy in pitch black. She groped for her flashlight and found it underneath the mattress. She turned it on, and there was light for about one more minute, and then the flashlight died. Tracy, who was used to everything being new, had not considered that the batteries in the flashlight might have been about to expire the minute the flashlight became available to her. She had no idea how long a battery would last because she had never had to worry about it. In fact, she had never before the tall one and the short one came into her life, ever had to use a flashlight. Lots of things she had always taken for granted were rushing forward into her excessively pampered mind.

Tracy began to feel panic overwhelming her, this time worse than ever. She rolled over on the mattress and started to do push ups, counting out loud, "One two, two, three two, four two." She didn't know what day it was, and she didn't care. She wanted her father to find her; she wanted Jack to help him, but now she knew this might not be possible. Breathe in through the nose, breathe out through the mouth. Breathe in, breathe out. She did this until all of her anxiety subsided then she fell into a restless sleep. She dreamed about her father, and she dreamed about Jack. *They were looking for her; they were calling out her name, but she couldn't answer them. There was something blocking her from answering. What was it? She was being restricted by something. It was something she could feel but couldn't see! It was dark, very dark. She couldn't breath, why couldn't she breathe? It was the tar. That was it, someone was pouring black tar all over her, and she was swallowing it, inhaling it.*

"We did good, huh, Willie!"

Shorty was waiting for him at the top of the steps. He lifted his hand to give his brother a high five. Willie didn't respond to the high five.

"We did all right, I suppose, but there is still a lot of work to do."

"Come on, Willie, I did a good job on this one. Can't you say so?"

Shorty was starting to feel unappreciated. "I don't think you give me enough credit."

"Go change your clothes. I'll give you all the kudos you need when the job is done, but for now, I want you to change. Dress up because we are going out, I need to get out of this run down place for a few hours. My adrenalin is running in high gear, and I need to get moving. Are you going with me or staying home?"

"What about that girl downstairs? What are we going to do with her? You have never said what we are going to do with her. We can't keep her down in the basement forever, you know."

Willie was well beyond any sort of staying power with his brother, as was usually the case; he was trying to think, and his brother wasn't helping him one little bit with all of his nagging questions.

"Go change your clothes. Do what I tell you, damn it!"

"Well, how am I going to know how to dress if you don't tell me where we are going? I need to have some idea, don't you suppose?

Shorty sat down at the kitchen table, waiting for his brother to answer him. Shorty was getting that stubborn look on his face, the one that Willie knew better than to provoke.

He gave his little brother a fond pat on the head and said, "Get dressed. Put on your best shirt, pants, jacket and tie, we are going to go out and celebrate our success."

Shorty knew exactly what that meant. He changed into his best clothing and waited for his brother to inspect him, when and only when Willie gave his nod of approval were they on their way.

While Shorty was driving, Willie was calculating. This could be a very defining evening. Willie always allowed Shorty to do the driving because when Shorty drove, he could think, and he knew as well that Shorty handled a car with masterful skill. Willie loved watching his brother as he took control of the vehicle. His younger brother, unlike himself, was always completely focused on what he was doing in present time. Shorty was a man with a simple mind but also a genius when it came down to the need for his particular talents. Willie knew that he could always depend on Shorty to do what needed doing as long as he kept it within the vicinity of his brother's capability.

Shorty was slicked, all fresh and tidy and ready to go. He wasn't very tall, this was true, but what he lacked in height he made up for in the looks department. His hair was golden blond, his eyes the color of the sky on a clear day. He was well built from top to bottom, his wide muscled shoulders narrowed as they approached a slim waist, his arms and legs revealed incredible strength. His stomach was flat and as hard as a rock. The buckle on his belt remained as revealed when he was sitting as when he was standing. He reeked of childlike innocence. He was made of the sort of material that women loved to take home with them. His beguiling blue eyes and dimpled smile got them every time. Shorty loved to converse, especially with women.

Shorty veered right out of the driveway, heading north to St. Paul. They would have a night of it, a long night of it. Willie slid his hands into his pants pocket and pulled out a button. He wove it through his fingers with the grace of a magician. He rotated the large purple button from his right hand into his left palm and gave it to Shorty. Shorty removed the button from his brother's palm and automatically shoved it into his coat pocket. His eyes remained focused on the road ahead; he had a winsome smile on his face.

"Willie, do you think we'll ever get caught?"

"Not if we play our cards right, dear brother of mine, and if we do, we are going to go down in a blaze of glory."

"Blaze of glory, that sounds nice, Willie, that sounds really nice."

Willie settled his head on the back of his seat as he watched his brother drive the van into the parking lot of their previously selected bar and restaurant. He was getting tired. He closed his eyes to rest for a few minutes. He just needed to rest for a little while.

"Are you okay, brother?"

"Sure I'm okay, I just need a few minutes, and then I will be fine. I am just a little tired right now. Let me rest a couple of seconds. I'll be fine and then we will have some fun."

Shorty sat silently waiting for his brother to wake up. He waited for two hours and then four hours, keeping the engine running so as not to allow his brother to get cold while he slept. When the parking lot was empty, he put the van in D for drive and took himself and his brother back to the point from where they had started. Shorty was angry with his brother for getting him all hyped for nothing. He left his slumbering brother in the car when he got home, no longer concerned about him freezing to death. Willie was frowning as he watched his brother stomp into the house. This had all been one big test. His brother would take a kicking in the morning for leaving him outside to freeze to death. He needed his brother to be able to handle himself, and he hadn't done that tonight. Shorty should have not let him sleep. Shorty should have done a lot of things differently. He gave Shorty plenty of time to go inside the house and settle into bed, after which, he went in and did the same.

Chapter Thirty-Three

Dawn was nearly breaking when the doctor finally made his way to the stark white, sparsely decorated waiting room. He was a tall, large-boned man. His gray hair, mixed with black, was combed straight back from his broad forehead. He wore thick lenses in narrow-rimmed glasses that enlarged his equally gray black eyes. He lumbered into the waiting room, as though he was carrying the weight of the world on his massive shoulders. His not-very-handsome face was deeply lined and seemed to contain a perpetual frown. The furrows in his forehead were in keeping with the downward pull around his mouth. He wore his clothing with complete disregard for fashion. His white jacket was wrinkled. His black shoes were scuffed; he wore no tie to adorn or brighten up the dark gray shirt almost hidden underneath his overtly wrinkled jacket, which was noticeably tinged with gray from age or lack of bleach or even perhaps lack of cleansing altogether. The gray slacks that he wore had, without a doubt, seen many better days and had long since this day been ready for permanent retirement.

The doctor glanced sorrowfully around the room; when his eyes fell on the only two people in the waiting room, he said, "Which of you is Jack Ireland's wife Kirsti?"

Before either Brice or Vic could answer, he limped his way to a chair, sat down, removed his shoes and socks, and started rubbing his feet. He looked abstractedly at the two men and said, "Excuse me, but this has been a very, very long day. My feet are killing me. Everyone keeps telling me I need new shoes, but these old boys have been with me a long time, and I hate to get rid of them. Then there is always the painful thought of breaking in a new pair. I have had these shoes as long as I have had my wife, and I don't think I am going to toss her out because she gets a bit old and worn-out. What do you think?"

Brice was the first to regain his composure and spoke first. "I think I should introduce myself. I'm Brice Buchanan and this is Vic Melton."

"Ah, so I can assume neither of you are his wife? I would like to speak to her if I could. Is she somewhere in the building?" He gave each of them a gloomy look as he continued to rub his feet. "One never knows these days."

"His wife was here but has left. I would like to speak with Jack if I can."

Brice had unconsciously backed himself completely away from the doctor and was leaning up against the wall next to Vic. "How is he?"

The doctor didn't say a thing immediately. He put his socks and shoes back on, pulled two small paper towels wrapped in plastic out of his pocket; he wiped his hands thoroughly, placed the used wipes back in his pocket, stood up with a groan, and then reached out his hand to Brice.

All the craggy lines in his face lifted into a wonderful smile as he said, "I am Dr. Keath Larson. I would prefer you refer to me by my first name. Being called Doctor makes me stiffen up, and stiffness in doctoring is not a healthy idea for either me or the patient."

"All right, Keath, how is our boy doing."

"Cranky, very cranky, why don't I take you to his room and you can find out for yourself. I've had a busy night. With Jack coming in and three babies to deliver, I have had my time keeping up. I have one more delivery, and then I am going home. Follow me.

"So what is your reason for being here, Mr. Buchanan, if I may ask? Are you a relative?"

"No, I'm just his boss. The guy with me is his partner."

"His boss, huh, from what I can gather from this lad, he doesn't take to bossing very easily." The doctor reached out and shook Vic's hand, "can't be easy being his partner either."

Brice chuckled approvingly, "No, Jack doesn't take any bossing at all. He works best when I allow him to be his own boss."

Keath was lumbering on down the hallway ahead of them, one heavy foot placed in front of the other with a deliberation that implied great effort. His large shoulders were stooped, and his head bent downward. He came to an abrupt halt in front of Jack's room.

"So, what sort of business is our friend Jack in that would cause this sort of thumping on the head, if I might be so inquisitive as to ask?" The downward furrows around his mouth seemed to appear even more downward, if that was possible.

"He's a police detective."

This answer brought about a wonderful uplift in the doctor's facial expression.

"Well, mates, have at him. My dear grandfather was a cop. He never did the family any good, but the world was a lot better for him. He was half Irish, you know, got it from his mother's side. My father was a doctor. We have as solid a home life as cops do. I haven't seen my wife for a week."

Doctor Larson did a quick about-face; his gait seemed to have lightened a bit or was that just a figment of the imagination? Brice and Vic were about to enter Jack's room when Keath turned around and said, "Oh, by the way, you can take him home. If you can get him to rest a few days, which I doubt, he will mend faster."

Jack was sitting in a greenish-black leather lounger, staring out the window, when Vic and Brice entered the room. He was dressed in the pants that he had on the night before and a white tee shirt, also from the night before. He had a plastic brace strapped around his right shoulder, a cast on his right wrist, and a large gauze bandage taped to the back of his head. On his lap was the sweater Kirsti had given him. He was mindlessly pressing the nose of Rudolph, causing it to blink on and off.

"How you doing Jack, my old buddy, friend, and partner. You don't look so good."

"Just great, Vic, I'm doing just splendidly. Where is my wife? Where is Kirsti? Did you call her and tell her I was here?" Jack was agitated.

Vic arched one eyebrow as though stupefied by the question, "Brice, have you seen Kirsti?"

"Kirsti, do I even know Kirsti? Now let me think, the name sounds familiar."

Vic could see that Jack was getting even more upset and this gave him profound feeling of gratification. He wasn't going to let the chance to dig at his partner pass him by. Vic had an axe to grind.

"Mr. Buchanan, you don't suppose she was the girl sitting in the waiting room when we first got here? You know the one. That dark, short-haired, blue-eyed looker that came in with another woman who was about your age that was equally as good lookin?"

Brice played along, "Oh, you mean the two women that you and I and Stanhope visited within the coffee shop? The one that stomped out of here in a fit of anger, taking that other good looking middle-aged woman along with her? You mean that one, Melton? She was pretty mad when she left the hospital. I sure hope that wasn't Jack's wife!"

"What in the hell are you guys talking about? Give me a fricking break, damn it. Have you seen Kirsti or not?"

Jack put his hand to his head and winced. His shouting was making his head pound harder than it was before his so-called guests arrived.

"My head feels like I have a jackhammer running wild inside it, and you are only making it worse. I would simply like to know where my wife is. You did call her, didn't you, Vic?"

"Now, Jack, you have to watch yourself. You can't have any painkillers until this evening, so don't be working yourself into a dither. The doc said you can go home, but you have to take it easy. Real easy, like lie-down-and-rest type of easy. So let's get you up and moving. You got no place to go but my place, which leaves you at my mercy, and right now, I don't feel very merciful."

"Where is Kirsti?" Jack hissed, now holding his head with both hands. I don't want your damn mercy, save it for someone else. I want to know about Kirsti."

"All right," said Vic condescendingly "but you're not going to like what I have to tell you, and you had better bear in mind that I am only the messenger. You must not shoot the messenger. That would be me, amigo."

"If I had my gun, which I don't, you would already be in the bed next to me."

"OK, boys, the fun's over. Answer his question, Vic." Buchanan wanted to get down to business.

Vic sat down on the edge of the bed. Brice was right; he had had his fun.

"Kirsti was here with her mother, but she went back home. She isn't happy Jack. I hate to be the one to tell you this, but she left me with a message for you, and I will quote it as closely as I can remember it."

"She said and I quote; you can call her when you get your shit together."

"She seems to think you are not telling her everything, which is true. She thinks I'm not telling her everything, which is true. If you want me to give you the grueling details, I will be more than happy to oblige because if the truth be known, I am about as pissed at you as she is."

Vic could see the pain in Jack's eyes as he spoke. His friend was hurting both physically and emotionally, but he didn't seem surprised, nor was Vic surprised that Jack wasn't surprised.

"I'm sorry, Jack. I shouldn't have been so callous. I guess I am a bit troubled by all of this too. I think I have a right to be, don't you suppose?"

Jack held out his left hand to his friend, "Just shut up and help me out of this chair, will yah? I need to get out of here. I hate hospitals. What's the story on my house?"

Ireland's eyes were clear and focused as Vic carefully assisted him to his feet. Jack had just slammed the door on his emotions. He had, also, in effect, just slammed the door on Kirsti. A cop's world has very little room for emotion. Vic had seen this before; Jack was a cop first and everything else second.

Vic studied his friend, "Again, you leave me to be the bearer of bad news. You have always been better at this part than me Jack; besides, I think you know the answer without me telling you."

Jack let out a groan as he shifted the harness back into position.

"Yah, I guess. There were three explosions from what I can remember, and when I last looked, before they lugged me off in the ambulance, there wasn't anything left of the house. There's a more than serious possibility that the explosions were not created by anything other than explosives. I would say with dead certainty that my house was bombed."

Brice was staring hard at Jack as he spoke, "Explosives? Why do you think it was explosives, Jack? What do you know that I don't know?"

Jack's eyes widened with surprise as he turned to Vic, "You didn't tell him?"

"I was waiting to talk to you first."

Vic reached into his jacket pocket, retrieved Jack's cell phone, and handed it to Brice.

"I guess I thought you would want to tell the Chief about this yourself. You don't have much appreciation for people telling tales out of school."

Jack knew exactly what he was getting at. He was referring to the pictures of him and Tracy and his violent reaction when Vic had opened his big fat trap, letting the cat out of the bag before Jack was ready.

"You're good, Vic, you are really good. Sometimes I forget how good you are. I should never underestimate you."

Jacks eyes started to spark as he fought off a strong urge to beat his good old buddy and partner into a bloody pulp. Now who's being the deserter?"

"Underestimating anyone is not a good thing in your line of work, Jack, and payback is hell, or so I have been told." Vic's voice was thick with trumped up superciliousness.

"Here we go again. The two of you acting like a couple of overcharged, undersexed teenagers. Knock it off or I am going to have both of you arrested for offensive foolhardiness."

The commander was getting no special kick out of the detectives' verbal bantering. Brice tossed the cell phone directly at Jack, who caught it, midair with his uninjured hand.

"You punch it up. I hate these damn cell phones. They never make two of them alike. Furthermore, I have this little voice telling me I am about to have an aversion toward your cell phone more than all others. Let's see what Vic is talking about, and I don't want to hear another word out of either of you until I ask a question." He was dead serious. The word explosives had put a whole different mood into play.

Jack pressed a few buttons, retrieved the message, and handed the phone back to his boss without comment. Brice read the text message on the cell phone, snapped the phone shut, put the phone in his coat pocket, and said deprecatingly, "Well now, isn't that just as sweet as Grandma's apple pie? I will see both of you in my office in the morning, you will bring your badges and your guns, and you will be prepared to answer a lot of questions. Now get out of here, go get some rest while you can, Jack, because after tonight, you won't be getting any. You had damn well better take painkillers that don't make you sleepy! Your maverick methods are starting to get downright unwieldy."

Daring not to say another word, both men viewed in silence as Brice strolled casually out of room number 333. He had a right to be miffed and both men knew it. If the two were worried about the repercussions, neither of them showed it.

When he was out of their sight, Jack suggested Vic grab his Rudolph sweater and his jacket. He placed his left arm around Vic's shoulder and said woefully, "There is something about you that really gets the old man ticked off. However, you also need to know that I can understand why this happens. It happens, because you have the same effect on me. Now tell me more about my wife."

"Not even if you beg," Vic said as he helped his partner slip his jacket over his shoulders. He left the Rudolph sweater lying on the chair and stated, "Right now you and I have enough baggage."

Jack couldn't have cared less about the sweater. He did care that Buchanan was miffed.

Chapter Thirty-Four

Brice Buchanan was deep in thought as he drove away from the hospital toward his mansion in Minnetonka. There was no doubt remaining in his mind that someone was out to get Jack. Who and why was what was puzzling the commander. He saluted Boyd as he passed through the large gate at the entrance of his driveway. Brice had considered going straight to the office from the hospital but decided he needed to get a shave, shower, and try to get some rest first. He hadn't had any sleep in over forty-eight hours. He also needed some down time to sort things out. Greta, his house manager, was waiting for him as he entered the front door.

"Boyd told me you were on your way up the driveway."

Greta spoke with a heavy Scandinavian accent. Greta and Boyd had been working for him a long time, he couldn't remember how long, so long that he knew he would never be able to get along without them. Greta managed all of his household affairs with such zest and energy that he had to wonder why no one had ever snatched her up before he got his grips on her. When he would ask her why she had never married, she would fire back, "Who needs a man to keep life lively? Men need women a lot more than women need them, if you ask me. Men never do anything for a woman that she can't do all by herself. I have seen this to be true all my life. Besides, now that you're asking, I need a raise."

Her body was short and plump, her face a mixture of expressions, and her determination to convince him of all truths, never ending; her sincerity and her willingness to prevail, as abundant as she was. Greta had always had, or at least as long as Brice had known her, long whitish gray hair that she wore braided and piled on top of her perfectly round head. She was ageless to Brice, and she was more importantly one of the most unchangeable and predictable persons, he had ever met in his entire life. In his world, this was something to admire and appreciate.

"Lord, Lord, Lord, you need a shower and a shave, where have you been all night?" She scolded with both hands firmly planted on her oversized hips. The question, of course, was nothing more than rhetorical.

"You get up to that bathroom while I fix you something to eat. When was the last time you put something into your stomach? You can't expect to be useful to anyone if you starve yourself. Food feeds the mind. Now get going, I will not have your food getting cold because you are hankering to dilly-dally around."

Greta firmly believed that the answer to all problems was good food. He couldn't argue that. She was a lot older than he was and in much greater mental health, always.

"I have fresh towels for you in the master bathroom. Now go then, go get yourself spiffed up. You look like the wreck of the Hesperus. I will have breakfast ready for you in a jiffy." Greta was mumbling to herself as she departed; she was always mumbling to herself. Brice learned quickly not to ask her what she was saying or ask who she was talking to. He did it once and got a resounding lecture on all of his short-comings. Once was enough.

Brice didn't go to the master bathroom per her instructions, he went into his den and mixed himself a strong drink, a double scotch and water in a tall glass. Greta, everyone knew, had eyes in the back of her head and when Brice didn't go up the stairs like she had told him to, she followed him on his heels into the den, and she was a-clucking.

"You shouldn't be drinking this early in the day; it isn't a good thing to get started. I have known many a man who lost everything from drinking. You put that drink down right now. I will not have you drinking before you eat. It isn't like you to do this, and I won't have it. You need to eat first and then get some rest."

Brice took a deep breath and exhaled slowly. He wasn't in the mood for this. The last thing he wanted right this moment was to listen to Greta carry on; he was going to have a drink and that was all there was to it. Sometimes she forgot who was boss, and in fact, now that he thought about it, most of the time she forgot who was boss.

"Greta, today you are going to have to indulge me and allow me to do things my way. I am going to give you the day off starting right this minute. I don't want to eat right now. I just want to have a drink, sit down, relax for a bit, and then I will take a shower. I might even take a nap. You can take the rest of the day off with pay, please leave now. You're getting on my nerves with your incessant nagging. I am a big boy, and I am very capable of taking care of myself." He was being deliberately harsh, this was the only method he could think of that would get her to back off.

Greta was stunned; she had never heard Brice speak to her this way. She backed out of the den on tiptoes. As she was about to put on her coat and make a hasty retreat, the doorbell rang. She wasn't sure whether she should answer it or not until she heard Brice bark, "Greta, for the love of God, go see who's at the front door. Please!"

Greta let the doorbell ring several more times, just for spite and didn't answer it until Brice hollered at her one more time "Answer the door and then go home, Greta!"

"Well hello, Ms. Greta, you're looking fit. You get younger looking every time I get a chance to see you. Are you heading out? You have your coat on. Is Brice home? If he is, I would like to speak to him."

The person attempting to charm Greta right out of her knee-high nylon stockings was Mac Durkin. He didn't look so good. Greta was tempted to remark on his appearance but refrained; he had a good reason for looking the way he did. What she wanted to do was feed both men and then send them to bed.

"I am not so sure you want to visit with Mr. Brice this morning. He has a case of the uglies, if you know what I mean."

"Oh, I think I can handle Mr. Buchanan and his uglies, Greta." Mac had a lot of appreciation for Brice's housekeeper; her job wasn't without complications. She had a lot of responsibilities on her hands, trying to keep track of her 'chief' and managing single-handedly the affairs of his household. "If Brice is giving you trouble, you just let me have at him. I'll see to it that he treats you right and proper."

Brice was getting a kick out of the conversation, thus he made no attempt to intervene.

"So be it, Mr. Durkin, just follow me, but if he bites you, don't ask me for a Band-Aid, and better you than me is the only thing I have to say. He's been nasty, since he got home, and I am not ashamed to say so. Drinking at this hour of the day, why, whoever heard of such a thing and a man of his caliber no less. He needs to get something to eat and go to bed for a while so don't stay too long, Mr. Durkin. I don't want him getting sick on me.

"If you are through with your nastiness, Mr. Buchanan, Mr. Durkin is here to visit with you. I hope you are kinder to him than you are to me. I will be leaving now." Greta glared angrily at Brice, curtsied impudently, and backed out of the room.

Brice raised his glass to Greta, grinned conspiratorially, and said, "Have a nice day, Greta, see you tomorrow, that is if you want to come back to this nasty, ugly place."

Brice moved toward his distinguished colleague, reached out his hand, grabbed him, and gave him a hug. Mac responded in kind. Both of the men gave out a grunt of understanding as they embraced each other.

"We are having tough times these days. To what do I owe the pleasure of your company, pray tell."

"Gloria is spending the day with her sister, and I needed to get out of the house for a while. I hope this isn't a bad time for you?"

Mac glanced at the drink Brice had placed on the coffee table when he walked in, "I know it's early in the day, but do you have another one of those concoctions for an old friend? I could use a drink, and I could certainly use a friend."

"Sure, sit down and make yourself comfortable. I just got home from a long night at the hospital. It's good to see you. I could use someone to talk too as well. In this business, it is sometimes difficult to distinguish day from night, especially now."

"I thought you looked a little travel worn, are you sure you don't want to get some sleep? I can come back another time."

Brice brought Mac his drink and pointed toward a chair.

"No, please sit down. I wouldn't be able to sleep right now anyway."

Mac sat down in a large overstuffed chair and watched as Brice added some logs to rekindle the dying cinders in the fireplace.

"I have always liked this room. It's warm and comfortable, masculine. My wife prefers everything fancy." Mac patted the arms of the chair, "This piece of furniture would never be allowed in our house. There is certainly a distinctive difference between a house and a home. I live in a picture-perfect house, I long for a place to call home. Do I sound a bit melancholy?"

"If anyone deserves to sound melancholy, it is you, Mac. You don't have to be shy about being honest here. I've been giving some thought to selling the place. It's too big for me, Mac, always has been. Were it not for Greta, I would have sold out a long time ago. I've been looking for something on the river, closer to Hastings. I want something smaller, more comfortable, less expensive, and I don't know. This has never been my style, Mac. There are too many ghosts lurking around."

Brice replenished their drinks and sat down in a chair across from Mac. He knew Mac's wife; she was high maintenance. The thought brought back flashes of his ex-wife. Brice hadn't thought about her in a long time. He didn't want to think about her now.

"You look as tired as I feel. I know you didn't come over this early in the morning to talk about how much you like this room. Why don't you take off your coat and tie, get comfortable, and tell me what's on your mind."

Mac did as Brice had suggested. He stood up, removed his jacket, his tie and positioned them neatly on the back of the sofa. He then sat down and removed his shoes, wiggled his toes, put his feet up on the coffee table, and let out a sigh of relief. Brice did the same after he had grabbed the bottle of scotch and placed it on the table between them along with the ice bucket and a pitcher of water.

"There now, this should save both of us some steps, and before we get started, I need you to promise me, that what we talk about, concerning your daughter and the ongoing investigation, stays right here; I cannot talk to you, and besides, it really isn't my case, it belongs to Washington County and the FBI."

"Of course," said Mac with understanding, "that's a given and vice versa. I am not here. As far as anyone else is concerned, you haven't seen me, and I haven't seen you, and if they ask I will say we were talking old times. You and I have been friends for a long time, Brice and that's precisely why I'm here. The FBI has had no success in finding Tracy. They are no farther ahead than they were the day she disappeared. I want to know what your thoughts are. I want you to give me the God's honest, undiluted truth. Can you do that? Do you think she is still alive? If she was abducted for ransom, wouldn't we have heard something by now? I'll give whoever has her, anything they ask if they will give me back my daughter."

Brice poured each of them another drink. The scotch was going down a bit too smoothly and coupled with lack of sleep, Brice was feeling the effects. He wordlessly studied Mac for a few minutes. He knew he owed him the benefit of what he knew and probably more to the point and importantly what he didn't know. On the other hand, he was walking a very fine line, and in the end, he decided to stick to what he didn't know. The commander could not afford to let emotionalism get in the way of an ongoing investigation.

The morning sun was broadcasting light through windows when Brice, in a thick mental fog, heard someone rattling pots and pans in the kitchen. He distantly, not quite awake yet, thought he heard Greta muttering to herself as she came into the den. When she caught sight of the two bottles, one empty and the other partially emptied, she began her harangue, which brought him to complete attention and the awareness that a new day was about to commence. With blurred vision, he tried to read the clock on the mantel, but he couldn't make out the numbers on the clock, which lead him to make the quantum blunder of asking Greta the time of day. This would turn out to be one of those regrettable decisions one makes without using better judgment. This gave Greta the opening she had been hoping for, the whole night through.

"Lord have mercy, 'uffda', what have you boys been up to all day and all night? Shame, shame, shame on you! I have never seen the likes of anything such as this. You get up right now, both of you, before I have to come after you with the broom. How do you ever expect to make anything of yourselves if you are going to drink half the day away? Now you will be useless to anyone and everyone for the rest of the day, including yourselves. You should know better, why men of your age and importance. I cannot believe this. Breakfast is ready, and I will expect you to eat every bite, shame on both of you!" Greta was bustling about, bristling with self-righteous indignation, and she was not fooling around. Brice could not recollect ever hearing her so angry or upset.

"Greta, please go away, you are making my head hurt even more than it already does."

Poor Brice and Mac had no conceptuality that she was only getting after them because she was still miffed about the way she had been treated the day before, and she had nothing to concentrate on from then until now but her own indignity and her anger, and therefore, it had built up a considerable amount of steam. When she arrived that very morning, she was bound and determined to crack a few heads.

"It isn't me making your head hurt, and it serves you right. Now get up and go eat before the food gets cold. Both of you!"

Greta went back to the kitchen in a huff.

"Well, Mac, we had better go eat, or she will be in here with the broom to give us 'what for.' She scares me to death when she threatens me with the 'what for' business." Brice was smiling as he said this. He loved the daylights out of Greta. He had known he would pay for his words the day before. A bit of peace-making was in order; eating breakfast and offering her a raise would be a good place to start.

Mac grabbed his jacket, coat, and tie. As he made a beeline toward the front door, he chuckled and said, "I think I will pass on the breakfast and leave Greta and her broom up to you, and you had better be good to her or she will tan your hide. Thanks for the conversation and the hangover."

As he closed the front door behind him, he heard Brice yell, "You coward, you get back here and face the music with me, you fair-weather friend!" He chuckled all the way home envisaging Brice being chased around his mansion with Greta close behind him swinging her broom.

Brice sat down in his chair and held his throbbing head. He needed a shower, a shave, fresh clothes, and a bottle of aspirin. The smell of fried eggs and bacon was making him gag. He ignored Greta's clucking as he groped his way up the stairs to the bathroom. If he hurried, he might be on time for his meeting. He had no choice but to be on time. Greta and her breakfast and her scolding would have to wait for another day.

Chapter Thirty-Five

The "war room" had taken residence in a vacant warehouse located in Apple Valley, chosen because the building was somewhat centrally located for all parties concerned. The Dakota County commander of the CDI department, Brice Buchanan had organized a special task force to investigate the Purple Button Case. On board for the first meeting was Vince Grossman from the Shakopee Sheriff's department, Dean Thomas representing the Washington County Division of criminal affairs; Doug Farland, medical examiner from Scott County, and FBI profiler Frank Stiles. Jack Ireland and Vic Melton were included to represent the Dakota County Criminal Investigators Unit. Also in attendance was Robert "Bobbie" Brooks in command of the Tracy Durkin investigation and Jamie Engle, who was responsible for setting up the computer system to be housed on the first level of the building that would now be the headquarters for the special teams working on these two cases.

The location for the meeting was in a large conference room located on the upper level of the warehouse. A large oval table had been brought in, surrounding the table were three large bulletin boards. At the center of this was a large screened television complete with a VCR/DVD player. Buchanan arrived exactly on the hour and found that everyone else had arrived before him and were already seated. The group had come prepared; each of the men had their file folders, notes, and yellow legal-sized notepads positioned in front of them and were engaged in conversation.

After Brice made the proper introductions, a formality, he asked the county medical examiner from Scott County, Doug Farland, to speak first. Doug got up from his chair and moved to a position in front of the television. He had the remote for the VCR/DVD player in his right hand. He pressed the play button. Two separate pictures popped up on the screen. Each held a full view picture of a young blond girl lying on her back, covered with a sheet to just above the breasts. Doug walked toward the television and pointed to each girl, calling attention to the bruises on their necks.

"These two girls died of asphyxiation from strangulation. The markings indicate that they were strangled from behind."

Doug zoomed in on each picture, bringing the bruises around the neck into close focus. "As you can see, on both victims, the marks around the neck are almost identical."

"The blood analysis report indicates the use of Halothane. Halothane is a general anesthetic. The drug will render a person unconscious. It also relieves pain, stress, and fears, though I highly doubt the person perpetuating these crimes had the latter in mind. Halothane is most often found in veterinary clinics, more so than any other medical arena. The drug is generally administered through the air passages, not by injection.

"There was no indication of sexual activity. We found no traces of hair left behind that did not belong to the victims or skin under the fingernails, nor was there any traces of blood found on either victim. There was no evidence of a struggle. By this I mean any unusual bruising, scratches, gashes, or broken bones."

Doug pressed the button on the remote again. Two different pictures of the same girls appeared on the screen. These pictures were taken at the crime scene.

"Note the positioning of the two bodies. They are laid out exactly alike with the button clinched in the left hand. The two girls resemble each other. Both have long blond hair and blue eyes. They are of approximately the same height, weight, and age."

Doug Farland placed the remote back down on the table.

"In summation, I believe these two young girls were killed by the same person, and this person has a lot of confidence in his knowledge of forensics. He knows how to clean up a crime scene. He has killed before, and I am convinced he will kill again."

Vince Grossman rose from his chair, picked up the remote, and went back to the first two pictures of the two girls lying on the table taken by the coroner's office. They were not pleasing to look at. He pressed the zoom button and brought the young girls' faces into full focus. The men around the table were staring at close-ups of two young girls who had just suffered a brutal death. Vince turned to the men sitting at the table; his sandy-colored eyes were filled with anger and indignation. He planted his hard-muscled body so that his feet were square with his shoulders. He folded his hands behind his back, in military rest. He was a Vietnam veteran. He had served four long grueling years in Vietnam; he had seen death before, lots of it.

"I have never had an opportunity to experience a crime of this sort, not in my territory. These young girls were in my jurisdiction, during my watch, and they have wound up dead. I'm doing all I can to find out who would think them this countless on the human scale as to kill them and do this in a manner so degrading as to make me, a man of hard core, shudder. These two girls were just getting started in their life, and to be a witness to such a travesty makes me literally sick to my stomach. I will not have any peace until the person who took their lives so brutally is brought to justice."

"I know who the girls are, but I don't know why they've been killed nor do I know who killed them, not yet." Vince moved toward the television screen and pointed to the first picture to the left.

"The first victim is Rusty Winter. She came to Minnesota from Chicago. She was twenty years old when she was killed. Her parents said that she left home two months before they put out a missing person report on her. They hadn't heard from her in that period of time and were beginning to wonder what had happened to her. I wondered why it took two months. Neither of the parents was willing to talk much about their daughter other than in an abstract manner at first. It took a lot of tough questioning to get them to talk about her at all. The mother told me that there was a lot of bad blood between Rusty and her father. He would lose his temper and fly off the handle. Rusty would get confrontational, and the fights would get downright nasty. The mother passed it all off as 'control issues' coming from both sides.

"One day, Rusty and her father had a huge fight. Rusty's mother considered this just another one of many. However, this time was different. The difference being that after this fight, Rusty just simply disappeared. Mom got up in morning and found her daughter gone, 'lock, stock, and barrel.' Rusty had packed what few personal belongings she owned and had left sometime during the night.

"When I asked her what 'flying off the handle' meant, she became vague. All she would give was, 'Well, you know, pushing and shoving and a lot of hitting, rough stuff with Rusty generally winding up on the shorter end of the stick.'

"Mom said she had no idea where she might be but she 'might' be staying with an ex-boyfriend of hers who had moved to Chanhassen a year ago.

"When I spoke to the dad, he was even less forthcoming than his wife was. His whole attitude was, 'So what?' He disliked his daughter, always had; she was nothing but trouble. He was glad she was gone and, hopefully, in his own words, 'for good'. When I told the parents that she was dead, they both acted like I was talking about a stray cat that had been left on their stoop and had decided to stray back out again.

"After I wrenched the name of the ex-boyfriend, out of the 'sense of duty' Mom, I tracked him down in Chanhassen through the motor vehicle department. If I thought the parents were bad, this guy was a real piece of work.

"He did get her a job at a sports bar in Eden Prairie. The name of the bar is in my report. The owner is fearful that negative exposure is going to hurt his business, so he wants us to try and keep the name of his business out of the mix, if possible.

"I interviewed the owner of the bar, and he said that Rusty was a great waitress and bartender. The customers really liked her; she did well in tips, and he was a bit surprised when she didn't show up one day, nor the next or the next, but waitresses come and go and generally without notice.

"I asked him how she got back and forth to work, and he said she drove a beat-up old Ford pickup truck that she bought for $250 when she came to town. The pickup has yet to be found. The ex-boyfriend hasn't got a clue about anything. He likes his crack, and according to him, he lost track of Rusty right after she moved in. He says to me, 'Hey man, I gave her a place to flop out, what more do you want from me? She and I walk in different circles, you know what I mean?'" Grossman's spontaneous imitation of the boyfriend brought a laugh out of the men who were sitting and listening.

"In the end, and much to my gratification, I did eventually get him arrested for drug possession. When we knocked on his door on our second interview with him, we caught him unawares. He was in a hurry to hide some cocaine he had recently purchased, with no time to think it through; he had stuck his stash in one of his boots. You know; the kind that cowboys wear when they're rounding up cattle each day? They were fancy ones. Snake skin and expensive. In my mind, this guy had no business owning a pair of cowboy boots, he was being disrespectful to all cowboys because he was no more a cowboy than Jack the Ripper was. I tripped over one of his fancy cowboy boots when I came in, knocked it over, and the drugs fell out. Well, you know what that did, guys, sure enough. We got ourselves a warrant right there on the spot, and with permission to search, we found enough dope in the apartment to keep all of us up in the clouds for the rest of our lifetimes. He'll be spending a little time in jail. I would have shot him for 'indifference' but then on second thought figured he wasn't worth the cost of the bullet, and besides, other things in consideration, I didn't want to take a chance on getting stuck in the same jail cell with that stupid asshole. That would have been just about my luck; me and that wild-haired, wild-eyed, dope-selling creep in the same cell, no way. I would have had to strangle the son of a bitch just out of pure principle."

By now the group of men sitting around the table, were crumpling up with laughter. Frank Stiles was laughing so hard, he got the hiccups. Brice had laughed his way out of a hangover. Farland was sitting in his chair, holding his throat; he was choking because he couldn't catch his breath. The only one who failed to see the humor was Grossman.

Vince reached into his pocket, pulled out a pack of cigarettes, and lit one while he waited for everyone to get serious again. When this didn't happen right away he lifted his voice about a half a decibel.

"Rusty's legal name was Rhonda Carly Winters."

He took a deep drag off his cigarette and set it down in the ashtray before he pointed to the second girl on the screen. The laughter in the room subsided immediately.

"This one is Anne Windsor Taylor."

Vince picked up his cigarette from the ashtray, took another drag, and set it back down in the ashtray again. The room became eerily silent; glumly and seriously silent.

I found out Anne's identity the same way as I did Ms. Winters; that would be by connecting with missing persons. This girl is from Des Moines, Iowa. She was nineteen when she was murdered. Her parents are divorced. Her father has had nothing to do with her since the day she was born. She was raised entirely by her mother. When her mother divorced, she never remarried. Mrs. Taylor had three kids that came from three different men, one girl and two boys. She said that she and birth control didn't get along very well, sort of like the way she got along with men. 'When it works, it works, when it doesn't, it simply doesn't.'

"Mrs. Taylor is a beauty and about as decent a person as I have ever met. I would trust her with my own kids.

"She has a nice home in the suburbs of Des Moines, clean, very clean and expensively decorated. This woman is no slouch.

"Anne was the oldest of three kids and was the most restless. Mrs. Taylor did all she could to provide on her own for the three kids by working as a waitress at the most expensive restaurants in town. She said she enjoyed being a waitress because she made a lot of money and could call her own hours, allowing her to be home when her kids were home.

"Annie, Mrs. Taylor calls her Annie, told her mother that when she graduated from high school, she was heading to Minneapolis. Mrs. Taylor wanted her to go to college, but Anne said that wasn't the life for her. She was sick of school. She wanted to go where the action was. Mrs. Taylor had a younger brother living in Chaska who was willing to take his niece in. Annie and her uncle had always had a very close relationship. He found her a job at a sports bar he frequented just outside of Chaska. One morning, he woke up, and Anne wasn't around. They always had coffee together in the morning. He got worried and called his sister who called missing persons.

"I have been working together with Jack Ireland and Vic Melton to try and find the killer of these two girls. Their investigative skills have been essential. These two men have assisted me in all aspects of this investigation and have been out there every day, helping me interview anyone and everyone who could lead us to the killer. I am now going to hand the podium over to Jack."

Jack and Vic had found a spot at the very back of the room because they felt more comfortable observing than participating. Jack was taken aback when Vince asked him to come up and speak, so was

Brice. The whole point of Jack and Vic being invited to this meeting was to observe, not participate in the procedure. Brice stood up to protest, but Jack waved him back down into his chair.

Everyone watched as Jack made his way slowly to the front of the room and towards the podium. His whole body was suffering numerous after-effects from the jarring it had taken from the collision against the unyielding windshield and hood of his vehicle. Brice noticed that he was limping as if his tailbone was misplaced. Had he re-injured it?

The bright fluorescent lights revealed dark bruises on the right side of his face, from his jaw line to his hairline. The whole left side of his face was bruised and swollen. His shoulder was in the brace and his right arm in a sling with the cast around his wrist. The dark circles around his eyes made him look drawn and sickly. He was ghastly pale. Brice regretted insisting he be at this meeting.

Jack was aware of everyone's eyes upon him, as they studied his injured body and the sympathetic gazes made him feel uncomfortable.

"Hey," he said with an attempt at a white-toothed, wide grin, "You should see the other guy!"

The audience might have laughed if his smile hadn't been so out of kilter and lopsided. The left side did all right; it was the right side that didn't move. He looked like he belonged in a mental ward, not there, standing in front of a batch of investigators.

Jack caught on right away to their discomfort and said, "All right, all right, so I'm not as funny as Vince Grossman. Give him a hand. You've done a great job, Vince, and contrary to what he is telling you, he has been the person doing the hardest work on the Purple Button Case. I just tag along and take a lot of notes. His eyes went over the men at the table and settled on Vic, laughed and said, "All right, so I don't take the notes, my cohort, --Jack used the word cohort intentionally-, Vic is the note taker. He gets upset when I take credit for what he does."

Jack was not smiling as he continued with, "I am going to make this short. We are all here today to catch a serial killer. The very word's serial killer puts the fear of God into all human beings. They strike without warning, and they are hard to catch. The history of a serial killer means just what it says, multiple deaths, and as we all know, some of them never get caught. To catch a serial killer means we have to step outside the box, we have to use methods that we are not accustomed to using; we have to be as innovative as the person doing the crime, and we have to be even more determined than he or she is. We cannot afford to assume anything nor sleep while he is awake, and we don't know when that will be."

Jack pressed a CD into the VCR/DVD player, picked up the remote off the table, turned toward the television, and pressed the select button. A picture appeared on the screen.

"We have two more. These two have not been identified yet. We don't even know where they are. These pictures were sent to us by their killer. How kind of him to keep us up to date" Jack inserted caustically. "These two pictures are new. We just received them."

Jack said nothing more. He shuffled his way slowly to the back of the room and sat back down.

The assembly of men sat quietly for a long time as they studied the pictures on the television screen. Brice allowed time for all of this to sink in before he rose to speak.

"Gentlemen, we have a problem that needs resolution. These deaths are unrequited. We have to catch the person who took these girls' lives before we can sleep one more night. Doug was correct when he said the killer would strike again. He has struck again; now there are four. I have something else you need to see. I think what I am about to show you is related, in one way or the other."

Brice removed Jack's CD and put in another. He turned off the interior lights; the only light remaining came from the television set. The CD displayed a sequence of pictures starting with the first victim to the last taken from the CD Jack had received from the killer and the ones delivered to Brice. However, there was more; lots more because next and very unexpectedly, showing, in full hue, were the pictures of Jack and Tracy together; the ones he had given Brice and included was the note from the killer, and last but not least, pictures of Jack's house burning to the ground. Jack sat silently watching; sweat was visible on his brow; his jaw was tightly gnarled, and it wasn't from pain. When he could no longer stand to view what was happening on the television screen, he prodded Vic and nodded his head toward the back exit door. He hadn't been prepared for this; he was visibly fuming.

Brice had been watching Jack, and when Jack moved, so did he. He switched off the television and said, "Let's get working on this, folks, all of this is somehow related. We need to get this solved before things get worse. The person who is doing this is sending a message. I want to know what it is. I want him found. If you want copies of these CD's talk to Jamie, he'll get it done."

Jack stood up and worked his way slowly out of the room toward the back door. He had no desire to speak to anyone. Brice was one step ahead of him. He had made his way unhindered and quickly to the back door and was standing there, his arms crossed in front of him, intentionally blocking Jack's exit. Buchanan's concern for Jack was enormous, and he didn't want Ireland leaving the building without some indication on how Jack was responding to what he had just put him through.

Jack was quick and concise with his reaction.

"That was quite a display, if you ask me. I'm surprised you didn't have the press sitting at the sidelines, watching this disclosure. You might as well have. By the way, you left out the tape recording I received, why did you withhold the tape, Brice? If you were intending to give it all to them at the expense of yours truly, why didn't you give them the whole damned business?"

Brice met Jack's fierce gaze with equal might. He stood his ground firmly almost casually. This wasn't the first time these two men had gone toe-to-toe. Brice wasn't Jack's boss because he had a pretty face. He was Jack's boss because when push came to shove, Brice never capitulated. Brice at no time made a move, especially where his job was concerned, when he didn't know exactly why he was doing what he was doing. This time was no exception. Brice was fully aware of how the pictures were going to affect Jack, and he wasn't disappointed, not at all. In fact, quite the opposite, he was pleased.

"I didn't ask you nor am I going to ask you how I should handle this investigation. I am going to tell you that you might want to consider going home and getting some rest. You are no good to me in your present condition. I don't want to see your face until after the New Year. If I see you, I am going to fire you, and that is no threat, it is a promise."

As Brice was turning to walk away, Jack said, "I think you told me the same thing in about the same words yesterday morning." Jack fired back. "You told me to be here, and so here I am. You flashed the picture of what is left of my home, the rest was necessary and fine but why my house, why did you bring that in before I had a chance to go out there myself and take a look around? What home are you talking about, exactly? I don't have a home to go to, you know it, and I know it and now, thanks to you, so does everyone else involved in this flipping investigation."

"Take care of yourself Ireland, and I mean it and again, I had better not see your face anywhere or hear your name until after the first of the year. If I have to put you on suspension I will." Brice had his back to Jack as he spoke, and then he was gone.

Jack was seething; his head hurt, his shoulder hurt, his wrist was throbbing relentlessly.

"I think you had better get me out of here, Vic, and get me out of here fast. I need some air."

Frank Stiles was, by this time, also standing by the exit door as Jack was negotiating his way out. He was a profiler and part of his job was keeping a close eye on all active participants of any crime situation he was brought into. Jack had gathered his attention. His instincts told him that Jack was a major player in the whole scenario and more than likely in a way that even he wasn't aware of. He had a hunch; he needed to interview Jack.

"I would like to talk to you if you wouldn't mind."

Stiles had been the only person included in the special team's unit who hadn't put in his two cents' worth. Jack found something in this to value. Jack's mind was getting a bit distorted from the pain that was coursing through his body. Every square inch of his body was protesting his movements. He was desperately fighting off the onslaught of nausea.

"Sure, here's my card, use my cell phone number; I don't have a land line any longer. It's temporarily out of service."

Vic was following Jack as they left the building, he noticed his friend start to stagger a bit.

"Are you all right buddy? You look like you are about ready to take a long nap."

"I'm not doing worth a shit."

Jack was chalky white and sweating profusely. His face was beaded with perspiration, and the hair around his temples was swirling into cute little ringlets.

Vic grabbed Jack around the waist, hoisting him as they walked toward his car.

"I'll have you back to my place and in bed before you know it. Lord, Jack, don't pass out on me. I need you to hang on for just one minute can you do that? Just three more steps and we're there."

"Sure I can." Jack's speech was barely audible.

Vic could feel Jack slipping out of his arms as he opened up the passenger door. With a final surge of willpower, Jack sat down in the bucket seat of Vic's car and by his own determination not to pass out; he fastened his seat belt.

Vic got behind the steering wheel, started the engine. He pressed the gas pedal to the floor and peeled out of the parking lot, leaving a long line of rubber behind him.

"Very funny Vic; very funny" Jack murmured as he fell into a dead sleep. By the time Vic arrived in Hastings Jack's color had returned to normal. He carefully tucked Jack into bed in the guest room not bothering to remove his clothes, closed the door, picked up the phone and called Tory.

"Can you come over? I'll fix you dinner." The clock on his mantel told him it was noon. It had already been a long day.

He slept in his chair until he heard the doorbell ring. Tory was the one who fixed dinner, and then they went to bed. Jack never stirred for the next twenty-four hours.

Chapter Thirty-Six

Grandma was sitting in her recliner, reading a magazine when Kirsti came down the stairs. She walked over to her grandmother and gave her a kiss on the cheek. Her grandma granted her a beaconing smile and pointed for her to sit down on the couch. Grandma was on the phone. The couch had to be at least a hundred years old if it was a day. Everything in Grandma's house was old and worn-out. Kirsti glanced at the floor to ceiling shelves that encircled her grandmother. They were filled with books older than she was; some of them were even older than Grandma.

Surrounding her grandmother's chair were stacks upon stacks of magazines. Grandma referred to them her friends. Kirsti's parents had lived with Grandma until she was fourteen years old. When they bought the adjoining property and moved into a different house, Kirsti had elected to stay with her grandma until she graduated from high school.

The fact of the matter was that Kirsti had always resented not being an only child. She never took kindly to sharing anything with anyone, and the fact that she had seven younger siblings to contend with made her all the more determined to have a special place in one person's life, and her grandmother gave her this. Eugene and Mary went along with this arrangement because it served two purposes. Grandma would not be alone, Kirsti would be content and they, as parents, noted that Kirsti thrived well under Grandma's influence. Kirsti was a well-behaved child, a serious student, and Grandma was more than just a little willing to have her granddaughter under her dominion. Living with Grandma gave Kirsti a distinctive advantage over her siblings because Grandma became her private coach and mentor. Kirsti was a smart and cooperative pupil.

"Your legs look more swollen today, Grandma. Can't the doctors do something for you?"

Grandma suffered from massive varicose veins in both legs. Her ankles were swollen to the size of grapefruits; her legs swollen three times their normal size with thick, protruding black snakelike veins intertwined around her feet, ankles, and calves.

"I sit too much or so I'm told. I'm too stout"—Grandma refused to use the word fat—"so it's hard for me to get around like I should. I hardly eat anything. I should be as thin as a rail for what little I eat."

Grandma was always lamenting about her weight; those closest to her knew it wasn't how little she ate but more in keeping with how often she ate, and what she ate. Kirsti observed that she had a large glass of buttermilk sitting on a small table next to her recliner.

"I am going to fix you something to eat."

Watching Grandma struggling as she tried to hoist herself out of her chair was a painful sight to behold. Kirsti felt the need to help her, but she knew from experience that Grandma would only wave her away. Grandma didn't take kindly to people offering her assistance if she hadn't asked for it. When she had finally managed to accomplish the grueling task of standing up and correcting her balance, she walked slowly and stiffly to the kitchen, motioning for Kirsti to follow her. She seemed to be getting more hunched over with each passing day.

She ran her fingers through her fine gray-white hair as she plopped herself heavily into her worn-out wooden chair. Grandma had had this chair, at this same table, since the day Kirsti was born. The tablecloth, also predating Kirsti, was covered with a clear plastic sheet, now yellow with age. The plastic had patches of tape over various cuts and holes caused by knives and forks over the many years of usage. It wasn't as though Grandma didn't have newer tablecloths or clear plastic because Yvonne and Lynne were always trying to improve Grandma's ambiance. She had lots of them, all folded up neatly and stored in the closet right along with every other birthday present and Christmas present she had received over the past fifty years. Every room in her house, upstairs and down, were packed to the rafters with items still new in the box that she had been given overtime. It wasn't as though she was ungrateful because she wasn't. She was very grateful for any gifts she received from her family and friends, but she had come through the Depression and was saving all of these things for a rainy day.

"I need your mother to come down and fix my hair. She is the only one who can do it the way I like it. I miss your mother, I never see her anymore."

This wasn't true, but this was Grandma, she was always complaining about one thing or another. Grandma was a brilliant woman, razor-sharp, interested, and interesting. She had been and still was active in civic affairs and church activities, most of which she chaired, but she was always lonely. She wrapped herself for some inexplicable reason in loneliness and needless, unending, and unproductive worry. She seemed to have made up her mind somewhere along the line that to be happy and to be satisfied was the ultimate undoing of mankind and though the world might find some sort of bliss in life; she wasn't going to be a participant in anything that required having fun. She had no time for silliness and yet, diabolically, she encouraged others to have fun.

"Laugh," she would say, "Laugh! Start every day with a good laugh and a song. You will feel better if you do."

Her knowledge of human nature was considered by some as paranormal. What these persons failed to consider in the equation was that Grandma had spent all of her lifetime studying human behavior. To find the truth in this, would be to notice that every book she owned and all the books she read had something to do with enlightening herself to the how comes and why's of human history and civilization, or lack of. This is what made her a leader in her community. She knew what made people tick. She knew how to motivate people into doing something they ordinarily wouldn't do or didn't think they could. She believed that right could prevail over wrong and that right should always be studied and applied daily. She could be stiff and stern, and yet she has an extra-ordinary capacity to be liberal-minded.

"Grandma, I don't want anything to eat, I am not hungry, so please don't trouble yourself with cooking anything on my account."

Kirsti may as well have been talking to the wall, the refrigerator, or nobody.

"I'm going to fix us a good cup of coffee and something to eat and that's all there is to it" was Grandma's predictable and all too familiar reply, "So sit down and visit with me now."

"Sit," Grandma commanded. Kirsti sat.

Grandma took some bacon out of her forty-year-old refrigerator and got it frying over medium heat in her century-old cast-iron frying pan on her century-old stove. She put the coffee on to boil, no electric coffee pots for her. She took out the loaf of bread that was stored in a bottom drawer of her century-old cupboards. She made some toast after the bacon was done frying and cut up a grapefruit. She made enough for both of them. The breakfast was delicious. Grandma could make a plain tuna sandwich something to remark about. The coffee was rich and full flavored, the bacon fried to perfection, extra crispy. The toast was probably made with special bread; Grandma favored the German variety and the butter specially blended probably with a bit of honey. The grapefruit was fresh and sweet. Grandma believed that eating was a social affair not just a thing to do to fill up your stomach and be done with it.

Grandma kept the conversation light while they ate. She was a believer in not disturbing the digestive system with a lot of heavy conversations while eating; meals were supposed to be enjoyed. They talked about food, they talked about the upcoming fashions, they talked about books, and they talked about famous people. When they had finished eating, Kirsti cleaned off the table and did the dishes while Grandma made another pot of coffee.

After she had the coffee set up and was waiting for it to boil, Grandma sat down in her chair, and as she stared out her kitchen window, she said with hint of melancholic reflection, "Not much has changed around here in the last fifty years. The buildings are in need of some repair, but they have held up well, thanks to your father and your brothers constantly paying attention to them. I don't know how I would have managed without your dad after your grandpa passed away. He is exceptionally bright, you know. He would have done much more with his life had he not had so many responsibilities as a youngster."

Kirsti knew her father was bright; she had heard this a thousand times if she had heard it once. Grandma worshiped her only son. In her eyes, he could do no wrong. She never tired of telling anyone who crossed her path about how bright a child Eugene was. "Why, he was so smart they passed him through two grades, second and third. He could read when he was three and would have graduated valedictorian of his class had he not had to miss six months of his senior year. He was sick for part of that time, very sick, he almost died, you know, and then he had to help out with the farm. Eugene didn't have it easy, you know. Grandpa was way too hard on him. He expected too much from him. In spite of all of this adversity he graduated salutatorian."

"Grandma, you have mentioned this to me before, can we possibly talk about something other than Dad?" Kirsti was mad at her father and that Grandma was taking this course in conversation was irritating her.

"I had a rough time of it with your grandfather. He was a determined man with many ideas that didn't coincide with mine. We came from opposite sides of the world, you know. He was a good man, but he was harsh. His upbringing was harsh. I was raised in a world of the more genteel. My family never agreed with my marriage to your grandfather. My father was especially adverse to the thought that I would marry a 'lowly' farmer." Eventually, things worked out, but it took time. In time, my family came around to accepting things and even liked to come out here for a visit, but this didn't change things between me and your grandfather. He and I had a controversial relationship; we were not well suited for each other. We had some happy moments, but we could never seem to agree on anything. We had horrible fights. I would not want to relive those moments."

Grandma's eyes became vague and distant, as though she were viewing something or someone far away, "He never understood me. I understood him, but he never tried to understand me. He had no patience you know. Your father is a lot like him. He has no patience either."

"Did you love him? You must have loved him some to have stayed with him."

Grandma's eyes narrowed to small slits, her mouth tightened into a straight line, "Marriage isn't always about love, Kirsti. Love is for the wide-eyed innocent. Our purpose is more about taking responsibility than it will ever be about love. I hold a deep respect for your grandfather, but to say I ever loved him would not be my way of describing it. I learned to cope with him and how to coexist with him. I learned many things by being married to him, but love was not one of them. You have to remember, Kirsti, these were different times. Divorce was completely out of the question. My family would have disowned me entirely. Society did not tolerate this behavior. I would have lost everything, including myself-respect. I would have been regarded as a loose woman. I would have become a social outcast. No, Kirsti, no self-respecting woman would have ever considered divorce as a solution to their marital problems. I never considered divorce as an option. I had to learn to get along."

Grandma looked out the kitchen window again and said quietly, "But he was a good man, incredibly intelligent, and well regarded by the community. Things might have been different had his mother not had to live with us. She was an impossible woman and was constantly interfering and causing problems for me. Your grandfather always took her side, which made life very difficult for me."

Kirsti was getting uncomfortable with the way this conversation was going. She was an idealist, and Grandma was telling her things that didn't fit her image of her grandfather. She wanted to escape this conversation, badly.

"What exactly are you getting at, Grandma?"

"I talked to Eugene this morning. He's not very happy with you right now."

Grandma gave Kirsti a shrewd once-over, "He told me about the fight that you, and he had before you came down here."

Kirsti's defense mechanisms kicked into high gear.

"I should have known he would call you. I should have known he would tattle to his mommy. The very man who hates tattling of any sort calls his mom instantly, how, and oh, so very hypocritical of him." Kirsti was literally spitting out her words; her face was flushed with self-righteous indignation.

Grandma rose from her chair, Kirsti was getting out of hand, but Grandma knew how to manage her granddaughter. She had a lot of experience with Kirsti's little tantrums and quick with the tongue retorts.

"That's pure nonsense. Your father is right, now settle down. You have a lot to think about at this particular moment in your life, and you are not going to get this done by defying the people who love you. You will stop this defiant business right now, or I will see to it. You and I have things to discuss. Your rampage isn't going to make life any easier for you or for me, so be silent."

Grandma slowly and deliberately left the kitchen and went back to her recliner, leaving Kirsti alone, for the time being. She knew that Kirsti would, in due course, come into the living room and join her. Kirsti had always shared her every thought with Grandma, this time would be no different; Grandma knew Kirsti better than Kirsti knew herself. What had happened between Jack and Kirsti came as no major surprise to either her or Eugene. They had had their misgivings right from the beginning. If anyone had Grandma's sympathy right now it was Jack, not Kirsti.

Kirsti's mind was in a swirl. The last thing she wanted or needed was to have an argument with her grandmother. Grandma was not wrong; they did have lots to talk about. She had invaded her grandmother in the middle of the night. Without any need for explanation, her grandmother had taken her in and given her sanctuary.

Kirsti sat for a long time, thinking about the previous night. She had been in an emotional state of mind when she had returned to her parents' house with her mother. She had never been this distraught or at least not that she could remember. Her mother had been appeasing, but her father wasn't. He was up waiting for his wife to return. He had been totally surprised to see Kirsti following her mother into the house, and he hadn't been exactly pleased to see her; the expression on his face made words unnecessary. Her father had been even less delighted when she told him that she was through with Jack. She had tried to explain to her father that she was tired of playing the role of second fiddle to Jack's job and his life. She detested his job, and she hated that she was always excluded from the major part of his life. She was tired of him, and she was tired of their marriage, for whatever that was worth; she was done, finished, and there was nothing he could say to change her mind. She told her father, she could never be married to a man who would deliberately lie to her, and Jack had lied by omission. Jack should have forewarned her about the danger on Christmas Eve. He hadn't told her anything; he had just left her there at the farm.

Her father had laughed at her. He hadn't only laughed at her but told her she was acting irrationally. She was insulted by his mirth, which she considered caustic, and his insinuations. When she knew she wasn't going to be granted anything but a fight to the finish, she grabbed her only belongings left after the fire, her purse, and stomped down the hill to her grandma's house. Grandma had been sitting in her chair, watching the early morning news, when she came banging through the door. Grandma had said nothing as Kirsti stormed up the stairs to her old bedroom at five o'clock in the morning.

Kirsti heard the chime of the mantel clock. Her grandparents' century-old, very faithful mantel clock which had been chiming since the day Kirsti was born and had since that time sat on top of a shelf in Grandma's kitchen, just above the double door leading into the dining room. She whistled the tune in her head as the clock rang out the tone of its own music ending with three distinctive gongs. Grandma was sitting in her living room, waiting for her.

Grandma held a tacit alertness as Kirsti entered the living room. She held her stillness as Kirsti situated herself, once again, on the overstuffed maroon velvet sofa; only this time, her granddaughter didn't sit down, she laid down, pulling a multicolored afghan from the back of the couch, wrapping herself into it from head to toe.

"I am sorry, Grandma, I have no place else to go, can I stay here for a while? I need some place to call home. I promise I will make peace with Dad, but I cannot go back to Jack right now. I can't do that. You have got to help me, Grandma. I feel so alone. My life is such a mess." Tears filled her soft blue eyes. "I'm tired, Grandma, I want to go to sleep. I don't want to think about this anymore."

Grandma forced herself out of her chair and went to her dearly beloved granddaughter. She revealed no emotion when she said, "Hush now. Dry your tears and sleep. There is nothing that needs to be done right now."

She gathered another blanket from the closet that adjoined her bathroom. With arms that ached from rheumatoid arthritis, she covered her granddaughter, tucking the blanket tightly around her. She sat back into her recliner, exhausted from the efforts of the day. She picked up the phone, called her son, and said, "She's sleeping. The poor girl is exhausted. How awful this is for her. Of all things to have to happen, why is this happening to her?"

"No, don't come down now, I think she is going to need a day, Eugene. I hope she sleeps until morning."

The early sun was dawning when Kirsti awoke. As she gathered her senses, she noticed that she was sleeping on Grandma's couch. Upon further glancing, she noticed that Grandma was sound asleep in her recliner. Kirsti was moved that her grandma had stood vigilant over her all night long. She was in need of a shower and was in desperate need of a toothbrush. Her mouth felt like the bottom of a bird cage, and she was uncomfortable with her odor. She had slept in her clothes, twice, and they reeked of body odor, stale perfume, and cigarette smoke. Her mood shifted immediately from bright to dour when her mind registered that she had no change of clothing or a toothbrush or toothpaste, which reminded her that what she was wearing were probably the only material possessions she had now. This reminded her of the fire and the fire reminded her of Jack, and thinking about Jack made her furious again.

"Hello, is anyone up yet?" It was Mary. She was carrying three different plastic bags containing everything Kirsti would need to get her day started off on the right foot.

Mary hugged her daughter and said, "I brought you several changes of clothing, makeup, blow drier, and a curling iron, toothpaste and toothbrush—I think I thought of everything."

"Oh, Mom, you are totally magnificent! You have just saved my day. Let me see what you brought." Kirsti was already removing items from the plastic bags. "These will do just fine, it's a good thing we wear the same size and have the same taste. You are a lifesaver." She gave her mom a big hug and then was gone.

"Grandma, did you sleep in that chair all night?" Grandma was now wide-awake but a little disoriented. "You did, didn't you? You have a bed just around the corner, but you slept in that broken down old lounger. We need to do something about getting you a new chair." Mary was as practiced at scolding as her mother-in-law was. "Sleeping in that recliner is not good for your back."

"No one needs to do anything about my stuff. Don't get any such notions. I am so glad to see you Mary. You never come and visit me anymore. I don't suppose you could give me a haircut and style it for me? I look terrible."

"Sure, I can fix your hair for you," Mary said compliantly.

Mary grew wary of Grandma's physical stability as she followed her into the kitchen, "Grandma, you need to start using your walker. One of these days, you're going to fall, break a bone, and wind up in the hospital. You can't afford a broken bone at your age. I don't want to scare you, but it wouldn't take a lot for you to wind up in a nursing home. You know it, and I know it, so be careful and use the walker Yvonne got for you."

"Eugene told me about the fire. I think it might be wise for Kirsti to stay here with me for a while." Grandma was intentionally changing the subject. "I always use my walker, I just didn't this time."

As Mary ran a comb gently through her mother-in-law's soft white hair, she said in words barely above a whisper, "I am afraid that is how things might have to be for now. Where's your walker, Grandma? I want you to use it while I wash your hair at the sink."

Grandma couldn't remember.

Chapter Thirty-Seven

The Crawford and Crawford law firm had always thrown an annual Christmas party for their employees and clients on New Year's Eve. Ordinarily, the party was held at one of the better hotels in downtown Minneapolis, but this year, Kirsti had persuaded Samuel Crawford to have the party at the Orchard Lake Country Club. At first, Samuel had been adverse to the idea because he didn't want any of the guests to drink and drive. He had always provided a room for each guest to avoid any issues with the strict drinking and driving regulations in the state of Minnesota. Kirsti had countered his reluctance by finding a motel that was near the Orchard Lake Country Club that would provide shuttle service. Hannah and Joe had offered a deal that Sam simply couldn't refuse, and the total cost of the rooms was considerably less as well.

Patti, Samuel's personal secretary, attended to every detail of this event—as she had for the past twenty-some some years—right down to the color of the napkins. Patti could gather butterflies for a group picture if she set her mind to it. She was without any doubt Samuel Crawford's greatest asset where his law firm was concerned and his right arm in all matters concerning him. He relied on her almost exclusively to steer him when he needed steering. She was his best friend and closest confidant. Their birthdays were on the same day and of the same year. Samuel would have married Patti long ago and vice versa if it weren't for the fact that she already had a husband that she loved more than she loved Sam.

Kirsti hadn't seen or heard from Jack since Christmas. He was, she had heard, living with Vic. She had made no attempt to call him; she had made up her mind that when he was ready, he could call her. She had no intentions of calling him first, none. It was, after all, not she that had created the problems in their marriage. If there were going to be amends made, they would have to come from his side, not hers.

She hadn't gone to see the damage done to what she now referred too as Jack's house. She was told the house was gone, so what was the point. She was working hard at avoiding any further unpleasantness. She had made it clear to everyone willing to listen that she needed "time to heal." No one pressed her. She spent what little idle time she had shopping with her mother or Maggie. Hilde refused to shop with Kirsti. She had sworn off these activity years ago, and Glenda was back in Oklahoma. Glenda wouldn't have gone shopping with her either for the same reason as Hilde's. Shopping with Kirsti demanded a lot of time and excruciating stamina. Kirsti would travel from store to store and could and very well might take a whole day just deciding on a pair of socks. Neither Glenda nor Hilde had the wherewithal or the desire to endure what they referred to as the torture treatment. Kirsti had to bribe Maggie to go along after their first excursion, promising to buy her lunch. The girl just loved to eat.

Maggie and Kirsti were the first to arrive at the Orchard Lake Country Club for the Christmas Party. Maggie had been hired by Crawford and Crawford to replace a girl who had decided to be a stay-at-home mom after her baby was born. Maggie, with her sparkling, intellectual wit, fit in well at the law firm. Jerry had hired her as a Girl Friday a couple of months after Kirsti first met her. She sorted and delivered mail and took on the boring task of filing with an unusual amount of enthusiasm. She kept the coffee flowing and assisted willingly anyone who needed her. Even Reed, who liked and trusted no one, had warmed to her. She was the only one in the office who could put him down and get by with it. She didn't pick on him often, but when she did, she made it count and generally in a manner steeped in sarcasm. She had a clear, uptight, and personal feeling about the difference between idle chiding and deliberate insults. She had been on the brunt end of the latter all of her life. She wasn't the least bit fooled by Reed's insufferable arrogance. She had quipped to Jerry and Kirsti that he was nothing more than a shy little lamb in wolf clothing. She stood alone in this assessment because everyone else in the office viewed him as a weasel in wolf clothing.

Hannah was standing by the back bar when Kirsti and Maggie arrived arm and arm. Hannah and Kirsti hugged each other, and then Kirsti introduced Maggie to Hannah. Kirsti looked around, taking in every inch of the room. She couldn't believe her eyes. Every inch, nook, and cranny spoke of a New Year's celebration, including the bartenders and waitresses donned in black-and-white with gold-littered vests and black top hats.

"You have done a wonderful job, Hannah, the place looks absolutely exquisite."

"My thanks should go out to you for landing this one for us, Kirsti. Joe is really appreciative. He gave me full rein without his usual whining. "Spare no expense, he said because this party will be our last. Let's go out in style!"

"How is the old goat anyway? Is he here?"

"He's doing a lot better, looking forward to retirement. I don't know if I am, though. He said he was coming, but he didn't say when other than he wants to be here for last call. I didn't encourage him to come; he needs to relax for a while. A heart attack can slow a guy down. I was glad to be working during his recovery. He was a bear to deal with after the surgery. I left that job up to his mother who knows exactly how to handle him."

Kirsti smiled sympathetically. "When does the new owner take over?"

"Right after this party actually. Tomorrow morning, we get the cash, and they get the keys."

Kirsti hugged Hannah again. "What are you and Joe going to do with yourselves after tomorrow?"

"Joe bought a motor home. I guess we're going to travel. He wants to go out to California and spend a little time with our son and then east in the spring to visit our daughter in New York. We are planning on leaving in a week. After that, who knows?"

"Well, everything looks wonderful, Hannah. Maggie and I have to go back to the motel and change. Are you going to be hanging around all evening?"

Hannah gave Kirsti her infamous toothy grin and said, "Now, Kirsti, would I be anywhere else? I wouldn't miss this party for the world. Remember, this is my last hurrah! Joe and I will be on the dance floor at midnight. You will know us when you see us. I will be the one celebrating the loudest and hopefully making a general fool out of myself. Joe can't drink, but I can, and I intend to. Tonight, we are leaving the party in the trustworthy hands of our staff. Don't be surprised if they don't do a bit of celebrating as well."

"I want to say hello to Budrick, is he working tonight?"

Hannah's face dropped into a sorrowful frown, "No, Kirsti, his wife passed away yesterday. He begged off, understandably. He didn't think it would be appropriate."

"Considering the circumstances, that's gracious of him. She was awful to Budrick. How he tolerated her all of these years is beyond me. I should think he would be dancing in the streets. Even Grandma who will not say a bad word about anyone said she was 'contrary'. If that aint an understatement, I don't know what is!"

"Kirsti, sometimes your bluntness is downright unsettling. Now get out of here, I have to make my final rounds before the party starts."

The parking lot was filled when Kirsti and Maggie arrived two hours later. Kirsti wasn't part of the planning committee, so she had no idea how many guests had been invited, the rumor was well over 250 people. She recognized some of the faces, those she worked with, but many were unfamiliar to her. Men came in dressed in their black tuxedos, white shirts, and black bow ties; the women in long gowns in a captivating array of styles and colors.

Jerry Lucas was the first to greet the girls when they entered. He looked at them both, up and down, from top to bottom, and back up again, "Wow, you girls look absolutely gorgeous tonight."

Kirsti had selected a clean-cut, formfitting, floor-length strapless gown of a gold-shimmering lightweight silk material with a matching shawl. She was wearing the diamond necklace and earrings she had received from Jack as a Christmas gift. She had gold glitter sprinkled in her hair and lightly powdered on her freckled face and tips of her long eyelashes.

"I have been waiting for you and Maggie. I have a table reserved for us over near the dance floor, if that's OK. Adam is holding down the fort." Jerry gave Kirsti a wink. Everyone in the office knew that Adam had a huge crush on Maggie.

Maggie noticed the wink but made no comment. She liked Adam. "Lead on, dear boy, lead on."

Adam stood up as they approached the ornately decorated table. "Maggie, you look absolutely stunning!" Adam gushed, nearly tipping over a glass of water in his haste to pull a chair out for her.

Her long brown hair flowed down in casual waves to the middle of her back. The lighting in the room brought out the soft red highlights. Kirsti had helped her apply her make up. Maggie had a flawless complexion, requiring only a light touch of powder for a perfect look. A bit of mascara to her long, thick lashes and a touch of eyeliner to the corner of her lids gave depth to her dark brown eyes. The gown she wore was also strapless, black and of a soft-flowing velvet material. The gown fit tight at the bodice and waist then draped loosely to just below the ankle, complimenting her ample, lush figure. She wore a diamond-shaped black onyx pendant around her neck with matching earrings. *She did look stunning*, Kirsti thought approvingly.

"Well, thank you, Adam, you look mighty attractive yourself. I only hope I can get through the evening without ripping out the seams in this getup. Remind me never to go shopping with Kirsti again. My feet still hurt. I believe we hit every shop in the metro area three times before we found this dress, and I am still not convinced this is the right garment for me, but most all of this is completely out of my element." She waved her arm taking in the room. "This ghastly get-up cost me two weeks pay, and I'll probably only wear it once."

Maggie plucked at the sides of her dress in despair. "This thing is so tight that I'm afraid to inhale, let alone eat. I think I need a drink. Adam would you get me a vodka tonic with a twist of lime?"

Adam rose from his chair, bowed, and said, "I am at your service, madam. Does anyone else want a drink while I am flying and buying?"

Kirsti ordered the same, Jerry put in an order for a bottle of beer, claiming no preference. After Adam returned with the drinks, the foursome lifted their glasses to Jerry's toast. "Here's to friendship, now let the games begin."

Dinner was served at precisely eight o'clock. After the dishes were cleared off the table, Samuel got up and spoke to his employees and esteemed guests. He thanked all of them for another successful year. As he spoke to his audience, the waiters and waitresses passed around neatly wrapped gifts to all the guests.

"The gifts that you have now received are of personal importance, thus I am going to insist that you do not open them until you get home. Anyone who breaches this humble request will have to buy everyone drinks for the rest of the evening. So please, someone open their gift!" The crowd broke into laughter and thunderous applause.

"I now want to introduce the group who will be entertaining you for the rest of the evening. Please welcome the Roving Cowboys." The leader of the band made the proper introductions, took a bow, and opened their performance with "Bed of Roses" made famous by the Statler Brothers. This was definitely going to be a country and Western night, which would and did remind Kirsti of Jack. This would have been their first New Year's evening together, and he wasn't around.

"Would someone please ask me to dance?" She directed this edict straight toward Jerry, who was caught entirely off guard. He had wanted to, but he wasn't so sure, by reading her present facial expression, that she would even be willing had he asked her.

As Jerry held out his hand to take Kirsti to the dance floor, she noticed someone striding briskly toward her. It was Reed. He had his sights set exclusively on Kirsti.

"Oh no, you don't, Jerry. I get the first dance with this girl."

Without any regard or consideration to what Kirsti had to say about any of this, he grabbed her firmly by the hand and dragged her out to the dance floor. She felt herself being swept up in his arms, and soon she was moving stride for stride with the man who was holding her tightly against him. He carried her with a force that startled her, holding her unfalteringly, guiding her, and controlling her every movement. He danced rapidly, confidently, and by design, staying in perfect rhythm with the music. He seemed to be challenging her to keep up. His method of dancing became more complicated with each circle around the dance floor, but she followed him anyway, knowing that if she made a miss-step, he would ridicule her with those luminous blue eyes. Before she could think these actions all the way through, the song was over. The band had stopped and so had they. Reed held her firmly against him as he called out, "Kirsti and I request one more spin, and give us a slow one please."

Kirsti attempted to rip herself away from Reed as the band began to play "Sentimental Journey," but Reed held on to her, his strong arms wrapped around her, his body pressed intimately against hers. He hummed the song suggestively into her ear as he moved her gracefully around the dance floor. He placed his lips to her ears and whispered, "Don't fight me, Kirsti; enjoy the moment. You and I could make beautiful music together. I want you, I need you, and honestly I think I love you." Kirsti knew he was teasing her. Reed was totally incapable of loving anyone, let alone wanting or needing anyone.

His bold words startled her and made her extremely uncomfortable. She didn't want to be the laughing stock of her group. Kirsti glanced toward her table and sure enough, Maggie and Jerry were grinning from ear to ear. She tried even harder to pull herself away from Reed and make her escape, but to no avail; his hold on her was too inflexible and not until the he had her where he wanted her, did he release her. He escorted her back to her table, bowed, and said, "Until next time, and there will be a next time, Kirsti. You can count on it." He looked at her boldly in the eyes, turned on his heel, and disappeared into the crowd.

Jerry was standing, looking very perplexed, as Kirsti sat down at the table, "What was that all about?" He had seen something in Reeds eyes that he didn't like.

"I am not quite sure," Kirsti responded, equally perplexed. "Well, never mind anyway, I think I need to sit for a moment. This dress is making me hot, and the air around here is getting sticky."

Maggie had caught the look too, but she wasn't confused nor was she perplexed.

"I think Reed has been bitten by the lust bug and not by Andrea. I would say love, but I don't think Reed is capable of loving anyone, and it isn't your dress that is making you hot nor is the air in here getting sticky, Kirsti. Reed has had his eye on you for a long time."

Jerry was stunned by what Maggie had just said. He needed some fresh air. He quickly excused himself and left.

"What in the world is the matter with Jerry? He looks ill."

Maggie seized Kirsti's arm as she went to follow him, "Leave him alone, Kirsti. He needs to be alone right now."

"Why? Is he sick? I need to know what's going on. If Jerry is ill, I'll take him home." Kirsti's innocent, lovely face was overflowing with genuine concern.

Maggie was torn between anger and sympathy for Kirsti. Never in her short life had she ever met anyone as utterly egocentric as

Kirsti nor anyone more naïve. Her tunneled vision was downright maddening.

"If you can't see what's happening here, Kirsti, I have to wonder the virtue of explaining it to you."

Soon Jerry returned, back to his usual, cheerful self. He asked Kirsti to dance, and away they went. Adam shyly requested a dance with Maggie, and away they went. Maggie liked Adam; she liked her job; she was starting to like herself. She was, however, wishing she hadn't said what she had said. She might have opened up a kettle of worms that she couldn't close back up again. Kirsti didn't need any more male distractions than she already had. And most certainly Maggie didn't want her friend's attention heading towards Reed.

At eleven forty-five, the waiters and waitresses placed hats, noisemakers, and graffiti in front of each guest. Kirsti and Maggie helped each other get their hats on and then did the same for Jerry and Adam. As the clock was ticking down to midnight, there came a rumble of voices from the direction of the front entrance. Maggie turned to see what the noise was all about, and what she saw caused her to do a double take. She poked Kirsti in the shoulder and pointed towards the double doors.

Jack Ireland had entered the country club. He was hailing everyone loudly as he passed the first bar; he had obviously been drinking, a lot. He was wearing a black tux; his bow tie was dangling from his shirt collar. His wavy hair was slicked back from his forehead; if there were a man more handsome on the face of this earth or entire universe, for that matter, Maggie couldn't imagine who that would be. Jack's keen eyes cursorily reviewed the large dining hall as he entered. He was perceptibly searching for someone in particular. That person had to be Kirsti. When his eyes found her, he beamed.

He gave Maggie a friendly greeting and then took his wife by the hand. His gorgeous smile would have melted an iceberg as he said, "Hi, darling, looks like I am a little late for the party. I thought you and I should have the last dance of this year together. I have come to take you home."

Kirsti was nothing short of flabbergasted to see her husband standing before her, but she was not quite so impressed with his disarming good looks or his charm as everybody else seemed to be.

She yanked her hand away from him like he had touched her with a hot iron.

She was seething as she said, "You have no right to be here. Who do you think you are to come waltzing in here like this and assume anything? I have no intention of going anywhere with you, not now, not ever! How dare you, you are not invited to this party, so please leave."

Kirsti was shouting, trying to make her voice heard over the noise of the band, "My last waltz for this year will be with Jerry, and then I will be leaving with Maggie. So you might just as well turn around and go back the same way you came. I don't want you here, and I don't want you in my life, so go away!"

A half-drunk and amused Jack took another step toward his wife. She responded by grabbing an empty beer bottle by the neck from the table and thrust it toward him as though it were a sword. When he did nothing more than laugh at her, she started yelling at him again to back away and leave, but he was by now completely enthralled as to how all of this was going to end and had no intentions of backing off.

The band had discontinued playing because everyone had quit dancing. All eyes and ears were on Jack and Kirsti. Reed was standing next to Andrea with a sly grin on his face. He was enjoying the show. Samuel was looking at the spectacle with complete bewilderment, and was not quite sure how to handle the prevailing situation. He sat back and decided to wait, with one eye on Jack and the other on Reed.

Jack grabbed Kirsti around the waist and picked her up. He looked at the band and said, "This is my wife, and if she is going to leave me forever, how about a song for the two of us? 'Auld Lang Syne' will do nicely." The timing seemed to be perfect; it was ten seconds until the clock would strike midnight.

The leader of the band brought Hanna and Joe up on stage to do the countdown, and with gusto, the band began to play the infamous year-ending Scottish melody. Soon the dance floor was crowded with couples. When the song was over, Jack leaned down and kissed Kirsti hard on the mouth, "Happy New Year, darling."

Kirsti accepted his kiss awkwardly and without emotion. She did not hug him, and she didn't kiss him back.

"I have to go now, Jack." Tears were glistening in the corner of her eyes.

Jack held her tightly for a moment longer, and then let her go.

"Come home with me, Kirsti. Please."

Kirsti wiped her eyes and took a deep breath before she spoke again.

"I can't, Jack. I wish I could, but I can't. You shouldn't have come here. All of this is very romantic, and before my life with you, I might have been impressed, but I know better now. You have a life that is yours, and you deserve it. I want things from you that you will never be able to grant me because I want you and only you, not your job and then you. I need a man who can share his life with me and a man who is willing to share mine with him. You can't do that. I know that now."

Kirsti grabbed her purse, collected her coat, and walked out the door, leaving Jack standing in the middle of the dance floor as the band played on. They had one more hour before they would shut down. The crowd was getting louder and more boisterous as the evening wore on. This was an expected behavior and, without difficulty, contributed to a tradition that most all Americans found satisfactory and well deserving. This was a time for celebration that was as engrained in the fabric of American culture with as much significance as the colors of red, white, and blue were engrained into the American flag. And what were people celebrating? Who cared? Anything and everything was a reason for celebration. Pick one. For one brief, fleeting period in time people set aside all of their differences, except Kirsti. Maybe and just possibly had she decided to set aside her differences with Jack that evening life would have turned out differently for her. This would be a thought for the future; right now, Kirsti was living in the instant mode and Jack was not going to be a part of it. Her fury had turned to ill-tempered stubbornness.

Reed was watching Jack and Kirsti; he was smirking and thinking, *Well now, and there now, that's half the battle won.*

"I'm heading home Andrea, you can catch a cab or take the shuttle, makes no difference to me either way."

Reed reached in his pocket for his money clip and extracted a one hundred-dollar bill; he tossed it on the table in front of her, and said snidely, "This should cover your cab."

Andrea had seen this coming. She wasn't the dimwitted blond that Reed had always taken her to be. Indeed she wasn't. She knew that

Reed was after Kirsti and had been for a long time. He thought he wanted her, but in the end, she knew that Reed would probably—for the first time in his life, ever—not get something he wanted. This made her day. She was bored with Reed anyway. He had only been a dalliance to her, and besides, there will always be plenty of other fish in the sea, lots of them, big ones, very big ones. Well, if Kirsti wasn't interested in Jack, maybe she could get to know him better. He was a big fish in a big pond. The man might be in need of some consolation. Not tonight but soon. Give him a few days to recuperate and then make your move. She had no difficulty visualizing herself in Jacks strong arms. Kirsti's loss would be her gain. Let Reed have Kirsti, she was as arrogant and self-centered as he was. They were a perfect match.

Andrea picked up her empty glass and moved toward the front bar. She sat down next to a man she had noticed earlier in the evening. He was cute. His beguiling, and up-turned mouth exposed deep, elongated dimples in both cheeks. His shy green eyes revealed something mysterious, dangerous, and yet so very enticing, especially to a woman who liked living on the edge. His thick blond hair was cut to flatter its pronounced natural wave with a lock that fell casually over his forehead giving him a boyish, disarmingly child-like appeal. He was entertaining the bartender by singing along with the band. He had an exquisite, rich tenor voice that needed no professional to critique. Andrea needed no one to tell her that this stranger sitting beside her had unusual talent. He stopped singing the minute she sat down beside him.

"Don't stop singing on my account, you should be up there on stage, you have a fabulous voice."

The man grinned bashfully, flashing his pronounced dimples, "Thank you. I like to sing, and the Statler Brothers are one my favorite groups. I think I own every album they have ever made. The band is doing a really good job of imitating them. Can I buy you a drink?"

"Sure, I suppose you can, why not? One for the road, what about you? Will you join me?"

"Bartender, please bring this lady a drink."

"I'll take a martini, straight up in a frosted glass. *Please.*" Andrea very rarely said 'please' to anyone.

299

The blonde man stood up. Andrea couldn't help but notice how lacking in height he was. He couldn't be over five feet four, but oh, those eyes of green were so very nice. Andrea was a sucker for compelling eyes.

"Let me introduce myself. My name is Mike. I'm not from around here. I was just passing by, noticed the crowd and, decided to stop in and see what was going on."

Mike reached out his hand to Andrea, who took his into her own small impeccably manicured hand.

"It's a pleasure to meet you, Mike. This is a Crawford and Crawford law firm Christmas party. I didn't think you were one of their employees. I know all the people employed by Crawford and Crawford because I am Reed Crawford's personal secretary."

Andrea lifted her hands and did the quote sign, "I thought you might be a client."

"No," the young man said, his dimples deepening more yet. "I try to shy away from the law, in all capacities. Have you got family around here?"

"No. I moved here from Missouri several years ago. All of my family, what little there is of it, lives out of state. I am one of those proverbial runaways. I haven't seen or spoken to them, since I left. I don't like my family very much, and they certainly don't like me; end of story, I didn't have a favorable childhood."

The blond-haired man placed a twenty dollar bill on the bar and got up to leave.

"I don't have family here either." He glanced at his watch, "I guess it's time for me to get going. It's been nice talking to you."

Andrea was tempted to ask him to stay, but didn't.

"Perhaps we will see each other again?"

The blond man flashed his dimples once more and said, "I am sure we will."

He grabbed his coat from the back of the bar stool and patted Andrea on her shoulder. Andrea kept him in her sights on him until he disappeared into the assembly of people waiting for the shuttle to take them back to their motel rooms. She glanced at the Rolex that Reed had given her for her last birthday. The time was 12:50.

Andrea finished her drink as the bartender gave last call.

"Its hotel/motel time, you don't have to go home, but you can't stay here, last call."

Andrea brushed her long blond hair over her shoulders and made her way back into the dining room. The place was empty. Everyone had left, but the staff. They were busy bustling around, cleaning up the litter left from the party. She gathered up her purse, put on her long sable coat—another gift from Reed—and left by the front entrance. Her car was the only one remaining in the front parking lot. She had come late and it was now extremely dark where her car was located. She was starting to wish she had asked the bartender to escort her. Reed had given her a hundred dollars for taxi. Had he forgotten she had driven, or had he done this simply to insult her?

Andrea was feeling a little tipsy as she made her way to her car. Whew, it is cold, she hated winter in Minnesota. It was miserable to get into a stiffly frozen car in the middle of the night. She was feeling rather unstable. She had never been one to have more than one or two glasses of wine in an evening. She wasn't overtly worried about being picked up for drunken driving until this minute. The drive between the country club and the motel was only a mile. She could negotiate that easily enough. Her thoughts were on the blond, dimpled man as she opened her car door and slid in.

As she pressed the key into the ignition a nagging thought ran across her mind. Had she forgotten to lock the door? She hadn't needed to unlock it. Habits are hard to break; she always habitually locked her car. Who was that cute little man? Andrea wished she had pushed for a phone number. She turned the key and as she did so, she glanced in her rearview mirror. She was terrorized to see a visage other than hers, staring back at her. She had no time to think before she felt strong arms grabbing her, gripping her from behind and a mask being pressed over her nose and mouth. Before blackness enfolded her, she thought she heard a gentle, masculine voice whisper, "*Night, night, Andrea. Sweet dreams.*" The voice sounded hazily familiar.

Chapter Thirth-Eight

Doreen Landers was waiting for Jack. According to her calculations, it seemed as though she had spent one half of her life waiting for him. She had spent New Year's Eve with some of her single friends and had just gotten home when her phone rang. The clock on the wall read 1:36 AM. The call consisted of three words. "I'll be right over." Before she had time to react, the line went dead; she would have said yes anyway because she always said yes to Jack even when she didn't want to or think she should.

Doreen hadn't heard anything from Jack, since he had married Kirsti Poval, and now she had to ask herself why he was coming to see her. Why was he coming this late at night and on New Year's Eve no less? But then she knew the answer; he was coming to see her because she was the one person in his life who would never say no to him. Jack had always come to her first and last over many things with one notable and understandable exception, his marriage to Kirsti, and she didn't have to ask why about that either because she knew the answer. He didn't have the heart to tell her, or so she told herself over and over again. They had been seeing each other on and off for over a decade. She knew Jack, and she loved him unconditionally. Doreen wasn't lacking in male attention and never had been, but Jack was the one that made her heart throb. Jack was the man she wanted. Any idle mention of Jack's name made her weak in the knees. She knew about the fire and had heard rumors that he and Kirsti were having problems in their marriage. She had suffered when she heard the news and read the paper about the fire. She knew how much his home meant to him. She wished she could have been displeased to hear about his marital problems, but she wasn't. She could find no reason to be. Kirsti was her contender.

When she opened the door, Jack was standing there with a bottle of champagne in his left hand, in the other, he was holding his shoulder brace. He seemed to be unaware of the cast wrapped around his right wrist and hand. She had heard the rumors, and she had read the newspaper. She had even ventured out to take a look at his obliterated house. The sight of charred mess had scared her. She had tried frantically to call him but to no avail. Both his cell phone and land line was temporarily out of service. She had finally called Vic, and only after he had reassured her a hundred times that Jack was fine did she stop worrying.

Now here he was, standing at her door, looking mighty pathetic and in need of assistance. Doreen melted to mush when she saw her lover. She grabbed the bottle of champagne, the shoulder brace, and his suit jacket, which was hooked in his belt by the sleeve and trailing behind him like a dirty old rag.

"What in the world are you doing out in this cold weather without a coat, and why don't you have this shoulder brace on, Jack? What in the world is the matter with you?"

"Well, darling 'Happy New Year'. Hi, long time no see" he slurred and that gizmo wouldn't fit under my tux. Here, give it back to me, I'll show you."

Jack swayed a bit as he tried to take the shoulder brace back from Doreen. "How about you open that bottle of wine, fruit of the vine, and you and I can bring in the New Year properly." Jack had, by then, staggered his way into Doreen's living room.

"You're a bona fide mess, aren't you, Jack? I really don't think you need any more to drink."

"True enough, my dove but this boy is going to have another anyway so are you going to do the honors or should I. I have a lot to celebrate. This has been my best year ever!"

"You're in no condition to do anything, Jack, just sit down before you fall and hurt yourself. I don't have the strength or the desire to be picking you up off the floor." She took him by the arm and propelled him to the couch. "You sit, I'll pour."

Doreen popped the top of the bottle like an expert, filled each glass to the top, *Why not?* for each of them; she then handed one to

Jack, lifted hers to her lovely mouth, took a sip, and said, "So, Jack, here's to those who wish us well, those who don't can go to hell; Happy New Year." She put the glass to her lips once again and, in Irish tradition, emptied it.

He raised his glass and touched hers with the edge of his and said, "To my beautiful Doreen, may our friendship never die, Happy New Year, I have missed you."

Doreen was significantly attractive; in fact, she was downright beautiful. She stood before Jack in a soft fleece robe of a lime green color; her slender feet were bare, her toenails manicured, but unpolished. Her abundant, shoulder-length auburn hair was pulled back in a knot behind her head with loose, unmanageable tendrils falling around her face. She wore no makeup. She had never needed to wear makeup to enhance her natural Gaelic beauty. She had dense auburn lashes that surrounded incandescent emerald eyes. Jack loved her eyes; they spoke of hidden wisdom that he rarely saw in any other women. She was tall and model thin, almost bony, but not quite. She moved with the grace of a swan. She was a woman who gave the impression of someone in complete control of herself and everything around her. She and Jack, as many had stated, were made for each other, not only in attractiveness but also in compatibility. There were more than a few who knew them both who were unpleasantly surprised when Jack had dumped Doreen for Kirsti and wondered why. The person who topped the list was Vic.

Jack pulled Doreen toward him with his workable arm, maneuvering her so that she was positioned across his lap and facing him. Doreen didn't resist him when he kissed her. She didn't resist him when he slid his hands up her thigh and underneath her robe. She didn't protest when he whispered passionately, "Let's forget about everything for tonight. Let this night be just you and I."

Jack looked deeply into Doreen's beautiful green eyes; they seemed to be welcoming him to enter, enticing him and leading him to a place that only a few very special souls could enter.

"You are my beautiful Doreen. I do love you, and I guess I always have loved you, and I have missed you and I together, like this, as we are now. Tell me you love me, tell me you need me." She had never seen Jack desperate, but now he seemed desperate and weak.

304

She wrapped her arms tightly around him. She buried her head in his strong, masculine shoulder; she was crying from a longing she could never express.

"I will always love you, Jack, it seems as though I have loved you forever. I ache for you even when you're here." Her words were tender, kind, and forgiving.

Jack gently wiped away her tears, "Yes, I know. I'm sorry I have hurt you. You are my angel and my salvation. Will you forgive me?"

He leaned down and kissed her again. She gave herself to him as freely and as openly as she always had. She opened her heart, her soul, and her body to him without reservation. They made love for hours, forgetting anything and everything but each other. This time he was gentle and easy with her, not like the last time.

Then, with arms and legs wrapped around each other, they slept. Doreen's passion for him was the balm he had needed to soothe his injured body and tormented mind.

Maggie had followed Kirsti out the door of the Orchard Lake Country Club. Kirsti was upset, distraught would be a better word, and in no condition to be going anywhere alone. With a lot of argument and persuasion, Maggie finally convinced Kirsti to allow Jerry to drive her home.

The distance between the country club and Grandma's house wasn't very far, less than a fifteen-minute journey; however, on this cold, frigid night, it was probably one of the longest stretches of time that Jerry had ever, in his life, experienced. He was at serious odds with himself over the events of the evening concerning Kirsti and had no real desire to be with her at all, let alone be volunteered as her designated driver. He was processing all of this while Kirsti sat beside him as soundless as a stone. He had one thought on his mind, take her where she needed to be and get back home; post haste.

Tiny flakes of snow were starting to swirl across the hood of his car as he circled around the windmill and parked the car next to the cracked cement walkway leading to the entry door. The porch light was on and shining with a yellow glow which permeated the interior of Jerry's car. Grandma always left her porch light on during the night, and she never locked her doors. She was a member of the days when the trusted belief was 'locking doors only kept the honest men out'.

This was a deeply embedded concept in the Poval mentality. Locked doors portrayed fear and fear of any kind was unacceptable to the Poval approach to life.

Kirsti made no deliberate attempt to get out of the car after Jerry had brought it to a stop. She just sat there wide-eyed and taciturn. She seemed to be waiting for someone or something to happen, so finally, Jerry spoke, trying hard to be patient, "Kirsti, I have to go home now. I think you need to go in the house. Do you want me to walk you to the door or do you want me to take you to your mom's?"

His words brought her out of her trance-like state; she turned to him and said with unhesitating conviction, "No. I want you to take me home with you. I need some time to think and sort things out, and I can't do that with my family. Please, take me to your place. Please, can you do that?"

In all of his wildest imaginings, this was the very last thing he had ever expected to come out of Kirsti's mouth, and because of this he was completely lost as to how to react. His first reaction was to deny her; his second instantaneous reaction was what he went with.

"So be it. If that's what you want, that's what you get."

Act in haste, repent at leisure crossed his mind. He didn't know why. Had he been afforded the opportunity to ask Maggie this question she would have said, "Jerry, you don't have a spontaneous, impulsive bone in your body. She caught you off guard and you had no time to think it through. Thus, and now you know the reason for that particular metaphor running through your mind at that particular fragment in time. You were working against your natural grain."

Jerry put the car in forward motion and drove back out the long driveway leading to the main road. His mind reverted back to the porch light and Grandma. He was troubled as he drove onward. The idea of Grandma waiting made him extremely uncomfortable.

"I think you had better call and leave a message for your grandmother, I wouldn't want to cause her any worry."

"I don't think so Jerry, I was supposed to stay at the motel. She won't be expecting to hear from me until tomorrow."

"I'd feel better if you called her anyway. She might be waiting."

"Jerry, get off it. She isn't waiting up for me. If I call her now, I will wake her up, and then she will worry. She isn't expecting me until sometime tomorrow, but it's nice of you to be so considerate of her."

Kirsti looked at the dashboard, "It really is getting cold, isn't it." The gauge on the dash read minus 21.

"Look, it's starting to snow again. Cool! I love snow storms."

Large snowflakes were starting to cover the windshield as Jerry kicked the windshield wipers into high gear. He didn't share her sentiments.

"The weatherman might be right for once. We are supposed to get six to twelve inches of this by noon tomorrow, and judging from the way it's coming down now, it will likely be closer to twelve inches than six." Jerry was not pleased.

"I love Minnesota winters. I hope we get snowed in. You and I can sit and watch the parades, the football games, and spend the day together. I hope you have a spare set of sweats. I like New Year's Day even better than Christmas Day."

Jerry made no comment. He wasn't quite sure what to say, so he kept his eye on the road and concentrated on his driving. He let Kirsti do all the talking. She kept the conversation convivial, which was fine with him. When they arrived at his house, he opened the front door and said, "Here it is, such as it is. Welcome to my humble abode."

Kirsti entered first and was fascinated by the décor. There wasn't any. What there was to her sooth her troubled soul were books and papers scattered everywhere. Mostly books, coupled with magazines and newspapers piled everywhere. Jerry's house resembled an out-of-sorts and deranged library. Jerry's house resembled Grandma's. Kirsti fell in love with his habitat instantly.

Jerry led Kirsti into the main part of the house then he showed her the kitchen. The kitchen was stark in contrast, completely void of any appearance of daily use. Kirsti doubted he ever used his kitchen, but she did notice a coffee pot, this was good. She would want coffee first thing in the morning.

"I suppose I should apologize for the clutter, but I didn't expect a guest and especially not you. Had I known you were coming, I would have tried to tidy the place up a bit."

Jerry watched and waited as Kirsti unflinchingly inspected his private dwelling. He was not accustomed to having guests and wasn't comfortable with how she was paying attention to every detail of his personal life. He had law books lying around in random order, obviously being used for something he was working on. There were hunting magazines, sports magazines, computer tech magazines, and people magazines in the mixture. His walls were lined with bookshelves from one side of the room to the other; the shelves were stuffed from top to bottom with books of all sorts.

"This place is perfect, Jerry. It is so you. I would describe it as organized clutter. Does your whole paycheck go towards books and magazines? Is there anything under the sun that you don't want to know something about? You are amazing, this place is amazing!"

Jerry grimaced and said, "I wouldn't know. I think there has to be, I just have yet to find it. You can call it what you want, but I'm embarrassed. Sometimes I can't even find my computer. Where is it, by the way?"

Jerry disappeared into his bedroom. When he returned, Kirsti was sitting on the brown tweed older-than-God sofa, engrossed in one of his books.

"Here are your sweats; I have seconds if you need them. You will drown in them, but what can I say. Had I only known? I have a spare toothbrush in the bathroom. Anything else you need your going to have to find on your own. My bedroom is off limits." The sharpness in his tone of voice clearly indicated to Kirsti that Jerry was truly uncomfortable with her invading his world so unexpectedly. "Never mind what I just said. You take the bed, I'll take the couch. What was I thinking?"

Kirsti rose from her seated position and gave Jerry a fast hug and a kiss on the cheek.

"No, I don't think so. I am going to take this book you have about Clarence Darrow and read a bit before I go to sleep. I haven't read this one. In fact, I didn't even know it existed. Thanks for letting me stay here tonight, and I mean that from the bottom of my heart. You are a wonderful and refreshing friend. I sincerely apologize if I'm putting you out, but I can see now that you are a true gift from God and exactly what I need right now. Thanks, Jerry." Her sincere gratitude wasn't lost on him.

Upon more of Jerry's insistence, she took the bedroom, he took the couch. He had never sat on the couch let alone slept on it. Jerry gave Kirsti another hug; he didn't dare to do more. He didn't want to accumulate any false notions on either side; after all, Kirsti was still a very married woman.

Jerry couldn't get to sleep. He started to toss and turn, trying in futility to think that if he could find a comfortable position, he could shut off his mind, but he couldn't shut off his mind. It had to be the couch. He got up and sat in his chair, thinking he was a bit over-stimulated. He couldn't get comfortable in the chair so went back to the couch and did a lot more tossing and turning, trying to get his mind off Kirsti, but she kept creeping back in like a cat in the shadows. Maggie's words kept popping back into his mind. "It isn't the dress making you hot, Kirsti, nor is it the sticky air in here."

He had seen for himself how Kirsti had responded to Reed; she was far more uncomfortable than she should have been and that Maggie had made a comment to the obvious was dreadfully disconcerting. Not Kirsti, not Kirsti with Reed. The combination of these two was an amalgamation for disaster. He wanted to save her, but how? By early morning, he had convinced himself that there was little he could do but be what he was to her already; a good friend, and yet he seriously doubted that this would be enough. He couldn't shake the sense of foreboding he was feeling. Thoughts of Jack, Kirsti, the fire, the newspaper articles, the killings and the changes being prevailed upon him at Crawford and Crawford were all enclosing on him as he finally surrendered an agitated and light state of unconsciousness.

Chapter Thirty-Nine

The beginning of the New Year was bringing about a lot of changes that very few who were involved from the Povel side of the world had anticipated twelve months ago. If someone, anyone, had mentioned to Kirsti that she was going to get married and then separated in less than three months, she would have said, simply, "Hardly!"

A year ago, marriage was the last thing on her mind. She was living in her own little apartment and finishing up college. If anyone had told her that she would not only be married for only a few months but that her husband would be living with one of his old girlfriends by the end of the year, she would have thought this totally absurd. Life only works that way in cheap novels or bad movies and maybe one of Mom's favorite soap operas.

Yet here she was, less than a year later, separated from her husband with her mind on divorce and her husband was indeed living with one of his old girl friends. Jack had just text messaged her to tell her he had a new cell phone number, and if she needed to reach him for any reason, he could be found at a Farmington address. Kirsti knew where Doreen lived. Jack had told Kirsti all about Doreen. In hindsight, she was wondering why he had been forthcoming about Doreen and not other things in his life, but she really wasn't willing to give it a lot of thought, just a question for argument and debate. *One lie at a time, thank you very much.*

What he hadn't told her about was Tracy. She had heard about his affair with Tracy through the grapevine but had never paid the gossip any mind. To Kirsti, gossip was gossip and didn't deserve any sanctioning or encouragement from her. She hadn't paid any attention until someone sent her a CD loaded with pictures of Jack and Tracy, revealing in detail the fun they were having while she was in the mode of planning their wedding. This was the last straw; she had flipped out. Kirsti had no idea who sent her the CD, nor she did care; she was far too furious and upset to care. What got under her skin more than anything else, truth be known, was that she had been forewarned about Jack and his propensity to have multiple affairs going at one time. She had been amply forewarned, but she had thought she would, could be, and was the one and only woman in his life; she had been crazy enough about him, to believe it.

Jack had seriously faulted in two departments: one, he had hit at her strongest and weakest characteristic, which was, her self-centered view of herself; commonly referred to as ego; and two, her total incapacity to be considered wrong about anything. That others were right and she was wrong was not a point of acceptability and never would be. She had to be right, or she had to be wrong; she couldn't be both. Jack had lied to her. He had abused her trust and these two criterions were enough for her to plant all the blame and wrong-doings squarely on his shoulders, case closed. What galled her to no end was that others could and might, with all sincere justifications, say to her, "I told you so. You were amply warned."

The possibility of her being thought of as foolish and blind-sided was more than her ego could stand. Jack had placed her in a position of being where she had to back track a bit and reflect on how she had treated others for being ignorant, stupid, and not very insightful. She was her family's greatest critic, the first to say, "You shouldn't have done that and now look what has happened, you brought this down on yourself and have no one else to blame but yourself." She was unbending and unyielding and all too often insensitive. She had always prided herself in being the one who could and did learn by other people's mistakes. Kirsti, for the first time in her life, found herself in the pickle of philosophical controversy of her own making.

The CD had been dropped on her desk with the morning mail the day she returned from work after the New Year's holiday. She had popped the CD into her disk drive, and there it was, picture after picture of Jack and Tracy together, each picture had been dated. She had been fascinated at first and then angry and finally totally and completely disgusted.

Jerry had been there; he had seen it all, including the last picture of a note that said, *"Happy New Year, Kirsti. I hope you enjoyed the show. What do you think about your Jackie now?"*

While Kirsti was busy venting her anger toward Jack, Jerry had other concerns, but Kirsti wasn't hearing them. He wanted to know who had sent the CD and why. These were logical questions. Jerry's curious mind had many questions about the CD. It worried him that someone had been able or had taken the time to get that close to Jack without being noticed. He needed time to think, so he called Hilde to come and collect her distraught sister. He knew there were only two people who could control Kirsti, one was Hilde and the other was Glenda. Glenda would have been his first choice, but she was out of town.

Hilde, who wasn't known for her easy manner, had listened silently while Kirsti ranted and raved. When Kirsti had succumbed to exhaustion and had nothing more to say; Hilde deadpanned, "Are you done now? Really finished? Because I am going to bed, unlike some people, I have to work tomorrow."

Kirsti had finally fallen asleep on the couch. Hilde covered her up with a blanket, gave her a kiss on her brow, and went to bed, thinking all the way up the stairs, *whew, when is all this going to end?*

"So then, old buddy, old friend of mine, what do you think of the joint?" Jerry had come early; he was sitting cross-legged on the floor, drinking a cup of coffee with his back resting against an empty wall.

Kirsti was standing next to a large window, in the living room, facing the street. "Jerry, are you sure that joint is the proper adjective to be using?"

Jerry grew pensive and a bit defensive; he had grown weary of Kirsti's need to get into word games. "Whatever, Kirsti, a yes would have worked. I need to get out of here and get a breath of fresh air. I'm going outside to have a cigarette and walk around a bit. Let me know when the movers arrive."

"Please, Jerry, hold up a minute. I'm sorry. I know I'm testy these days."

Kirsti grabbed Jerry by the shirt and pulled him toward her and gave him a kiss on the cheek, "I like it a lot. It's just the right size for Abby Kitty and me. I can ride my bicycle to work if I want to, and you have made it affordable. I only wish that this benefit to me didn't have to come at the expense of your aunt."

"She doesn't know where she is, Kirsti, and hasn't for a long time; the nursing home is the best place for her. They'll take good care of her. Having you rent the house and my aunt in a nursing home, will take a lot of stress off my dad." Jerry stood up and joined her at the window.

"The movers are here, looks like we can start setting up your new home, and look whose coming; your sister has just arrived. She found the place. I hope she's in a good mood, if she isn't, I'm heading out!"

Kirsti gave Jerry a push on the shoulder. "You like Hilde, and you know it, so just knock it off. Try to be nice for once in your life."

"Be nice to your sister? You have got to be kidding me!"

The movers had backed a large panel truck up to the driveway. Two very strong-looking young men beat Hilde to the front door. When Kirsti opened the door, one of them said, "We have a delivery for a Kirsti Poval, would that be you?"

Hilde pushed her way past the two young men before Kirsti could respond to the question. As Hilde entered, her cell phone rang. Kirsti heard Hilde say, "Yes, I'm here, where are you? Good, you will be here in about an hour. Yes, I love you too." Kirsti guessed Hilde was talking to Mom.

"Hi, Jerry, I see my sister suckered you into helping her. One day, we will learn, won't we?"

"Hi, Hilde, nice to see you too; I haven't decided yet if I have been suckered or am just being a nice guy."

Hilde gave Jerry a mocking grin and said, "Process of elimination: one, you are not a nice guy, there is no such thing, thus you have been suckered."

"Hilde," Jerry was now on his knees and kissing her outstretched hand, "Your kind and gentle words are always so inspiring."

Hilde let out an exaggerated sigh and said, "Yes, I suppose so, but to be inspiring is so exhausting. Let's see if there's a bed in the moving van. I think I need a nap."

Jerry, Kirsti, and Hilde followed the strong husky movers to the truck. As one of them thrust open the back door. Hilde gasped with astonishment. "Lord, Kirsti, could you spare the expense a bit, for crying out loud? Where are you going to put all this stuff?" The truck was loaded from front to back with brand new furniture.

Hilde was appalled at the spectacle and hadn't quite gathered her wits about her when another truck pulled up. This one was loaded from front to back with boxes.

"Poor Jack! You really have been on a shopping binge. Have you no mercy for the man at all?"

Hilde wasn't kidding. "Lord, Kirsti, have you no shame whatsoever?"

"Look at the sky towards the west, Hilde, and tell me what you see." Kirsti was standing at the end of the driveway by the mailbox and pointing westward. There was an expression on her face that Hilde had never seen before; it was something she couldn't describe, and yet she recognized it.

"Come on, Kirsti, what are you getting at?"

"Seriously, tell me what you see. Study it and look at it hard, and then tell me what you see."

"All right, if you insist. How detailed do you want me to be?" Hilde asked. She was more than willing to play this game with her sister; she thought she knew what Kirsti was getting at, but she wanted to be sure.

Hilde rolled her eyes and looked at Jerry, who was giving her a time-out signal, better not to get Kirsti started on the Jack-thing again. Hilde ignored him. She couldn't help herself. This was going to be a grappling of the minds that was long overdue between two sisters.

Hilde walked casually toward the west, and when she reached the middle of the street, she stopped. She looked right and then left. She turned around and gave her sister a mocking grin. She then sat down, facing the west, with her legs crossed underneath her. She spoke loudly and clearly for all to hear, "Don't anyone come near me because I will not be moved without a fight. Off to the west I see the sun setting. Kirsti wants me to tell her what I see."

"Today, the sunset is brilliant with colors of radiant red. 'Red sun at night, sailors delight.' We are going to have a pleasant day tomorrow, but that is not what Kirsti is thinking about, is it, Kirsti?

"This is not what Kirsti is thinking at all, is it Kirsti? You are saying that with the end of this day ends something forever. Watch as the sun goes down because when the sun comes up, there will be a new tomorrow. What is here today dies with the sunset and will never be revived. That is what you are thinking, aren't you, Kirsti? What you are saying is that your life, as of this day, with Jack Ireland is over. All of this spending is your way of saying good-by? Honestly, Kirsti, sometimes I don't get you at all."

Hilde was getting a cold butt, so she stood up, brushed the snow off her hinder, and started to walk back to the house. At that moment, as though on cue, a car came to a screeching halt, about three feet away from Hilde. She just stood there on the snow-packed pavement seemingly unaware of the danger she was in. The driver got out of his car and started screaming, "God damn it, Hilde, I could have run over you! What are you doing standing out here in the middle of the road?"

"Nothing much, Charlie, I wasn't doing anything out here but proving a point to my sister."

"Well then, damn it, can't you find a better way to do it? Must your tutorials always require a heart attack on my part? What if I had run over you?"

Hilde shivered and said with far more aplomb than the world—especially hers—was ready for, "You didn't, and that speaks for itself."

Kirsti stood there frozen as though everything was moving around her in slow motion. She didn't realize that she was in this state of paralysis. She had seen the car coming toward her sister, she had visualized herself running to try and save her sister from being crushed underneath it's wheels, she could not comprehend that it was Charlie that was in that car. Not Charlie the chef? Couldn't be! How had Charlie gotten into the act? Was she dreaming? What was her sister trying to prove? She had only been trying to tell her sister that her life with Jack was now over and a new world was coming around for her.

She could not comprehend much of anything and especially that her younger sister seemed to be telling her, with guarded satisfaction, that she and Charlie had been dating for months and were going to get married. How could this be?

Kirsti had the wild sensation of being completely outside of herself and feeling of detachment when her sister showed her the engagement ring. She had no concept of time or location. Jerry took her into the house and made her sit on the floor while the furniture was being moved in. She went back outside and studied the sunset as he set up her bed, trying to focus on her younger sister's words. She was trying to lock in on the message; it was there, she knew it was, but she could not find it. Or was that just Hilde being Hilde.

When had Hilde and Charlie gotten together and they were planning on getting married? How could that be? How come Hilde had never told her about any of this? She couldn't ask Hilde because she was gone. She had left angry and had said something but Kirsti couldn't remember what she had said.

She studied the star-cluttered sky. She thought back to her astronomy classes and tried to pick out the constellations. Then while she was looking for the small dipper, she saw it; a shooting star flashing across the horizon and something small, very remote, clicked within her, *a falling star, how appropriate.*

"Come on Kirsti, you have to come in the house now. You're freezing cold! I have your bed all set up for you." Jerry had to literally carry Kirsti into the house. She was incapable of moving on her own.

"I think I get the message, Jerry. I think I've got it. Hilde wasn't just trying to scare the wits out of me for no reason, but what about Charlie. I cannot, for the life of me, figure that one out. Was he really here, or was I imagining it?"

"Try not to imagine anything right now, Kirsti; you need to get some sleep. You are all worn-out."

After he had tucked Kirsti in to bed, Jerry laid down on the sofa. It would be hours before he would fall asleep; he felt like he was in the "twilight zone". He would call Maggie in the morning. She would know how to deal with a fraught Kirsti. He wished he had the guts to call Ireland.

Chapter Forty

The sky was a crystal clear, ocean blue with not a cloud anywhere to be seen from one side of the horizon to the other. The temperature, however, was a solid twenty below zero, relatively typical for Minnesota in January. Jack was dressed in a pair of heavily lined bib coveralls and an olive green parka with a fur-lined hood pulled over his head. His newly grown mustache was frosty white from condensation created by the mere exercise of breathing. He was enjoying the crunching sound his heavily lined boots made as he paced through the frozen snow.

When he saw Vic driving into the drive, he removed the heavy clothing and tossed it in the back end of his Jeep. He grabbed another jacket and sauntered slowly toward Vic. Vic had barely come to a complete stop before Jack was seated next to him on the passenger side.

Vic let the jeep idle as he took in the show of the large machine moving one way and then the next, the large scoop moving and lifting and cleaning up what was once Jack's home. A large pile of crushed concrete sat to the right of what used to be the house and an equally large pile of dirt was situated to the left of a large gaping hole.

"What's he doing?"

"What does it look like he's doing? He's excavating."

"Well any dumb bunny could figure that much out, but what is he actually doing besides moving things from here to there and back again?"

"Precisely what it looks like; he is going to mix that pile of dirt with the concrete from the foundation and fill up the hole of what used to be my basement."

"Oh."

"Oh? What do you mean 'oh'? Why are you drilling me with these pointless questions when I know, and you know exactly what is going on? Your father was one of the best excavators in the state of Minnesota, and you ask me what the guy is doing? You were born and raised on one of those damned machines, and you are asking me what the guy is doing? Really, have you lost all of your powers of observation? You must be in love again. Every time you fall in love you lose sight of yourself, and it is downright stressful."

"Sorry, I didn't mean to upset you my darling, just checking to see if you knew what was going on. One can never be too careful these days."

With the normal verbosity behind him, Jack leaned his head back, shut his eyes and let Vic take control of the wheel and the conversation. He hadn't seen Vic in a few days, not since he had moved in with Doreen.

"How's Doreen these days?"

Jack had known this question was coming. They rarely argued but when they did it was usually over Jack's relationship with Doreen.

"Fine, Doreen is fine, and I suppose you are going to reacquaint me with your thoughts on how wrong it is for me to be moving in with her this soon after my separation from Kirsti?"

Vic shifted gears, both mentally and physically. When he hit the open road toward Farmington, he slipped the car into high gear and let the engine hum. He loved speed, and he loved his four on the floor 1957 Thunderbird.

"Nah, Jack, I think I have already said all I can on that score. I like Doreen, I have always liked her, but why she still puts up with you is a question that crosses my mind now and again. Not that it's any of my business."

The last part was said with zero sincerity. In fact, the sincerity was in equal margin with the temperature, minus zero.

Jack sat up in his seat, rolled down the window and spat before he said blithely, "I hate to say this, buddy, but this car is a pile of 'womanizing' crap. This console is a nightmare for holding a woman close, and the backseat is impossibly small for any great action that might come to a man's mind. No small wonder you are so lacking in female attentions."

With that said, he spat out the window again.

"And besides, I don't take kindly to a man messing in my personal life, be it kindred or friend."

"Well, the truth be known, Jack, there are other places in the world that can provide all of those conveniences. I don't have to resort to making love to a woman in the backseat of a car nor do I have to worry about women in my life. Most women I have encountered, which I might add, is in no short supply, love this, T-bird with bucket seats. And if I might add, what do you know about my lack of female attention anyway. You have no clue. In fact, as far as I can tell, you are clueless, period. Jack 'Clueless' Ireland, now that fits and besides I wouldn't get into your personal life at all were you not always in the business of making such a mess of it."

Jack leaned back in his chair, looked out the window and replied dryly, "Yah, whatever."

Anyone on the outside over-hearing the conversations might be inclined to think that these two held some animosity toward each other, but that wasn't the case at all. They were closer than most brothers and as honest with each other as two people can afford to be.

"And if you spit one more time, I'll throw you out the window."

Jack closed the window, and said, "OK, you win."

It had been almost a week since Jack had been into the office. Lulu was sitting at her usual position in dispatch; she was filing her fingernails as the two men passed by her. Her hair color had changed; it was a bright orange with a mixture of dark brown stripes mixed in. Along with her narrow gray eyes and pale complexion, this was a startling vision to behold. Both men stopped dead in their tracks as they approached her. Vic was the first to utter something that sounded like, "Lulu, you have done something with your hair."

Lulu smacked her gum, blew a bubble, poked it with a pencil, and said, "Great observation, Sherlock. Do you like it?"

Vic knew better than to speak his mind, "Looks just fine to me, Lulu, just fine. It sure does catch the eye. It sure did catch my eye!"

Lulu turned her attention to Jack, who was grinning like a New York schoolboy fresh out of detention hall.

Jack didn't wait for the question but walked up to her, grabbed her hand, kissed it, gave her a dashing smile, bowed, and said, "You look absolutely remarkable, remarkable indeed, Lulu, it is only to dismal a thought that all of your beauty and talent is wasted in this unappreciative environment."

Brice came out of his office to see what the commotion was all about; the whole office had been waiting for this moment with satisfaction guaranteed. Everyone in the office had their ears directed toward the two men and Lulu.

Lulu tossed her pencil at Jack and suggested that he be more careful, or she might have to take him home with her and give him a taste of real remarkable.

Jack acknowledged with, "I would, Lulu, but as you can see, Brice is on his way to lead me astray from your wonderful persona. I must now leave the beautiful light of your glowing beauty and go into the darkness of the world beyond."

Contessa was sitting at her desk, feigning indifference. Perhaps there was a hint of jealousy involved; if there was, it was only because Contessa would think Lulu unworthy of all this attention from these two great men. She disliked Lulu immensely, and besides all that, Lulu looked ridiculous. Contessa was eagerly awaiting Jack and Vic as they approached her. Each of them gave her a proper greeting. As they passed her, they said, "But you know, Contessa," said Jack, giving her a flirtatious wink, "All of our love belongs to you." Vic nodded in earnest agreement, gave her a peck on the cheek and strolled into Brice's office.

Contessa was amply satisfied, gave each a casual wave with her heavily ringed fingers, and went back to her work.

"You watch out for her fella's because she's a harlot," Contessa muttered under her breath. Jack and Vic heard what she said. They gave her another nod of the head and a knowing wink, and this time not for appeasement.

"Well, could you guys possibly spare the speed?" The commander was not long on sitting around and waiting and had never been, but than, neither were his two top investigators.

Buchanan was grabbing his heavy jacket and hat as he spoke and moving rapidly down the corridor.

"We have to be in Apple Valley in less than an hour. I'll drive while you guys read these files. I want you up to speed when we visit with the investigative team."

Vic wound up carrying the files because he was standing closer to Buchanan than Jack was. Both Jack and Vic took pleasure in teasing their boss; and could because Buchanan was receptive to bantering. This sort of give and take was necessary and was what made Buchanan the highly regarded man that he was.

As the thick files were tossed in Vic's general direction, he said with complete and convincing despair, "What have we here, reading material to keep us from annoying you on the way, Chief? I know it can't be a coloring book because there isn't any color crayons, and I know you wouldn't do that to us now, would you, Chief. Jack and I don't like to color."

"Is it "Goldilocks"? I hope it isn't "Goldilocks" because I'm tired of that story! My mother read "Goldilocks" to me every night until I was eighteen. I got so sick and tired of "Goldilocks" I had to move out, go to college, and get a job."

Buchanan didn't miss a beat when he said, "I would suspect that by the time you are done reading that file, you will be wishing it was "Goldilocks," but then that's only my take on things, you read, and then you can give me a little report, how about that, Melton?"

Jack fell into pace with his long lean, blond-haired, blue-eyed, handsome friend and said, "What do you mean moved out? You are still living with your mother, the gracious lady that she is. You never moved out of any place in your entire miserable life. That woman cooks for you, does your laundry, and all but wipes your rear end. Maybe she reads you "Goldilocks" every night to teach you something, ever thought about that? Or maybe she thinks you are so slow, she needs to read you the same story repeatedly with a slim hope you might learn something however hopeless this is because your real name is, or should be, Vic "Hopeless" Melton."

Vic no more lived with his mother than Jack did.

Brice was smiling to himself as he listened to the two men go back-and-forth all the way to his car. He had been with these two detectives for many years and knew that the more rein you gave them, the better they were. This was their way of letting off steam. He actually envied their relationship. If there was ever a team that was equally harnessed, it was Jack Ireland and Vic Melton.

"Jack, you sit in the backseat. Vic, you sit in front and start reading, both of you get to reading, you have a lot to cover before we get to Apple Valley, and you can put in the back of your minds this is more about "Goldilocks" than either of you want to imagine."

Jack climbed into the backseat and wrapped his feet around Vic's head. He had the file open in his lap, had removed his boots, and had already started to read. Vic pushed Jack's feet away from him with an overstated shove.

"Get those putrid, smelly things out of my face."

Brice ignored both of them as he put the car in gear and made his way out of the parking lot.

Jack stretched out on the soft, black leather seats.

"You know, Vic, I think Caddies are highly overrated. This backseat isn't much larger than yours, no wonder Brice hasn't got any women in his life. I have pondered this phenomena but I won't any more."

"Shut up, Jack, I'm reading."

"Shut up, Vic, I'm sleeping."

Brice glanced into his rearview mirror. Jack's lithe body was folded in half, the file open and resting against his thighs. His eyes were intently focused on the pages in front of him. Vic was slumped down in his seat with his knees braced against the dash, the file open and resting against his thighs. His full attention was on what was in front of him. You could have heard a pin drop on a carpet floor for as quiet as the threesome were as they traveled to Apple Valley.

"Pretty engrossing stuff" was Jack's only comment as Brice brought his car to a halt in front of the large warehouse. Vic didn't say anything. He didn't need to. His partner had said all that needed to be said.

Chapter Forty-One

Reed Crawford was a little disappointed that he hadn't heard from Andrea by the end of New Year's Day. He thought he would have heard from her if for no other reason than to give him an earful about his deliberate mistreatment of her. She was always good at this. He could almost count the seconds, but this time had been different; she hadn't called. She would, he had faith in that; all the shallow women he gathered into his life called him. They loved his money. Andrea wasn't his only playmate, but she was his favorite. She was less plastic than the rest, less obvious, more challenging. As he cranked up his Jaguar, he visualized her long, flowing blond hair; her sea foam eyes; and long, graceful body. She would be waiting for him, she would come into his office, he would close the door, and then everything would be just fine, like always. Andrea knew how to please a man.

With that set right in his own mind, Reed moved his next thought towards what was ahead of him. The case of the three misguided boys was coming up rapidly, three imprudent boys. Reed knew all about foolish, ill-advised boys. These youngsters were no more misguided than he was. They had just been having a little fun and fun was something Reed understood. The girls had been willing to associate with these young gentlemen; they had had their fair share of booze and even used a bit of cocaine. Reed had been there and done that, a time or two in his years as a college student. He understood. He related to these mischievous young lads.

The very youngest girl, only sixteen, had died of a head injury. This was most unfortunate, but it was, according to the boys involved, strictly accidental. When she was running away, after the poor boy realized he had frightened her and released her, she had stumbled and fell. She hit her head on a rock. She had had sex with the boy several times that night, and what triggered her to run and fall was more than likely caused by the drugs and the booze she had *willingly* ingested throughout the night. Did the boys provide the drugs? Of course not, the girls brought their own medicine. How could anyone suggest these clean-cut boys could or would think about such a dastardly thing as murder and rape? They were the epitome of virtue. Just three young boys who were led down a dark path by three very experienced girls.

Reed had pictures of the girls. Pictures of them dressed very provocatively in short skirts and tops that barely covered their sweet young bodies. He also had pictures of these girls partying with their friends; drinking and doing drugs was part of their scene. He had three million dollars riding on the line and his reputation as a winning attorney riding on this case, and he would win if he had to drag the accusers into the darkest corners of their lives.

Reed's biggest problem was Jack Ireland. He had to find a way to discredit Jack's testimony. Last night at the party, Jack had revealed a glitch in his armor. *I need to use Jack's passions against him.* Reed had heard rumors that Jack might be the prime suspect for the serial killings in the, now notorious, Purple Button Case. This improbability could be very helpful to Reed and worthy of a long look. All he needed was an element of doubt, a thread to grab on to. He needed to discredit Jack. With this latest bit of information, it would appear that Ireland was lending him a helping hand. *How considerate.*

Kirsti and Jerry were at their desks, reviewing trial transcripts, when Reed came into the office. They were only halfheartedly trying to help Reed with his assault against these three young party-loving girls. They had spent all of New Year's Day discussing the case and trying to find a way to get this to work for Samuel, their real boss. They had devised a plan. The plan was to use sabotage and, of course, this would be considered mutiny; they could lose their jobs, and the company might even suffer; but they were going to go ahead anyway. To accomplish what they intended to do meant long hours and hard work, but to Kirsti and Jerry, every second spent to bring this to a just end was worth the effort, time and reputation. "Let justice be served" became their pact.

Reed rushed into the building, skipped up the stairs and went immediately to his office. He noticed on his way in that Andrea was not at her desk. He pondered this for a moment and then yelled to anyone who was listening, "Where is Andrea?"

Samuel's secretary, who used the desk adjoining Andrea's, was the first to respond. Samuel came out of his office at the same time, motioned his secretary to be quiet, and walked up the stairs and into Reed's office. "She hasn't come in, nor has she called to let us know her intentions."

Reed picked up the phone and dialed Andrea's cell phone; when he got the answering machine, he said, "Call me." He dialed her home phone number, and when he got the answering machine, again, he said shortly, "This is Reed, call me."

"You treated her shabbily last night, Reed."

Samuel was standing in front of Reed's expensive oversized desk. "She might be trying to give you a message."

Reed looked at his father with a grin and said, "Dad, you have no idea what women think. We play this game all the time. She'll be in later or tomorrow, that is if I don't fire her first."

Samuel sat down in one of the three expensive chairs in Reed's office. He looked sadly at his son and said, "I didn't come in here this morning to discuss your love life. I'm here to tell you that I've returned the three-million-dollar retainer to its rightful owners."

"I don't think you can do that, Dad, not without some serious repercussions."

"Oh yes, I can and I did. I own this company, and you went ahead of me on this one. I wouldn't have taken the case no matter how much money I could be paid or would be paid. The boys probably deserve a strong defense, but it isn't coming from this office. I'll shut my doors first.

"If you want to be a defender of brutality, then, I suggest that set up your own office with your own money, create your own law firm. You flaunt my money like it's your own. Well, let me set you straight on this particular issue right now, my money isn't your money, this company isn't your own company to do with what you will, the reputation of this company belongs to me."

Samuel rose from his chair and left before Reed could say anything more. On his way back down to his own office, he instructed Patti to get Jerry and Kirsti into his office, immediately.

Reed was neither surprised nor worried by his father's words or actions. Surprise and worry were not part of Reed's basic makeup. This wasn't the first time that Sam had threatened to expulse him. Reed knew there would be ramifications of the legal variety in returning the retainers; he was a bit curious to see how his dad was going to work around this little itty-bitty problem.

Reed couldn't have cared less about what his father thought at this point or any other point, for that matter; he had his inheritance he could back up to. Maybe it was time for him to break away from his father and start up his own law firm. He had given this some thought many times and now could very well be the perfect moment to make his debut. Three million dollars worth of retainer could go a long way in helping him become independent of Crawford and Crawford. He knew without any uncertainty the person he needed to talk to, L. L. Benton, Esquire. Reed made a quick phone call before leaving the office. As he passed by Patti's desk, he asked, "Any word from Andrea yet?"

"Not a word."

"Well, you tell her when she does call that she is fired."

"No thanks, Reed, you can tell her that yourself. I'm not going to do your dirty work for you."

"Whatever you say, Patti, if anyone wants me tell them I'm going to be gone for the rest of the day. Can you do that or is that to dirty a job for you as well?"

Patti didn't look at Reed, nor did she answer him; she knew what was happening. Samuel intended to stick to his guns this time. Reed had better shape up, or he was out, and Sam had the power to do exactly as he was threatening. Patti knew everything that went on in Samuel's law firm. There had always been office gossip about Sam and Patti. There was not an ounce of truth to any of it. Patti and Sam had never had an affair. Sam, unlike his son, didn't believe in interoffice relationships. In fact, there were no similarities between Sam and Reed whatsoever. They were so entirely different that there had been many occasions when Patti had to wonder if Reed was Sam's son at all. She also often wondered if Sam had ever asked himself the same question.

Leo Langley Benton had his law office in the finished basement of his two-story, split-level home located on the north shore of Lake

Marion. He and wife, Katie, had resided in this house since the early '60s. Benton had lived in Lakeville the majority of his seventy-eight years of life. What set him apart from all other people in Lakeville and in the legal profession was the well-known fact that anyone who had ever crossed his path grew, in a short period of time, to dislike him, if not detest him. He was a man who was utterly and completely void of anything even closely resembling scruples. Leo Benton was wealthy. He came from humble beginnings and was, as he loved to boast, a self-made man. To find another human being more obnoxious than Benton would take a lot of searching. He was crusty, abrasive, filthy-minded, and foul mouthed. Many questioned how his petit, dark-haired wife, sweet wife, had tolerated him; but she had managed somehow. And to the bewilderment of anyone associated with the couple, not only did she manage, but she seemed to adore him, even dote on him.

Benton made all of his money in the late '60s and early '70s. He specialized in divorce cases. This was a time before "no contest" was brought into play and if ever there was a person who had probably paved the way for "no contest," it was L. L. Benton. He fought hard, and he fought dirty. One of the grounds for divorce being used and abused during this, 'freedom to do whatever you want', period was infidelity. This "free lifestyle" thrust half the population of married couples into divorce court. Sleazy private investigators hired by individuals or by attorneys came out of their sludge pots by the droves, stalking and hiding and taking enough pictures to make Kodak stock soar through the roof.

L. L. Benton enjoyed his occupation. He charged by the hour, knowing the longer he could prolong the divorce, the better for him. His trick was to keep both sides charged up by making unreasonable demands and creating an impossible field for negotiations. If he wasn't playing the infidelity card, which was rare, he would use the "abuse" card. This one was his favorite. More often than not, he used both in one fashion or another; and if kids were involved and this was invariably the case, so much the better because there was no such thing as joint custody yet. He would never settle, he would never negotiate nor would he ever, ever capitulate. He would set the child support so high that the father would invariably find it less costly, in the long run, to fight for full custody. Leo would smirk and say,

"Good, now we will prove infidelity, unfit father, abusive, etc., etc. Let the battle begin."

There was one custody case, the most talked about in the legal circles, where Leo had the parents so hostile with each other and into court so often that the exasperated judge finally warded the children to the grandparents on the mother's side. Both parents had to pay the grandmother child support, and the parents were granted reasonable, but regulated visitation rights. That was fine with Benton because he got paid by the hour. It wasn't so fine with the parents or the grandparents, but Leo didn't care; he had no reason to care. In his warped mind, he had done his job with fortitude and could hardly be faulted for what the judge decided. Unlike any other lawyer in the metro area, the vast majority of his divorce cases wound up in front of a jury.

There was another L. L. Benton case where the judge, after two years of haggling over personal possessions, demanded that everything be divided in half, literally. He demanded and angrily commanded that everything be cut in half-chairs, tables, sofa, pictures—everything. A date was set for this unusual event, the judge promised to attend and provide the chainsaw. Leo just laughed, he got paid first, and that was all that counted with Leo. What also counted was winning; winning kept the clients coming in. He understood better than anyone that in the legal game, winning was everything. He also knew that the money was on the side of the women because divorce, during these times, was a losing proposition for men. He never took a divorce case initiated by a man. In fact, he never represented one single man in divorce court during his entire career as an attorney.

When the laws of divorce changed to "no contest" and joint custody for simplification and expediency, Leo lost interest in doing divorce cases and turned his attentions to civil suits. He lived frugally and had invested wisely so money became secondary to picking and choosing cases that he found interesting. At the age of sixty-five, he and his wife rented out their house and moved to Arizona. He applied for his license to practice in Arizona, got it, and set up his practice in a small office in the downtown area of Phoenix. Rumor had it that when he moved to Phoenix, the entire judicial system in the state of Minnesota was so happy to see him leave, they celebrated for weeks.

He was back in Lakeville within three years. Rumor again had it that he had blundered a case, big time, and had lost his license to practice in the state of Arizona. The southwestern judges didn't appreciate his mud-slinging ways, especially when the mud was being thrown their direction. There were some back home bold enough to ask him directly if the rumors had any ring of truth to them, and all he would say, with a wink, "When you substantiate this idle chatter, let me know."

There was an article in one of the metro papers stating that L. L. Benton was returning once again to Minnesota to practice law. One judge was quoted to have said with much venom, "Perhaps he will be back, but he will not be welcomed in my courtroom." The name of the judge was not revealed. L. L. Benton took this as a compliment.

Leo greeted Reed jovially. He shook his hand with a vigor that Reed hadn't expected. Age hadn't changed L. L. Benton. He looked the same now as he did thirty years ago, maybe a bit whiter haired and more wrinkled in the face, but just as crusty and gruff as ever.

"It's been a long time, boy! The last time I saw you, you were knee-high to a grasshopper. Come on in my boy, and grab yourself a chair."

The man was remarkably spry for a man his age. He had to be pushing eighty-five and still practicing law as vindictively as ever. His office was as neat as a pin. There was a slight musty smell permeating the air that came from the furniture that had been around since the early '60s and stuck in a dank basement.

Reed looked around the office and then sat down in a high-backed black leather chair. He watched as Leo made his way to a well-supplied bar.

"You look like a brandy, man."

Leo poured two shots of expensive brandy into a snifter and handed it to Reed.

"A bit early in the day for this, don't you think?" Reed knew better than to turn it down.

"At my age, nothing is too early for anything. So what brings you to my doorstep? Let's get right down to it. I have an appointment with my barber in about one hour."

"OK. Let's get right down to it."

Reed shifted uneasily in his chair, feeling childish and awkward under the pressure of Leo's tough, scrutinizing gaze.

"I want you to work with me on the *Wallace/Parish* case."

Leo's eyes narrowed as he leaned over his desk toward Reed, "Well, that's refreshingly straight forward. I thought that this was a Crawford and Crawford case. Why would I want to be involved in a Crawford and Crawford case? I think you and your dad ought to be able to handle this one just fine."

Reed cleared his throat anxiously. He wasn't crazy about the way this conversation was going.

Dad returned the retainers. He seems to think he can get out of it but I don't think he can. That's why I came to see you."

Leo laughed and said confidently, "You're not partners, so sure he can. He can get out of this if he fires you. Is he going to fire you?"

"If push comes to shove, I believe he will. He has no interest in connecting Crawford and Crawford with anything this volatile. He was angry when I accepted the retainers without consulting him first. He considers this case to be a loser for the firm. He calls it 'dirty business,' and he wants no part of it."

Leo went to the bar and poured himself a brandy with water in a tall glass.

"Your father has never been interested in criminal law. He likes fighting for the underdog, and these boys wouldn't qualify in his eyes. He and I are a lot alike, you know. I have always fought for the underdog. The only difference between your dad and I is tactics. I don't mind getting down in the trenches and slinging a little mud around. Your dad likes a clean fight, that's the difference between us."

"Listen, Leo, I'm not here to get into a philosophical discussion about the distinctions between you and my father. I have no interest in the past disparities between you and my dad, and I couldn't give a rat's ass about your similarities either. All I want to know is one thing, will you work with me or not?"

Benton sat back down in his overstuffed chair, flung his long feet on top of his desk and took a sip of his drink, taking his sweet old time in doing so before he answered Reed, and when he did his tone was relaxed and lazy.

"Well, you certainly are an arrogant puppy, aren't you?" Benton drawled his words.

He lifted his left wrist and with staged deliberation, looked at his Timex watch, "Time's a-ticking way. What do you want from me? Get on with it, boy, get on with it or I am going to have to start charging you by the second. I have things to do, places too go, and people to see, so you might want to quit wasting my time with your immature, impertinent, dillydallying."

Reed was feeling a bit of anger rising from his belly. He was starting to comprehend why people found this man so utterly insufferable, but he had a situation, and he wasn't going to let a bit of offensiveness get in the way of his long-ranged goals.

Reed decided to go straight to the reason for his visit.

"There is three million dollars worth of retainer sitting out there, waiting to be collected. I have a full grasp of this case, and I want it. The parents hired me once, and I think I can persuade them to hire me again. I want you to take me on as your partner. I need a shingle. We'll split the difference fifty-fifty, after that, I will be on my way. You won't have to do anything but provide me with a place to hang my hat."

"Benton and Crawford; has a nice ring to it, doesn't it? I'll only do this if you are willing to come in as a full partner, and I want five hundred thousand dollars up front, in my bank account before the papers are signed. That will be what it will cost you to buy into my law firm. I can have my secretary draw up the papers and have them ready for you to sign by tomorrow morning. In the meantime, call the parents of these poor darling boys and get them committed back to you. If you can't accomplish this, then the deal's off."

L. L. Benton stood up and pointed to his computer.

"I have to go see the barber and catch up on all the local scuttlebutt. You can use my machinery to write your formal resignation to Crawford and Crawford. I want your resignation on Samuel's desk by this afternoon, signed, sealed, and delivered. I think we're going to make a great team, you and I."

As he reached the top of the stairs, he turned to Reed and said offhandedly, "Oh, by the way, did I mention I knew your mother very well? She was a lively one, that girl was. Pretty as can be. Indeed she was. She was especially fond of having sex in the bathroom while a party was going on in the next room. Sex with your mother was the closest thing to heaven I will ever experience. I knew her before your dad married her, you know. We had a real history together, she and I did. I would be interested to know if she ever had blood tests done on your paternity. I hope to run into her again in the afterlife. You can let yourself out and don't bother to lock the door when you leave."

Leo laughed heartily as he closed the door behind him. Reed sat silently gaping at the closed door, as what Leo had just implied slowly seeped its way into his consciousness, *paternity test?*

Chapter Forty-Two

Buchanan, Ireland, and Melton entered the warehouse from the south entrance door. A tall middle-aged, overweight guard stopped them. If he could have acted any more bored, disinterested, and lethargic, Jack didn't know how.

"Show your badges please and sign in over there at that table."

The sleepy disgruntled guard pointed in a vague direction, glanced at their badges, and let them pass.

Vic nudged Jack and said, "Look at this place. Would yah just take a look? If this doesn't resemble a computer geeks' convention, nothing does."

"Pretty impressive, isn't it?" said a familiar voice from behind the three men.

"Jamie, well, I might have known you were behind this. What have you done to our warehouse? What'd you do, drag every computer possibly known to man into one central location for your idle amusement? Hey, you look like you've lost some weight." Vic grinned at Jack as he continued his verbal onslaught. "Jamie must have found himself a girlfriend."

Jamie refused to dignify anything that Vic was saying with a comment as he led the investigators to the center of a huge room.

"We, in the industry, call this networking. The FBI has their section over on that side of the room, yours is on the other. All the information that comes in on the kidnapping and missing persons is channeled through the FBI section. Your computer system takes in everything concerning the Purple Button Case and then everything meets in the middle. I have the best of the best working on this. We should get results if everyone shares their information and does a thorough job of entering their data."

Jack glanced warily around the room. He had to agree it was impressive. However, he also knew that in every investigation he had ever been involved with, to date, computers couldn't replace pounding the streets. He also knew that the exchange of information was not always forthcoming and only as good as the person entering the data. He didn't have a lot of trust in computers or the people who ran them.

In a serial-murder situation, it wasn't the computer that caught the perpetrator. He had studied the spreadsheets; they hadn't revealed anything he didn't already know about the Purple Button Case or the kidnapping of Tracy Durkin and as far as he was concerned, he knew as much if not more than the computers were spitting out, but he wasn't going to get into this with Jamie, at least not right now he wasn't. He could save that debate until after the cases were solved and the killer was either dead or locked behind bars.

Robert "Bud" Neilson, chief of police for Pine Bend, had been the first to arrive. He was sitting at the conference table on the upper level, watching the activity below, when Brice, Jack, and Vic arrived. He watched as the three men slowly made their way through the bottom level and up the stairwell, taking time to greet everyone they knew. He introduced himself to Brice and Vic and shook their hands firmly. He didn't need to introduce himself to Jack. Bud had met him, by chance, at the VFW, shortly after Jack had moved into his house, located just outside of town.

Bud was born and raised in Farmington. He graduated from Farmington High School. He married his high school sweetheart two weeks after graduation. Pam was a brown-haired, brown-eyed, pretty little thing with a dynamic personality. She was a cheerleader while Bud was Farmington's star football player; they were in the same graduating class. These were the days when all girls wanted to date the star football players. She nabbed Bud in her freshmen year of high school and never let loose of him. When asked how his marriage had survived the wily '70s movement, he would say in all seriousness, "Pam has always been my girl and always will be." Then he smiles slightly and says, "And if you don't believe me just ask Pam."

Bud enlisted in the marines immediately after he graduated from high school. It was either enlist or get drafted. He survived the Vietnam conflict by the grace of God and pure dumb luck. After four years of faithful serve, he came back to Farmington and began what would become a long career in law enforcement. He had been with the Pine Bend police department for thirty years. He had been chief of police for twenty-five of those thirty. Bud ran a tight ship in Pine Bend. He knew his town, he knew who the troublemakers were, and he handled them accordingly. He wore the trappings of a cop with pride. He stood tall, though he wasn't exactly tall, he was about five feet, ten; his greenish blue eyes were sharp and alert. He had experience under his belt and wore it with ease. Bud was a man to be reckoned with. Anyone who took his casual demeanor seriously could be in for a shock when the going got tough. Bud had been shot at many times and stabbed twice. These were things he never talked about; others did, but not Bud. He was, in his mind, only doing his job.

After everyone was seated at the oval table, Brice stood up to speak.

"I am not going to linger with introductions. We're here to discuss new developments in the Purple Button Case. Bud, would you come forward please?"

Bud stood up and made his way around the table until he was standing in front of the large television screen. He turned on the television and picked up the remote for the DVD/VHS player. He pressed a button and the picture of a poem came on the screen.

"Jack Ireland was the first one to suspect that two of the victims were dumped somewhere in Pine Bend. He thought this because of a poem that was written and sent to Mr. Buchanan. The killer gave us an approximate location of the bodies. But, because of the unusual amount of snowfall this year, we have been unable to get back into the area and do any searches for fear of doing more damage than good. We found the bodies yesterday and almost precisely where Jack thought they might be."

Bud pressed the button again. Appearing on the screen were two pictures, side-by-side, of two different women, one blond the other dark haired. These were the graphic pictures of the two girls that had been dumped on Brice's desk by Lulu. Bud placed the cursor on the second picture, and with a click, the picture disappeared. He placed the cursor on the remaining picture and clicked to enlarge it. Jack recognized the pictures. He had studied these pictures hard and long. He had his own file on the Purple Button Case that contained everything that had transpired to date, the file was three inches thick.

"This girl's name is Amber Linn Koech. She was twenty-three years old and had been living with her grandmother south of Farmington. She moved in with her grandmother after her parents died. Her mother passed away when she was just a child. She had a stroke at the age of thirty-nine. Her father died a year ago from cancer at the age of fifty-three." Bud took a sip of his coffee and lit a cigarette.

"Amber graduated from Farmington High School and was considered by everyone who knew her, to be extremely outgoing, popular, and liberal minded. One of her best friends moved to Chicago after graduation, but they kept up their friendship through weekly phone calls and e-mails.

"Her grandmother told me that Amber was scheduled to work the night before Christmas Eve at the Fireside Inn located just north of Farmington. Amber had told her grandmother that after work, she was going to travel to Chicago to visit a friend over the holidays. Her grandmother wasn't expecting her back home until after the New Year. When she didn't return, her grandmother called missing persons.

"Amber's grandmother isn't what I would call on top of her game. I think she is either really slow, or she is on drugs that make her lethargic. She seems to fall short in the awareness department. She wasn't exactly depressed about her granddaughter coming up missing, nor was she really overly concerned. When I asked her where Amber worked, she said, 'I don't have a clue, someplace north of town.' Grandma let us search Amber's room, and while searching her room, we found a pay stub but little else of any help. We talked to people at the Fireside Inn, but they had little to contribute. I went out to Chicago to visit with the friend that Amber was supposed to visit, and she had nothing to contribute either. She thought Amber had simply changed her mind. Amber was like that.

"I, personally, made the trip out to the farmhouse to let Amber's grandmother know that her granddaughter was dead. She didn't seem to react in an ordinary fashion. In fact, she just looked at me with glassy eyes and said, 'Thanks for letting me know' then slammed the door on me. She didn't ask for details. She appeared to be aggravated, angry, like she didn't want us bothering her anymore. The sad thing about this is Amber has no other family around here. She was an only child, ironically, so were both of her parents."

Bud then pressed the button on the remote again, bringing up the second girl in the pictures. She was there, her face in full view, just like the last one, her medium brown eyes glazed and staring into some spot in outer space. Jack had also studied this picture for a long, long time. He had asked himself, many times, why did this girl have dark hair while the other girls were blonde? She didn't fit the archetype or the pattern of the other victims. This was not typical of a serial.

Bud stepped closer to the television screen, as though he was seeing the picture for the first time. He grabbed a file off of the table and began rummaging through it when he finally found what he was looking for; he looked at the men around him, walked to the bulletin board, and hung another picture up of the same girl. He turned around; with his eyes on Jack, he said, "Everything you need to know is in the file in front of you. I have to leave now." Neilson's abrupt departure surprised everyone but Ireland. He saw what Bud had just seen.

Jack knew instantly what Bud was up to. Bud was going back to the crime scene, and he intended to follow him, but he had no car. He grabbed Brice by the arm. "We have to leave now."

Vic and Brice had by then also noticed the difference in the photographs. The purple button was missing from the forehead of the second victim, the dark-haired girl. The killer had been back and had removed it, this was certain, but they needed to be sure.

Down on the lower level, one of the phones rang. Jamie, filling in for someone taking a lunch break, answered the phone.

"I wish to report a missing person."

"What's the missing person's name please?"

"Andrea Pennington."

"How long has she been missing?"

"She's been gone for over a week."

"What is your name, sir?"

Click.

Jamie thoughtfully placed the headset back into its cradle and logged the phone call into the database. He wanted to mention this to Vic; but he, Jack, and Brice were already on their way out the door. His cumbersome body would never be able to catch up with them. He picked up his cell phone and entered Vic's number. Vic answered immediately.

"What's up, my fat and under loved friend? You miss me already?"

"You have another missing person. The guy who made the call, hung up on me."

"Did they, I mean, he give you a name?"

"Andrea Pennington, sound familiar?"

"Not to me, but hold on, let me ask Jack."

Jamie heard muffled voices on the other end and soon after, Vic was back on the line again.

"Did you tape the conversation, Jamie?"

"Sure, it's on tape; everything that comes in here is recorded."

"Ok; be a really good man and do a voice analysis for us. We want you to compare his voice with the voice on the tape you have of Jack's, can you do that and get back to me on the results?"

"I can, but I don't think it's going to help much, the person calling, muted his voice."

"I don't care, Jamie, check for background noises, anything, we need something here, give it your best. We need a break.

Thick black, ominous clouds were building on the western horizon as Brice followed Neilson from Apple Valley to Pine Bend. Bud was taking them on back roads to cut off distance and avoid traffic. Brice was having all he could do to keep up.

Vic was staring out the passenger window, deep in thought. "Look's like we have another storm moving in."

"We don't need that right now, please, God, no more snow."

Brice, too, was anxious about the pending storm and about having to follow Bud at this break neck speed.

"Give me the particulars on the second victim found in Pine Bend, the dark-haired one, will you, Jack? Bud gave you a file, read it to me."

"I have it right here, Chief. I'd have an easier time reading it if you could cease with the swerving."

"Take that up with Bud."

"The second girl, fourth victim's name, is Shawn Mickel Parker. She was thirty-one years old. She had spent the day Christmas shopping with her sister who lives in Farmington. Now get this, after they were done shopping, they stopped at the Fireside Inn to have a couple of drinks and dinner.

"Shawn's sister, her name is Charlene by the way, goes on to say that she left first. When Charlene left, Shawn was visiting with a high school chum she hadn't seen in a long time. Charlene states she left around twelve thirty. This was the last she saw of her sister. Charlene was the one to call her in to missing persons. They were supposed to have their family Christmas gathering on Saturday, and when Shawn didn't show up, Charlene got worried but thought she might have been called into work over the weekend, this wasn't uncommon. She tried over the weekend, numerous times, to reach her sister, but never got an answer. On Sunday evening, Charlene went to Shawn's house, the doors were locked, and her car was gone. That's when she called missing persons.

"Shawn and her husband were divorced about a year ago. He had found a job in Fargo, ND, and when Shawn found out that he was taking another woman with him, she filed for divorce. She was living in their house located about a mile south of Pine Bend. They had no kids, she was living alone. She worked for a bottling company in South St. Paul and had been working there since she graduated from high school. She worked the graveyard shift. That would be from midnight to eight AM, for those of you who don't know what the graveyard shift is. That would be you, Victor; you wouldn't know anything about the graveyard shift. You have always been a pampered child and have never put in an honest days work in your life.

"Now get this. I have the medical examiner's report right here in front of me. This girl was hit on the head with a blunt object, knocked unconscious, and then strangled. According to this report, the blunt object had all the markings of a tire iron. The girl apparently survived being struck over the head because she died of asphyxiation. She was apparently knocked unconscious and then suffocated."

Mitch Garrison, the Dakota County medical examiner, didn't look old enough to have graduated from college yet. His red hair, blue eyes, and youthful freckled face bore a strong resemblance to Opie Taylor from the Andy Griffith Show. Mitch greeted the men with a wide-eyed friendliness that strongly resembled Opie as well. He apparently loved his job; his enthusiasm was infectious.

"I'm glad you called ahead. I have everything ready for you. Let's go take a look at the victims now this is always the hardest part."

Brice shook his head. "I don't think we want to start there. I want to see your pictures of the crime scene.

"Are you looking for something in particular? Our photographer is very thorough."

"We're going to be looking for two purple buttons."

"Really, well that's interesting. Someone else had the same question about a half an hour ago. I just finished researching that very question before you arrived."

"Who called, was it Bud?" Brice asked the question.

"Yes, it was Bud, how did you know?"

Mitch was looking at Buchanan as though he had some sort of mysterious prophetic skills that were worthy of his scientific attentions.

Brice dashed him unintentionally with his logical answer of, "We followed him here. Tell me what you told him."

"There was only one purple button found at the crime scene. I scoured the pictures taken by the photographer, and there was no purple button anywhere around the scene of the crime other than the one found on the blonde girl. The button was embedded into her forehead, and by embedded I mean pressed in hard. It left a deep indentation on her forehead when it was removed."

Jack showed Mitch the picture he had in his folder that showed a button on both of the girl's forehead. Mitch shook his head and said with conviction, "There was no button on the dark-haired one's forehead, nor was there a second purple button anywhere near the crime scene. I have magnified all the crime scene pictures, and if there was another purple button, someone took it from the scene before we got there, or it was carried off by some wild animal, but I don't think so because the bodies hadn't been touched by animals yet. They were deeply buried in snow. We found them in nearly pristine condition. The cold weather and the four feet of snow covering them preserved them, as though they had been in a freezer."

"You're sure?"

"Yes, I am very sure. I was there. I was in charge of that scene. There was no second button anywhere near the crime scene. I also checked with Hank. He said he had only found one purple button at the scene, and it was on the blonde girl's forehead. Hank was positive. He even made a notation of this in his notes because he has been keeping himself up to date on the Purple Button murders. You haven't discussed any of this with Hank yet?"

Jack gave his boss a questioning glance.

"Hank was the homicide detective on this one? Why wasn't Hank brought into the meeting today?"

"I did tell him to be there, but he said that I didn't need both of you at the same place at the same time. He said he had a date with a lovely lady, her name was sleep, and if we needed him, we should call him in the morning."

Jack chuckled with appreciation. "Sleep, huh? I know all of his girls, and there isn't one that has the name of sleep. He's probably ice fishing. What do you think, Melton?"

"Let me put it your way, Ireland, 'Button, button, who's got the button,' and what do you know about Andrea? I hope she isn't another one of your long-lost loves."

Chapter Forty-Three

"For the life of me, I cannot understand why you chose to bring that girl back here to the house. Do realize what you have done, Shorty? Did you give any thought to this before you brought her back here? She *is not* part of the plan." Willie was seething.

"How many times have I told you not to mess with the plan; I cannot believe you did this! I think you might just have screwed everything up beyond repair, and for that I could kill you. In fact, I might just have to."

Willie was not the least bit happy with his little brother. In fact, the truth of the matter was he wanted to strangle his little brother with his bare hands. Willie was pacing back and forth in the kitchen, his face distorted and flushed with anger.

"What do you mean?" Shorty retorted back. "I haven't screwed anything up. I'm doing what I want to do for a change. You always get to do what you want to do, why shouldn't I do what I want? I never get a chance to find someone of my own. You always pick the ones you want, and I never get a say-so on anything. I just get to do all the dirty work. It isn't fair! If you want to kill me, go ahead and then see who you have left. You won't have anybody. You'll be all alone, and it would serve you right."

"Did it ever occur to you, my stupid, asinine brother that perhaps I pick the ones I do for a reason? That's two now that you have done without any conference with me. You are being reckless, and you know it. If you keep this up you're going to get us both strung up by a rope and that definitely is not part of *the* plan!" Willie was growling; his voice was harsh and coarse.

Shorty was busy taking down the Christmas tree, boxing up all the decorations carefully and getting them ready for storage. Willie was still attired in his round-two robe and Shorty was wearing a black-and-white horizontally stripped, long-sleeved t-shirt, bright red suspenders and black jeans that were too short for him; his feet were bare.

"Besides you look like a clown in that getup. Where did you find those clothes anyway?" Willie was giving his brother a head-to-toe once-over.

"I liked her, and I wanted her for my own. The other one is a certifiable brat. She isn't a pet at all. She is vicious and mean. I don't like her. You don't look so hot yourself in those ugly slippers and your boxing-match robe. Where did you find that getup?" Shorty was mimicking his brother's condescending pitch.

"Damn it, Shorty, you picked the same damned type. The other isn't any better. She comes from a place way beyond you, and besides, she isn't even pretty."

"She is too pretty and she likes me. I know she does. She wanted to go with me last night, I could tell."

"Cripes Shorty, get over yourself and help me carry these boxes out to the garage before I beat you within an inch of your miserable life. I hope you got the shoveling done, otherwise, we'll be walking through six inches of snow, and I won't help you."

"You get over yourself before I clobber you within an inch of your life! Why do I always get stuck doing the shoveling? I have to do everything around here. You don't do anything. All you ever do is come and go as you please and give me orders. I'm getting really sick and tired of having to do all the hard work."

Shorty knew full well that he was walking a very dangerous line, but he couldn't help himself. He was worn-out with having to be considered the dumb one of the bunch. He wasn't dumb, and if his brother would leave him alone, he might even be able to live a normal life.

"Someone has to make a living, Shorty, or we would be back out there, thieving and not having near the fun we are right now. So be a good boy and help me carry these boxes out."

Willie had calculatingly changed tactics on Shorty. He had said what he had to say, and now it was time to console him and bring him back into the fold. They played this game all the time. He had to keep Shorty under control because he needed him, for now. Getting him all riled up and angry didn't work out well in the long run.

Willie gave his brother a hug and said, "You be a good boy and store this stuff while I get dressed. I like your outfit, I really do. I was just angry when I said that."

Shorty gave a little sniffle and hugged his brother back. "We shouldn't fight like this, Willie. It makes me sad."

"I know, brother, I know. We'll figure it all out, now you get to work, and I'll get cleaned up."

Shorty wound up carrying all the boxes to the garage by himself as Willie showered, shaved, and brushed his teeth. The sidewalk had been meticulously cleaned of all snow and ice.

"There's a storm moving in, so get a wiggle on, Shorty. We have a lot to get done today. You have a mess to clean up here, a big mess. I know you like her, but it is time for us to finish this. I'm going to depend on you to do the right thing. Can I count on you, Shorty?"

"Yes, Willie, you know you can count on me. I just want you to say that I didn't do anything wrong."

"You didn't do anything wrong, Shorty, you just made an error in judgment, we all do that now and then."

Tracy's senses had sharpened by her long stay in this very gloomy, distasteful place. She could hear those now familiar footsteps and muffled voices upstairs. Darth and his short partner had come down sometime during the night. The short one had pinned her down while Darth drugged her. She had a large swollen spot on her hip where he had thrust in the needle with unnecessary roughness. They had given her little time to react or to fight, but after further thought, she knew that wouldn't have made any difference. She was glad to be awake to see another day. Soon, hopefully, the short one would turn on the light and bring her something to eat. She was starving. She couldn't remember the last time she had eaten, as one day passed into another. She had lost all track of time.

Tracy was lying on her back, listening to the sounds coming from above, when she thought she felt something stir beside her. How quickly insanity takes over. There should not be and could not be anything stirring beside her; her heart quickened as she felt the stirring again. At this exact moment, the door from above opened wide. Light came pouring down into the pitch-black cavernous basement, blinding Tracy momentarily. By the time the short one hit the light switch, her eyes had readjusted. She wasn't insane! There was a person, a female person, lying next to her.

She jumped off the mattress in one very agile leap; her heart was thumping, pounding, hammering with excitement. She was totally dazed by what she saw. The chains from her ankles had been removed, and another person, lying in deep slumber, was now wearing them. The girl seemed to be sleeping restfully, totally unaware of her surroundings and the peril she was in. The girl wasn't anyone she knew. Tracy stared down at the blonde beauty, as though she were some alien from outer space. She rubbed her eyes, shook her head and looked again.

Then another thing happened, which put the fear of God into Tracy. Her two captors came down the stairs, the tall one in front of the short one; they were not wearing their hideous black garb. Neither of the two men were wearing their masks. She threw her hands over her eyes as though to shield herself from seeing them. She didn't want to see them; she did not want to know who they were. Her pulse quickened even more, the pounding in her chest accelerated, she felt faint. They had decided to reveal themselves to her. Tracy took three deep breaths, and then she started to cry uncontrollably. She tried to wake the girl next to her but got no reaction.

Tracy stared at the taller man in disbelief; tears were streaming down her face. She couldn't quit sobbing. She knew him.

"It's you? But why? I don't understand?"

Darth ignored Tracy's question and said with a snarl "Don't worry, she will wake up momentarily. Shorty gave her enough drugs to get her here and have her sleep through the remainder of the night. He thought you might need a roommate for a while.

"He thought you might be losing your mind and in need of another woman to share your woes with, and if I was about your shape and your size, I wouldn't be asking any questions, none. Let me introduce you. Her name is Andrea."

Shorty was moving around the room, randomly taking pictures with his digital camera. He was smiling all the while, a meaningful satisfied smile. He spoke not a word. Click, click, click, click went the camera, as though he were trying to stay in rhythm with Tracy's beating heart.

With eyes filled with stark horror, Tracy studied the girl on the mattress. She could not remove her eyes from the girl's naked body lying there, not moving, serene in her unconsciousness.

"Who is she? Why is he always taking pictures? Who is Andrea?"

Tracy was asking, not because she was expecting any answers, but to avoid the thoughts that were lurking in the back of her mind.

"Why is she here?"

Tracy had not come to realize yet with all of these other things to concentrate on that she was naked too.

Darth's ugly face twisted into a convulsive, twitching smile.

"You're here because of Jack Ireland; she is here because she looks like our mother. If you ask me one more question I'm going to have Shorty beat you to a bloody pulp. He'll be happy to beat you to death because he doesn't like you very much. In fact, he doesn't like you at all.

"Oh, I see she is stirring. We'll depart for now. You will be in charge of keeping her under control, Tracy. This means, I didn't want her here in the first place, she was Shorty's idea, one scream out of her, and you're dead. One scream out of either of you and you're both dead. That's a promise."

The cruel tone in Willie's voice convinced Tracy that he meant it.

As the two men climbed the stairs, Tracy asked without thinking, "Can I have something to eat? I haven't had anything but water for days."

She was so hungry she had to take the risk, bloody pulp or not. They had been slowly starving the energy right out of her. In the following instant, she regretted the question. She doubted that she would be able to keep anything down at this point. She had no idea why she had asked such a frivolous question.

Garth stopped mid-stairs and said without turning around, "Why would you want to wreck your perfect figure with food, Tracy? The last time Shorty brought you something to eat you complained he was giving you too much starch, too much fat. You hurt his feelings, Tracy. You should be more appreciative of the gifts you are granted and not so critical and demanding. Now you are hungry and want him to do your bidding. I don't think so, Tracy. You deserve everything you are getting right now, which is nothing, and for what it's worth, you don't even deserve that."

This was true; she had said this. When would she ever learn to keep her big mouth shut? She had been denied further showers when she had made a request for shampoo for her hair rather than using a bar of soap. When she had asked for some more reading material to occupy her time, they had cleaned out everything she had and brought her none. When she had asked for a change of clothing, they had laughed at her. When she asked for fresh bedding, they howled.

The scent of mildew had long been replaced with the scent of old sweat. Her long blonde hair was grimy and thick with grease. Her once-beautiful skin was now marked with raw sores and crusty, her full lush lips were dry and cracked. She was bone thin. How long had she been in captivity? A few weeks probably, but to Tracy, it seemed like forever. Speaking of clothes, why was she naked? She grabbed the blanket and covered herself. She pulled the sheet over her naked roommate. She had a headache; nothing was making sense to her. They had left the light on, it must be daytime. Her stomach was churning; she was starting to feel sick. This was no time for weakness She took a deep breath, swallowed hard and waited.

Tracy kept a close eye on Andrea as she gradually came out of her drug-induced slumber. Andrea didn't move or say anything at first but rather looked around the room with a quizzical expression as though trying to absorb her surroundings. Tracy waited for the right moment, the moment when panic would inevitably come into Andrea's eyes, when she saw it she jumped on top of Andrea, straddling her and placed her hand firmly over her mouth.

"Hush, be quiet, don't make a sound. If you do, we are both dead."

Andrea shook her head violently, trying to escape the hand holding her mouth shut; she struggled to remove the person holding her down but Tracy held her firmly in place. She wasn't physically stronger than Andrea, in her weakened condition. She had a desperate fear that the girl might be able to over-power her and this enabled her to do what she had to do. Andrea fought with all of her might to remove herself from the woman on top of her, but she couldn't; finally she relented, her eyes were stark with fear.

The woman held her fast and kept hissing words at her that she couldn't understand, didn't want to understand. Words like "Don't scream, don't scream; don't scream. Please don't scream."

When she could fight no longer, she listened to the woman who had her pinned down; she was a madwoman, no doubt, and this was nothing more than a nightmare she was having. She listened with her eyes closed tightly as Tracy said, as though the weight of the world was behind her words, "When you are done fighting me, I will let you loose, but if you make one peep, I will break your neck. I can and I will. Do you understand me?"

Gasping for air, Andrea nodded her consent, her beautiful eyes wide with undiluted fright. When Tracy finally released her Andrea rolled over to the side of the mattress and threw up, a reaction from the drugs she had been given and raw gut fear. Tracy was empathic. This had been her first reaction too. She was having a bit of a problem herself. The additional odor of vomit combined with the foul scent of old sweat was making her gag. Yet this was much easier to contend with than the rising bile in her throat being generated by the horrible thought that her life was very near to being ended. The incomprehensible image that today might be her last day would not go away.

Willie removed his hooded parka from the coat closet and slipped it on. He grabbed the keys from the kitchen counter and slipped them into his pants pocket.

"Where are you going? You're leaving me again without telling me where you're going?"

"I just got a call from Lulu. I have to head to Hastings, when I come back, I will expect all the excess baggage to be gone. They've found the bodies in Pine Bend."

"What do you mean excess baggage?"

"You know exactly what I mean by excess baggage. You have a mess to clean up, and I want it done before I get back here. I want all of it gone and the basement stripped bare."

"Where do you want me to dump this excess baggage? What about all the other stuff? What do you want me to do with it? This is sort of short notice don't you think? You expect me to do it all by myself?"

"You know where! Damn it, Shorty, why do you keep making me run things over you, time and time again? You are acting stupid on purpose. Knock it off, or I'll clean up the mess and then clean up on you as well. Don't push me."

"What if I don't want to do this Willie? What if I just do one and not the other, what then?" Shorty was getting down right brave. He knew this type of belligerence could get him throttled if not worse, but he couldn't help himself. Willie had been aggravating him all day long with his bossiness.

"I'm leaving now, and when I come back, you had better have cleaned everything up or be gone before I get back. You know what you have to do. We've discussed this many times, brother. It isn't going to be good for either of us if you let me down, Shorty. I have to leave now. Shorty, I am depending on you, do not let me down!"

"Whatever you say, boss, whatever you say," Shorty replied sarcastically.

Andrea was curled up in a ball on the bed with the sheet wrapped tightly around her. Tracy was sitting on the toilet stool. Both she and Andrea had developed a chronic case of diarrhea. The air reeked of excrement and vomit. Tracy felt as though all of hell was breaking loose.

"How much trouble am I in?" Andrea asked in a benign tone of denial. She really did not want to know the answer. She was scared witless and shocked beyond all reason. She would blink and everything would be back to normal. This was a bad dream happening to someone else, not her. Tracy was about to take this state of complacency away from her in the *blink* of an eye.

"I don't know about you, Andrea, but I see no way out of this predicament we are in, no means of escape. I have had weeks to work on this, so if you have any bright ideas, now is the time to share them. It seems as though I have been down in this basement for an eternity. I think that the only chance we have to survive this, is probably zero. Today is the first day that the men who have been holding me captive revealed themselves. That is not good Andrea. Not good for you and not good for me. If you have any last prayers, I would say them now."

Tracy crawled her way to the bed and wrapped her arms around Andrea. She had never held another woman in her arms before. She had never wanted to. Somehow, comforting Andrea helped comfort herself.

"Tracy, have we ever met before now?"

"No, we have never met before."

"This is a very interesting way to meet, isn't it?"

"Yes, Andrea, I guess it really is a very strange way for people to get to know each other. Just sit tight, I'll think of something. I just need a few minutes to think."

The blue-eyed blondes watched with lackluster hope as Shorty made his way down the stairs. His demeanor was calm and friendly, his blue eyes bright; his dimples were deeply creased. He pointed a gun, a .357 magnum with a silencer their direction and pressed the trigger four times. He checked their pulse to make sure they were dead and then carefully planted a purple button, number five and six, on their foreheads. He took several pictures of the dead bodies, wrapped them in plastic and carried them up the stairs. He carried out the mattress along with their clothing and burned them. He stood there vigilantly as the fire burned until it extinguished itself. When there was nothing left but a charred metal frame of the mattress and ashes, he placed the bodies of the two women in the trunk of his car and drove off down the long driveway leading to the main road. Shorty knew exactly where he was going. His route had been planned long before this day.

It was starting to snow; large fat flakes were falling heavily on the windshield. He had come to like Minnesota. He wanted the snow, lots of it. Snow would suit his purpose, but he had no time to waste. The temperature, according to the thermometer in his car, read minus twenty-one. He was glad he had dressed warm. Willie had told him to dress warm and be careful not to take too long. He didn't want him caught in a blizzard.

Shorty hummed a tune as he drove; his mind on places of the future, way beyond the dark horizon to a place where his life could begin all over again with his mother, his dear, beautiful blond-haired, blue-eyed mother. He went from softly humming to singing out loud. His exquisite rich tenor voice resonating through the interior of the car, keeping in time with the rhythm of the windshield wipers elevating in volume with each stanza, his rendition almost identical to the original version done by Michael Nesmith a few years back. His soul sang out the dream closest to his heart.

Beyond the blue horizon, waits a beautiful day.
Good-by to things that bore me,
Joy is waiting for me.
I see the blue horizon.
My life has only begun,
Beyond the blue horizon lies a rising sun.

Shorty would have liked Michel Nesmith to be proud of him. Maybe one day, beyond the blue horizon, he would meet his favorite singer of all time, and Michael would offer to sing the song with him. Maybe, maybe they could sing the song together for his mom; that would be nice. She loved beautiful music.

Chapter Forty-Four

Time was scurrying like rats in a harbor, one day bleeding incessantly into the next. Those who were in the process of investigating the Purple Button Case and those investigators working on the disappearance of Tracy and Andrea were but vaguely aware of the passage of time. They hardly noticed that the weather had become warmer and that the snow was starting to melt or that the spring flowers were pushing their noses up through the dirt and the trees were getting little tiny green leaves on them. Spring had arrived unannounced and without commotion. Time had slipped by the team of investigators because their thoughts and minds were on the problem at hand, not on the calendar. One would think they might have noticed the change in season because this had been a long hard winter with near record snow accumulation, fifty-six inches; and a subzero cold snap that lasted, continuously, through three long months, from the beginning of January all the way through February and March. It might have been that while they were trudging painfully through the muck and the mire of resolving one of the most challenging cases of their careers, the weather hadn't offered any glorious performance of being anything other than the same, impossible.

What they all were aware of was their lack of success in finding the Purple Button Killer or in finding Tracy Durkin and Andrea Pennington. As spring arrived, or should one say what should have been spring arrived with the spiteful reluctance and belligerence of a teenager, the teams of investigators were filled to the maximum with frustration and exasperation.

Jack, however, knew one thing for certain one unusually bright spring morning in April; he knew he had to find a way to reconcile his situation with Kirsti, one way or the other. She had been out of his life, almost entirely, since New Year's Eve. He had been living with Doreen, and he knew without her saying anything at all that she wanted something more than a bed-partner. In fact, she wasn't in the market for a bed-partner or a roommate and especially where Jack was concerned. Doreen had been exceedingly patient, non-prying, cooperative, and loving. Jack knew that Doreen was good for him, Lord knows, Vic reminded him of this often enough.

What Jack wasn't so certain about was how good he was for Doreen. He wasn't being fair to himself or Doreen by allowing this phase of living in limbo to lag on indefinitely. It was time he made a decision, and he couldn't do this without having a heart-to-heart with Kirsti, who had been doing her level best to avoid him. Try as he did to get her narrowed down to having a one-on-one conversation with him, she would not, couldn't, or didn't want it. She seemed determined to hold him at bay, so it was time to lay the old proverbial hammer down.

Kirsti was entering the Crawford and Crawford law office when her cell phone rang. She flipped her cell phone open, her caller ID indicated that it was Jack. She really wasn't surprised; she had been acerbic and rude to him every single time he had tried to communicate with her. Basically, she had hung up on him, or she wouldn't take his calls at all. She didn't want to talk to him now either. This was a beautiful, sunny spring morning. She didn't want to have anything dampen her cheerful spirits in any way whatsoever and Jack would, could, and did do this to her just by his mere existence. The simple thought of him made the hair stand up on the back of her neck. She hadn't carried her grudge with him to the finish line yet and no amount of family pressure had made her change her mind.

She answered the phone abruptly, "What do you want, Jack? I'm busy. I have a meeting in about one minute, so that's all the time you have."

"Well then, if I only have a minute I will use it wisely. I need to talk to you. Will you meet me tonight at the Lakeville Municipal?"

"That isn't possible."

"Why isn't it possible?"

"Because I don't want to see you, I don't want to talk to you, nor do I want to see you. It's as simple as that."

"So I guess you are in the business of repeating yourself, but I am going to have to insist that you meet with me Kirsti. I am not asking you this time. There is no other answer but an affirmative to this question. I will expect you to be there at seven sharp. We need to get this business over with once and for all, one way or the other. If you don't show up I will track you down. One way or the other, I am going to have a meeting with you before you go to bed tonight."

Jack hung up on Kirsti before she could reply, and as he did, he grinned a little. Kirsti had a real thing about people hanging up on her. She could do it, whenever she felt like it, but she detested anyone hanging up on her. Over the past few months he had discovered a lot of little quirks about Kirsti that he hadn't been aware of before he married her. "Act in haste, repent at leisure?" He was finding out that repenting wasn't something that Kirsti accepted at all. She didn't want repentance because she didn't want to forgive. She seemed to be totally unwilling to give him any hearing at all. Jack was determined to meet with her. He was going to have his hearing by the end of the day.

Jack was sitting on a stool in an obscure spot at the end of the bar when Kirsti arrived. He hadn't laid eyes on her in three months; she seemed to have lost the innocence that had made her so appealing to him. She had garnered a tough look through the eyes, a hardness that hadn't been there before. What hadn't changed was her immaculate appearance. She was dressed in the latest style available. The dark gray pin-stripped, double-breasted suit fit her small body flawlessly. The blouse underneath was a startling white made of a soft silk material. Around her neck was the diamond pendant he had given her for Christmas. Kirsti had taken on the aura of a highly successful, well-paid woman; her stride was confident, purposeful, her expression was serious. Jack, no slouch at reading people, could plainly see that she had already determined the outcome of this meeting.

Jack purposely opened the conversation with a compliment knowing full-well that Kirsti was a sucker for compliments. She thrived on them.

"I like your hair. You have it styled differently. The blonde streaks are a nice accent, spiked. I see that style a lot these days. Kind of cute, I suppose. Sorta makes you look like a kid though and the look doesn't really match your suit very well. The secretary at the office has a suit like that. She told me she got rid of it because everyone, and their sister, was wearing one." He had granted the compliment and as rapidly had whisked it away.

He knew Kirsti hated to be held in comparison with mass mentality concerning anything and everything. She had once said to him, "I do things differently because I hate to see myself coming down the street." Probably not a good way to get things started, but he just couldn't help himself. He needed to wipe that smug look off her face. It was annoying him.

She pretended to ignore the insult, greeting Jack coolly, she said, "I'm here, and I am hungry. Let's sit over there."

Kirsti pointed to a booth right behind them. "I don't have a lot of time. I have a meeting with Jerry at eight; we have business to discuss."

Jack barely noticed the waitress as she came and took their order; his attention was on Kirsti. He was fascinated by how much she had changed since the first day he met her. She was not the Kirsti he had loved or the person he had married. She was now something entirely different but equally as appealing, if not more so.

After the waitress delivered their drinks and had taken their order for dinner, Kirsti got right down to her usual, predictable directness, "I think I know what this meeting is all about. You want a divorce so that you can be with Doreen."

Jack lifted his glass to her appraisingly and responded, "Not exactly. I came here to meet with you to see if there was a possibility that you and I could get back together. I don't want a divorce; in fact, I never did want a divorce. I want to see if we can work out a different arrangement, like maybe getting back together again. I'm a Catholic, you know. I would be excommunicated from the church and two excommunications in one year is a bit more than my poor heart can handle."

"You're shacked up with Doreen and have been for months now." There was heavy emphasis placed on her use of Doreen's name, "This says a lot to me, Jack, and as far as you being Catholic goes; come on, give me a break! Don't insult me with that pile of crap. You haven't been to church in centuries."

Kirsti was heated, this was nothing new, she had been infuriated for so long that Jack was starting to get used to it.

"What does my living with Doreen say exactly other than I can live with another woman besides you? Doreen and I go back a long way. We've always been very good friends. What did you expect me to do, sit around and twiddle my thumbs waiting for you to make up your mind? What about you and Jerry?"

Jack was amusing himself; he knew Kirsti had him by the gonads on the Doreen issue, but that wasn't what he wanted or intended to get out of this conversation. It was going to be reconciliation or nothing. He was fighting fire with fire.

"Don't you dare to try and turn the table on me, Jack Ireland. Jerry and I don't have anything to do with you and I, and you know it! Don't even try to drag him into this. I am not living with Jerry. He and I are friends and nothing more. I work with him, for God's sake."

Kirsti sounded defensive, leading Jack to believe there was something going on here besides just pure as the driven snow innocence on her part, but on the other hand, she was right about Doreen. He was probably reacting to his own guilt about moving in with Doreen so quickly after their separation.

"All right, you win on the Doreen business, so I will get directly to the point." Kirsti also thrived on concessions, especially if they were made in her direction.

"I want you and me to try again, Kirsti. We have had a lot of pressure surrounding our marriage, which I think caused our present situation. I wasn't completely honest with you, and I regret that. I promise this will not happen again. I can't change my job, but I can change how I deal with my job and you. I'm willing to try if you are."

Kirsti sat there for a long time pondering what Jack had just said. Her flashing blue eyes were intense as she studied him. She took a sip from her glass of wine before she spoke, "You and I both know that's impossible, so what are you up to Jack? I don't believe you and even if I were dumb enough to believe you, which I'm not, I still wouldn't come back to you. It's too late. Too much water has gone over the bridge. I don't love you anymore, maybe I never did."

Jack sat back in the seat, picked up his drink, put it to his lips and drained the glass of its contents.

"I usually drink scotch. I don't know why I ordered vodka. Maybe change is a good thing" he said as he set the glass down in front of him. He stared into the bottom of the empty glass, gave it a couple of spins, raised his hand to the waitress, and ordered another.

"I've been hearing things about you, Kirsti."

Jack's voice was as cold as ice, his expression even colder. "Not good things, not good things at all. I hear that you have been having a little fling with Reed Crawford. Is that what you mean by impossible?"

Kirsti's eyes grew wide for just an instant but it was only for a split-second and then the self-righteous expression returned. She reached for her black leather briefcase, a very expensive black leather briefcase. She snapped the lid open, reached in and retrieved a set of neatly bound blue legal papers.

"Ah, you always did like to listen to the gossip, Jack, but this time the gossip is true. I have been dating Reed, and what we have going is something a lot more than just a fling. You might want to call it that, but it isn't. In fact, he has asked me to marry him." This wasn't quite true but it close enough and besides, with Jack, truth didn't matter. He had already proven that.

Jack responded by laughing until he had tears in his eyes. Everyone in the room was now staring their direction, this made him laugh all the harder. When he regained his composure, he said with a sneer, "And then I suppose you are going to quit Crawford and Crawford and become his little paralegal? Go to work for Benton and Crawford?"

"No, Jack," she said "I'm going back to law school, and you're going to pay for it, and when I am done with law school, I am going to partner up with Benton and Crawford."

Jack burst into another fit of laughter; he could not believe his ears. She couldn't be serious. He waved at the waitress again. He pointed to his glass and gave her two fingers. The waitress got the message. His laughter stopped abruptly; his mirthful expression changed into something dark and portentous.

"Benton and Crawford deserve each other, but that you are walking side by side with them, Kirsti, is downright embarrassing, not for me, but for you. Reed is every bit as unscrupulous as his new partner. What those two men did to those poor girls in the Wallace/Parish case is downright sick. They dragged the names of those three girls through every mud hole they could find. They should be ashamed of themselves, but they aren't, and they never will be, and that is what makes them so unworthy of even being regarded as human beings let alone representatives of the law you have thought to make yourself a part of."

"They won, didn't they, and that has to really gall you. The boys are back out on the streets again in spite of you and all of your theories and so-called evidence," Kirsti spat back. "You said they were guilty, you arrested them, but a jury of twelve thought otherwise. This is how our judicial system works, Jack. We have to take the good with the bad."

Now the conversation was getting down right ridicules so Jack switched gears, "How's Eugene and Mary?"

"Don't even start with that, Jack. You know exactly how they are. You and Dad talk almost every week. He told me he has invited you to go fishing with him up at Big Elbow next weekend, more power to the both of you, have a good time." Kirsti's self-possession was starting to slip. He had hit a sore spot.

"Your Dad doesn't know about your plans and your relationship with Reed, does he?"

Kirsti stood up and flung the divorce papers at him. "That's none of your damned business. Look these over and sign them. You have thirty days to respond. I don't think you will find any reason not to sign them."

Jack stood up to, picked up the papers, folded them in half, and stuck them in his coat pocket; he took a fifty out of his wallet and threw it on the table.

"Ok, fine, I guess we don't have anything further to discuss. You'll receive my response to this in twenty-four hours. I'll have my lawyer look it over in the morning. If he thinks it's all right, I will sign it, if he doesn't, I'll have him call you. From here on out, all our communication will be channeled through our attorneys."

As he walked toward the bar, he turned back and said, "One more thing, Kirsti; I hope, for your sake, you don't get yourself too tangled up with Reed Crawford. He doesn't know how to love anyone. He will only use you and than cast you aside like a dirty old dish rag."

"Sounds like the old proverbial 'pot calling the kettle black' to me, Jack," Kirsti hurtled these words over her shoulder as she strolled out the door with her hips swaying a little more than usual.

Jack went up to the bar, sat down, and ordered himself another vodka tonic. He pulled the divorce papers out of his pocket. Bannered in bold letters at the very top of the first page was the name Benton and Crawford Law Firm. Reed's signature was at the bottom of the last page. He folded the document in half and placed it back into his pocket again, thinkin, *figures.*

Doreen was at home folding laundry when he came ceremoniously through the door. He was stumbling down drunk and singing at the top of his lungs. She knew that he was having a tough time with the case he was working on, but not in a long time, had he come to her in this condition. In fact, she hadn't seen him this bad since New Year's Eve.

"I need another drink, Doreen, fix me a drink, please."

She did as she was asked. She filled a tumbler with ice and then water. In his condition, he wouldn't know the difference.

He was sitting on the couch and beaconing for her to join him. When she sat down Jack fumbled in his coat pocket with his right hand; when his hand came out of the pocket, it contained a maroon-colored velvet ring case. He thrust the case at Doreen, and next, with an enormous amount of inebriated effort, he pulled a set of papers out of his other pocket and thrust them at Doreen. She knew what they were. She didn't need to be told. He was getting his divorce and was he now going to propose to her? If so, she would have preferred he would do so, when he was sober.

"Open the box. I bought this a couple of weeks ago and was waiting for the right moment and now seems to be as good a time as any."

"Where have you been, Jack?" Doreen set the box and the papers down in front of her, unopened.

"I met with Kirsti in Lakeville." Jack was slurring his words badly.

"I wanted to make things right between Kirsti and me. You know I had to do this Doreen. I asked her if there was a chance for reconciliation, and do you know what she told me?"

Jack didn't wait for her to answer.

"She told me that reconciliation was impossible. Those were her exact words. No explanation, nothing; just a, 'see-ya-around' and without further ado, came the papers. Can you believe that Doreen? Can you believe it? You and I know nothing is impossible, is it? And get this; she is sleeping with Reed Crawford; that is if you want to call it sleeping. How did they ever come up with that one? Sleeping? She says he has asked her to marry him. Now get a load of that one. Ain't it all just too funny? I think it's funny, very funny. It's all a bunch of shitty, crappy, smelly, ridicules kind of funny."

Jack was laughing hysterically and leaning forward so far he almost fell flat on his face. Doreen gave him a shove backward, saving him from the possibility of a displaced nose or a cracked head.

"Thanks Doreen, you are really good to me. I'm a little drunk, aren't I? I must be rambling a bit. Open up the box. I want you to see what is inside of it. Talk about impossibilities."

Doreen picked up the small box lying on the coffee table and opened it. It contained a three-carat, at least, diamond ring.

"Is this ring for me, Jack; or was it intended to be for Kirsti?"

Jack doubled over with drunken laughter, "Damn it, Doreen, who did you think it was for? Why would I want to give Kirsti another ring; she didn't like the first one I gave her."

His strong handsome, tormented face went into complete relaxation as he fell into a deep alcohol-induced slumber; in short, he passed out.

Doreen sighed, put the ring back in the box and called Vic. When he answered, she said softly, "I want you to come and pick up your buddy."

"Now? You want me to come and get him now? What the heck time is it anyway?"

"He's passed out on my couch. I want him out of here, bags and baggage, before the sun comes up. I'll leave the key under the mat. I'm going to bed. When Jack wakes up, tell him I said he can go straight to hell."

"You don't mean that, Doreen, you can't."

"Oh yes, I do. I have never meant anything more in my life."

Jack woke up to Vic staring him in the face.

He noticed right off the bat he was sleeping in his clothes from the night before. His blurred vision was preventing him from clearly identifying much of anything else around him.

"Where in the hell am I?"

"Oh, shut your fucking mouth, Ireland. You have managed to piss off everyone who ever remotely liked you, including me."

Jack grabbed his pounding head. "Wow, this is a bad one. I think I have the hangover of the century."

Vic strolled into the kitchen and fixed Jack an orange juice mixed with vodka.

"You deserve it, buddy, here take a hair of the dog that bit you. We've got a big day ahead of us, and I don't need you hanging around me with after effects of the night before. Drink this, take two aspirins and then a hot shower and don't talk to me."

Jack took several sips of the drink, more because Vic was standing over him, insisting than from any personal desire to put the concoction into his system. His stomach was feeling queasy.

Isn't the 'hair of the dog that bites you" drink supposed to be made with tomato juice and Tabasco sauce?'

Vic turned on his heel and left the room, "I told you not to talk to me."

Jack placed his head between his hands, rubbed his cheeks, and said meekly, "OK, thanks, pal. I think things are coming back to me now. I screwed everything up with Doreen, didn't I?"

Vic reentered the bedroom and said with disgust, "It was inevitable. Drink your drink because we need to get going. I don't have time to discuss your female relationships, which are at this present time, a complete and absolute zero, zilch, none. I received a call from Buchanan. He wants us in his office as soon as we can get there. You had better get a quick grip on yourself because he got another video from the killer this morning, and he has invited you and me to come on down there and take a gander and don't say another word to me, or I am going to hit you so hard your whole family will fall over."

Jack knew Vic meant what he said, he didn't say another word to Vic as they traveled to the courthouse. Brice was impatient with both guys when they came into the office. He took one look at Jack and scowled. Jack looked like he had been run over by a truck. He had a thick, five o'clock shadow; his eyes were glazed, red-rimmed, and vague.

The commander, who had more than earned the title, didn't stand on formality but got straight to the point. "Jack you look like shit. What in the hell is the matter with you? Never mind, I don't wanna know."

"I received another group of pictures from the killer, and I don't think you're going to like what you are about to see. That is, Jack, if you are capable of seeing anything right now. What in the hell is the matter with you? You look like death warmed over. I need you to be sharp today. Damn it, Jack. Never mind, I don't wanna know."

Brice, through Jack's dim vision, seemed to have aged twenty years. His face was pale and deeply lined. His mouth was drawn down as though being tugged by an invisible gravitational force.

"You're repeating yourself boss. You don't look so hot yourself. I don't mean to be insulting but you look worse than I feel. Have you looked in the mirror lately? How long has it been since you've slept?"

"Just be quiet and look at the monitor. I want your full attention, Jack, quit clowning around." Jack was standing up and shaking himself, as though he were trying to disengage himself physically from his hang-over.

The computer was up and running. Brice turned the screen ninety degrees so that both Jack and Vic could get a close look. There were sixty-three pictures in all. Jack wasn't prepared for this, neither was Vic. By the time the video had ended, both Jack and Vic resembled Brice: pale, haggard, and downright miserable. Jack put his head in his hands and let out a deep sigh. Just as he had suspected, both Tracy and Andrea were dead, and just as he had suspected all along and voiced more than once, they did indeed belong inside the Purple Button Case.

"I knew it. That son of a bitch! I knew it. I want a copy of the last picture."

As Brice was making a print out of the last picture, someone knocked on the door. Brice answered with a bark as he was handing the printout to Jack, "Come in."

The person, who had knocked on the door, was Irv. Jack studied Irv as he came into the office and placed a pile of papers on Brice's desk.

"These are the printouts you wanted."

Brice nodded absently and replied absently, "Thanks."

Jack was thinking Irv seemed unusually cheerful, almost haughty. What was it about that guy that he disliked so much? There was something sinister about him, something sly and sleazy, slippery and shady. Jack got a case of the chills, the hair on the back of his hands had risen, and he let out an involuntary shudder.

After Irv left the office, Jack commented again to Brice, "Who is that guy anyway. What do we actually know about him? He is always lurking about. I don't like him, I don't trust him, and I wish you would fire him. I'm serious, I don't like him. He gives me the willies."

"You're starting to sound like a stuck record, Jack. I can't do that without a basis, and so far he hasn't given me any reason. He's just weird, that's all. We've sort of gotten used to him around here. He doesn't bother anyone; he does his job and goes home. I think you need to cut him some slack."

"Yah, if you say so."

Jack turned his attention back to the piece of paper in his hand. Another taunting poem from the killer directed at him personally.

> Ireland is where our lost ones lie,
> People who know him soon will die.
> We cannot bury our past, you know;
> For revealed it will be with the
> Fast-melting snow.

Brice had no idea how he was going to tell his good friend Mac the bad news. Jack had no idea how he was going to carry on with the burden the killer was laying on him. Who would be next?

How many is that now; we have six buttons, six purple buttons that have been used. How many are there, how many buttons are left? How many were there to begin with? Why Tracy, why Andrea, why anyone? What did this killer want? Every serial killer wants something. What does this one want?

Because Jack was currently without a home to call his own, he asked Vic to take him back to his place. He showered quickly, borrowed some clothes from Vic; Doreen had intentionally skipped packing him a bag. He all but beat the keys out of Vic for his Thunderbird and then went to Apple Valley. He needed to make contact with Jamie, the computer man. He had a copy of the disk with him, it was time to start from the beginning again and go over everything line by line, picture by picture, document by document.

As Jack drove, his mind was searching for something, anything that would reveal the nature of the killer. There had to be something they were missing, there always was. His mind came back to the poem; he recited the poem out loud several times. He stomped on the brakes so hard he almost caused a ten-car pile up behind him, did a rapid lane change, spun down through the median, kicking up a multitude of dirt and mud in the process, and then headed back in the same direction from which he had just come. He paid no attention to the helter-skelter of cars he had left behind him or the angry horns blaring at him as he sped away.

Jack knew where Tracy and Andrea had been dumped. What troubled him enormously was that the killer had wanted him to know. He couldn't have made it any more obvious, if he had called him up and told him where to look. The killer had been keeping him informed from the very beginning. *Why and why now?*

Chapter Forty-Five

Kirsti was winding her way back home on her bicycle. She had decided, now that spring had arrived, the time was right for her to start pedaling her way back and forth to work. She needed to tone up and get rid of some of the fat she had accumulated over the winter months. She had stepped on the scale a week ago and realized by the numbers, she had gained three pounds. She didn't want those three pounds to become six. As she pedaled, she was thinking about her plans for the evening with Reed and her ideas about planting flowers around the house now the weather was starting to warm up. She loved to garden. She might even put in a vegetable garden if she could talk Jerry into coming over and tilling up some ground. He would, she knew he would because he always did whatever she asked him to do.

Reed had decided she needed to learn how to golf, play tennis, and manage a sailboat. She had no objections. Reed was keeping her busy every moment of her waking hours with one thing or another. He wined her and dined her, taking her to all the fanciest restaurants in town. He lavished her with gifts, expensive gifts, very thoughtful gifts. He never seemed to tire of taking her shopping. Last night, he had suggested he pay for a breast implant. Kirsti had been somewhat shocked by the suggestion at first and then grateful. She appreciated that Reed was aware of how self-conscious she was about her body. She had often thought about getting a breast implant and would have before now had she been able to justify the expense. When she had mentioned to Hilde that Reed thought she should get a boob job, Hilde had been revolted and said that Reed was now way over the top in his desire to control and manipulate her. Kirsti didn't see it that way.

"I love your body," he had said carefully. "But a bit on the top would really make you look wonderful in your new bikini. We also have to get you tanned up a bit. I'll pay for it. Just say the word."

He had kissed her long and deeply, and had made love to her with a passion she had never received from Jack. She had, through Reed's coaching, learned how to respond, reciprocate and enjoy sex. He would hold her for hours until she went to sleep. He was with her in the morning. He had promised he would never leave her in the middle of the night, and he never had. She had no doubt she was bringing the very best out of Reed Crawford. All the nasty things people said about him were fading into the distance as she got to know him better and better. Kirsti had come to blame all of his errant behavior on his upbringing, on his mother in particular. She was convinced that with her, he would become a better person; the person she knew he was, not the person he portrayed to the world. He made her feel like she was the center of his world, and this was exactly what Kirsti needed for a long-term relationship. Jack was now behind her, and she was glad. She was happy.

As Kirsti rode her bicycle around to the back of her house and parked it next to the garage, she glanced at her watch. She had two hours to get ready before Reed would be spinning into her driveway to pick her up. She was having a difficult time deciding what to wear because she didn't know what the arrangements were. Reed had suggested casual, but how casual?

She entered her house through the back door; her mind was occupied with thoughts of Reed and her wardrobe. Whoever had designed this place had a thing for entrances. There was the front door, there was a back door, and then there was a door off the kitchen that allowed her into the garage. She had been nagging Jerry to get a garage door opener for her, but lately he had been acting somewhat aloof, which wasn't the least bit surprising to Kirsti. She knew that he didn't like her relationship with Reed. He'd get over it, because he had too.

Kirsti turned the key in the lock and then tried to turn the knob. The door was still locked. She twisted the key again, this time the door opened for her. Had she forgotten to lock the back door when she left? Jerry was always getting after her for leaving her doors unlocked. She was sure she had locked it, but maybe that was yesterday. Oh well, what Jerry didn't know wouldn't hurt her. She had been in a mad rush to get to work this morning. Reed had made her late.

The remnants of her previous night with Reed were scattered all over the house. She had no time to clean up anymore, but she wasn't concerned. She picked up a pair of Reed's socks and threw them in the laundry room. She was aiming for the clothes basket but missed it entirely. Last night's dishes were soaking in the sink; they would have to stay there another night; she didn't have time for them. She smiled when she saw his clothing lying haplessly all over the living room floor. They had undressed each other on their way to the bedroom, leaving a trail of clothing behind them. Reed's white terry bathrobe was slung over a kitchen chair, reminding her of the sex they had had that morning, interrupting their breakfast and making her late for work.

She needed something cold to drink. She felt a bit dehydrated from her bike ride. She opened up the refrigerator door and spotted the pitcher of ice tea. This was just what the doctor ordered. She filled a tall glass with ice and tea but couldn't find the fresh lemon she had sliced up the day before, so she added a little concentrated lemon juice. She took a sip. *Fresh lemon would have been better*, she thought.

She glanced at her watch again. Reed would be here in less than an hour and a half; it would take her every second of that to get ready, she couldn't wait to see him. Tonight she would tell him 'yes' to the question she was certain he was going to ask her. Jack would sign the divorce papers, he had no reason not to, and soon after, she would be free to marry the one *true* love of her life.

Kirsti turned around and gasped as strong arms grabbed her from every direction. There seemed to be black masks everywhere. She felt herself being dragged to the floor. She tried to scream but couldn't. Her constricted throat wouldn't let her. She felt more than saw something being put over her face. She struggled to get loose but couldn't; she was overwhelmed with fear; she couldn't breathe. Now there was nothing but darkness. As she fell off into a place she thought she ought not to go, she heard a soft, pleasant tenor voice whisper in her ear, "Sleep, little one, go to sleep and have sweet dreams."

The rumbling of the excavating machine was adding to Jack's headache. He was convinced that Tracy and Andrea were on his property someplace. Where was the question, and for how long had they been there was the other unanswered question. Jack had halted the excavation of his house after the basement had been filled and hadn't been back since. He had been waiting for spring to arrive before he began the process of rebuilding. He was glad he had waited because now he was having second thoughts about reconstructing at all on this site. There were too many bad memories here. The possibility of Tracy and Andrea being found on his property was more inductive to his present headache than his over-imbibing the night before. He was hoping upon hope that he was wrong.

Jack was slowly making a wide circle one direction while Vic went the other direction. They had started at the basement and were working outward toward the woods that surrounded what used to be his house. There were no unusual sounds to be heard in the woods as he made his way step by small step through the sprouting thickets. The ground was soft and mushy from recent rain and spring thaw. Jack edged his way in a crisscross fashion, covering every inch carefully, always looking down, to the left, to the right, and then forward. Jack couldn't have been fifteen feet into the seclusion when he spotted something about ten feet ahead of him that he instinctively knew didn't belong there. His stomach lurched as he drew closer. He might not have spotted the body from such a distance a month ago. The white stood out well against the green of the new undergrowth. He moved his way toward the form, being careful to mark his steps as he went. When he was right next to the body, he spoke into his two-way radio.

"You can tell the excavator to stop digging, I've found them. They're both here. I'm coming back out. You had better give Hank a call. I don't think I'm going to be able to handle this one, Vic."

Jack tried to maintain a sense of stability as he walked back toward the clearing. His legs felt like rubber. He plopped himself down on a log as he waited for Vic who was presently running toward him in what seemed like, slow motion. Everything seemed to be moving very, very slowly. His vision was getting fuzzy, and he was seriously wishing his heart would slow down a bit; the loud thumping in his ears was making him feel dizzy. Vic noticed immediately that Jack wasn't looking too good. His face was the color of ash.

"You think you're going to be all right, buddy?"

The question was purely oratory; Vic could see that he wasn't going to be all right.

"That's it, Jack, put your head down between your legs."

Vic pushed Jack's head down for him because Jack wasn't able to grasp much of anything at the moment; Vic didn't need a doctor's degree to see that his buddy was on the verge of passing out.

"Take deep breaths, Jack. Try to breath slowly and deeply. That's a boy, you're doing just fine. I don't want you passing out on me. Are you going to be sick? You look like it, you son of a bitch. Are you going to be sick?"

The words were barely out of Vic's mouth when Jack threw up all over Vic's boots, both of them.

"You know, Vic, I think I am going to be sick, and you can stop yelling now."

Vic started jumping around, shaking one leg and then the other in a hopeless attempt to remove the ill-scented vomit from his boots. The sight of Vic's long lanky body moving up and down in a hip-hop fashion, made Jack laugh. He laughed so hard he actually threw up again, spewing more smelly stuff onto the ground in front of Vic. On the brighter side, Jack's coloring had returned to normal, and he was now standing up on his own two feet without any assistance.

"Damn it, Jack, one of these days I am going to have to trade you in for a different partner. You are nothing but a big fat freaking annoyance! Where's a damned mud puddle when you need one?"

"That's OK, Vic, you can swear at me if you want to. Don't hold back on my account and Dave here, he's heard a few swear words in his life too. I suppose we had better call in the first responders." Jack had regained his bearings in a shorter time than Vic had expected.

Vic started to laugh and didn't quit until he was gasping for air.

"Forgive me, Jack, but in case you hadn't noticed because you've been a bit preoccupied with throwing up all over me, I need to tell you, we are the first responders. If you don't think so, take a gander at my boots. Yuk! If this ain't responding, I don't know what is. If you got any of your smelly stuff on my pants, you and I will be undressing and redressing from the waist down. We will be exchanging clothes."

Jack looked Vic up and down, scowled, and said, "What are you talking about? Your ugly green-colored, boat-sized boots are knee high. We ain't going to be exchanging anything any more and that includes women."

"No sweat, you ain't got no women in your life to share, never did."

Vic regretted saying this the second it came out of his mouth.

"Sorry, pal, I didn't mean anything by that."

Jack punched a number into his cell phone while nodding his head with apparent understanding. He knew Vic was only trying to humor him out of any thoughts of despair.

"We need first responders here immediately. We have two dead bodies at 1913 Victory Lane, Farmington, Minnesota. This is Dakota County Homicide Detective Jack Ireland speaking."

Jack looked at Vic and said sharply, "Let's get back to work. I don't take kindly to people leaving dead bodies in my back yard. In fact, I don't take kindly to anyone leaving dead bodies anywhere, let alone my back yard."

Vic grabbed his friend by the arm, "I think we ought to hold up until the first responders get here. I don't want you going back in there, Jack. I don't think it's a good idea, your too close to it, could taint your objectivity."

"Thanks, Vic, I appreciate your concern. I truly do, but I can't just stand around here twiddling my thumbs. We can work the outside perimeters for now. At least we'll be doing something."

The two partners were strolling down the long driveway when they heard sirens off in the distance, heading their direction. Jack said to his partner, "I suspect this place will be a real zoo in about three minutes. Every precinct in the Twin Cities is going to want to be in on this one."

"And let us not forget the press," Vic added deprecatingly. "Oh, by the way, how did you like driving my T-Bird, huh?"

"It's a piece of crap, a pile of junk. Nobody in their right mind would have bought that rattle trap, but then no one ever said you had a mind, let alone a right one."

Vic slapped Jack on the back hard enough to make him choke on his phlegm. "I'm so glad you approve. We make a good team, so why don't you get the hell out of here while the getting is good. Hank and I can take it from here. You, my friend, need to get your ever-loving ass out of here, and I mean right now, before you get tied up here forever. Go do what you were going to do before you got side-tracked."

Chapter Forty-Six

The pictures, those horrible pictures, of Tracy would be printed indelibly in Brice's mind for the rest of his life. As he eased his way in and out of traffic, many thoughts raced through his mind, none of them serene. He tried hard to push the mental pictures out and away so he could concentrate on what he needed to do next. He had to have those ugly visions gone before he met with Mac. There were too many questions and not enough answers; and while the entire police force in the whole of Minneapolis, St. Paul, and surrounding areas were looking for answers, bodies were piling up fast.

The pictures that the killer had sent him of Tracy and Andrea had been vivid in detail, far too vivid for the mind to grasp or even want to grasp. There were a lot more of Tracy than Andrea, but that was probably because Andrea had been taken later. The pictures were tormenting and painfully taunting. Brice once again tried to take his mind off the pictures and think about how he was going to tell Mac that his daughter was dead. He had decided not to call Mac ahead of time but try and catch him at home; he didn't want to alarm him. Mac still held out faith that they would find his daughter alive.

As he veered off of Highway 62 to go north on 494, his cell phone rang. The caller ID told him it was Walt Stanhope. He felt a tingle creep up the back of his neck.

"Brice Buchanan here, what can I do for you, Walt? Please tell me this is a courtesy call. I'm really not in the mood for any more bad news."

"I wish it were, sir. I was instructed by Jack Ireland to call you immediately and tell you that we have found the bodies of Tracy Durkin and Andrea Pennington."

Brice felt an electrical current bolt up and down his body. He could feel sweat starting to bead on his brow; his heart started pounding so loud, he could barely hear himself think.

"Are you OK, sir?" Walt's voice was rich with concern. He had sat in on several meetings and was aware of the close connection between Buchanan and Durkin.

"Yes, I'm OK, I just need to get out of traffic, give me a second."

Brice caught sight of a McDonald's parking lot to his right. He pulled in and parked his Cadillac in the closest available slot. He loosened his tie, removed his suit jacket, and undid three buttons of his shirt. He was disturbingly hot. He rolled down all the windows in his car and let the fresh cool air pass over him before he spoke again.

"You talk, I'll listen."

"Jack Ireland and Vic Melton found the bodies of the two girls about twenty minutes ago. The two bodies were dumped roughly sixty feet from Jack's house or what used to be Jack's house. All the proper teams are out here now. Everything is tied up tight all the way to the main road. There are no back entrances into the place which is a good thing. It'll make it easier for us to protect the scene from curious intruders. You know, press, the curious and anyone else who should decide to nose around uninvited. You know better than anyone what protecting a crime scene can involve, and this one is going to be especially nasty."

"Jack's place?" he gasped. Brice was stunned beyond words.

"The killer dumped the bodies on Jack Ireland's property?" Brice couldn't believe his ears. "What the hell is going on?"

"Quite a shocker, isn't it? This doesn't play too well for Jack, Mr. Buchanan."

"Listen, Walt, if Jack is there playing detective, I want him removed immediately. Tell him I said so."

"He isn't, sir. He removed himself right after he found the bodies. He called Hank Streece in. Hank and Vic are covering this one."

"Hank Streece and Vic Melton, that'll work for now. Where's Jack? Is he still there? If he is, put him on the line for me, I want to see how he is holding up."

"Sorry, sir, Jack has already left. Last I heard he was on his way to Apple Valley to meet with a person called Jamie. We gave him a pass. I hope that's all right. He was looking a little green around the gills, so I thought he might need to get out of here for a while and concentrate on something else. Were it anyone else, well, you have to know I wouldn't have played it that way."

"Thanks, Walt, you did the right thing. I'll catch up to Jack in a bit, but I have one more question, and then I have to get off the phone. Did you find a purple button anywhere on the bodies?"

"Yes. Yes we did, sir. They each had a purple button clutched in their left hand."

"Oh, before you hang up, there's another thing I need to know. Have you got any idea of how they died?"

"They were shot sir, two times through the chest. The rest will be up to the medical examiner to determine."

Brice hesitated before he asked the next question. He didn't want to ask it, but he knew he had to, so he spat it out fast and then held his breath, "How did they look? I need to know what Jack walked into."

Walt knew better. Brice wanted to know because he had to brace himself for Mac. Brice didn't want any surprises. Walt chose his words very carefully. "The girls have been out here for a while, Mr. Buchanan. We know they were placed here before the spring thaw. I think you know exactly what I mean."

"Good work, Walt, thanks for calling me. I'll get in touch with Ireland. I want a meeting set up with all core investigators in Apple Valley in the morning, seven sharp. I want everyone who is remotely connected to the Purple Button Case in on this meeting. Tell them to be ready to answer some hard questions. No one sleeps tonight, no one, including the medical examiner. Oh, is Bobby Brooks out there?"

"You better believe he's here, and he is livid. He thinks he's been left out of the loop. He thought Ireland and Melton should have called him first before they ever came out here."

"Well, they probably should have, but then there is no point in arguing about that right now. Jack isn't going to do that if he is working on a hunch. I'll deal with Bobby. Tell him to call me on my cell. He has my number."

"The press is lined up and ready for the kill. There are hundreds of them lined up out there for at least a mile, up and down the main road, what should I do with them?"

"Send them to me. I don't want anyone talking to the press right now, and I mean no one. Anyone who ignores this order will be fired immediately after they are tarred and feathered!"

"I think they intend to camp out here until they find out what's going on. They are being pretty persistent." Stanhope did not want to be the one having to deal with the press.

"Let them camp away. I don't care if they make the place their permanent residence, just don't serve them coffee and donuts and don't speak to them. I'll set up a press conference for sometime tomorrow afternoon. Tell them that, maybe they'll go home and let us do our job."

"I don't think that's too likely, but I like your optimism."

Mac and Gloria Durkin were waiting for Brice as he wound his way up the splendidly landscaped drive to their equally breathtaking mansion situated on the shoreline of Lake Minnetonka.

Today would prove the case, in point, that money simply cannot buy happiness. Mac and Gloria had been together for as long as Brice had known them, and he seemed to have known them forever. They, like all the rest in this exclusive area, had inherited their wealth. Mac Durkin was a judge because he wanted to be, not because he had to be. He was not a self-made man. He was controlled by the world in which he was raised. He was lofted to his position by his world of the wealthy, the enormously wealthy. He married Gloria because she fit what was expected of him. She came from a family of equal if not more wealth. Brice appreciated Mac because he didn't allow his money to drive his thoughts or his ambitions. He had the mentality of a pauper packaged in rich man's clothing.

Mac was generous, kind, understanding, and gracious with everyone, rich and poor alike. Gloria was his exact opposite. She did nothing for anyone, unless it benefited her. She was all about position and especially her position. Gloria and Mac had so many differences of opinion that she had quit sleeping with him after Tracy was born. How Mac had existed with Gloria for as many years as they had been together was a common query among their peers. Everyone knew there was only one answer, and it was because Mac was a State Supreme Court justice. Then there was Tracy, how was he going to tell them about Tracy?

Another question that crossed Brice's mind as he drove up the drive and parked his car in front of the gigantic pillars in front of the mansion was, *why are Mac and Gloria standing outside as though they are expecting me?*

This answer was easy for his detective mind. There was only one explanation. Someone had informed them he was coming. Someone had beaten him to the punch. How much the informant had told them was another subject that had entered Brice's already overly-burdened mind.

The expression on Mac's face made Brice want to weep. "She's gone, isn't she? My beautiful Tracy is gone."

Mac's gentle baritone voice was barely above a murmur. His eyes spoke the horror of the imaginings that had been lingering there for months. He seemed to sag from within as if something or someone sucked the air out of him.

Mac said, almost as if he were reading Brice's mind, "We received a phone call about fifteen minutes ago. The caller didn't give his name, he just said you were on your way to deliver some bad news, and then he hung up. The voice was disguised, muffled, and gruff, as though he were wearing a mask of some sort that would distort his voice."

Brice wished he could have been surprised by this, but he wasn't. The killer was having a good time at a lot of people's expense. Here he had been worried about beating the press! He hadn't even given a thought to the possibility that the killer would be the one to leak the bad news to Mac. Worse yet, he should have known he might. This perpetrator had made a practice of keeping the whole operation in motion with his phone calls, pictures, and poetry. *Why wouldn't he be the one to call Mac?*

Gloria, gracious as always, spoke next, "Mac and I have known for quite some time now that we weren't going to get Tracy back alive. Sure, we have tried to remain positive. We had to be positive, or we wouldn't have made it through each day, but underneath all the positive thinking, we knew. Parents know these things without being told. I suppose we have had more time to brace ourselves for this than you have. You look as though you are about ready to collapse. Let's go into the house, it's chilly out here."

Gloria was well trained in how to handle difficult situations but her off-the-cuff manner was almost unnerving to Brice, but then, it had only been fifteen minutes. Gloria was the picture of elegance as she led them into their enormous foyer. Most people's houses weren't as large as this one area of the mansion was. The average person's lifetime income wouldn't cover a tenth of the cost of a single picture that was hanging on the walls. Yet Brice knew that both Mac and Gloria would gladly give all of this up for one more day with their daughter.

From the foyer, Gloria took them into the den located straight forward off the main entrance. Brice accepted the scotch and water that Gloria mixed for him. He didn't need to remind her of what his preference of beverage was. They had known each other a long time. He reflected on the conversation he had had with Mac a few months ago. Mac had been accurate in his description of his den; there was not a hint of anything masculine in the room. The chairs were there for decoration, not comfort. It was a work of art and a showpiece for every serious art collector in the world. Expensive bookcases lined each wall. The shelves were immaculately lined with leather-bound books, each of them worth hundreds of thousands of dollars. He sat in a white satin chair of a vintage unknown to him, holding his drink carefully so as not to spill on the pristine white carpet, contemplating what to say next. He needn't have worried.

Mac watched as his friend gazed around the room in complete awe.

"Frightful, isn't it? All this stuff, all this expensive stuff, never to be used, never to be touched, so what's it all worth? I have to think about that, you know, especially now. You don't look very comfortable. Why would you? I hate this room. I hate every room in this house. Let's go out by the pool; it's a beautiful spring day, and I need some fresh air. Tracy loved the pool. I want to be where Tracy wanted to be while she was with us."

As they made their way to the pool, which was no short jaunt, Brice noticed that Gloria was speaking to someone on her cell phone as she made her way out the front door. She never said a word to Mac about where she was going or why. She left without a murmur or a farewell.

Mac's sharp, sad eyes observed Brice taking note of his wife as she was leaving and explained, "She's going to see her sister. She hasn't been home much since Tracy disappeared. She was here today only because she needed to drop off her laundry and pick up some things. Now that Tracy is gone, she won't be back. Our days together are over."

Mac frowned at the exasperated expression on Brice's well-formed and intelligent face. Brice had aged a lot since their last visit. His dark wavy hair, once only gray around the edges was peppered throughout. Deep crevices lined his brow. He had dark blue circles underneath his golden-brown eyes. He looked as though he hadn't slept in weeks. He had also lost weight he could ill afford to lose.

"Don't worry about it, my friend, she and I have been heading down this road for a long time. She has been living her own life since Tracy was born. Our marriage, like many others in our culture, is in name only, and I suppose it always has been, but that's not what you came here to talk about. Nor is it something I want to discuss now. I want to know what happened to my daughter."

Brice allowed Mac to serve him another drink. He hadn't finished the first one yet and didn't intend to, but Mac didn't need to know this; Mac needed special treatment right now, and if it took until morning, so-be-it. Brice leaned back in his chair and studied the crystal clear blue water in the pool as he waited for Mac to settle down. His mind seemed to be dancing from thought to thought like the sparkles of the sun glancing off the water in the pool. He needed time to recompose his thinking and so, he suspected, did Mac. Too many things were happening all at once. The finality after months of waiting had to be taking its toll. Mac took his time making each of them another fresh drink. He took his time in deciding where to sit. When he finally spoke, his eyes were fixed hard on Brice but he really wasn't seeing him. He was staring right through him.

Mac leaned back in his chair, "How long before you can give me all the details about my daughter?"

He was strumming his fingers on the solid glass table impatiently. This was the first time that Brice had noticed that he was a nail-biter. He had bitten them down to the bleeding point. However, on the flip side, maybe he had never been a nail-biter before losing Tracy. Unusual stress causes many uncommon reactions.

Mac curled up his hand; he had seen Brice looking at his fingernails and said, "It's a hard habit to break."

"It isn't a habit, Mac, it's a condition. Now do you want the long version or the short version?" Brice didn't wait for Mac to respond.

"I have a meeting at seven in the morning. I'm meeting with everyone involved with the Purple Button Case. Your daughter and Andrea are now part of this investigation. Before I arrived here, I got a call from the Farmington Chief of Police, Walt Stanhope; he told me that it was Jack Ireland, who found Tracy's body." Mac knew all about Jack Ireland and his relationship with his daughter. He read the paper every day.

Mac stood up and poured his drink on the cement. "You're ducking the question, Brice. Are you driving or am I?"

"Where are we heading, Mac?"

"You are going to take me to see my daughter. If you aren't willing I will have someone else take me, and I know just who to call. I have a driver ready and waiting."

Mac was not threatening Brice, he was telling him. Hell would freeze over before Mac would change his mind about seeing Tracy one last time.

"Let me make a phone call, and then we will be on our way."

Brice wasn't quite sure he wanted Mac driving anything, not even a tricycle at this stage of the game, so he opted to drive. Mac didn't argue with him, which was a good thing. He lived in the same vicinity so bringing him back home again was no inconvenience. None of what he had to do for Mac this night was an inconvenience, it was a requirement.

The men were silent as they headed out of Minnetonka toward Hastings. The bodies were in the process of being transported to the Dakota County medical examiner's office building located at the Dakota County Courthouse.

Brice picked up his cell phone and checked for messages. He snapped the phone down and said, "There are twenty-seven new calls, all from the press."

Mac threw his head back, laughed, and said, "Of course. I keep forgetting that this isn't personal to the media, this is big news for them."

"It is, Mac, this is going to be big for them. I didn't want this to come at you this soon, but now that you're traveling with me, we're going to have to greet them head on. They will be at the courthouse, by the hundreds."

"How are you planning on handling this, Brice?"

"I don't know, I was thinking about using a semi-automatic to drive them back a few paces."

"I don't think a semi-automatic is going to be effective enough. I think we need to create a diversion."

What sort of diversion did you have in mind?" asked Brice, not entirely believing what he was hearing.

"Let's have Bobby Brooks get on the air and state the bodies are being transported to St. Paul. He's great with the press. He'll do it for me because he knows it would be the right thing, besides," Mac chortled, "this diversion will help him out just as much as it does us."

"Why, Mr. Supreme Court Justice; that would be an out-right lie. I am challenged by your deceit and more than willing to oblige."

"Then be challenged, young man, be challenged and consider yourself fortunate that you can be. I have it on the best authority that a bit of deceit never hurt anyone, and at this point, myself, especially. Unusual circumstances require unusual actions."

Mac called Bobby and Bobby called the network news media, and before long, it was a done deal. Money buys power, and power buys everything.

There was not a soul around when Brice and Mac arrived at the Dakota County Courthouse. The halls echoed the sounds of their steps as they made their way to the medical examiner's section of the building. An attendant met them at the door and led them to the refrigeration unit. Buchanan left Mac alone with his daughter, so did the attendant. His cries of anguish could be heard up and down the empty hallways; they seemed to last forever. In the hearts of many, those horrible cries of complete desolation would, indeed, last forever and reverberate into infinity.

Chapter Forty-Seven

Jamie had selected an area off the main ground level, far to the back part of the building, to set up the place where he, Jack Ireland, and Frank Stiles would be meeting. The room was small but adequate. He had coordinated all the information he had, to date, in a variety of different ways for the two men to review. As far as he knew, there would be no one else attending this conference. He had no clear idea what Jack was hoping to accomplish. Instinct told him that Jack didn't either. This was going to be a search mission to see what might have been overlooked. He had the room lined with pictures of each victim that he had taken off the computer disks. Each victim had their own particular area in order of their death. He had a large chalkboard ready for notations should Jack want to use them. He had heard that they had found bodies on Jack's property. He had to question what condition Jack would be in when he arrived.

Frank Styles was the first to show up; Styles was an FBI profiler and, to this point, had been kept more or less in the background. This was normal. Profilers are called in when they are needed and not until. He came well prepared for this meeting. He had done a lot of research on his own, interviewing the investigators and the FBI personnel involved in what had now become known as the Purple Button Case and also the Durkin and Pennington cases. He was particularly curious to find out why Jack had insisted he be here and not any of the other investigators involved with the case. He would just have to wait and see. Styles never assumed anything, nor did he guess.

Jamie had met Styles in a previous meeting and liked his easy manner. Styles had straight, pure white hair, always freshly cut and neatly combed to the left. He stood about six feet tall and was the right weight for his height. Jamie had never seen the man in a suit. Styles was generally wearing a polo shirt and casual slacks of either tan or olive green and wore white tennis shoes with black trim of whatever brand was the cheapest. He had the look of a college professor about him. He hid his sharp intelligence behind a veneer of a light heartedness. He told jokes, one right after the other, to keep the atmosphere elevated when the going got bogged down and tension got tight. Today he was serious. He took a seat in one of the three chairs positioned around an eight-foot rectangular table, pulled some files out of his briefcase, a yellow legal pad, and a lead pencil. He was arranging some papers on the table when Jack arrived.

Jack greeted Frank and Jamie in a subdued but friendly manner. He took a quick gander at his watch, frowned, and said, "Let's get started. We have a lot of ground to cover before the press conference tomorrow morning."

"I want to start by going over everything line by line, picture by picture, detail for detail. Thanks for laying all of this information out for us Jamie, you've surpassed yourself. Let's start with the first girl. I want to see what we have that is similar, and I want to see what is different in each case. I don't want any more bodies, and we will not get him stopped unless we understand him. Somewhere in this stack of files, pictures, and database printouts, there is an answer to these horrible deaths, and we're going to go over them until we find it. I hope you guys brought no-doze with you.

"Frank thanks for coming on such short notice." Jack acknowledged Frank without a smile or a hint of apology.

"I'm glad to oblige, Jack. I'm as anxious as everyone else on the team to get this one solved. I'll do whatever it takes." Frank removed a packet of no-doze from his pants pocket and waved it in the air. This broke the ice. Jack and Jamie chuckled favorably.

"Good, I might need to borrow some; I didn't have time to stop along the way and get my own." Jack picked up a piece of chalk and moved to the blackboard. He wrote in bold letters: Purple Button Victims before he started to speak. The notes he had in front of him were meticulously written in longhand; his longhand. Jamie had set up the machine and screen so that he and Frank could follow along. He hadn't been sure if Jack would use it and was pleased that he decided to. Jack cleared his throat and began his presentation. He spoke in a dry, monotone voice, using a retractable pen for a pointer.

First Victim:	Rusty Carly Winters
Age:	23
Description:	Blond hair, Blue Eyes, 5' 6" in height.
Body found:	Credit River, Scott County, May 17
Occupation:	Waitress in Chanhassen
Cause of Death:	Drugged and then manually strangled from behind.

"She was found in a ditch. We know her body had been deliberately positioned. She wasn't killed where she was found. There was a purple button found in her left hand. She had been dead for approximately five hours before she was discovered."

"She came to Minnesota from Chicago and had no family in the surrounding area."

Jamie brought up the pictures that the killer had sent to the investigators. All three men watched as he flashed one picture after another.

"She was stalked by her killer. If you study the pictures, it becomes very apparent that the killer knows how to use a computer and how to run a camera. The pictures are edited to eliminate all backgrounds. There were no bruises or scratches on the body and nothing under the fingernails to indicate a struggle. The drugs found in her system explain why there was no struggle. She had been doped into unconsciousness before she was strangled. The marks on her neck indicate she was strangled from behind. There were no hairs or fibers found on the body. There was no evidence of sex."

Jack moved on rapidly scrawling information on the board.

Victim 2:	Anne Windsor Taylor
Age:	22
Description:	Blond hair, blue eyes, 5' 5" in height.
Body found:	One mile north of Chaska on Highway 169. Scott County. October 17 last year
Occupation:	Waitress at the Blue Duck 3 miles west of Chaska.
Cause of Death:	Drugged and then manually strangled from behind.

"This girl was found lying by the side of the road, in plain sight. She had also been planted and was not killed where she was found. Her body was deliberately positioned, the same as the first victim. She also had a purple button clutched in her left hand. She had also been dead approximately three to four hours before she was found. Both of these girls were butt naked. Again there was no evidence of a struggle, there were no hairs or fibers found on the body, nor was there evidence of sex."

Jamie was putting the pictures up on the television screen as Jack continued in the same monotone voice.

"She, like the first victim, had no family in the surrounding area. She was from Des Moines, Iowa. She was stalked by her killer as indicated by the pictures."

Jamie continued his slide show: vivid pictures of the girl's shopping, of them walking, one of them dancing, and then the death scenes. Jamie was having a hard time. He was a computer man. The pictures were making him feel ill. He was developing a new admiration for cops.

"The killer sent us these pictures via a Web site which he has chosen to ignore since these first pictures. Give us the tape, Jamie."

Jamie punched another button, this one leading to audio. A muffled voice came over the speakers.

"*I am your man, Jack; I am the one with the purple buttons, and I have several. You will not know how many until the day of your death. When I am done with the buttons, then I am coming after you. Have fun trying to find me, Jack. I am your nemesis. Check out the Web site, Jack, I have dedicated this Web site to you, just go to your own name, jackireland/visit/murder.com. Have fun.*"

"This call came in via my home phone at the same time as the second victim was found. The exact dates of when I received this call is in the file, Frank, but, for now I am only interested in looking at an overview. We can be more comprehensive later.

Victim 3:	Amber Linn Koech
Age:	23
Description:	Blond hair, blue eyes, 5' 6" in height.
Occupation:	Waitress at the Fire Side Inn, Farmington.

Found: Pine Bend, Dakota County, April 6 this
                year
Approximate time of death: Possibly late December
Last seen: December 23rd, last year.

"Amber disappeared from sight a couple of days before Christmas. She was found in Pine Bend just a few days ago. The approximate time of death is late December. She was drugged and then strangled from behind. She was living with a disinterested and somewhat senile grandmother at the time of her death. Because she has been so recently discovered we are not quite sure of all the details yet. We do know that she had a purple button planted on her forehead. Her body is in remarkable shape because of the hard cold winter we had this year. Five feet of snow didn't help us find her, but it did keep her refrigerated."

Jack nodded his head at Jamie. Pictures of Amber Linn Koech revealed themselves on the large television screen Jamie had borrowed from the conference room above them.

"There are no pictures of this one prior to her death. If the killer was stalking her, he didn't take pictures. If he did take pictures, he didn't send them to us. The medical examiner's report states that she was drugged and then strangled from behind. There was no indication of a struggle, there was no hair or any fibers on her body, her fingernails were clean, she was naked when she was found, and there was no evidence of sexual activity. Unlike the other two, she was positioned on her back and the purple button placed on her forehead rather than in her left hand."

"The killer had these pictures delivered directly to Mr. Buchanan's office right after the New Year. This is twice he has moved in right under our noses."

"I think it is interesting to note that the killer has moved from one side of the Twin Cities to the other. I have a feeling he has moved his activity closer to home with each victim. I also suspect the first two were done in Scott County to lead us away from him. However, I am only speculating.

Frank spoke for the first time, "When was the first time he moved in under your nose? You mentioned he has done it twice."

Frank had been sitting quietly up to this moment, taking notes and listening intently.

"You have to be patient, Frank, and quit interrupting me." Jack said, casting a bit of humor. "The next one will knock your socks off, so pay attention."

Jack had worn down one piece of chalk; he picked up another and continued writing.

Victim 4:	Shawn Mikel Parker.
Age:	31
Description:	Short, dark brown hair, dark brown eyes; 5' 8" in height.
Occupation:	Factory worker, Glass Company in St. Paul.
Found:	Pine Bend, Dakota County, April 6 of this year
Time of Death:	Unknown
Last seen just before Christmas	

"Amber and Shawn disappeared just before Christmas. What is most noteworthy is that these two women were at the same location at the time of their disappearance, the Fireside Inn just north of Farmington. Amber was working as a waitress, and Shawn was there having dinner. She was out shopping with her sister, and they decided to stop at the Fireside Inn to eat and have a couple before they parted ways.

"The cause of death is different as well. Shawn was hit over the head with a heavy object. The medical examiner says she was probably hit with a tire iron. She was than strangled; her cause of death was asphyxiation. She had been hit over the head from behind hard enough to knock her unconscious. The blow on the head was not hard enough to kill her. Marks around her neck indicated that she was strangled from the *front*."

Jack nodded once again to Jamie.

"The first picture sent to us by the killer shows her lying on her back with a purple button on her forehead. Shawn is lying next to Amber, who also has a purple button planted in the middle of her forehead. The pictures have been cropped so that there would be no evidence of blood around Shawn's head. However, there is enough in close-ups to show that it was snowing the night these two young women lost their lives." Jack added wryly, "However, this isn't much help at all because we have had near-record snowfall this year. From November through March, it has snowed more days than not.

"Now take a look at this picture."

Jamie brought up the picture taken by the forensic photographer. It was a close-up of Shawn's face. Her dark brown eyes were glazed over in death and were expressionless. Clearly missing was the purple button on her forehead.

Jack cued Jamie again with a nod, a picture of the poem appeared on the screen.

Frank shifted in his chair ever so slightly as Jack set the chalk down on the rim of the chalkboard and said, "Let's take a break here."

Frank Styles declined the offer to join Jack and Jamie for a cup of coffee. Rather, he sat at the table and thought about all that had been presented so far. Through Jack, he was starting to get a feel of the killer. He got up from the table, walked toward the pictures on the boards, and studied them one at a time. The killer was clearly somehow connected to Jack, but how and why was yet to be determined. He stood back and studied the poem intently.

Jack made his way to the front of the room and nodded to Jamie to start the next series of pictures. He didn't stand this time, but rather opted to sit down in a chair as though casual would make this easier for him. He was sitting so that he could see the screen and yet have a view of Frank.

"These pictures of Tracy Durkin and I were delivered to me, to my home, in December, just before Christmas. I found them after I came home from visiting my wife in the hospital. They came to me right on the heels of Tracy's disappearance.

"Just before Christmas, Tracy Durkin, daughter of State Supreme Court Justice Mac Durkin, came up missing. As you can see, I had a personal relational relationship with her."

"Because this was being treated as a kidnapping, I wasn't involved with the investigation. I was, at one time, considered a part of the investigation, but as a suspect because of my involvement with Tracy and because of the mysterious manner in which the pictures had been given to me. I was cleared eventually, but there are still those who think I might have had something to do with Tracy's disappearance."

Frank turned his attention from the screen to Jack. He felt Jack's discomfort and said, with no malice intended, "I have looked at you, also. I had the same thought and the tables being turned, I think you would have to agree. You wouldn't have let this one slide by you, not ever. You should be proud that your associates were on top of things and feel downright grateful that you are not the only credible cop on the block. You are not out of the woods yet, Jack. There are still a lot of good reasons to make you the prime suspect in these killings. You know it, and I know it. However, let me say this, I don't believe it."

Jack took Frank's comments in proper stride.

This part of the presentation had been the toughest for Jack. He gave Frank a slight upward turn of his mouth and continued. Frank gave Jack a nod and turned his head back toward the screen.

"On New Year's Eve another young blond disappeared. Her name is Andrea Pennington. This one also went to the FBI because it was considered a possible kidnapping. She worked for Crawford and Crawford, the same legal firm my wife Kirsti works for. Today, Brice Buchanan received a display of pictures of Tracy and Andrea in captivity and a poem directed to me and for me. Vic Melton and I discovered the dead bodies of these two girls on my property early this afternoon."

"Bring up the poem again, please, Jamie."

Jamie clicked a button and up popped the poem that was sent with the last batch of pictures.

Frank's eyebrows lifted markedly as he read the poem.

> Ireland is where our lost ones lie,
> People who know him soon will die.
> We cannot bury our past, you know,
> For revealed it will be with the
> Fast-melting snow.

Frank stood up, stretched, and yawned. He felt as though his mind was being deprived of oxygen.

"Let's leave everything as it is right now and go have a cup of coffee. I need to give my brain a break. That was a great presentation, exceptional, actually. We all need to take a breather for a minute before we get back to work. I have a few questions that need answering, but things are pretty clear in my mind. I think I might be able to help give you a real visual of who this killer might be. I think you know him, Jack. He has crossed your path many times. I am worried about that missing button. I think we need to start there. If indeed the killer removed it, and I think he did, then he has plans for it, and he has someone very specific in mind."

As they made their way to the employee rest area to get a cup of coffee, Frank's mind was processing.

"Andrea got the button, but she doesn't fit the profile. She fit the description, but not the occupation. Most serial killers are stiff about these exact details. Nor does Shawn fit. Something happened I believe, that wasn't supposed to happen. They were not part of the killer's initial plans, but before I say more, I need to work on it a bit further.

Jack stopped short.

"You said killers, not killer."

Frank was startled by Jack's abrupt stop.

"Did I say killers, plural?"

"Yes, you did, Frank, are you toying with me?"

"No, I don't think so, Jack. You belong somewhere in his past. That's why he has picked you out. Do I think there is someone working with him? I guess I do. I can't say that as a fact, but I can certainly say that I have a strong inclination to think that there is more than one person involved. I am really worried about the missing button."

"Do you think he is saving this button for me?"

"I don't think so, Jack. The target always seems to be young, long blond-haired, blue-eyed females. You don't fit that description. What worries me is that he seems to be changing his modus operandi; the killer or killers are not using strangulation any longer. They have moved to a gun. You carry a 357 don't you Jack, and therefore, what concerns me, even more, is that he seems to want you to take the rap for his misdeeds. We have a lot of work to do before the sun comes up and our meeting with other core investigators. Everyone is under a lot of pressure right now, and as you and I know, shit flows south. How much faith do you have in Buchanan?"

"I have ultimate faith in Brice Buchanan. He and I go back a long way. He would never send me down the river, not for any reason; that isn't Buchanan's way of doing things. Why do you ask?"

"I ask only because I know for certain that there are those on the state and federal level who are watching you very closely. The daughter of a State Supreme Court justice has been found dead. Someone is going to have to pay the price. The press is already rattling their sabers for a conclusion. The whole metropolitan area will be clamoring for an answer, and they will not be abated until the crime is solved. Someone will have to be blamed. Thus far, the fingers seem to be pointing your direction. Now with the two kidnapped victims found on your property? Jack, you have got to be careful. You could very easily become a scapegoat, and the real killer will walk away free and clear, and I am convinced that this is exactly what he wants.

"Thanks, Frank, for the heads-up, but that isn't going to change what I am doing one little bit. If I get strung up by a piano wire for deeds I didn't do, so be it, but in the meantime, I have a killer to catch, or killers if you're right. I'm not concerned about me. I'm worried about his next victim. I can agree with you all day long, but the main point, to me is that whoever is doing this isn't done yet. I feel it in my bones. I feel as though I have already come to know him. He is the darkest side of me. He is the darkest side of human civilization. If he wants me, then I have to draw him out, now let's get back to work and see how we are going to make it happen."

When the three men were back in the cubbyhole of a room and in their perspective positions, Jack said, "All right, Jamie, let's start from the beginning. I want it all in chronological order, including the phone calls, the Web site, everything. You just get it up there, one picture at a time. Frank and I will take notes and hammer this out to a fine point. I know I'm not the one doing this, so let's find out who it is." The last comment was for Frank's benefit.

Jamie glanced at Jack appraisingly while Frank let go of a small chuckle and clapped Jack on the back. "Did I tell you the joke about Ole and Lena on their wedding night? I didn't? Well, Ole and Lena got married you know. Sven being Ole's best friend stood up for them. After the wedding, they and all their friends went to Ole's house where Ole in the spirit of celebration got drunk and passed out. Sven asked Lena if she wanted to go to bed seeing as how Ole wasn't going to do her any good, and she said "Vell sure, Vy not. About the time they were getting started and having some fun, that Ole stumbled in through the bedroom door, saw Sven and Lena going at it and shouted, "Well, will you look at that!! Sven is so drunk he thinks he's me."

Chapter Forty-Eight

Reed was running a bit behind schedule as he spun his red Jaguar out of the Benton and Crawford law firm located in downtown Lakeville. He was on top of the world, and he was humming. The best thing that could have ever happened to him was to separate himself from his father. After winning the Wallace/Parish case, business was booming. He and J. T. Benton had wasted half the morning gloating over how they had won this one. It wasn't brilliance on their part, but a complete breakdown of communication on the part of the prosecution. The district attorney had put a young, eager rookie in charge of the case with all confidence that it was a slam-dunk case. The press, with a lot of underhanded assistance from Benton and Crawford, had a heyday planting the guilty without a doubt into the minds of everyone in the greater twin city area. Benton worked at the press hard, one way than the other, but what he really wanted was what he got, control of the case. By the time he was done, thanks to his feeding the press bogus information, the whole state of Minnesota was convinced these boys were guilty as hell.

On the first day of the trial, he walked into the courtroom with a stack of newspapers that was twelve inches thick. These poor innocent boys were being tried by the press and found guilty before they ever reached the courtroom, Benton cried in contrived hopelessness. The defense filed for a change of venue, the exasperated judge denied the motion. The prosecution was so confident in their string of witnesses that they didn't bother to bring in the DNA evidence, stating this would only confuse the people on the jury. Benton loved the underestimation the prosecution had for the intelligence of the common man. Such arrogance had won him more than one case in his long-existing career as an attorney. Be that what it was, this particular young prosecutor was no match for L. L. Benton and with Reed's vicious nature added to the mix, there was no way she could win. By the time the district attorney realized what was actually happening, the damage was already done, and it was all over with but the hollering. Benton, with little or no effort, had upended the whole case against his three young clients in a matter of weeks.

"There is nothing like a blizzard to keep everyone confused. I love blizzards, keeps everyone on their toes," Benton quipped as he walked out of the courtroom on the last day of the trial. "A not-guilty verdict was appropriate."

The only one in the whole bunch who wasn't confused, aside from Benton and Crawford, was Jack Ireland. However, his testimony was only as good as the prosecution would allow it to be. She never did ask him the right questions, nor did she bring up the DNA evidence to support his testimony. Benton handled the witnesses (the victims), himself and made absolute mincemeat out of them. One mother was so distressed, she screamed at Benton, "Have you no shame?"

Benton hurtled back, "The shame of this belongs on these harlots who wish to do nothing more than destroy the lives of these three young innocent men, and if you were a decent mother, you would know that. If you were a decent mother, none of us would be here today."

When the verdict was brought in and the boys were exonerated from lack of evidence and utter failure to prove guilt beyond a reasonable doubt, the press turned their vengeance on the prosecution. Jack agreed. His quote to the press was "You don't put a kitten up against a pair of jackals and expect the kitten to survive."

The cost to the parents of the boys exceeded six million dollars in total. The bill was paid without any itemization. The parents never asked for one. They were only too glad to pay every penny to have their boys set free. This amount of money barely made a dent in their pocketbooks. Then there were Benton and Crawford, they certainly had reason to celebrate. Samuel Crawford refused to answer any questions directed at him and refused to be interviewed. He remained silent, stone silent.

Reed had hit a high wave and was riding it with relish and delight. He was extremely pleased with how things were going for him since he left his father's office. He was going to celebrate his grand success with Kirsti. He couldn't wait to see her. For the first time in his life, he was in love. His mind went to her, and soon he was consumed with pleasure, a type of gleeful pleasure he had never known before.

Reed had called Kirsti many times after she left Jack, and she had cut him short. He barraged her with flowers, and still she had resisted him. She had laughed at him and scoffed at him. Soon he began calling her every day; he sent her flowers every day, and still she denied him. She resisted him until he sent her an invitation to take a weekend trip with him to Aspen, Colorado. She consented to go under the provision that they would have separate rooms. He agreed to this. She refused to cave into his sexual advances on this trip, but shortly after, they were seeing each other every night. She was now his lover and his best friend. She showered him with attention and made him feel like he was the only person in life that counted. She was his Kirsti now, his and only his.

Reed glanced at the clock on his dashboard, he was halfway there; he was running late. Kirsti hated to be kept waiting. He didn't want her upset with him. He picked up his cell phone, punched in her number, but didn't get an answer. She had probably shut it off. He tried her land line but got no answer. Perhaps she was in the shower. Kirsti always took great pains with her outward self. He wondered what she would be wearing. He hadn't told her where they were going but had suggested she dress casually

Reed had bought a brand new yacht and his first trip down the St. Croix was going to be with Kirsti, the love of his life. He couldn't wait to be with her. The crew was getting everything ready for them. A little dinner, a little wine, some dancing, and then he would ask her to marry him. Reed had the engagement ring in his right-hand pocket. The ring had set him back twenty-five thousand dollars; she was worth every penny. He knew it might be too soon and harbored an undeniable thought that she wouldn't accept his proposal, not because she didn't care for him but because her divorce from Ireland was still pending. Reed grimaced at the thought of a rejection. He tried her phone again, still no answer.

Reed spun his car into Kirsti's driveway. He liked the small modest house she lived in. He had never thought that there could be a life outside of extremely rich. He had never paid any attention to people who lived in small houses; they were not of his world. He was sublimely fascinated when Kirsti would mention that she had managed to get all of her bills paid and put some aside without any help from Jack. He couldn't help but pay attention when she would balance her checkbook and run her fingers through her short spiked hair, sigh with vexation, and say, "So much for a haircut this week. I guess it will have to wait until next week."

Reed would beg to give her money. Kirsti would always decline, saying, "No, I want to make it on my own."

She would place her hands around his face, kiss him, and say, "But thanks for offering anyway."

"Jack has plenty, or so I hear," he had mentioned to her in one of these precious moments. "He owes you something, doesn't he?"

"I have taken as much from Jack as I am going to take. All I want from him is a signature on the divorce papers. My family thinks I have taken too much from him already, and they are probably right. He would give it to me; I know that and so does everyone else. I could, by law, take half of what he has, but if I ever did that to Jack, my father would never forgive me, not ever."

"Will he forgive you for being with me?"

Kirsti slammed that door faster than he had opened it, "Don't mention my father, Reed. He likes Jack; he isn't going to be receptive to you now and maybe not even later. Dad has nothing to do with you and me, nothing, and the sooner you get that through your thick skull, the happier I will be. I don't want to talk about it."

And she wouldn't. With Kirsti, persistence did not prevail. He had learned this very early in their relationship. She did exactly what she intended without any sort of encouragement and didn't do what she wasn't going to do regardless of any sort of persistence, pressure, or persuasion applied to her. She was like no female he had ever met before, and thus he was enthralled and drawn to her like a moth to a flame and piteously in love. Yep, he was going to marry this one before she changed her mind. If he liked her, then there was a world of wolves waiting and scratching at her door.

Reed parked his Jaguar in the driveway and walked up to the front door. He got no answer when he rang the doorbell. He rang it again, still no answer. The drapes were drawn, blocking all vision into the house from the front, so he decided to walk around back and see if the back door was unlocked, it wasn't. He peered into the garage and noticed her car was parked in its usual spot and her bicycle was standing next to the back door. He pounded on the back door; he wasn't worried about neighbors, there wasn't any.

He shouted, "Damn it, Kirsti! Let me in, what's going on? Open the door and let me in, please! I'm sorry I'm late. I'll make it up to you, I promise!"

Nothing. He walked around to the front again and pounded on the front door until his fist hurt. Nothing. Reed walked back to his car, got in, and sat behind the steering wheel and strummed his fingers; he was confused. None of this made any sense. He tried calling her again, still nothing. She couldn't be standing him up. No one had ever stood him up. Then again, he had never known anyone like Kirsti before. Would she do this to him? His mind went backward to a conversation they had had while making love, one of their first times together. She had looked at him and said, "Don't ever make the mistake of taking me for granted, Reed, I am all done with that line of thinking. Jack took me for granted, and I will not ever go there again. Not ever. Not with you or anyone else."

He was getting nervous now; he took another look at his watch. He had been twenty minutes late. Was she testing him? He believed Kirsti was capable of that. His mind was spinning. He started up his Jaguar, backed out of the drive, and spun off into the sunset. He had only been twenty minutes late, he had tried to call her several times to let her know, but she hadn't answered her blasted phone. His mind was torn between guilt and self-serving rage. He had never felt this much emotion all at one time, and he had no idea how to deal with the whirling of emotions surging their way through his mind, thus he got angry. If it was games she wanted, games she would get.

Reed was frustrated, he was hurt; he felt, intolerably, rejected. Where in the hell was she? There was no one he could call because no one knew about them. Kirsti had insisted on this. He spun his car around and went back to Kirsti's house. He would wait for her. She had to come home eventually. He parked his car across the street from her house and waited. He fell asleep around midnight. He woke up at daybreak, still no Kirsti. She didn't answer her phone, and she didn't answer the door. Reed was becoming overtly worried. He was starting to think of the worse case possible. He hoped this wasn't her way of giving him the boot. He was radically befuddled for the first time in his spoiled-rotten life.

No one, not anyone, had ever gotten by with this before. Not one woman in his present or past life had ever even considered standing him up, let alone dumping him. He loved her. Didn't she know that he loved her with a greatness that could move heaven and earth? Where was she, and why was she doing this to him?

He turned the key in the ignition, the Jaguar let out an impressive roar as he pressed on the gas pedal. Suddenly, Reed felt dirty and in need of a long hot shower. It was time to get moving. His love for Kirsti was now a whisper in the wind as he reconstructed his thoughts. He made up his mind. He wasn't in love after all. He blew a kiss to the house, gave a solute to the mailman, put his car in high gear, spun the tires, and moved on, leaving a trail of burning rubber and smoke behind him. He would never again let any woman get under his skin and into his heart. This decision was final.

Chapter Forty-Nine

There had never been a single day of Kirsti's employment with Crawford and Crawford when she had not notified them if she was going to be late or not show. Jerry glanced at the clock, it was eleven thirty, and Kirsti hadn't arrived yet, and there had been no phone call. He knew that she had been planning to spend the weekend with Reed. He knew all about "that" relationship. He disapproved, but Kirsti wasn't listening to him, and the more he tried to discourage her, the more remote she was with him. He wanted Kirsti in his life, so he had decided to back off. There were those who chided him about his love for her, but they were wrong. He loved her, this was true, but he had no desire for her. He knew her too well. Kirsti had a bite to her that put him on edge, a hardness that went to her core and made him feel uncomfortable. Jerry had come to find Maggie to be his woman of choice. There was nothing intense about Maggie except her sense of humor and her wit. They had been seeing each other since the New Year began.

Speaking of Maggie, she was now entering the law library to give Jerry his lunch. She always brought him lunch, otherwise, he wouldn't eat. She clucked over him worse than a mother hen. She catered to him, and Jerry loved every minute of it. He had once said to her, "You keep this up, and I am going to have to ask you to marry me."

To which Maggie had dryly, "We'll get married after I get back from Detroit."

"Maggie, I didn't know you were going to Detroit, when are you going to Detroit?"

Maggie had said with elaborated emphasis, "I ain't ever going to Detroit."

Jerry's Aquarian mind couldn't decide whether his Gemini Maggie was serious or not, so he let the insinuation fly right on by him.

Maggie opened up an insulated cooler containing their lunch, placing the sandwiches on paper plates that she had brought with her. She took out bottled water for herself and a diet coke for Jerry.

"Where's Kirsti?" she asked with indifference. The unusualness of this, hadn't dawned on her yet. "I brought you a piece of strawberry-rhubarb pie my mom said you had to try, a new recipe of hers."

"I have no idea. She didn't come in this morning nor has she called to let us know whether she will be in or won't be in. Maggie, this is very unlike her. I'm getting a little worried. This isn't like Kirsti. Give me the piece of pie first. I'll eat the sandwich later. I love your mom's cooking, but her baking is much better. How did she know that strawberry-rhubarb was my favorite?"

Maggie laughed her deep throaty laugh.

"She was spending the weekend with Reed perhaps she has gotten cluttered for the first time in her perfectly organized life. I wouldn't worry too much if I were you. Kirsti has Reed to worry about her now. Eat your sandwich, and then you can have your pie."

Jerry looked at Maggie a bit shocked by her irrelevant tone, "You sound a bit caustic there, girl! She's one of your very best friends, remember?"

"Did I sound caustic? Well, please forgive me for the nastiness, but Kirsti has been getting on my nerves a lot lately. I don't think I like the person she's becoming. I would have never guessed her for taking on Reed as her partner in exchange for Jack. There is no comparison. I don't know what's gotten into her."

Maggie shrugged her shoulders as though trying to shake an invisible weight off of them before she added ruefully, "I don't know, I really wish I did. Maybe I'm being too judgmental, I hate it when I'm judgmental, maybe I'm jealous."

Jerry studied Maggie thoughtfully. "Now stop it, Maggie; never have you ever been either of the above. What does she tell you when you are alone with her?"

"Well, not a whole lot except that she is sick and tired of everyone trying to run her life and that what she does with her own life is nobody's business but her own. Then, again, we haven't seen much of each other outside of this office, since she started dating Reed. Man, does he shower the gifts on her."

Jerry leaned back in his chair and rocked back and forth as Maggie gave him her take on things.

"So tell me, who does Kirsti think is running her life but herself?"

"Well, who do you suppose?" Maggie sat down in Kirsti's empty chair. "Who do you think?"

"Must be her father, who else would it be."

Maggie nodded. "Of course she thinks it's her father and her grandmother and her aunt Yvonne, the dog, the cat, and the good Lord too. Anyone who disagrees with her these days is trying to run her life, and by the way, you can add your name to the list as well."

"Is she correct, do you think? She tells me the same thing. She says she is tired of her family having control of her, but I don't know that this is the total truth of the matter, or if she has just decided that she is tired of being the self that she created on her own. Maybe she doesn't think she has to be perfect anymore. Her sisters are certainly under the same jurisdiction as she is, and they don't act like her or even really think like her. Maybe she wants to be more like them. If anyone has influence over Kirsti, it's her sisters. Kirsti has always been more uptight than either Glenda or Hilde."

Maggie gathered up a bunch of files she had dropped on Kirsti's desk, "That's true, Jerry, the other two are far more relaxed about life than she is, one does have to remember, she is the oldest and that, 'they' say, makes a difference. Besides, with those three, it is hard to determine who influences whom. They are so intertwined that it is almost impossible to distinguish where one stops and the other starts."

"I guess you're right, Maggie. They are quite an intricate bunch those Povals, but if Kirsti isn't here by the time this office closes, or if we don't hear from her, I am going out to her house and see what's going on. This isn't like her. I have a bad feeling which I have no intention of ignoring."

Maggie turned as she was leaving the room and said, "If you haven't heard from Kirsti by the end of the day, I'll go to her house with you."

"Thanks, Maggie that would be appreciated. I truly hope I'm wrong, but I have a really, really bad feeling about this."

Hilde was sitting at her desk, working on a client's account when her phone rang. It was the business line, not her cell phone.

"Have you heard from Kirsti over the weekend?" It was her mother. She sounded a little agitated.

"No, why would you ask?"

"Your dad and I stopped by there yesterday, and everything was dark. Her car was in the garage and her bike was sitting by the back door, but there was no sign of Kirsti. Your dad and I were just wondering if you had heard from her, or if you had any idea where she is.

"She told me she was spending the weekend with a friend."

Hilde heard her mother relate this to someone else.

The voice on the other end changed quickly; her father had taken over the conversation.

"What friend, Hilde?" Eugene's voice was stern. There could be only one explanation for his angry timbre. Dad had found out about Kirsti and Reed.

Hilde knew where this was going; she had anticipated it long before now and had been dreading the moment. Hilde had been the first person to find out about Kirsti and Reed. It was Kirsti, who had told her. A huge fight had ensued. Hilde had threatened Kirsti and had said if Kirsti didn't tell her father, she would. Kirsti had pled with Hilde to let her handle it on her own. She would tell Dad when the time was right. She threatened severance of their relationship if Hilde betrayed this trust, and of course, Kirsti had prevailed. She had made Hilde promise never to tell anyone, not even Glenda. Hilde had promised, not because she wanted to, but because she felt she had to. She had stuck to her promise, with one exception, she had told Glenda.

"I really think you need to talk to Kirsti about where she is, not me. If she can't be reached, then she doesn't want to be reached. You have to wait until she becomes available, I guess."

"All right, if that's how it has to be, Hilde, then you tell your sister to call me when you hear from her. In the meantime, I am taking you out for lunch. I'll be there to pick you up at noon."

Hilde hung up the phone knowing the proverbial "bear was about to hit the buckwheat". Where was Kirsti, by the way? She picked up her phone and dialed Crawford and Crawford. The clock on the wall read eleven thirty.

Glenda and Nick were standing at the exit gate, waiting for Yvonne and Ray to disembark from their plane. Glenda had been pleased, yet nervous, that her aunt was finally coming to visit her. Yvonne had decided there was little left for her to do with her mother and her sister who was still on her consistent drinking binges but get out of Dodge for a few days. Glenda was just one of her stops on her way to Phoenix to visit with one of Grandma's brothers who lived in Glendale, Arizona. Their plane landed, and when the couple walked through the gate, Glenda was surprised at her own delight to see her aunt. Yvonne had always favored her two sisters; this wasn't a contrived thing, it was something that was because it was and for justifiable reasons.

In the view of her superiors, Glenda had some serious character flaws. First of all they considered her to be far too strong-willed and independent for her *own* good. Secondly, she could not or would not tend to business. As far as Glenda was concerned, school was one great big fat social event and so was life. Her grades had been deplorable and had it not been for Kirsti riding herd on her she might not have graduated. Last but not least and *aghast,* Glenda had a tendency toward rubbing shoulders with all the wrong people. Not only did she rub shoulders with them, she embraced them. Contrary to her two sisters who walked the straight and narrow, Glenda did the exact opposite, causing a lot of people in her life much worry and many sleepless nights. Most everyone in her family breathed a huge sigh of relief when she married Nick. Glenda, in short, was *the* Poval misfit. They didn't understand her and she didn't understand them but now, since she married Nick, all of that seemed to change. Glenda was back in the fold. *Whew.*

Glenda suggested they go check out her shop first. The guys weren't all that excited about the idea, but Yvonne was. Glenda was fairly sure she would be. She was right. Yvonne had always had an interest in antiques and anything that had to do with history.

While Yvonne took her time strolling down the isles of books and antiques, Glenda told Veronica, her manager, to fix them a sandwich and serve them outside. When asked what to serve, Glenda said, "Surprise us."

When Nick's cell phone rang, she thought nothing about it. His cell phone was always ringing. He was a man in demand. This would be the last complacent thought Glenda would have for years to come, if not the rest of her lifetime. With this phone call, the earth would quake underneath the entire Poval family. With this phone call, the very depth of their existence would collapse beneath them, and nothing would ever be the same again.

The caller was Eugene. He was abrupt when he told Nick that Kirsti was missing and had been for several days.

There was no more time for pleasure as arrangements needed to be made for all of them to return to Minnesota. Nick decided he was going to fly them back, himself, in one of the company jets. He called the owner and got permission to use the plane. They swung by the house, packed up a suitcase, and soon they were on their way to the small private airport located a short distance south of the city limits. The small airport was owned and operated by the company Nick worked for.

En route to Minneapolis, Glenda called Hilde to let her know they were on their way. Hilde was wearing her emotional hard hat, "Don't you think coming back right now is a bit premature?"

"You're probably right Hilde. I'm thinking the same way but what the heck, I was due for a visit anyway. No time like the present for a family reunion! Let me know right away when Kirsti checks in. By the way, has anyone talked to you-know-who?" Glenda had moved to the back of the plane so no one could overhear their conversation.

"You-know-who is unavailable. No one has been able to get in contact with him. I think the two of them are together and don't want to be disturbed. When Dad found out about you-know-who, he went ballistic. I wouldn't want to be in Kirsti's shoes when he finds her. I have to go. I'll see you at the airport."

Glenda knew Hilde would be in denial, she was feeling the same way. Kirsti was all right; she had just taken off to be by herself for a few days. She'd be back by the time the plane landed. Glenda had to tell herself this because any other thought far to much to think about. Yvonne made a few phone calls of her own. She was going to get to the bottom of this before the plane landed. Yvonne had lots of important connections, but none of them would be of any help. She didn't know any more about Kirsti when the plane landed as she did when they took off, but it gave her something to do other than think thoughts she didn't want to think as the plane carried them to the Minneapolis-St. Paul airport.

Part IV

Tlot tlot, tlot tlot! Had they heard it? The horse-hooves, ringing clear;
Tlot tlot, tlot tlot, in the distance! Were they deaf that they did not hear?
Down the ribbon of moonlight, over the brow of the hill
The highwayman came riding—
Riding—riding—
The redcoats looked to their priming! She stood up straight and
    still.

Tlot tlot, in the frosty silence! Tlot tlot, in the echoing night!
Nearer he came and nearer! Her face was like a light!
Her eyes grew wide for a moment, she drew one last deep breath,
Her musket shattered the moonlight—
Shattered her breast in the moonlight and warned him with her death.

He turned, he spurred to the West; he did not know who stood
Bowed, with her head o're the casement, drenched in her own red blood!
Not til the dawn did he hear it, and his face grew grey to hear
How Bess, the landlord's daughter,
The landlord's black-eyed daughter,
Had watched for her love in the moonlight, and died in the darkness
    there.

Back, he spurred like a madman, shrieking a curse to the sky,
With the white road smoking behind him and his rapier brandished
    high!
Blood-red were his spurs in the golden noon, wine-red was his velvet coat
When, they shot him down in the highway,
Down like a dog in the highway,
And he lay in his blood in the highway, with the bunch of lace at
    his throat.

Chapter Fifty

The sun was setting on the western horizon as Jack made his way to his car parked in the Dakota County Courthouse parking lot. It was five thirty in the afternoon. He was on his way to Lakeville; he was meeting with Frank Styles again. The task force had spent the entire weekend going over the material they had on the Purple Button Case and had come up with nothing, at least nothing new. Frank had been working hard to get a grasp on creating a profile of the killer or killers. Frank was convinced there were two people involved in the crimes, and this is what they were going to discuss. Jack was exhausted, both mentally and physically. He hadn't slept well since the day they found Tracy and Andrea; he couldn't get the vision of them out of his mind. The press was trouncing the story every single day, morning, noon, and night. Panic was gripping the Twin Cities at the thought of a serial killer roaming the streets. The press was right in alerting the public that they were in danger, people needed to know, and young girls needed to use caution; but the daily coverage was creating havoc with their investigation. Thousands of calls were coming in, many from nut cases who claimed to be the guilty party. Jack's biggest concern was that press coverage might cause the killer or killers to pick up stakes and move out of area only to start up again someplace else.

Frank had suggested they meet at the Lakeville VFW Club. Jack observed Frank's Buick parked out front as he pulled into the small parking lot located across the street from the club. Frank was always early and seemingly always in control, but perhaps, he could afford to be. After all, he was nothing more than an observer in this case. Other than a few regulars sitting at the bar, the place was empty. Frank was sitting in a booth next to the door. He stood up and graciously shook Jack's hand as he approached.

"It's a pleasure to see you again, Jack. You look like you're about ready to drop."

"I am. It has been a long year. I need something to eat."

"Well, you came to the right place. They have excellent food here and I would be the first to recommend any one of their steaks. Their ribs are also exceptional. Let's have a drink, something to eat, and then we can get down to business."

As the waitress came near their booth, carrying two glasses of water on a tray, Jack's cell phone rang. Jack's face lost all color as he spoke to the party on the other end.

"You're there now? Don't touch anything; I'll be there in a half an hour, if not sooner. Don't, and I repeat, don't touch anything!"

Without a word to Frank, he made another call.

"Vic, meet me at Kirsti's immediately."

When Jack turned to Frank, his brown eyes had lost their tired glaze; his adrenaline had kicked him into overdrive. As he jumped up he said, "I have to leave right away. I think I want you along on this one. Do you want to ride or follow or neither?" The question was allegorical because Jack couldn't have cared less, one way or the other.

Frank had no idea what was happening or where he was going but quickly replied anyway, "I'll drive. You can fill me in on the way."

Jerry and Maggie were sitting on the front doorstep of Kirsti's house when Frank brought his car to a screeching halt in the driveway. Vic stormed in right behind them. Fifteen minutes had lapsed since Jerry had called Jack.

"I swear that there is no one in the world that drives faster than Vic. Where were you anyway, down the street? You couldn't have come from home, not with that ugly bucket-of-bolts."

Vic knew that the next few moments would be critical ones for Jack and his sanity. Vic knew he had to push Jack past where he was at this moment, and he did it in the only way he knew how.

"Jack drives like a grandma. I was about fifteen miles from here, if that's any of your business. I was on my way to pick up Hank because we were going to do a bit of night fishing on the river. What's happening, Jack, you can't tackle this one on your own? You keep telling me you're the 'super cop.' If this is true, why do you need me here. I know you need me, Jack. You really, really, need me; all you had to do was say so. Tell me you can get along without me. Go ahead say it and I'll go away." To Vic's enormous relief, Jack bought into this notion of exchange, immediately.

"Fishing with Hank, that's a laugh. I know exactly what sort of night fishing you and brother Hank do and as far as needing you goes, forget it. The only reason I let you hang around is because there might be a remote possibility that you might learn something. I have high hopes for you Victor. I always have had."

In no mood for any further distractions, Jack immediately switched his attentions to the others and said, "Jerry, this is Frank Styles from the FBI, you already know Vic. Why don't we take a look around while you tell me what you know and don't know? You haven't touched anything, have you, such as doorknobs, any windows, or anything that is surrounding this house from a half a block away? You have to be precise about this because we don't want things to get all muddled up before we ever get started, now do we? I want to know exactly where you walked and what you touched."

"I touched the doorknobs and the doorbell, but that's all. I wanted to see if the doors were locked. I haven't touched any windows." Jerry sounded defensive. He was a bit put off by Jack's superior attitude.

"You're a good friend of Kirsti's; did she give you a key to her house?"

"No, but I know where she keeps the spare key. She was always locking herself out, so she put one under a rock in the backyard."

"You follow me and walk exactly where I walk. Vic, you go around the other way. Maggie, you stay where you are."

Jack went around one side of the house while Vic went around the other, they were careful not to disturb what might have already been disturbed by someone else. They were looking for footprints and found none. Jerry pointed to a rock next to the back door. Frank remained in front of the house. He took a leaning position against Vic's T-bird and was jotting down notes in a small spiral tablet. Maggie had nothing to do but sit on the steps and watch him do his thing, wishing she had something useful to do.

The garage had a back door containing a normal-sized window. The window was spotless. Jack knew that Kirsti had a thing about clean windows. In this case, it was a good thing, no discernable fingerprints; the door was still firmly locked. Kirsti's car was in its usual spot, parked in the center of the garage. The detectives decided to search the house first. Kirsti's bicycle was standing next to the back door. There was a small entry way on the other side, commonly referred to as a mud room. The bicycle was being held upright by its kickstand. The back door was locked.

It was starting to rain; this was unfavorable, a soft light mist but enough moisture to make Jack swear. "Shit, the last thing we need right now is rain! What's the forecast, Vic?"

Vic smiled at his partner and said, "Clear skies until sometime into the middle of next week."

"Damn it, can't those people get anything right?" Jack had diverted his attention back to the bicycle. "So she didn't leave here by her usual mode of transportation."

Jack reached into his pocket and pulled out a pair of white rubber gloves. With a gloved hand, he lifted the rock and picked up the key that was lying underneath it. He gave Vic a knowing nod.

"Front door or back door?" This question was directed at Jerry.

"Front door."

"When was the last time you saw or spoke to Kirsti?"

"At work on Friday. She had a date with Reed on Friday night."

"She told you that?"

"She mentioned this to both Maggie and me. I got concerned when she didn't show up for work this morning."

"Has anyone talked to Reed?"

"Not that I know of. I didn't, nor has Maggie. I thought I should come by here first, and then I called you."

"Why did you call me instead of Reed? She might still be with him."

"If she was with him, she would have her cell phone with her. She never went anywhere without her cell phone. I thought it would be better to call you."

"How do you know she doesn't have her cell phone with her and just isn't answering it?"

Jerry thought for a moment, "Good point, I guess I don't know. I just had a hunch, I suppose. She didn't call in this morning and that is what got me worried because it is so out of character for her."

Jack offered an acknowledgement with a slight nod of his head. "Jerry; and I are going to walk around the house in the same path we took to get back here. I want you to follow me using my footsteps in the same manner as before. Vic, you do what you know you need to do back here. I think and if what I am thinking is accurate, they drove in through the ally."

Jerry felt a surge of electricity causing the hair on the back of his neck to stand up, "What are you thinking, Jack? Do you think she was abducted?"

"No need to panic, Jerry. Cops always think worse case scenario and then move in from there. It's possible she is with Reed and forgot to call home, we're not going to jump to conclusions or assume anything."

Jerry's response was barely audible. "Ok, that's wise."

Frank slipped his notepad and pen in his inside jacket pocket when he saw Jack and Jerry came around the north side of the house. Jerry was walking so close behind Jack that had Jack stopped, Jerry would have slammed into him, probably knocking both of them over.

Jack held up the key and said, "I'm going in, Frank. I want you in there with me. Vic is securing the back parameter. Maggie, I want you to call Eugene Poval and get him get over here right away. Tell him to be discreet. We don't want to start a panic."

Maggie's eyes grew wide with fright.

"Why are you asking me to call him, what's wrong, Jack?"

Jack became instantly impatient, he barked louder than he intended, "Jerry, call Eugene and get him over here now. I have no time to answer questions."

Jerry grabbed Maggie by the shoulders, looked her straight in the eyes, and said, "They think or Jack thinks that Kirsti has been kidnapped, and we need to help him. We don't have time to think right now, so are you going to call her father or should I? We really don't have time to think about any of this, Maggie. I don't want to think what you are thinking either. Imagine how important this is to Jack. If he can make his way through all of this, so can you and I. We will not be able to help Kirsti if we don't remain calm."

"I think you better do it Jerry. I think I need to sit down, I'm feeling kind of queasy."

Maggie slumped down on the steps, placed her face into her cupped hands, and started to sob, and between inconsolable sobs, she gasped, "This can't be happening, it can't. I should have been more attentive. I should have come here right away this morning when she didn't show up for work. Where could she be?"

"I need you to move, Maggie. I'm sorry I was short with you, but this is no time for sentiment. Frank and I are going in, perhaps you and Jerry should go wait in one of the cars for now. You're going to get all wet, sitting out here and besides," and in a more consoling voice he said, "I didn't say I thought she was kidnapped. Jerry is jumping the gun. Its way to early to assume anything, so just be calm and go to some place where you are out of the way and can stay dry."

Maggie got up but was a little bewildered about what to do next; she couldn't believe how harsh Jack had sounded. He had spoken to her, as though she were a stranger. She was so affected by the shock of all of this, she had no thought or presence of mind to even remotely consider how this might be affecting Jack, and Jack couldn't have cared less what Maggie thought at that particular moment of his life either. She decided she had better do as Jack commanded, or he might tell her to leave.

Jack shoved the key into the lock and gave it a twist. The sound of the door unlocking reverberated in his overly sensitive ears. He opened the door and stood there for a few moments before he entered. His trained eyes moved from side to side, looking for anything that was out of place. Behind him was Vic, and behind Vic was Frank. Vic was carrying a camera. Frank was carrying his spiral notepad and pencil. Jack unsnapped his holster containing his gun.

After he had removed his pistol from its holder, Jack moved swiftly from room to room. Evidence of Reed's presence was spread from one room to another. His clothes hung in Kirsti's closet next to hers. There was a trail of her clothing and his clothing, all intermingled and strung out from the living room to the bedroom. He found this to be irritating but not disturbing, what did disturb him was seeing Kirsti's purse sitting on the kitchen counter and a full glass of ice tea sitting on the counter. There was a puddle of water around the base of the glass from condensation.

The light on the answering machine was flashing. Jack glanced at Frank and gave him a heads-up. "Let's see who has been calling her. We might get lucky."

Frank pressed the play button with a gloved forefinger. Instantly, the machine started speaking to them in a female sing-song voice, "You have twelve new messages."

The first eleven were from Reed Crawford. He wanted to know where Kirsti was. This caused a reaction from all three men. This is not good. By the eleventh message, Reed sounded very upset. So now the investigators had it figured that Kirsti was probably not with Reed. The concept of this likely-hood wasn't the least bit reassuring. While Jack searched Kirsti's purse for her cell phone, he listened to the twelfth message; the last message froze everyone in their tracks.

> *"What do you say Jackie? I know your there. I knew you would be. I warned you, Jackie, I have been helping you, but you are way too stupid to figure any thing out. Cops are useless, when it comes right down to it. You gotta know that by now. You're a useless, dumb son-of a bitch.*
>
> *Look around, Jackie, many have died, and you guys just don't catch on. It has been a year, and you still don't know who I am. Doesn't say much about you, does it, Jackie.*
>
> *I have Kirsti now. Perhaps this will make you act faster; taking care of someone you think you love. It was as easy to get her as it was all the rest of them Jackie.*
>
> *To protect and to serve, well, Jackie, how many of these women have you been able to protect? How many have died, Jackie, at my hands alone. Not you, the state, or the FBI have been able to stop me. Kirsti is in my hands now. She is a spunky little thing, a real spit-fire. I will be talking to you again, very soon."*

The silence in the room was excruciating as Frank popped the tape out of the machine and placed it in a plastic evidence bag.

Vic grabbed his partner by the arm and said, "Steady, boy, you have got to be steady now." Jack's face was beet red. "You can't help Kirsti by losing control of yourself."

Jack's face had turned to granet, he yanked his arm away from Vic and said, "Get the hell out of my way. I will not be responsible for my actions if I don't get out of here. I need to get some air!"

He was blind with anger, grief, and frustration. He hadn't hit the ledge of the door when he ran smack-dab into Eugene. Jack's father-in-law had seen him coming and stopped him with a full body block. Jack felt himself being propelled backward by a force a lot stronger and more determined than his.

"Oh no, you don't, you're not going anywhere, Jack. I have been standing here for quite awhile. I heard the tape. My daughter's life is on the line, this is no time for dramatics. You and I and your boys have a lot to discuss."

Eugene's, normally blue-gray eyes were almost black. His demeanor was menacing. His tanned face was lined, his jaw rigid. His mouth was set in a firm, inflexible line.

Jack's feverish, hostile eyes met his father-in-law's with equal fervor. The two men stood glaring into each other's eyes for what seemed like an hour. No one in the room dared move, let alone take a breath. Finally, Jack backed up and away from Kirsti's father.

"You're right, Eugene. We have a job to do, and there is no one who has more reason than me to get this one solved and get your daughter back to you. I have let you down and Kirsti. I believe this one is bigger than me, Eugene. I thought I could handle it, but now I don't know anymore. I don't know. The guy is after me, and he is using Kirsti. I know that now. I didn't know that until a minute ago. I never thought that he would hurt her or harm her. I guess I should have known, but I didn't, I was too hung up on his MO. God, I'm sorry, Eugene."

Eugene relaxed a little, "I know you are Jack but that ain't going to help us now. "Sorry" isn't going to get Kirsti back nor is it going to appease Mary. I want to know what you *boys* are going to do about it. I want to know, and the sooner the better, how you plan on proving to that fellow, who seems to think he's got you by the balls, that he is wrong."

With some of the tension behind them, Frank picked up the phone and called missing persons alert.

Jack placed a call to the Apple Valley Police Department and another to Brice Buchanan.

Frank placed a call to Bobby Brooks of the FBI and within what seemed like minutes, the place was swarming with experts from all parts of the police spectrum.

Jack was frightened beyond sensibility for the first time in his life. He didn't know why, but he knew he had a part in all of this as much as the killer did. He knew what he knew, and thus he confessed to his partner the thought which he had hoped he never, ever, even remotely would have to consider. It was too horrible a thought to consider, let alone verbalize, but he had to now and he did.

"Kirsti is going to get the last purple button. The last button is intended for her, and I don't know how to prevent it, and what's even worse is, I am not sure that anyone can."

Vic shook his head. His countenance was in no better shape than Jack's. Yet he knew that if there was ever a time in life when words would matter, this was the time, so he chose them with great care.

"If anyone can, Jack, you can. Damn it Jack, you and I can. We just need to make sure this does not happen. I don't want her to die any more than you do, so let's get moving on this. If we weaken now Jack, she will surely die. We have to get her back; we have no choice."

"The guy is right, you know, and that is what is so terrible about all of this. He is right. He has killed and killed and killed again. He has communicated with us. He has taunted us, and he has deliberately tormented me, and I can't seem to stop him. I can't find him. I have tried. I have used every resource available to me without success. This guy is making all of us look like a bunch of bungling idiots, and right now I feel like one. I don't know where to start."

"He has had the advantage, Jack. We can't put everyone under lock and key for their own protection. This guy lives in the underbelly of life and has made killing his career. We will get him, Jack. You and I will get him."

Frank was listening to the two detectives conversing and pitched in. "Jack, he will be calling you within days. He wants you, for some reason. All of this is about you. I don't know why yet, but it is. We have to bring him out of his cozy place, and I know of only one way to do it."

"Right now, I am concerned that we might not get him before he takes out Kirsti. I don't want to find her lying in a ditch some place or in a remote wooded area. I don't want to find her chewed up by the animals or frozen solid from the winter cold. I could never live with myself if this happens. I couldn't handle it." Jack was visualizing the two girls found on his property. He shuddered so violently that his entire body shook.

Ireland sat down on the couch. He seemed to be slipping away and losing his bearings all together. Frank decided this was the right moment in time to pressure Jack. It was now or never. Jack had to be yanked out of his state of shock and the only way to get it done was to force him back into action. If this didn't happen soon the world was going to lose a great cop.

"Then you have to invite him towards you. I think we might be able to lure him in by having you arrested. Serial killers hate it when someone else takes credit for their crimes. Think about it, Jack."

Jack and Vic studied each other and as Frank spoke, he noticed the light coming back into Jack's eyes. He was thinking. His wheels were turning. Jack had researched serial killers and knew that Frank Styles might have come up with the only available course of action that could work. It would be dangerous and it was risky, but the rewards might be worth it.

"Frank, you're going to have to be the one to run this by Brice. I'm willing to give it a try, but if I know my boss, man, he isn't going to want to have it done this way. He hates the press, and he will have to convince the press this is legitimate. He isn't a very good liar, you know."

Frank stood back, grinned and pointed toward the front door, "Speak of the devil and who should appear? Here comes the man now, and with him comes Bobby, well this couldn't be more perfect. I'll walk them through it. You get prepared to be arrested for crimes you didn't commit." With this said, he gave Jack an appreciative nudge on the shoulder.

Jack found Eugene, standing outside, having an animated conversation with Maggie. Maggie was crying and laughing at the same time. This was a good sign that it was getting late in the day or rather early in the morning. Jack had to marvel at how well Eugene was taking all of this. He had to have ironclad grit. His self-containment was downright inspiring. As Jack approached them Maggie quit laughing and Eugene quit talking. They greeted him with the reserve of a stranger.

Jack really wasn't sure what to say so he got straight to the point, "Maggie, I think it's time you and Jerry went home. Before you go, I want to impress upon you that it is important that neither of you speak to the press about anything that has gone on here today. We're going to get Kirsti back or die trying, and you can serve us well by not speaking to anyone about anything. If anyone from the press should want to talk to you, and they will, refer them to our office. Can I trust you on this? I don't care what happens from this second on, you speak to no one about being here, or what you know and don't know. Kirsti's life depends on your absolute discretion."

Maggie nodded. She was worried and tired. She started to cry again as she signaled Jerry.

"I mean it, Maggie," Jack repeated, "no comment, no reaction, nothing. You know nothing, you have heard nothing, and I haven't talked to you about this. You have to give me your word that no matter what happens from now on; you will not offer your opinion or observations to anyone, not the press or anyone else."

"Did Jerry get the same instructions?"

Jack was too tired to say much more than yes; he was starting to look forward to his arrest. Maybe, just maybe, he could get some sleep once he was in jail and couldn't do anything else.

After Jerry and Maggie left, Jack talked to Eugene and told him what they had decided to do. Eugene was skeptical, at best. He especially didn't like that the press was going to be involved, but Jack was persuasive.

"By morning, I will be in jail for crimes I did not commit. Getting in is easy, Eugene, getting out is what I worry about. If the killer is going to be convinced, then this has to be treated as a reality, and this is dangerous for me because only certain few will know that this is a ploy to drag out the killer. Right now there is enough evidence lined up against me to give any good prosecutor a reason to have me arrested. That is exactly why this could work. The down side is that the killer might not buy into it and take off leaving me hanging out to dry. Styles thinks this is what the killer is intending, but there is a chance that the killer might have a change of heart. It's risky but it is the only thing we have right now."

"You're willing to put your life on the line for my daughter? I don't know think that's so wise." Eugene was not thrilled nor was he impressed, "This is a huge gamble and I don't like it."

"Sure it is, but unless you have a better idea, this is what we're going to do, like it or not."

Jack was aggravated by his father-in-law's propensity to dispute most everything that crossed his path. He had forgotten, momentarily, that it was Eugene's daughter that they were talking about and Eugene had the right to argue. This case had become personal to the point of obsession with Jack and now the same went for Eugene.

"I am going to do this with or without your approval Eugene. I am only forewarning you, not asking for your permission."

Eugene flashed Jack a warm smile, and as he planted a firm grip on Jack's arm, he said, "I like you, Jack. I don't want to lose you or Kirsti. Another thing I am not looking forward to, is going home. This is going to rile up my entire family, and I am not sure how I am going to handle it. First they will have to know about Kirsti, and then they will soon learn that you have been arrested. This is not going to be easy. Kirsti being kidnapped is one thing, you getting arrested for it, is going to create extreme confusion that I might not be able to explain satisfactorily enough to convince them."

Jack shook Eugene's hand and said with his charming grin added, "Just be tough there, Dad, remember, as they like to say, whoever they are, 'It isn't over until the fat lady sings.' I will bring Kirsti back to you if I have to dig my own grave doing it, and that's a promise. The hardest part is going to be convincing your tribe that this is a legitimate arrest. On the other hand, maybe it won't be."

Eugene grabbed his son-in-law around the shoulders and said confidentially, "Oh you can bet it will be. Good luck, my boy, good luck for you and good luck for me, and may the luck of the Irish be with all of us."

Jack was moved. Eugene rarely hugged anyone and never men. Showing any sort of emotion was, after all, a sign of weakness, and it was completely unlike him as a Norwegian to depend on the silly luck of the Irish. The sad and trusting expression on his father-in-law's face would remain in his mind for the rest of his life; those strong, unwavering clear blue-grey eyes staring at him without duress, without anything but definitive knowledge that if there was a prayer in his life, his prayer and his answer to getting his daughter back alive was now with Jack. It was more than Jack could bear. He wept and as he wept Vic stood vigilantly beside him. Eugene got into his car, placed his hands on the steering wheel and cried like a baby. He was all alone in his anguish and had to be.

Chapter Fifty-One

Shorty was sitting on a black beanbag chair with his legs and feet sprawled out in front of him. He was staring at the blank screen on the television, upset because his brother wouldn't let him turn it on yet. He wanted to watch his favorite cartoons, and he could not comprehend why his brother chose this day to deny him his daily ritual. He wasn't going to ask again because his brother was agitated. He was pacing the floor, and every time Shorty opened up his mouth, Willie told him to shut the hell up. Shorty didn't like it when Willie got in these moods. It hadn't slipped by Shorty that these dark moods were coming more frequently now than ever before.

"That girl downstairs isn't like the others, is she, Willie? I don't like her at all."

"You don't have to like her. What makes you think that any of this has anything to do with what you like or don't like, Shorty? She is here because I want her to be here. I have a plan in mind and have had one in mind for a long time, but you keep making my job more difficult by the day with your incessant whining, crying and questions. In fact, you have spoiled most of my plans already by adding your own twist to things."

Shorty ignored his brother's statement and said, "She isn't like the others. Why do we have her here? I don't want to go down there any more. She spits at me. She snarls at me, and she is impossible to deal with. The others were easier. You can go down and take care of her from now on. Yesterday, she pooped on the floor right at the bottom of the stairway. I stepped in it when I went down to bring her some food. That was disgusting."

"Don't let her get to you, Shorty. She's a fire cat alright, but she ain't worth getting upset about, no woman is. What you have to remember is that she is Jack Ireland's wife. That's the only reason why she is important to us. Don't feed her; just bring her water for the next few days. That'll bring her around. Leave her in the dark until she begs you for light. She isn't as tough as she thinks she is, and besides, none of what she is or isn't should concern either of us. She won't be down there for very long anyway."

"Turn on the television; I want to see if there is anything on the news about her disappearance."

"Damn it, Willie, I wanted to watch my shows. What difference does it make whether they find her missing or not? She is missing. I can tell you that much. I don't have to turn on the television to let me know what I already know. I want to watch my programs. Why do you have to have the final say-so on everything that goes on around here? The girl is in the basement, what more do we need to know?"

Willie wrenched the remote from his brother and turned on the television. He hit the local channel first. He stood back and waited; he didn't have to wait long. Every major network had cut into their normal broadcasting for what they were calling a special news bulletin.

"CID, Jack Ireland has been arrested by the FBI in connection with what has now been dubbed the Purple Button Case. Sources tell us that there is enough evidence to cause the FBI to believe that he is responsible for the deaths of six women and the disappearance of another. FBI agent Robert "Bobbie" Brooks will be here in a few minutes to make a brief statement."

Willie watched with incredulity as Brooks took center stage to explain how they had come to link Jack Ireland with these killings and the kidnapping of Tracy Durkin and Andrea Pennington.

"He was closely associated with a number of the victims. He cannot explain where he was on the night of the crimes. He had the ways, the means, and the motive. We have always suspected that these crimes were committed by someone within the police force because of their knowledge of forensics. We can tie at least three of the woman to him directly, and we cannot discard that he had an association with the others. We believe we have caught our man. That's all I can give you for now."

Willie started stomping around like he was doing some type of Indian rain dance. He twirled and he spun, his face was bright red with emotion. Shorty watched him warily from his black beanbag chair. His brother was delighted! He had to be! Jack Ireland was under arrest. Shorty didn't understand why his brother wanted to slay Jack, but he was happy because his brother was happy.

Then he heard a voice come down on him; a shrieking, screaming, angry voice, "No, no, no! He can't take the credit for this. Not in my lifetime. Those stupid ignorant cops think he did it. No, no, no! Ireland, you son of a bitch, you are not going to get by with this! What the hell is he pulling, Shorty? This has to be a ruse, it has to be. Ireland is not going to steal my thunder!"

Willie's voice rose to a high pitch as he shouted and stomped. Shorty moved himself into a corner of the room and away from his brother's wrath. He hated it when his brother got this way. He was remembering the night before when he had defied his brother, and Willie had literally knocked him unconscious and then strung him up by his wrists and beaten him until he passed out again. He hoped this wasn't going to be another one of those moments. He had no one to protect him from this, no one, and he never did.

Shorty scrutinized his brother from the corner of the room until he was finally seemingly in control of himself before he asked, "What's the matter with Ireland taking the blame? That works for me. I thought that was the whole idea. I just want to know, don't get mad at me, I'm just asking. What if this really isn't, what did you call it, Willie, a ruse? I think I know what that means. The cops are trying to fool us, right? What is wrong with them arresting Ireland anyway? I thought that was what you wanted. Now we can leave here. I don't like this place anymore. I want to go someplace else."

Willie sat down in front of his brother who was by now curled up like a mouse trapped in a corner. He grabbed his brother's hands and kissed each one of them, and said as though both of their lives depended on what he was going to say next, "Shorty, this has nothing to do with placing the blame on anyone else. I want them to think about things, I want them to be smart. I don't want them to arrest the wrong guy. None of this is about that. Jack is going to suffer badly, but I want the world to learn a lesson. I want to show the cops how stupid they are, how inept they are, and how totally useless they are.

That's what this is all about. I have decided I want Jack to suffer a fate worse than death. He deserves it. I'm not finished here yet. We have one more mission to accomplish, and then we will leave and go somewhere where it's warm and sunny. Maybe we'll go to Mexico. We'll find you a little senorita down there to play with. How would you like that?"

Shorty leaned back against the wall, removing his hands from his brothers. He stared at the floor as he said, "I get it now, Willie. This is all about teaching the world a lesson. I guess I am not sure I understand the lesson right this minute. Maybe I need to think a little longer, huh? Because I think you have proved your point. I don't want to go to Mexico. I want to find Mom. What happened to her Willie, where did she go?"

Willie stood up straight, whacked his brother on the side of his head, and sneered, "There isn't enough mental capacity in that pea-sized brain of yours to conceptualize what it is I am doing, Shorty. You will never understand, not ever, and if you don't get up off the floor right now, I will gladly beat you within an inch of your life, and then I will gladly kill you. It doesn't matter to me, one way or the other, just make up your mind right now because I don't have time for people who defy me or question me. What are you going to do, Shorty? Are you going to get up or not?"

Shorty stood up slowly; he was afraid that Willie was about to strike him back down again, "Sorry, Willie, I'm sorry. I do make life difficult for you, don't I? I don't mean to."

Kirsti was lying on the cold cement floor in the basement. Her hands were tied behind her back, her feet were tied together, and her mouth was taped shut. The door opened up, and light came pouring down. This sudden action startled her and blinded her.

The man, the taller one, her captor, said these words before he slammed the door shut again, "You have one more day, Kirsti, just one more day, so start praying that your husband finds you before I slaughter you. I don't think that they will, and because they are all a bunch of bumbling, stupid idiots, I am going to help them find you. Those jokers couldn't find the broad side of a barn if they bumped into it, and I am not saying that to be funny. You had better start praying Kirsti and if you shit on the floor one more time, it will be your last time."

Kirsti had so much tape wrapped around her body that she could barely wiggle her fingers and toes. At first they had her in cuffs with long chains. At least then she had some maneuverability; she could walk around. Last night, she had decided to get even. She had shit on the floor in front of the stairs and spit on the short one. This had incensed him more than she had expected. He had made her clean up her mess; and then he had grabbed her by the hair, shoved her into a chair, and taped her up from head to foot. The short one had enormous strength for his size, especially in his hands. He had been able to contain her using only one hand around her throat while he taped her up with the other. When she struggled against him, he had squeezed her throat, blocking off all air into her lungs. She had never envisioned that anything so horrifying as this could ever happen to her.

She was losing track of the hours and days. The parts of her body that were not stiff and sore had no feeling at all. She was hungry and very thirsty. She was running out of ways to keep her mind preoccupied and away from thinking about her demise. She knew if Jack didn't find her soon, she was going to die. They were keeping her alive for one reason, to kill her later. She knew this; somehow she knew this. She didn't want to know this, but it came to her mind in the dark hours that she had spent in this black, black hell-hole.

Her mind kept going back to Jack and how he had tried to talk to her about the Purple Button Case, and she had insisted he keep his work at the shop and not bring it home. Perhaps if she had listened to him, she might have been able to see this coming, Jack might have seen it coming. She had been selfish. She tried to reassure herself that Jack and her father would find her. It was inconceivable that they wouldn't. She wanted to scream, to cry out in pain, but she couldn't; she couldn't do anything but sit there and wait in this underground cavern that smelled of sweat, urine, and vomit; her sweat, her urine and her vomit.

Jack and her father had one day to find her. Kirsti felt her stomach lurch; she gasped as panic swept over her. She felt like she was being smothered as pure, raw terror consumed her. Soon everything went mercifully black. She had passed out cold.

Brice Buchanan had just sat down at his desk when his secretary informed him there was a call on line three, requesting his attention.

"Who is it?"

Contessa had tried to gather a name without success.

"I can't tell you, sir, but he sounds serious, and he says it's about the Purple Button Case."

"Put him on. This had better not be another crank call, or I'm going to fire you and everyone you love!"

Brice put the phone on speaker.

"Why, hello, Mr. Buchanan. This is the Purple Button serial-killer speaking. How are you doing over there in incompetent-villa, USA?"

Darth was back.

Brice stood up and walked toward the window, contemplating his next words. He needed to be cautious.

"We have already arrested the Purple Button killer. We have him sitting in jail right now, and he is confessing to everything."

"You have the wrong man. I want a conference with Ireland. I want you to put him on the phone."

"I can't, he's locked up in county at the moment, and besides, we have had about three thousand people calling in and claiming to be the Purple Button killer, what makes you different from all the rest?"

"I'll give you one hour to get him back in your office. One hour, or Kirsti dies. If you ask your secretary, she will tell you that she has a fax coming in right now. I think this fax will encourage you to co-operate with me."

One second after the caller hung up Contessa flew into his office with a picture she had just taken from the fax machine. It was a picture of Kirsti. It was a close-up picture of Kirsti. Her mouth was taped shut, her eyes were filled with fright, and she looked like she hadn't slept in months. Brice slid the picture into his top drawer and told Contessa to forget she ever saw it. She would never, ever, not remember, that horrible picture.

Frank was right. It had taken less than twenty-four hours for the killer to call. The ploy had worked.

They dragged Jack out of jail and brought him to Buchanan's office in cuffs. The show must go on.

Buchanan waited by the door of his office as Contessa took the call. When she gave him the signal, he walked back to his desk and punched the speaker button.

"Well hello again, whatever you name is, what can I do for you?" Buchanan's question reeked with sarcasm.

"First of all you can clear everyone out of your office but Ireland and yourself, and you can turn off the tracers. They aren't going to do you any good anyhow."

Jack instinctively turned around in his chair; he had a weird sensation that the killer was watching them. He nodded his head toward Brice and then toward the outer office. Buchanan got the message instantly. He signaled for Brooks, Styles, and Melton to leave the room. They took positions outside the commander's office where they could view everyone in the area, looking for that someone inside who was sending signals to their killer. While they were watching the area, Lulu had her eye on them.

"The tracers are off, now what?"

"I want to talk to your chief detective in private. Shut off the speaker."

"I don't need to shut the speaker phone off, it's already off." Buchanan was testing.

There was a caustic chuckle on the other end, "Shut it off, Buchanan, or I'm going to hang up, and you won't hear from me again. How did you like the picture?"

Brice handed the receiver to Jack, "You have my attention, Mr. Purple Button man. What do you want?"

Jack was speaking to the madman on the other end of the line, as though they had known each other for years.

The Darth voice came through loud and strong. He had removed his distortion equipment. The voice sounded vaguely familiar.

"No more games, Jack. I want you. I want you in exchange for Kirsti. It's as simple as that."

"I want to know if she is all right first."

"How standard is that, Jack? I'm sorry, asshole, but your negotiation days are over with. I want you and you alone to meet me at a place north of the Pine Bend Refinery. I will e-mail the directions to you. If anyone is with you, Kirsti will die, you can count on it. If I see one other person there, then Kirsti is goner, and you will have no one to thank but yourself, Jackie. This will be our showdown, Jackie boy. Don't cheat. You cheat me, I will cheat you and that's a promise."

"If I meet with you, one on one, are we going to have a shoot-out or what? Is this going to be like the OK Corral?"

"No, I am going to kill you, period. I plan on shooting you straight through the heart, Jack. It's as simple as that. Not one thing complicated about any of this. Your life for Kirsti's, it's a trade-off, even-steven, a life for a life."

"I don't suppose you are going to explain all of this to me." Jack was buying time. The FBI had tracers running from the basement. A few more seconds and they would have him.

"You're a bright boy, Jack or at least some people think you are, I don't. You figure it out. You know the score."

"You sound a bit impatient, Mr. Purple Button, where are we going to meet and what time."

"I guess you don't want to wait for an e-mail, huh? So much the better! There's a vacant warehouse just north of the refinery in Pine Bend, meet me there tonight, twelve o'clock sharp, and come alone, Jack. Do I have your word on that, Jackie? I need your very explicit words on that Jackie my boy or Kirsti dies. I am going to be holding you on your honor and that honor belongs to you, not me. If you lie, Kirsti pays. Oh, by the way, tell the FBI that a trace on this number isn't going to help them find me. This number is untraceable. I've seen to it. Modern technology works both ways, sport."

Jack didn't answer right away, and when he didn't, the killer said in a relaxed, easy voice, "Use your imagination, Jackie. I was not nice to the other girls. I will be a lot harder on Kirsti. She is waiting for you to come and get her. I would hate to see you let her down."

Jack set is jaw hard before he said, "You can count on it. Just you and me, and don't *you* cheat! You hear me, asshole?"

"I promise you, Jackie, if you come alone, there will be no problem. If you don't, then your wife is goner."

The line went dead.

Brice calculated his investigator; Jack was seething with anger and yet excruciatingly calm.

"How do you want to handle this, Jack?"

"I'm going in alone. I don't want to take any chances with Kirsti's life. If it is me he wants, it is me he will get. Now get me out of here."

Lulu smiled as the FBI dragged Jack out of the CID department in cuffs and chains. It wouldn't be long now, and she and Willie would be on their way to Florida, and Shorty would be history. Willie had promised. Shorty, bless his heart, had to go; he knew too much. He was unreliable. She had no idea why Willie held such animosity toward Jack; she only knew that she loved Willie. He was as ugly as a mud fence, but what a lover he was. He knew exactly how to treat a woman. He was her man.

Chapter Fifty-Two

Jack had no difficulty finding the old dilapidated solid brick warehouse located about a half a mile north of the refinery. He drove through the parking lot at normal speed until he had circled the entire area. There wasn't anyone around. He turned his jeep so that it was facing the entrance into the parking lot. His illuminated watch told him it was eleven forty-five. He was somewhat amazed at how calm he felt. He was finally going to meet the monster who had caused so many people so much misery; he was actually looking forward to it. He strummed his fingers on the steering wheel as he waited.

"Curiosity killed a cat."

"Yah, and satisfaction brought him back."

Vic was lying under a blanket on the floor in the backseat.

"Is it a bit snug back there?"

"Something better happen pretty soon or I won't be able to move when the time comes. My legs are starting to cramp up. You know, Jack, this is the moment we have all been waiting for. I hope you don't blow it."

"Ah," Jack sighed. "Ye of little faith, it is hard to function under such a heavy cloud of doubt."

At that moment, headlights appeared on the horizon, coming from the north.

"Looks like our man is here, early no less, this guy is in a rush. He's driving an old van. I would say '70s vintage. So stay low, my man, stay low."

The van pulled up directly in front of Jack's jeep, the glare from the headlights caused Jack a moment of concern but soon his eyes had adjusted. Jack removed his gun from its sheath with his right hand and opened the door slowly with his left.

"Careful, Jack, God, be careful" Vic whispered. "This guy is ruthless."

Jack's eyes caught sight of the door of the van opening on the driver's side. The figure of a man stepped out, closed the door, and moved forward toward the front of the vehicle. The headlights of the van obscured Jack's vision, allowing him to see only a shadow moving.

"Well, Jackie, we meet at last. Close your door and move around to the front of your jeep so I can get a better look at you."

It was Darth; he had his mask back on again.

Jack did as he was told. He held his gun down to his side.

"Why don't you do the same? I wouldn't mind getting a good look at you either. I want to see you without the mask."

Darth moved into the headlights.

"There, can you see me now?" Darth coughed out a mordant chuckle. "Or are the headlights getting in your way?"

"I can see you just fine. Why don't you remove your mask? Are you afraid to show me who you really are?"

"Cut the crap, Jackie. I want you to place your gun on the ground and kick it away. Then I want you to remove your jacket and bulletproof vest. I want a nice clean target."

Jack had expected this; he did as he was instructed. He placed the gun on the ground about six inches from his right foot. He removed his outer jacket and then the vest. He dropped them down behind him. He looked upward; there was a full moon. This could be helpful.

"Nice try, Jackie. You know, you're not as smart as you think you are."

"You want my life for Kirsti's, right?"

Jack knew he had to buy a little time, not much but just a little. He had to keep the guy talking. This guy had an ego, and guys with big egos love to talk, especially about themselves.

"That's right, Jackie."

"Are you going to tell me why?"

"That's too long a story, Jackie, and really depressing. I don't have the time nor do I have the inclination."

"Ok, I can live with that; so, if you're going to kill me, don't you think I have the right to face my executioner or are you too cowardly to reveal yourself." Jack knew he was pushing where he probably shouldn't be pushing.

Darth switched the gun he was holding from his right hand to his left. He grabbed the mask and removed it.

"Can you see me now, Jackie?"

Jack's eyes blinked several times, first to help adjust his eyes and secondly because he now knew the name of the killer. He recognized the voice. He didn't need to see him to know who he was.

"Well, well, well, so it was you after all, you dirty, rotten, son-of-a-bitch. I knew there was a good reason why I didn't like you, Irv, you sniveling, low-down rat of a coward. I should have taken my first impulse and shot you the minute I laid my eyes on you. I knew you were nothing but a no-good sorry example of a human being." Just a few more minutes was all Jack needed, just a few more minutes and everyone would be in position.

Irv cackled like a sick rooster, at Jack's response.

"Jackie, Jackie, Jackie, now you're resorting to name calling, how trite of you. You sound so much like John Wayne. You watch his movies a lot? He always comes out on top doesn't he Jackie, but we are living in the real world now, just you and me. This isn't a movie, Jackie, this is the real deal. You failed, buddy. You failed big time. But, I guess none of that matters anymore now, does it, Jackie? I never liked you much either. Do we have a mutual appreciation society going on here or what? You don't like me, and I don't like you, so what? The girls are still dead and Kirsti is still waiting for you to come to her rescue. How are you going to manage that Jackie? It's hard to move around when you're dead."

Irv laughed again. His laughter had a shrill, grinding sound, like a wheel without grease. Jack could tell from the sound of the laughter that Irv was on the verge of hysteria. He was getting nervous, and that made him unpredictable.

"So now that we have all of this discussed, it's time for me to bid you a final goodbye, any last words for Kirsti?"

Irv drew up his handgun and aimed it at Jack's chest. He was toting a .44 high-powered magnum; this was not the way Jack wanted things to end. He needed just a few more seconds.

Jack glanced up towards the sky. The moon had moved into the right position. He could see Irv very clearly and if he could so could the sniper. "Before you lay me down to rest, Irv, answer me one more question. Who was your inside helper on this? Who did you have at the office feeding you information?"

As Jack spoke, he was keeping his eyes planted on Irv's right trigger finger. His eyes had adjusted to the light, and he could see Irv as clearly as though it were broad daylight. Perhaps it was his adrenaline, maybe it was the moonlight but either way and for whatever reason, Jack could see Irv, and that was all that mattered.

"Why now, you know who that was, Jackie; it was Lulu. I don't suspect she is going to make out very well in all of this, either. She's going to meet me in about an hour, and then she is going to join you in the great beyond. I have all the details worked out. I am really good at details, as you must know by now. The swamps of Florida are a great place to hide dead bodies. She's packed and anxious to leave, and I will not see her disappointed, just yet anyway. She is expecting me, so we must get on with this Jack. Got any last words?"

Irv quivered hideously and laughed again, his cackling was now more like an unhealthy cough. Irv hadn't been paying attention to his own physical stance as he was talking. While he spoke, he had lowered his gun slightly, "She thinks I am going to trade Shorty for her. I will never fail to be amazed at how totally ignorant women can be. Whatever and who cares, because, now it's time for you to go. Are you ready, Jackie? Are you prepared to meet your maker? I hope so, the good Irish Catholic that you are."

When Jack saw Irv lift the gun towards his chest, he raised his right hand. A shot rang out, and Irv fell to the ground. As he went down, he reflexively pulled the trigger on his gun; the shot went wild and missed Jack by a country mile.

Jack leaped toward Irv as Vic untangled himself from the backseat of the jeep.

"Damn it, Jack, conversation is nice but that was too close."

"The sharpshooter was only supposed to wing him!" Jack shouted with frustrated rage. "He shot him right through the damn chest!"

Jack grabbed Irv by the shoulders and hoisted him to a seating position. Blood was running down the side of Irv's mouth. Irv gave

Jack a weak smile and whispered, "You cheated, Jack, you cheated. This will cost you. I warned you."

Irv lifted his left hand weakly, and then he was gone.

"Damn it. Damn it. Damn it! What in the hell just happened here?" he yelled.

Jack had jumped away from Irv's now-dead body and was screaming at the shooter.

"You were supposed to wing him, not kill him! What sort of an operation do you guys run anyway! If Kirsti dies, I will have your heads, and I won't bother with a silver platter. You were not supposed to kill him!" Jack, in outrage, was franticly pounding his fists on the hood of his jeep.

The sniper placed his gun down on the roof. He had done as he had been told; his orders had been specific. His instructions had been "*Save Jack Ireland's life, at all costs.*"

While Jack was throwing euphemisms at the sniper, Vic was going through Irv's pockets. In the left side of his pants pocket, he found a carefully folded-up piece of paper. On one side was a map and on the other was a printed note that said, "Cheaters never prosper."

They looked at each other. This was not good. The map was a good thing; the words on the back side were not a good thing.

Chapter Fifty-Three

The two homicide detectives left Irv lying in a heap in front of his van. Jack got into the passenger side, leaving Vic to do the driving. "Here's the map, amigo, tell me which way to go."

Jack retrieved a flashlight from the glove box, shined the light on the map and quipped, "I have a really bad feeling about this map."

Vic spun the jeep out of the warehouse parking lot, as though he were being pursued by the devil himself. As he was swerving, he was saying, "Jack, give me directions."

"We need to head south for approximately two miles and then turn left on a gravel road."

"He wrote gravel road on the map?" Vic asked incredulously.

"Sure enough he did, and that is about as spooky as life gets."

Vic buried the needle of the speed-o-meter and covered the two mile stretch at break-neck velocity.

"There's our turn, turn left, turn left!" Jack shouted, while still trying to read the map and hang on for dear life, as Vic fought to keep the jeep upright while negotiating the tight curves of the road. "Where are our FBI boys? We might need them!"

Vic didn't have time for questions, as he cranked the steering wheel hard to the left, hit the break pedal and the gas pedal simultaneously, and made a ninety-degree turn onto the gravel road. He had done this plenty of times in his car but never in a jeep, that would be down right insane, so he wasn't quite sure what the results would be.

After they landed on course and Jack had righted himself, he shook his head and said, "Damn, you're good. Have you ever thought about a career as a race car driver?"

"Nah, who wants to spend their life driving around in circles?"

Jack watched with special appreciation as four or five cars went racing on by them. Ah, the FBI boys. He did like the team; he seriously did and appreciated every ounce of their efforts, but it was fun, nonetheless, to see Vic, without any intention, give them the shake. They had seen them turn; they'd be back. They had better be; his and Kirsti's life might depend on it.

"Slow down a bit, Melton, we have to take another left real soon. The map says the road will be marked with a yellow ribbon wrapped around a tall oak tree. This guy is really sick."

No sooner had Jack said this, and there it was, a tall oak tree completely wrapped in yellow ribbon from the bottom of the trunk to the lowest branches of the tree. Vic stopped at the turn into the driveway.

"Does that resemble a skinny person having a bad hair day or what?"

"Funny, Jack, that's funny but quit with the funnies. I am as nervous as a cat on a hot griddle, and am not in the mood for your jokes right now. You can joke all you want to after we have Kirsti, but for now, we have to get her out of there alive."

"Might I be the one to remind you, Detective Melton that this is my wife, we are talking about, not yours? So, if anyone has the right to be nervous, it is yours truly. Now with that said, let's take another look at the map the scum ball was so kind as to share with us, and trust me, I have no reason to think that this map is anything but a pile of crap. It comes to me that this might be a bit too ingenious of him, but for the present, it is all we have.

"According to this map, we have about a half a mile of driveway before we reach the buildings. I think you should get out and walk in while I drive. I don't want to take any chances this time. You cover me from the left. The house is centered at the back of the yard. According to this drawing, we'll find Kirsti in the garage, which is connected to the north side of the house."

"Got you covered. Be careful, Jack. Take it slow and easy. Running through this thicket is going to take a little doing. You had better not get the party started without me. I'll give you an owl hoot when I have you in my sights."

"Let's hope a real owl doesn't come along and confuse me!" Jack said humorously, trying, unsuccessfully, to shake the jitters he was experiencing.

The dirt driveway was narrow, rutty, and rough. Jack had no choice but to take it slow. Vic veered off to the left, into the dense, wooded area, as Jack slowly and deliberately made his way toward the clearing. He pulled his jeep to a halt just short of the spot where the trees ended on both sides of the driveway. He could see the house from where he was, but not Kirsti. He was too far away to see much of anything clearly. The thick woods encircling him on both sides would give anyone who might be waiting for him, a suitable place to hide and a discomforting advantage. Jack was starting to feel like a sitting duck in the middle of the lake, all by its-self, during hunting season. Hell, he was a sitting duck during hunting season.

As he was reaching for the flashlight, he heard a pleasant voice speaking to him; the voice was coming from the left, and it wasn't Vic.

"Get out of the jeep, Jack. Do it nice and slow. Hold up both hands, and they had both better be empty."

Jack moved slowly. He tucked the revolver into his belt to his right side as he eased himself out of the jeep.

"Before you get out, shut off your headlights. You will not be needing them. Do it slowly Jack, nice and easy. I can see you better than you can see me."

As Jack's eyes adjusted to the moonlight, he saw a short man standing about fifteen feet away from him. He was holding a gun in one hand and what looked like a remote control in the other. The man moved a couple of feet closer and kicked something at him; it was then that Jack got a better look. The man was not very tall, about five feet four. He had thick blonde wavy hair. His broad friendly smile revealed deep dimples in the center of both cheeks.

It was time for some conversation.

"Who are you?" Jack asked genially.

"Please pick up the flashlight, turn it on, and point it towards the house. If you look close, you will see what you came here to collect."

Jack now knew that it had been a flashlight that the man had kicked his direction. *One question down another zillion to go.*

As Jack leaned down and picked up the flashlight with his left hand, he removed the pistol from his belt with his right. The short man started humming a tune, one that Jack indistinctly recognized but couldn't rightly remember.

Jack aimed the high-powered flashlight toward the house, and there she was. Kirsti was sitting in a chair on a porch in front of the house. She was wrapped from top to bottom with silver duct tape. She seemed to be holding something in her lap. Her hands were taped to the object in her lap. Jack's mind was racing and so was his heart. His worse fear was becoming a reality. She was holding explosives and the remote was the trigger.

"You can have me, just let her go."

The blonde man quit humming.

"It isn't like that, Jack. I have my instructions. Irv distinctly told me that if you showed up instead of him, then I would know that you had cheated. You cheated, didn't you, Jack? I know my brother is dead. You killed him didn't you, Jack?"

Jack shook his head back and forth slowly. *Careful, Jack, you have got to be careful.*

"No, your brother isn't dead. He is on his way to jail. He gave me the map and told me to come and get Kirsti. He said you would let me have her if I came alone."

The blonde man looked at Jack, flashed his dimples, and with a beguiling childlike smile, said softly, "I don't believe you, Jack. Irv would have made you bring him with you. He told me you would cheat, and he told me you would lie. Now it's time to get this over with. I'm tired. I want to go see my mom. You shouldn't have killed my brother."

Shorty lifted both arms; one hand held the gun, the other the remote. The porch light came on. Jack swung his head toward the house, his eyes were again on Kirsti; he saw her eyes. He whirled around, and lifted his revolver; he didn't have time to aim. As he pulled the trigger, two shots rang out, and then there was a huge, earth-shattering explosion.

Jack felt himself flying through the air. His mind was now on the song.

That's it! I remember now. I know that song. "Beyond the Blue Horizon."

I love that song. I need to buy the tape. Do they sell tapes anymore? Maybe not, then how can I get that song if they don't sell tapes anymore?

He looked up. In the black sky was a brilliant array of stars. *Where is the big dipper? If I can find the big dipper I can find the small one. Concentrate, Jack, just concentrate and you will find it. Was that his Dad's voice he was hearing?*

Look, Vic, there's a shooting star. It means something, what does it mean?"

Everything was getting dimmer and starting to turn black. He thought he heard someone screaming, a male voice screaming. A tortured, anguished person was screaming *"No, God, no, not Kirsti. Please, God, not Kirsti." Couldn't someone stop the shrieking, it was giving him a headache. Who was screaming? Please God, make it stop, make it all go away.*

Vic was running through the heavy undergrowth, trying to make his way to Jack when he heard two shots ring out and next came the cataclysmic noise of the explosion. He had made a huge mistake by moving away from the jeep to quickly, with too much distance. The thickness of the woods had slowed him down. The total darkness had caused him to lose his sense of direction. When he got to the clearing, he found Jack, lying unconscious next to his jeep. He was bleeding badly from the left side of his head. Sirens and flashing lights were coming in from every direction. Another person was lying on the ground about fifteen feet away from Jack. He was obviously dead. Jack had shot him squarely between the eyes.

From that point on, everything was a blur. Brice yelled at Vic to move away from the bodies. The paramedics took Jack. Vic's last recollection of the scene as he left in Jack's jeep was the pile of rubble that had once been a house. The explosion had obliterated it and everything else within twenty feet of it. Vic was following the ambulance to the hospital; the only thing on his mind was his best buddy, his friend, and his partner. He couldn't afford to think about Kirsti. She was gone, there was nothing left of her. He had to keep his mind centered on his partner, or he would lose it.

The medical examiner found a picture in Irv's pocket. Written on the back of the creased picture was, *"Mom and Dad, me and my brother."*

The mother was a beauty. She had long blonde hair and blue eyes. She appeared to be tall and slender. The father looked eerily like Jack Ireland. Irv was standing, unsmiling, next to his father and the youngest child, dressed in a stripped, long-sleeved t-shirt and black pants, with red suspenders, was grinning from ear to ear.

The medical examiner found an envelope in one of Shorty's pockets. The envelope contained a purple button wrapped in a single four-by-five-inch piece of paper. On the piece of paper were written, in bold print, these unfathomable words, **"This button belongs to you, Kirsti, because Jackie could not save you."**

Brice stuffed the envelope in his pocket and saw to it that the note and the purple button never saw the light of day. He could not afford to have Jack, should he survive, blaming himself for the death of his wife and all the other victims of these two insane individuals. The "Purple Button Case", according to the press was now closed. Everyone could go home and think about something else. But there would be many who would never forget this case. It would linger in the minds of those involved for the remainder of their lives.

Part V

And still on a winter's night, they say, when the wind is in the trees,
When the moon is a ghostly galleon tossed upon cloudy seas,
When the road is a gypsy's ribbon looping the purple moor,
The highwayman comes riding—
Riding—riding—
The highwayman comes riding, up to the old inn-door.

Over the cobbles he clatters and clangs in the dark inn-yard,
He taps with his whip on the shutters, but all is locked and barred,
He whistles a tune to the window, and who should be waiting there
But the landlord's black-eyed daughter—
Bess, the landlord's daughter—
Plaiting a dark red love-knot into her long black hair.

"The Highwayman"

Written by Alfred Noyes (1880-1958)

Epilogue

Dear Jack,

It has taken some time for me to find you, and find you isn't exactly right either, is it? Actually, I found a friend of yours who was willing to forward this letter to you. I hope it arrives and finds you doing well.

Not so very long ago, Mom and I were talking, and she said to me, "I wonder whatever happened to Jack. It's funny we have never heard from him. I would like to see him again."

I decided to make it my mission to try and get in contact with you. I hope you don't mind. Mom deserves the very best and especially from me.

Ironically, today is another anniversary of Kirsti's death. It is hard for me to believe all that happened then and what has happened since then.

I know that you have blamed yourself for Kirsti's death. I heard that at her funeral, and that is probably the way you would feel, Jack, but you were not responsible. You were more affected than any of us, and we were affected more than sufficiently. Vic told me that you wanted to get away from it all, and this is why you left the state, gave up your job, and bailed out. I think I might have done the same thing, had I been you.

I would like you to know that my family, none of us ever blamed you, especially my Father. All of us came to see you when you were at the hospital. Mom and I were there the day you came out of your coma. Vic, bless him, was standing guard and told me that you didn't want any visitors. We told him to keep us posted, and he did, in a very abstract way. He didn't want to have anyone hounding you. He had only one thought; to protect you.

I was invited to his wedding. I was glad to attend. Vic and Doreen are a happy couple, but I am sure you know all about that. The two dearest people in your life, your very most loyal loved ones together. I found it somewhat ironical. Doreen came to Kirsti's funeral. She and I have been close friends ever since. She is open with me, a better friend I could not want. She probably knows where you are, I am sure Vic knows, but your secret is safe with them and safe from me as well. If you want to remain incognito, that is certainly your business, not mine. (I sound a bit impatient don't I?)

I think about Kirsti today, and I think about you. I can't help but do that. We don't have Kirsti anymore, but we still have you to think about, and this is a good thing. What happened to you and my sister is something that rarely happens in anyone's lifetime, ever. Nor should it ever happen to anyone, ever. The repercussions of what those two men did to my family and many others can never be rationalized or modified.

Dad passed away a year after Kirsti died. His cancer came back, and he refused treatment. Lynn couldn't handle it either. She died a year after father passed away. She literally drank herself to death. Yvonne, who was also suffering deeply, tried her level best to keep the two of them going, but neither seemed interested in living any longer. I talked to several doctors, and they said there is more than one way to commit suicide. I don't think I need to know or even want to know if this is true. I do know it has been an uphill battle for me as one after the other of my family faded away to a place where I couldn't reach them or talk to them any longer.

I lost Nick a year after my father died. I survived this, but I still have to wonder how. He was my life. He got prostrate cancer and died of a pulmonary embolism. A clot the size of a walnut moved through his heart and lodged itself into the opening of his left lung. A doctor came in from New York, did surgery, but Nick didn't make it. I moved back home after he died to be with Mom. My brothers were still living at home, so was my youngest sister. I like to think that we were in the business of helping each other out. I have since moved on to other places. As you can see, I now live in Florida.

Hilde married Charlie; they might have lived happily ever after had she not had a massive heart attack. She never recovered from losing Kirsti the way we did. The shock of this was to much for her to deal with. It tore her up. She and Charlie had a son. He is with Charlie and doing well, so far. It is hard to lose a mom. I worry about him all the time, even knowing he is in good hands. I have never really accepted losing both of my sisters, and I doubt I ever will or even need to. We were a trio, you know. I think of them every time I pick up a book or crank up the tunes.

Grandma passed away the same month as Hilde, only a year later. She had a massive stroke that wiped her off the face of the map. One day, I will try and write a book about her. She was an incredible person. That she lived as long as she did, with the adversity she faced, is something to remark about. Who knows, it might be a best seller? Grandma was my lighthouse. Her beacon brought me through many stormy seas. I suppose, out of all of my departed people, I miss Grandma the most. I often think that I miss her the most because I cannot bring myself to miss the others. The thoughts of this are lonely and still too painful. I do know now that there is a limit to what the heart and mind can tolerate and continue to be strong. I sort of had it stuck in my mind that Kirsti, Hilde, and I would grow old together. I guess God had different plans! I, at one time, thought he could have had the common decency to send me a memo, but now after some thought; I am relieved that he didn't.

On the brighter side of this life we live in; Maggie, I am sure you must remember Maggie, she married Jerry. They are living in a small town just southwest of Lakeville. Both of them are still working for Samuel Crawford. His law firm is thriving. The last I heard, Reed had married himself a socialite, and he's doing better than ever. He is, I guess, practicing law in Europe, France, I think. If it makes you feel any better, none of us liked him very much, and he didn't come to Kirsti's funeral. Benton decided it was time to retire and go back to Arizona. None of us cared about that. In the life and times of the Povals, they were but a brief blip on the radar screen.

I will close for now and say one more thing. If you ever want to get back in touch with us, you will be welcomed with open arms. We really do miss you, Jack. Perhaps it is time to move on, but it is hard for us to do that without a lot of thought towards you. At least those of us who are left. I am free, white, and twenty-one (grin). If you want to give me a call, have at it. I am sure you haven't lost your investigative skills. You can find my address on the upper-left-hand corner of the envelope this letter came in.

Take care now. I hope your investigations bring you my direction

Glenda

P.S. It wouldn't hurt you or Mom if you were to give her a call. Her number is still the same. As for a philosophical notation, one needs to think almost daily that "time and tide waits for no man."

Jack folded up the letter, placed it back in the envelope, and tucked it in his back pocket.

"Well, what do you think, Abby-Kitty, do you think we need to get moving onward? This old log I am sitting on is getting a little worn-out and winter's coming on."

Abby-Kitty was not the original Abby. He had left the original Abby at the farm. He didn't know what became of her. He had left her in good hands, and that was good for him at the time. Jack had found this kitty at a humane society place in Golden, Colorado. He had stopped in just to look. He thought a pet would be nice. He was thinking a dog, but when he saw Abby, he had to have her. She looked just like Kirsti's kitty. She was sitting on her haunches, looking up at him with a look only an Abby-Kitty can give. She was just a baby, only six weeks old, when he got her.

Abby stood up and stretched as he reeled in his line. He patted the log he had been sitting on before he stood up and stretched. He made the long climb back up the hillside slowly and methodically. His mind was on Glenda. When he reached the front door of his modest cabin, Abby gave him a meow and scampered ahead of him. She wanted in. She wanted treats.

Before he gave her treats, he picked her up and nuzzled his face into her neck She fought him hard, but he knew she wasn't serious. She was purring loudly and steadily. She placed her pure white paws on his face and shoved him away.

"How belligerent you are, Abby."

He set her down and gave her the treats she was begging for. As she ate, he said to her, "What do you think, Abby, are you ready for a road trip? I think it's time you and I do some traveling. How about Florida? It's been a long time, since I have been to Florida. In fact, I haven't ever been to Florida, could be a nice place to be in the wintertime. If I can't be in Minnesota for the winter, I might as well go to Florida."

Abby meowed in protest as he swept her up off the floor and started dancing her around the room in a lively two-step.

"You and I are going to go to Florida. Maybe, just maybe, there *is* life after death.

About the Author

Gail Soberg - Sorenson was born and raised in a small community just south of Minneapolis proper. She is married and resides in a small community in Iowa. She has six kids and fourteen grandchildren. She and her husband have owned and operated their own business for the past twenty-five years, allowing her to be a stay-at-home mom. Her hobbies are reading, travel, and genealogy. She has traveled the United States from shore to shore by train, plane and automobile and visited parts of Europe, Japan, and Korea.

LaVergne, TN USA
03 May 2010
181361LV00002B/8/P